ZERO DAY CODE

A NOVEL OF THE END OF DAYS

JOHN BIRMINGHAM

1

A PROFESSIONALLY CAREFUL GUY

For James O'Donnell, it started at a Texaco on I-95, just a few minutes north of where the interstate takes that big swing east to hook up with the Beltway. James didn't need to fill up. His Camry hybrid had another two hours of battery power, and the tank was full, but so was he. The jumbo latte he'd picked up at Starbucks before leaving Baltimore was sitting heavy in his bladder. The slightly cheaper parking garage where he always pre-booked a spot had no bathroom facilities and was at least a twenty-minute walk from his appointment.

That'd be a long twenty minutes if he didn't pull into the gas station and get some relief.

James hissed through his teeth as the little hybrid hit the speed hump standing sentinel over the Texaco's entryway. He was cutting it close and cursed himself for buying the jumbo latte simply because the cost per fluid ounce was nearly half that of the more modestly sized regular takeaway. But he was a fool for a bargain. Always had been.

He drove past the pumps and took a bay outside the food court. Big windows gave a view into the seating area inside, where patrons sat at moulded plastic furniture with trays of McDonald's, KFC,

Dunkin Donuts, and the junk food refuse of all the lesser outlets, which made up the balance of the concessions. This was not his first visit. He knew from previous trips to the capital that because the food court was a popular, high-traffic stop just outside of the Beltway, there were large, unlocked washroom facilities, and he wouldn't need to buy anything to get a key.

James walked inside with his suit coat draped over his arm, locking the car and taking a messenger satchel with all of his documents, electronics and a cheese sandwich in a Ziplock bag. High summer had passed, but the brutal heat of June and July had not backed off during August. He started to leak sweat as soon as the steam press humidity fell on him. It was only a short walk to the entrance, but the chilled air that spilled out through the sliding doors felt like a first kiss, long anticipated. His nose wrinkled at the smell of hot grease and fried food, but it was just so pleasantly cool inside, compared to broiling out on the tarmac, that he considered getting a soda and staying a while. He was early, as always.

First, though, he hurried through to the washroom and took care of business. There'd be no clear-headed thinking about anything until that was done. After thoroughly washing and drying his hands —the drying is just as important as the washing, you know—he returned to the dining area. For somebody like him, raised on a farm, lunchtime meant noon. That was still half an hour away, but there seemed to be twice as many people lined up at the food counters as there had been when he walked in a few minutes earlier. James checked his watch again.

11.32 AM.

His appointment with Michelle Nguyen was at two, and there would be an unpleasant walk through the heat from the parking garage on 21st to get to her office at the Eisenhower Building. Unpleasant enough that he was open to the idea of booking a cab (but not an Uber) to make the short hop. And he did have time to kill before the meeting. Sitting here and reviewing his notes would definitely be cheaper than doing so inside the Beltway, where coffees ran to five bucks a cup if you weren't careful.

And James O'Donnell? He was a professionally careful guy.

The publisher, editor and only correspondent for *The Acorn*, a newsletter offering deep market analysis "but absolutely no tips", took his professional responsibilities very seriously. His subscribers paid him fifty dollars a month for his work—you got one month free with a year's subscription—and you had to be careful when you were taking that kind of money off people. Most of his subscribers were not wealthy. Not what James would call wealthy, anyway. They were like him: prudent.

He didn't need to check his phone to know it was hot outside, but he did so anyway.

Jeez! 100.4 degrees.

Okay. He made a prudent decision right then to drop a few dollars on a taxi and to spend half an hour here, reading over his notes for the meeting with Miss Nguyen. It would not do to turn up at the National Security Council dripping with sweat and reeking of BO. He'd been surprised that the researcher had even agreed to meet him and did not want to jeopardise the opportunity. Michelle Nguyen was the author of an unclassified paper on the increasing vulnerability of China's food security to industrial pollution. As bracing as her published conclusions had been, James suspected they'd been significantly watered down for release. Discontinuities in China's food supply could shock global supply chains and end markets. It could mean food riots and starvation throughout the developing world, shortages and price spikes in American supermarkets; threats but also opportunities.

Ever cautious, he took out his key fob and pressed the button to lock the Camry again. You couldn't be too careful.

He didn't want to sit in the main dining area. The smell was gross, and it was also very noisy in there. A large group of children were running wild, and their parents were too invested in the enormous McBanquet before them to bother with anything like supervision. Customers argued with counter staff at a couple of the concessions, and the music piping through the PA system was loud, tinny and awful. James didn't much like junk food. He'd been brought up to appreciate a simple but healthy fare on his parent's farm. There were a few empty tables away from the food court, in the small, separate area where motorists paid for their gas and shopped for the road. The shelves were brightly stocked with cookies, corn chips, pornography and motor oil. It would do.

He resisted the urge to lock the Camry for the third time. Already over-caffeinated, he fetched a small bottle of still water from a large commercial refrigerator full of Coke. The water, he knew, was also a product of the Coca-Cola Corporation, and its profit margin was considerably greater than on any bottle of soda. He resented that, just a little, but it was not fair to expect that Texaco should let him occupy valuable floor space without making something on the deal. The stupidly overpriced water was enough of a sacrifice, by his reckoning, to lease a little time at one of those unoccupied tables.

The line of customers waiting to pay for gas and pornography was long. The two women in Texaco uniforms serving behind the counter were both fussing about with one register. Waiting customers shuffled from one foot to another, checked their phones and grumbled about the delay. The long queue retained its coherent form for another minute until a stocky man in chinos and a white polo top cursed volubly, abandoned his purchases on top of a Dairy Queen freezer and stomped out. That seemed to signal the small crowd to collapse into a mass around the register, offering comments, technical advice, and demands for attention, a manager and more staff to appear and operate those registers that were working.

"None of them are working," snapped the older of the two women. She was a lumpy white matron with grey hair so tightly curled that James had a momentary vision of her sitting under a hair dryer with old-fashioned plastic curlers covering her skull. His grandma had done the same thing every day. She'd looked unreal in her casket at the funeral home because the morticians had tried to recreate the effect with a curling wand.

They had failed.

The name tag on the woman's uniform blouse read MARION, and Marion was having as much trouble with the cash register as that funeral home had had with Grandma's final do. She was punching tentatively at the keypad, frowning at a readout that none of the customers could see. Her co-worker, a much younger woman, Latina in appearance, stood stiffly off to one side, with the sort of terrified rigidity that spoke to her fear that something had gone wrong and it was all her fault.

Standing at the back of the now collapsed queue, James realised the small dramas he'd witnessed out in the food court and dismissed as the banal filler scenes of modern life—somebody complaining that they'd ordered large fries and only got small—were the opening moments of the same act. Texaco's data management system had crashed. Leaning back to look into the larger dining area, James could see that the crowds at the fast-food counters were two or three times as large and noticeably rowdier than they had been before.

He considered returning the water bottle but found that he wanted it now. His mouth was dry. He fetched out his wallet and removed a dollar note, the cost of the spring water. The old leather billfold, a gift from his parents when he had gone away to college, contained three hundred dollars exactly. Four fifties, four twenties, and the balance in tens and ones. When he travelled for business, as he was today, he always carried the same amount in cash. Not enough that losing it or being robbed would be a disaster, but enough to know that he could be confident of buying transport or shelter if the need arose. He'd once been stuck in Akron with a frozen credit card and no other liquidity.

Never again.

He always carried cash, and his Mastercard was linked to a debit account. He never used the card directly if he could avoid it, preferring to make any transactions via Apple Pay. He trusted the security of the tech giant's one-use tokens to protect him from scammers and skimmers.

There would be no using it today, however. Things were getting out of hand at Texaco. A man was screaming at the McDonald's counter that he had paid for his chocolate sundae, and by god, he was getting his chocolate sundae. Those unsupervised children were now running and jumping from tabletop to tabletop, taking maximum advantage of all the grown-ups being distracted.

Waving the dollar note for his water at the Latina girl behind the counter, James paid and walked the short distance back to the central food court. His success occasioned a small riot as the other customers suddenly remembered that paying by cash was still legal. People in the food court were now shouting at each other so loudly, some yelling that they'd been robbed, that it became apparent to James that he wasn't going to get any work done. Before stepping outside into the killing heat, he did take a moment to check out the motorists filling their cars at the dozens of gas pumps. They seemed oblivious to the chaos inside the roadhouse. The pumps appeared to be working without a problem. Traffic still flowed along I-95.

Just a glitch in the payment system, then?

He made a note on his phone to look into it when he was done with this interview. If the problem had occurred in the previous twelve months, he would have to block out some time when he got home this evening to do a deep dive into Texaco's payment processing architecture. FinTech was a sector that existed in a state of near-permanent disruption. It was the sort of thing his subscribers paid him to get ahead of. If needs be, he would sit up through the night in his modest two-bedroom apartment, writing a supplemental mail out for this week.

As it turned out, though, that wouldn't be necessary.

James O'Donnell never set foot in his apartment again.

2

THE CENTURION

T he weirdest two days of Jonas Murdoch's life started, as always, before dawn. One difference, though? He woke to discover he was famous. Or internet famous, at least.

Okay. Fuck you. Subreddit famous. But he'd take it.

Jonas lived in a small, dark brick house in the grey suburban wastelands half an hour south of SeaTac. Thorny weeds choked everything out of the garden, and grimy, unwashed windows rattled in splintered wooden frames when the big jets came in low from the south. He shared the rundown bungalow with Mikey Summers, a roommate he saw rarely and about whom he could give less than one grudging fuck. The dude helped pay the bills, which was about the best you could say of him. Jonas paid his share of the rent with the bullshit wage he made hauling crap around an Amazon warehouse down in Sumner, another five minutes south on Route 5.

The warehouse, or 'fulfilment centre' in the bizoid doublespeak of the company, was a massive facility, sprawling over half a million square feet to the west of the rail line. Working there was about a thousand fucking miles from fulfilling, but Jonas woke before dawn every morning knowing that he badly needed the job, at least for now. That was a sour fucking feeling, but it didn't make him special, did it?

No. What made Jonas Murdoch special was *The Centurion*.

Three days a week, he got up in the dark to hit a local CrossFit box – or, to be honest, a cheap copy of one, because who had two hundred bucks a month for the real thing, right? But four days a week, he rose before the first ray of light to prepare and record *The Centurion*.

He'd started the podcast in desperation after lighting out of Florida, where his pissed-off ex-wife, Trisha, had sued for alimony he couldn't pay, and she'd retained as her lawyer—get this— his pissed-off ex-boss, Hondo Alvarez.

That greasy bastard was probably doing the bitch too, because Hondo loved nothing so much as to fuck with Jonas Murdoch's life. It had been like this the two years he'd worked for him in Florida, running all of Hondo's shittiest errands, repping for his worst clients. Always on a promise of something better coming just around the corner.

Jonas stopped in the middle of the small, crowded living area. He was a big man, jailhouse-strong, and he took up a lot of space. There was crap all over the floor, and he was holding a cup of ice water to get his metabolism going. His way through the dark was poorly illuminated by the tiny red lights of sleeping electrical equipment and the ghostly glow of Mikey's stupid aquarium. Those fish and a hard-on for cycling hundreds of miles a week were what his roomie had instead of a life.

Standing there in the dark, surrounded by piles of Mikey's junk food refuse, it was only natural that Jonas would start thinking about Hondo.

The guano-eating tool was the reason he was stuck on the wet edge of nowhere, selling *Centurion* tee-shirts to dumbass Nazis to pay for his protein shakes.

But there was no point stewing on that. He needed to focus. If Jonas let himself pick at every scab and half-healed wound he had from Miami, he'd bleed out on the floor of this depressing little hovel

— long before Mikey Summers showed his ugly freckled face and started shovelling big handfuls of Cap'n Crunch into it for breakfast.

No fucking way did Jonas want to hang around for *that*.

He drank the ice water fast to clear his head, with a cold spike of pain if necessary. Hondo could suck him hard. Jonas would dial in on his shit. He would focus like a motherfucker. Fuck yeah, that's what he would do.

He'd been reading up on how the modern world conspired against focus. He'd heard a podcast with some physicist, computer science guy, or something fapping on about deep work, shallow shit, and digital distraction. And yeah, it was mostly bullshit, and the guy was obviously a cuck with a side hustle in self-help and personal empowerment for lesser cucks, but Jonas did take away one thing from the ten minutes he could bear listening to.

Phones, social media and the internet had fucked everyone up.

People with true focus were becoming increasingly rare. And what was rare was valuable.

Despite all the shit he'd gone through with his wife, his boss, the fucking Florida bar and the conga line of suppurating assholes he'd formerly known as clients, Jonas Murdoch prided himself on being a guy who could still focus.

And his focus was one hundred per cent on building *The Centurion* until he was as big as Alex Jones or Mike Cernovich — without flaming out like Jones, of course. The crazy asshole.

Jonas had zero doubts that he would get there. Doubts were what losers had instead of focus. He centred himself, let go of the rage which always burned just under the surface of things, and carefully picked his way through all the shit on the floor, heading towards the desktop computer where he recorded the podcast.

Fuck Hondo. Fuck Trisha. And fuck the Florida Bar Association.

The affiliate income from sales off his website was growing impressively (although to be honest, any growth was impressive when you came off a base of nothing). And downloads of his pod had exploded since *The Washington Post* cited it as an example of one of the newer, more imaginative Alt-Right media plays.

Still no Squarespace or Casper Mattress ads, though. And never would be, he knew. But he kept a spreadsheet of all the advertisers in the Alt-Right media world. When Jonas had grown his audience to a point where they were a viable sales channel for the purveyors of X-Treme Survival Urban Exfil Packs, Supermale Vitality Tonics and erectile dysfunction gel, he would be ready.

He might even leap to the real big time. A regular gig on Fox. Or his own patronage deals with some wealthy closet fascist who was too weak in the bladder to take on the Left straight up. Lots of guys had deals like that. Bannon. That Milo fag, until he flamed out like Jones.

No reason Jonas Murdoch couldn't make his own deal.

He was smarter than all of them, he knew, as he stood in front of Mikey's gaming computer in the cramped, messy room that did for a lounge, diner and kitchen in this shithole. He checked the tape over the desktop camera.

Still there. No morning wood for the CIA.

And Jonas was sporting some hard polished wood, too, because he had a great show today.

He sat down and woke the screen, his heart quickening. This morning, he'd follow up on his Guy Pendleton take-down from Monday.

That was a genuine coup. His first real scalp.

Pendleton, who had been in line to direct the first *X-Men* reboot for Disney, was your typical Hollywood liberal, which is to say, an egregious fucking hypocrite. Always whining about minority this and empowerment that. But Jonas had used his legal research skills, which were still razor sharp, to dig out a couple of multimillion-dollar settlements Universal had very quietly paid to three actresses Pendleton had assaulted, possibly even raped, while he was directing the *Duke Nukem* movies.

Jonas dropped that bomb during a convo with Joe Rogan in Monday's ep. (Rogan had no idea who he was talking with, but Jonas had carefully groomed the much bigger podcaster with six months' worth of dicksuck tweets and fawning blog posts on *The Centurion's* website). The shout-out from *WaPo* had been all Rogan's people needed to finally plug him into the pod for five minutes of burnishing his cred as a straight-talking guy who didn't give a fuck about PC bull-shit on the left or right.

It had gone well.

They'd segued from the latest Conner MacGregor arrest to the Pendleton reveal, and Rogan had been as surprised as Jonas had hoped. Being a thorough professional, Rogan was cautious naturally, but five minutes in and Jonas had what he needed. A viral audio clip of YouTube famous Joe Rogan what-the-fucking his way through the opening minutes of the latest #MeToo shitstorm.

It was trending on Twitter an hour after the pod dropped.

By the end of Monday, Disney had released a statement 'review-ing' Pendleton's role in any projects 'going forward'.

Jonas set up his 'sound booth' – a big ass cardboard box lined with packing foam – sat at Mikey's computer, adjusted his micro-phone and got ready to drop bombs all over the smoking crater he'd already made of Pendleton's and Disney's plans for *X-Men: Emergence*.

He almost didn't get there.

First thing that happened when he logged into his account on Mikey's computer was his notifications went apeshit.

He had thousands of hits from all over the net.

Messages from Cernovich and Rogan and...

Holy shitballs... from Tucker Carlson.

Tucker Fucking Carlson knew who he was.

Sort of.

Nobody knew that he was The Centurion, of course. He wasn't ready to have his name up in lights yet. If anybody at work figured out it was him, his ass would hit the gutter at high speed about two seconds later. Which sucked. But he consoled himself that at least he had health insurance and the job was a solid daily workout; cardio and strength, at least a coupla thousand calories.

Looking at the towering inferno of his Twitter mentions and the thousand-plus emails piled up in *The Centurion's* inbox, Jonas Murdoch wondered if this might be the day he finally escaped the fulfilment centre.

Which was pretty fucking ironic when he thought about it later.

THINGS GOT SO crazy after he fired up the desktop that Jonas almost missed the start of his shift. Hell, he almost didn't record the pod.

He read the messages from Cernovich and Carlson first. Or Carlson's producer, at least. That was a little disappointing, he'd admit. Not that Tucker had some bimbo to do his emails, but that she wasn't writing to invite him on the show. She said they loved his pod, just loved it, and Tucker was wondering if they could get copies of Universal's NDAs and settlements with the three women Pendleton had fucked over.

There was a part of Jonas that flared up at the presumption.

He'd done the fucking work; he should get the loot.

But the cooler, more rational part of his mind knew that just having Fox reach out like this, of being able to put one in the favour bank with them, was a significant payoff all on its own.

The next time he staged a coup of this magnitude, he could go straight to them with it.

And the time after that, they might have him on air.

He could imagine his name scrolling across the bottom of the screen already. He sent Carlson's producer a one-time link to an untraceable file dump where she could grab the documents. But first, he blurred out the actresses' names. He'd need them later and advised her to 'stay tuned'.

Cernovich was friendlier and less self-interested. He DM'd Jonas on Twitter to let him know he was already a fan of the pod, and he just wanted to say 'good job' on the Pendleton call out.

That was classy, Jonas thought.

The rest of the incoming was a mix of slavering fan mail and leftist abuse. Reading all of these strangers' thoughts about what he'd done was compelling. Even when it was enraging, he found it difficult to stop clicking through. It was only when Mikey startled him by knocking on the improvised cardboard sound booth that Jonas realised he was running two hours late.

"Shit!" he cried out.

"Sorry, man," Mikey Summers said, looking perplexed. He was wearing lycra. He always wore lycra when he wasn't in uniform for the Supermall Burger King. "Thought you'd be gone by now," Mikey said. "You still recording your thing?"

That's what this asshole called *The Centurion*. 'Your thing'. Or sometimes 'your little thing'.

Jonas clamped down on his annoyance, mostly with himself for losing focus.

"Yeah, sorry, man," he said. "Got caught up in fan mail."

Mikey laughed at that. The jerk. And again, Jonas forced himself to let it slide.

"Can you gimme another ten or fifteen?" he asked. "I need to record."

His roommate shrugged it off.

"Sure. I'm going out anyway. Gonna get some extra road miles in before work."

"Good for you," Jonas said, returning to his screen.

One thing he could thank his annoying roommate for was that Mikey had broken the spell of mindlessly scrolling through his messages and mentions. He had to lean into this thing now, or he'd be late for work, and there were no excuses for that. None that he could give the supervisor, at least.

He flew through the set-up procedure to record a new podcast.

Brought up his notes.

Chilled the fuck out and got into character.

The thing about the Centurion? The dude was angry, but he was chill with it. Like, murderously chilled.

Jonas took a breath, composed himself and started to speak with the slow, measured, ironic detachment that had gathered over forty thousand listeners to his podcast.

"Two days into the Pendleton scandal," he began, "Disney is still reviewing what role the rapist will play in their family-friendly business. This is the Centurion. Welcome to an imploding supermassive shitshow of desperate incompetence so violently bungle-fucked six ways from Sunday that even listing Disney's major oh-no moments feels like shamewanking over grief porn..."

He spoke for only ten minutes, leaving himself time to upload the files, but in the show's last minute, he squeezed off the money shot. Jonas Murdoch named the three actresses Guy Pendleton had raped.

Then he went to work.

3

THREAT ASSESSMENTS

Michelle Nguyen frowned. Twitter was down, at least on her desktop. She picked up the iPhone next to her keyboard and tried checking her account. Yep, down. That was annoying. She had a few minutes before she met with O'Donnell and wanted to dip into one of her lists. The latest edition of *Foreign Policy* had just this week cited her unclassified monograph on Chinese food security and set off a pretty willing debate in her 'Finding a Wonk for the End of the World' list. August Cole and Peter Singer were ragging on Hugh White for his 'aggressively naive' insistence that Beijing was a rational actor with too much to lose from subverting the rules-based international system. White and his crew, in reply, were all 'with-respect' and 'perhaps-I-was-not-clear-enough'; wonk speak for 'hey-dumbass-you-couldn't-be-more-wrong'. Michelle agreed with White about Beijing's power realism, up to a point, but Cole and Singer had given her a few new angles on the problem of China's deeply stressed agricultural sector.

Her landline buzzed, the front desk telling her that Mr O'Donnell had arrived for their two o'clock meeting.

"I'll come down and get him," she said.

Her office on the first floor was less than a minute from reception, but she had to stop by and let Admiral Holloway know that O'Donnell had arrived.

"The newsletter guy?" he said when Michelle put her head around his doorway to tell him. "Cool."

"Yeah," Michelle said. "I told him I could give him half an hour. When did you want to make your grand entrance?"

David Holloway smiled. He was three years out of the Navy and one of those military men who had relaxed so completely into civilian life that it was difficult ever to imagine him barking orders at anybody.

"Let's say... fifteen minutes? That enough time?"

"Sure. I'll soften him up for you."

Holloway thanked her, and she left to pick up her guest. The Eisenhower Building was a secure facility, belying the charm of its Baroque Revival architecture. Sitting next to the White House, it was, in Michelle's opinion, the much grander of the two structures, more closely resembling a palatial French hotel or casino than a federal government building. But it was full of Feds, including her tiny part of the National Security Council, and O'Donnell wasn't getting past the coat rack without an escort.

She found him waiting by the front desk, a plastic VISITOR card dangling from a lanyard around his neck. A messenger bag hung by a strap from one shoulder, and he'd taken off his jacket, draping it over one arm. She knew he'd driven down from Baltimore, meaning he'd had to park a few blocks away, but he didn't look like he was suffering from the heat. She clocked the expression on his face when he caught sight of her ink. Michelle Nguyen was a human canvas, a living tribute to the tattooist's art. She could see this guy struggling to put his shock and awe back in the box.

"Ms Nguyen," O'Donnell said, smiling nervously and stepping forward to offer his hand. His handshake was firm, and his hand was dry, even cool.

Must have caught an Uber, she thought.

Aloud, she introduced herself, "Mister O'Donnell, thank you for coming down."

She directed him through the metal detectors, which occasioned a brief delay as he had to empty the bag. Out came his laptop, a phone, a couple of smaller devices she didn't recognise and a snarled ball of dongles.

"Thank you for giving me the time," O'Donnell said as he collected all of his stuff on the through-side of the security barrier.

"My office isn't far from here," Michelle said. "Just follow me."

The young man, unremarkably good-looking in a sort of wholesome, corn-fed way, hurried to keep up with her. He dropped a couple of dongles and nearly tripped over his feet, picking them up.

"Do you mind me asking why?" O'Donnell said as he stood up again.

She made a face. "So you don't get lost?"

He responded with a confused expression.

"Oh no," he said suddenly, getting her joke. "No. I meant, why did you agree to meet with me? I didn't expect you to say yes when I emailed."

Michelle smiled. It was a genuine smile, and her eyes twinkled with it.

"Oh, we're big fans here, James. We have a subscription to your newsletter."

He frowned.

"You do?"

"Yes. We subscribe to several private bulletins, but we don't do so as the NSC. I understand that we used to, but a couple of the analysts started touting themselves as 'consultants'—" she sketched air quotes on either side of her head "—to the National Security Council. So instead, somebody came up with the idea of subscribing using the names of nineteenth-century Congressmen."

"Huh," he said, "You do learn something every day."

Michelle could almost see him filing the little factoid away in his head. He seemed the sort of guy who might sit up late tonight reviewing every name on his subscriber list.

They reached her office, and she showed him in, gesturing for James to take the chair in front of her desk, which was clear of papers. Her computer screen was similarly blank.

"I was happy to talk with you because I found that piece you did on the problems with milk formula for babies in China to be very helpful in framing my paper a month later. You were well ahead of the curve in identifying the issue with toxic melamine contamination of Chinese baby formula. And I must admit, I was curious to know how."

James O'Donnell shrugged as if embarrassed to be asked.

"I was looking at the business case for the German supermarket chain Aldi moving into Australia," he said. "Their operations down there can be seen as a proving ground for pushing further into the US market, where they're already significant disruptors. I found a couple of stories in the local retail trade press about sudden, unexplained shortages of milk formula."

He paused as though something had just occurred to him. When O'Donnell spoke again, the words came out in a bizarrely flat nasal accent.

"A dingo took my baby formula."

Michelle snorted at the unexpected pivot.

"Is that your best Meryl Streep?"

"Yeah, sorry. My Sean Connery is better. Anyway," he said, returning to his explanation, "Turned out Chinese students were making a lot of money, like hundreds of millions of dollars all up, mailing home as much Australian baby formula as they could buy. It was a tenth the price of the Chinese brands, and it didn't poison anybody."

"Nice," she said. "Your work, I mean, not the poison baby formula. Or your terrible Meryl Streep bit."

James fumbled with his messenger bag. "Do you mind if I ask you a few questions and take some notes?"

"As long you don't mind that I might not be able to answer freely. NSC has access to classified sources I can't talk about."

"That's cool," James said. "People underestimate the value of publicly available information even more than they overstate the value of information from, you know, other sources."

"They do," Michelle agreed.

James interviewed her about her research into China's food security problems, dialling in on the aspect of most interest to his subscribers, the money angle. She could tell he was circling in on the question of tariffs and the American farm sector when David Holloway rapped on the door.

"Sorry for interrupting," he said, with impressive artlessness, "But I heard that Mister O'Donnell was in the building, and I just wanted to say hello. I'm a fan."

James blushed and looked a little uncomfortable. Michelle found herself liking him even more. In this town, most of the guys she met were convinced of their own brilliance, but he had the grace to be slightly embarrassed by his. It was a pity this was a job interview, not a Tinder date.

Not that O'Donnell knew that.

JAMES HAD an awkward moment when Nguyen's boss interrupted them. He started to stand up, to shake the man's hand, when he remembered the open messenger bag on his lap and all of the crap that would come spilling out if he jumped to his feet. He fussed about for a few seconds, moving everything around before finally clearing the chair and taking Holloway's hand.

He knew who this guy was. Head of Threat Assessment for NSC. Retired US Navy admiral. Opted to continue in public service rather than farm his CV out to one of the K Street lobbying firms or big arms and aerospace companies, who'd have been more than happy to have him. But that was all he knew. Just a one-paragraph bio he'd mashed up from a Google search as part of his preparation for the meeting with Michelle Nguyen. He hadn't expected to run into Holloway.

Hell, he hadn't expected to set foot in this building.

"Sit down, please," Holloway said. He pulled a spare chair out of the corner and spun it around to face the desk. "Michelle told me you wanted to speak to her about China."

"I did, and she's been very helpful." He quickly raised his hands. "But not too helpful. All your secrets are still secret."

"That's good," Holloway nodded. "I'll admit I had an ulterior motive to dropping in, James. I am a fan, but I wanted to get your read on China if you don't mind."

James was a little taken aback, but he could hardly say no.

"Sure. What in particular?"

It would be something quite particular, he was sure.

"Supply chains. Specifically in the tech sector. Have you done much work on that?"

"You've read my newsletter."

Holloway smiled.

"I have. I wanted to get your take on how vulnerable some of our bigger companies would be if this trade dispute went sideways, hard."

James resisted the urge to ask whether that was about to happen.

"Look, you'd have to do risk assessments case by case. A company like Apple," he gestured at Michele's iPhone, "would already have their mitigation plans in place. Others with less exposure, not so much. But generally speaking, US tech companies and hardware makers are extremely vulnerable to downside risk from any disruption to trade relations with Beijing. In some cases, I think it's why you're seeing investments in downstream assembly that can't be justified as anything other than a hedge. Look at the iPhone. It's worth a couple of hundred billion dollars a year. If things got nasty, Beijing could turn that tap off. Of course, then they'd have the problem of millions of suddenly unemployed workers to feed... which circles back around to Michelle's work on their domestic supply chains. They can't feed themselves. Not from their agricultural base. They've built over too much farmland and poisoned most of what's left. Five years of drought haven't helped either. Unless they want to starve themselves to prove a point, they're stuck buying their groceries on the global market, specifically from Canada, Australia and the US, for grains, pulses and protein. And ASEAN for rice, fruit, vegetables, that sort of thing."

Holloway and Nguyen exchanged a look.

"James, would you be interested in writing a private briefing on this topic for the NSC?" Holloway asked.

James sat straight in his chair, blinking as if someone had just splashed cold water on his face. He could tell from Michelle Nguyen's expression that she wasn't surprised by the offer.

"I er... I..." he groped for a reply, suddenly understanding why he'd made it past the front door today.

"I don't need an answer right this minute," Holloway said. "But if you had capacity and you were interested, I would need to sign off the paperwork by close of business tomorrow. And I'd need the briefing by next Monday."

"Holy shit," James said quietly, then apologised.

"It's okay," Holloway smiled. "I know what an ambush feels like. But I'll explain. I have to coordinate a multi-agency presentation at the White House before the next round of tariffs goes into effect."

"The Doomsday round," James said without thinking, using the hashtag the media, new and old, had settled on for the looming avalanche of massive tariffs and quotas on Chinese goods coming into the US. He'd been writing about it in every edition for months now.

"Yes," Holloway said, his tone grim. "The deadline is two weeks off. We don't make policy, of course..." he showed them his open hands, a gesture of futility as much as it was a show of honesty, "but we still advise on policy."

"Is anyone listening?" James asked.

"These days, I fear nobody listens to anything but the counsel of their darkest angels," Holloway admitted. "But we must do as we would were our path through the world not a trail of tears."

"Admiral, you've been reading too much Whitman again," Michelle said.

"You can never read too much Whitman, Michelle," Holloway said. "James, thanks for coming in. And please, do think about it. We pay terrible government rates, and your work will almost certainly be ignored by those who most need to attend to it, but son, I've done some digging on you, and I know you're a young man who takes his responsibilities seriously. You're a private citizen, James, and you're free to walk out the door today and do what you will with whatever Michelle has told you. But you are also a citizen of the Republic, and I'd ask you to consider your responsibilities to—"

"I'll do it." James O'Donnell said.

Both Michelle and Holloway seemed surprised.

"Er... okay. Thank you," Holloway said.

"I would need to stay in Washington," James said. "I have a news-letter to get out tomorrow. I can do it tonight, but only if I don't have to drive back."

"I can get Marcie to take care of any bookings," Michelle said to Holloway.

"She might have to book by phone," said Holloway. "Internet's been flaky today."

4

ON MY SIX

N omi was snoring gently when Rick woke up. The curtains in their bedroom were parted, allowing a dusty beam of morning sunlight to stream through and gleam off her jet-black hair. She was beautiful. He was always struck by just how beautiful she looked when sleeping. Even her little snores were cute. He gently eased his massive arms around her shoulders and tummy and pulled her in close for a cuddle. She woke immediately, her eyes sparkling with delight, and she licked his face all over, from bristled chin to eyes squeezed shut.

"Oh... no. Nomi. Don't," he cried out.

The black Labrador barked and nuzzled in even closer, snuffling at his neck.

"Gah. Brazen hussy! No means no."

He pushed her away but playfully. Her tail wagging, she barked again. This was her favourite time of day, and there would be no respite for Rick Boreham until his best girl had all the cuddles she was due. He gave in. After five minutes of belly-rubbing and ear-scratching, Nomi conceded he had done enough to prove his love. The bare minimum, but enough.

She leapt from the bed, paws crashing and skittering wildly on the wooden floorboards. She spun around in tight circles, barking.

"Quiet," Rick said. He didn't raise his voice, but it was enough to silence her. She still panted with excitement and whimpered a little with the effort of keeping her feelings bottled up when the only reasonable way to start a new day was to bark and jump and spin about with utterly foolish abandon. But she had her orders, and she obeyed. Nomi was a good dog.

The reward for being such a good dog was a raw egg cracked over her bowl of venison kibble. Rick scooped a full measure from a ten-pound *Taste of the Wild* bag, poured the dry food into Nomi's stainless-steel bowl, and expertly broke open the egg with just one hand. Venison kibble sounded fancier than it looked, and the egg was straight from the factory cage. He couldn't afford no free-range organic cackleberries. But Nomi was salivating when he placed the bowl on the floor.

He looked at her.

She looked at him.

"On credit," he said.

She tilted her head slightly, frowning as if questioning his sanity.

"On credit," he said again.

Still, she sat, a small clear tendril of drool dripping from her lower lip.

"Paid for!" Rick declared, and she fell on her breakfast, wolfing most of it down in four or five noisy gulps.

He let her out into the small garden while he performed his own toilet, cleaned up himself and her breakfast bowl, and changed for their morning walk. Rick and Nomi lived in a small, one-bedroom bungalow in a thin strip of forest between the Potomac River and the southernmost fairway of the Bretton Woods Golf Course in Seneca, Virginia. The house, more of a shack, really, came with his job. He was a 34-year-old 'ball boy', which was just fine.

"Let's go, girl," he called out, slipping a worn canvas bag over his shoulder.

He locked the front door, then the screen door, set the burglar alarm, closed and padlocked the front gate, and gave Nomi a scratch behind the ear before telling her, "Go on."

She darted away, a flash of black lightning.

She was only two years old, and there was still a lot of puppy in her wild energy. Rick had once seen her leap six feet off the ground and pluck a crow out of the air. That'd been a hell of a mess to clean up, and he'd let her know that chomping birds on the wing was not something they did in this outfit. It would freak the kids out, and he could lose his job and the little cabin that came with it. Unlike the Trump National Golf Course across the river, Bretton Woods was child-friendly. There were always hundreds of families around on the weekend, the dads on the links, moms at the tennis club and the children scattered through adventure camps, the soccer academy, junior tennis and even swim coaching. They all loved Nomi, but that was because they'd never seen her tear apart a screeching bird or squirrel. And as long as Rick was training her, they never would.

Their morning rounds of the course would take them on a five-mile hike, north past the soccer fields and tennis courts, turning west at the aquatic centre, and out past the duck pond before swinging around to head home via the western links. He would undoubtedly collect a dozen or so stray balls, which he'd drop into the big bucket back at the driving range, but he would do his real work later, scouring all eighteen holes while Nomi took the first of her long naps.

Rick didn't delude himself into imagining he was a vital cog in the polished machine that ran Bretton Woods. He took his work seriously —besides gathering stray golf balls, he was also responsible for policing up rubbish and dead squirrels, some of them taken out by those stray golf balls, and general maintenance as directed by the head groundskeeper. But his work was also his therapy. The job and the cabin had been arranged by his old regimental CO, Colonel Farrugia, whose brother-in-law was the general manager. Rick had been riding in the Hummer behind Farrugia's when Sunni militiamen set off a roadside bomb four years ago. He did not care to think about what'd happened next, but when he came back from Iraq for the last time, invalided out of the Army, Farrugia, minus one leg, was waiting for him with a job offer and the keys to a quiet cabin by the Potomac.

"Nomi! To me," Rick called out as he emerged from the woods by a par three green. It was late morning, and the nearest golfers were two holes away. Bright morning sun flashed off the polished steel shaft of a golf club as Nomi came running out of the shadows into the light. She dutifully bounded over to Rick and sat down at his left heel.

"Good girl," he said, flicking her a piece of jerky from the stash in his shirt pocket.

It disappeared so quickly it was as though a small, mouth-shaped black hole had randomly opened up in front of him, consumed the entire mass of the jerky, and instantly winked out of existence again.

"Let's go," he said. "On my six."

Nomi fell in behind him, and they began the long route march around the grounds. Rick loved it here. Enough that on some very rare and special days, he could imagine it was almost worth the terrible journey that had delivered him to this place. He'd been surprised to discover that the first sod for Bretton Woods had been turned in 1968, not as just another exclusive retreat for millionaire businessmen and the politicians they owned, but as a place that didn't discriminate against anybody because they weren't millionaire businessmen and connected insiders. Farrugia explained that the International Monetary Fund had initially built the place for its staff, many of whom would never have been allowed into a whites-only country club. Half a century later, it retained a wide open, welcoming air. The winding trails and the green lawns, all resting quietly behind thick ramparts of remnant old-growth Virginia forest, it was so utterly removed from the heat, dust and horror of the sandbox that, if it weren't for the need to buy groceries and do his therapy at the VA, he would probably never leave.

But he had to go to the VA.

Nomi was part of a research program investigating the benefits of companion animals for veterans with post-traumatic stress. He could never have afforded the thousands of dollars for a pure-bred, highly-trained dog like her. He could barely afford the dried venison feed, and it was subsidised as part of the study.

Rick stopped to pick up a golf ball somebody had sliced off the seventh hole and onto one of the soccer fields. Sprinklers tick-tick-ticked away, shooting long jets of water over the playing field. He examined the stray ball. A Volvik Vista IV. Expensive. He dried it off with the small towel tucked into his belt and dropped it into the satchel at his hip.

It was a weekday, mid-morning, and he was surprised to see a group of young teens on the grass lawn between the tennis courts. You saw lots of kids out here on the weekend, but Rick assumed they were probably doing a school excursion. Bretton Woods had arrangements with some local schools to lease out sporting facilities as needed. The kids in this group seemed to be doing some sort of acrobatics or gymnastics class. He smiled as he drew closer and recognised the instructor.

Mel Baker.

So, no. They were learning jujitsu.

Melissa had them warming up at the moment, which meant a couple of dozen teenagers stretching and rolling and generally falling over themselves on the soft grass. Rick returned to scouting for golf balls, picking up another three before he reached the tennis courts, where Mel had the kids doing basic breakfalls.

"Why do we have to do this?" somebody whined. "When do we get to hit someone?"

Mel ignored the whining and waved at Rick and Nomi.

When the kids realised there was a dog (possibly even a puppy) nearby, all semblance of order broke down. Only a couple of kids made the initial break, but when Mel made no effort to restrain them, all of the others quickly followed.

"Sit. Stay," Rick commanded as they were rushed.

Nomi did as she was told, sitting in one spot, but her tail wagged furiously at the promise of so much lovin'.

Mel wandered over and joined the flash mob that had formed around Rick and his dog, asking him with a wordless glance and raised eyebrow whether he was okay.

He nodded.

There were times when suddenly getting mobbed like this would unravel him, put him back at a checkpoint in Ramadi or the souk in Fallujah, but he was feeling good today, and Nomi lapped up the attention as greedily as she'd wolfed down her breakfast.

"All right! Enough puppy time," Mel called out over the tumult after a minute or two. "Let's get back to it."

She rolled over the chorus of protests and complaints, clapping her hands together and shouting that the last one back would enjoy the privilege of racing her through a set of fifty push-ups.

Nobody wanted that, and nobody, especially not the boys, wanted to get beaten by her. They all raced back to the plot of grass she'd marked out as her open-air dojo.

"What's happening with you this morning, Master Sergeant?" Mel asked, shading her eyes from the morning sun.

"Same old, same old, Constable Baker," he replied.

"You got a few minutes for a demo?" she asked.

"Throws again?"

"You are a big boy. It does impress."

He chuckled and shrugged.

"Okay, sure."

They joined the school group at the training mats Mel had brought down from the gym.

"All right, listen up," she called out in her thick London accent. Or at least Rick assumed it was a London accent. He assumed everyone from England came from London. "You are in for a treat this morning," Mel said. "Mister Boreham, here, is a former Army Ranger. And he's going to help me show you a few things."

Rick heard the change in tone, especially among the teenage boys.

"Now we're gonna see some ass-kicking," somebody said in a stage whisper.

They had no idea. Rick sent Nomi to lie down under the shade of an old oak tree, and she happily trotted away to her assigned station, followed by the disappointed cries of her new fans. He slipped off the canvas satchel full of reclaimed golf balls and set it down on the grass.

"How much do you weigh, Mister Boreham?" Mel asked, dragging everybody's attention back onto them.

"Two hundred and fifteen pounds, ma'am," Rick said.

"And how tall are you?"

"Six-three, ma'am."

"You think you can take me?"

"Not even on my best day, ma'am."

His confession caused great amusement among the young audience.

"You're not much of a Ranger then," some little asshole called out from the back of the pack.

Mel turned on the heckler. Her smile was sweetly dangerous.

"Oh, would you like to try your advanced combat skills against Master Sergeant Boreham, Nicholas?"

An embarrassed silence followed by a few nervous giggles was her only answer.

"I didn't think so," Mel said before dropping into her instructor's voice. "As you can see, Mister Boreham is at least half again as big as me. He could literally pick me up and throw me over your heads. And now he'll try to do that."

Rick knew what was coming, and he mugged it up for the kids, suddenly dropping into character as a snarling, crouching monster. He went at Mel fast and hard, his arms spread wide as if to gather her up. He wasn't sure what the name of the throw she executed was called. Unlike her, he didn't have a black belt in judo or jujitsu. He simply knew it as 'the hay bale throw'. She dropped beneath his centre of gravity and used his mass and momentum against him, folding up before his assault and rolling with it. It worked every time. Rick felt himself magically take flight, and the world turned upside down. He tried to relax into the landing, exhaling fully, tucking in his chin.

He crashed down, heard Nomi bark, and the kids all cheer and gasp, and then he marvelled as Melissa somehow materialised on his chest, pinning his arms to his side and miming a flurry of punches that would have turned his face to blood pudding.

The kids broke into applause.

Nomi barked delightedly.

And for a few moments, Rick Boreham smiled as the sorrows of the world fell away.

5

MALWARE ATTACK

I t had not been that long since James had seen a mechanical credit card slide, one of those old models that took an impression of your card deets on a bundle of carbon-copied receipts. When you spent as much time in fly-over country as he did, you got used to old analogue technology. So he frowned as soon as he heard the unmistakable ratcheting *clack-clunk* at the front desk of his hotel.

The NSC guys had sprung for a room in a small, boutique hotel owned by the Marriott, a place called the Courtyard, over near Foggy Bottom. It was clean, modern, a little sterile for his tastes, and probably cost a hundred bucks a night more than federal government regulations allowed, which told him how much they wanted this briefing. It was also suffering from the same internet glitches that Admiral Holloway had grumbled about, and James had experienced first-hand at the Texaco on I-95. Unlike the poor clerks at the gas station, the front desk staff at the Courtyard by Marriott seemed to have the situation well in hand. It helped that there was only one other customer to deal with when James arrived at check-in. A businessman with a tiny overnight bag.

Clack-clunk.

"Thank you, sir," said the young woman in Marriott livery at the larger of the two counters. "We do apologise for the internet outage, but your room key will work, and AT&T assures us their techs are on it. You can take the elevators over on the left up to your room on the fourth floor."

The man said something James didn't catch and snatched up his bag before stalking off. Not a happy customer.

The check-in staff kept glassy smiles fixed in place until he was gone.

"You look like you're having a great day," James grinned as he approached the same desk, letting the cheeky glint in his eye assure the two women that he wasn't going to give them any trouble over something that wasn't their fault. Their professional masks slipped, just a little, to reveal the stress they'd been bottling up, possibly all day.

"Oh my word, it's been a day all right," the older of the women said. "Are you checking in, sir?"

James nodded and gave them his name.

"The booking might be in my name or the National Security Council," he said. "They made it for me. By phone this afternoon," he added quickly. If everyone's systems were glitching, the only record of his booking might have been scribbled on a Post-it note stuck to the side of somebody's frozen computer screen.

The staffer who'd spoken to him took control of his check-in, flipping open an old-fashioned hard-copy ledger and running her ink-stained finger down the most recent page. Her name tag read 'Wendi' with an 'i'.

"Yes, Mr O'Donnell," Wendi said. "We do have a booking from the NSC. They're covering all charges, so we only need to take an imprint of your card for the token holding fee. It's a dollar. Would you like a newspaper delivered in the morning?"

He almost said *no*. But after a moment's hesitation, James answered, "Actually, yes, please. Sounds like I might not be able to read the news on my phone."

Wendi shook her head and let her eyes roll, just a little in exasperation as she stage-whispered, "You would not believe what it's been like today."

"Tell me," he said.

Wendi looked as though she couldn't quite believe anybody was asking her opinion of anything, but when James smiled and nodded his encouragement, she leaned forward a little as if to share a secret.

"It's not just our booking system," she said in a voice just above a whisper. "I can't get on to Facebook to message my kids, and Deonie says her phone won't even make an old-fashioned call anymore."

The other front desk staffer, presumably Deonie, nodded with eyes wide.

"I think it's hackers," she said.

"Oh, you think everything's hackers," Wendi scoffed, but not harshly.

A man in a suit and tie appeared from a back-office area, an alcove hidden behind dark wooden panelling and an art installation of bright orange electric batons. His arrival instantly affected Wendi and Deonie, wiping out their real personalities, which were replaced by the bright, glassy grins and slightly too wide eyes James had seen when he first arrived.

He thought they both looked like they were screaming inside.

Wendi handed him a small square of folded cardboard holding two plastic room tags.

"Thank you, Mr O'Donnell, and welcome to the Courtyard by Marriott. Please don't hesitate to ask if there's anything we can do to make your stay more pleasant. You can take the elevators over to the left up to your room on the sixth floor."

James smiled as reassuringly as he could.

He did not ask about the Wi-Fi.

He would never use hotel Wi-Fi for anything.

JAMES' room afforded him a view over a small, triangular park where he could see a few people escaping the heat under the shade trees. A young couple shared ice cream cones, and a stoop-shouldered man in a black suit and a rather old-fashioned hat fed dozens of pigeons from a brown paper bag. James could feel the day's heat radiating through the window glass, but it was no match for the hotel's climate control. After his drive and meeting with Michele Nguyen, he was hungry and a little weary, but he took a few minutes to shower and change into a fresh shirt and underwear. James hadn't expected to stay overnight in the capital, but whenever he left home, even for a short road trip, he took at least two days' clothes with him in a sports bag. You could never be sure if a missed or cancelled flight, or even something as simple as a flat tire, might delay your return.

Rather than stinging the long-suffering American taxpayer for room service, he ate a protein snack from his overnight bag and made a cup of instant coffee from the complimentary in-room cafe bar. He set up his laptop and tried unsuccessfully to get online. Neither his phone's hotspot (AT&T) nor the T-Mobile broadband dongle he carried as a backup would work. James frowned, but he had expected that might be the case. On any other day, his natural curiosity and sense of responsibility to his subscribers might have led him down a rabbit hole as he tried to locate the source of what was obviously a critical failure of the national digital infrastructure. But he had a newsletter to get out and the commission from Holloway, and they would have to come first.

All the files he needed to complete the mailout and start Holloway's job were on his laptop. The shadows in the park outside lengthened, and the bright white light of high summer gave way to the softer, golden glow of sunset. He completed the newsletter, including an apology for the delay in sending it and a promise to investigate and report on any market inferences from the day's online disruptions. Problems with Amazon Web Services had caused similar issues just a few months earlier. (And yet AWS kept growing as an on-demand cloud platform.) He set up an auto-send command to get the newsletter out the moment his laptop detected a working connection and moved on to planning out the brief he would write for the NSC.

This was a little more challenging without internet access, but James maintained his offline archives on the MacBook Pro and a 256 gig flash drive that hung from his car keys. Using some of the stuff Nguyen had given him during their interview—he was scheduled to get access to classified data on-site tomorrow—James prepped a bullet point elevator pitch about US tech firms with supply chains running through China, a fifteen-minute small-group presentation and a much more detailed ten-thousand-word paper. It took a couple of hours. When he was finished, full night had fallen outside.

He hadn't noticed how hungry he'd been while he was hammering away at the keyboard, but within a few minutes of saving the files and backing up to the thumb drive, James found himself wondering which was worse; his rumbling stomach or the headache that always came on when he forgot to eat during a work binge.

The cure for both was the same.

Dinner.

He thought about walking down the street and finding a restaurant or bar where he could get a quick meal, but his usual guilt about spending other people's money had abated a little while he worked in his room. He thought that the NSC probably owed him at least a room service hamburger and fries. He ordered a cheeseburger and flicked on the television while he waited for the food to arrive, finding *Bloomberg Markets* after a few seconds of channel surfing.

The chyron at the bottom of the screen said it all.

MALWARE ATTACK SHUTS DOWN MILLIONS OF SITES.

Cristina Alesci looked as fearsome as ever, but she'd strayed far from her usual beat of mergers and acquisitions.

"The Department of Homeland Security is investigating the widespread outages as a massive hack on the backbone of the internet..."

James walked over to his laptop and checked whether the newsletter had gone out.

Nope.

No connection.

He frowned.

Flicking through all of the cable news channels, even the crazy ones like MSNBC and Fox, he quickly determined that the internet outage was the story of the day, having displaced the unlikely rescue of a boy scout troupe from a collapsed cave in Oregon, and the leaked CCTV video of disgraced Hollywood mogul Harvey Weinstein's prison rape.

James thought this had to be a little more serious than Twitter's fail whale coming out of retirement.

His burger arrived.

James tipped the room service guy and ate the food without tasting it.

Everywhere he looked, the news was all about the hack. It quickly became apparent that the malware had infected systems throughout Europe and Asia, but the US cable news channels weren't reporting extensively on those breaches. He flipped around until he found CNN Hong Kong and an Australian news channel.

The malware attack was the main story there, too.

It wasn't just social media and online shopping sites that had gone down. Critical infrastructure like hospitals, airports and even road networks were affected. Every traffic light in Auckland, New Zealand, was currently red and had been for hours. James finished his dinner, but he felt nauseous. His skin tingled, and his heart was racing. Not from the burger. It was excellent, he finally realised as he finished the last mouthful. He'd eaten it mindlessly.

Perhaps he was overly sensitive because he'd just spent hours thinking through the worst consequences of the trade war that was already raging across the globe.

Maybe he was freaking out because he'd just prepped the outline of a secret briefing about the vulnerability of US tech firms to catastrophic disruption by hostile state actors.

But this looked like the opening shots of a new kind of war to him.

"No way," he said quietly.

Given the scale of disruption, it was almost certainly a state-sponsored attack. Plenty of countries maintained deniable, arms-length strike capabilities, often disguised as digital security firms. Any of them could be responsible. North Korea earned more money from internet scams and cybercrime than it did selling weapons on the black market. Over a dozen 'private' companies in Russia, all with deep links back to the state, routinely broke into Western firms to steal data or money. Often, they just straight up shook down the victims by locking them out of their networks and demanding payment in crypto-currency for a key to get back in. That's what this would be, James was almost certain. Hackers fronting for a rogue state, short of cash, or maybe a terror group like ISIS, who were always looking for alternative income streams. Doubtless, tomorrow, he'd read about some hospital that had quietly paid thousands of dollars to get their patient records back or an oil company that dropped a couple of million in Bitcoin to recover their geological survey data. And there'd be others who paid who were still locked out. And still more who'd spent twice as much as the ransom demanded to pay consultants to tell them the genius conclusion that they needed a new server.

It was getting late. His eyes felt itchy and hot from all of the close-focus work. He needed to sleep—he was no good without his eight hours—but he had to make a call first. He couldn't leave it. He had no cell reception and didn't want to pay the hotel's long-distance rate, which he knew would be extortionate without checking. But what choice did he have? Sometimes, you just had to take the hit. He picked up the phone by his bed and dialled out.

The phone at the other end of the call, an old rotary dial unit in the kitchen of his parent's farmhouse on the other side of the continent, rang twice before his mom picked up.

It was always his mom.

"Hey, Mom. It's me," James said.

"Jimmy! What a lovely surprise. I didn't expect you to call until the weekend. Is anything up?" his mom asked.

James smiled. She had travelled directly from unexpected delight to matronly concern without drawing breath. Do not pass Go. Do not collect $200.

"I'm fine, Mom. I'm just fine," James assured her. "I'm in Washington for work and just wanted to check that you weren't having any issues with this internet thing. Is Dad there?"

Tom O'Donnell was the designated hitter for any technical difficulties at James's parents' place, the archivist of old technical manuals, keeper of all the cables, and guardian of the blessed passwords (which were written down and hidden in an old school notebook beneath a pile of tea towels, the third drawer down from the old coffee pot by the biscuit barrel). James could picture the scene as vividly as the hotel around him. His mother was calling the old man, telling him Jimmy was on the phone, and Tom – who would have been deeply embedded within his old TV chair – would be shuffling out to the kitchen in his socks, probably trailing a cloud of blue-grey pipe smoke.

"Jim, is that you?"

"Hi, Dad. Yeah. It's me."

"You okay, boy? You don't normally ring at this time?"

"I'm fine, Dad; I just wanted to check you hadn't been affected by this internet problem. Have you been online today?"

He tried to keep his voice light and free of anxiety, but his parents knew him better than anyone else. His father chuckled.

"Worried your old man was gonna give his credit card to some sharpie in Moscow, did you?"

"No, Dad, I just..."

"Well, don't you worry, boy. I haven't even turned on the computer today. Too busy helping Bob Waldrop re-stump the fence line down to Tillet Creek. Dry storm came through last week. Hell of a thing. Lightning bolt fairly blew the hell out of a stretch of fence line. Looked like an artillery shell had struck it. But not a drop of rain, of course. Still as dry as the devil's own dirt patch out here. Anyways I only just got in from Bob's, and your Ma was busy late at the library with the little ones' reading classes and..."

James didn't tune out, but he did come off the anxiety high he'd been surfing. He could hear his mother rattling pots and pans in the sink and, somewhere behind that, the sound of the TV news in the background. The real news, his Dad called it. Not that crazy cable stuff. When Tom O'Donnell was done telling him about the doings and a-goings-on around the county, James led him back to the reason for his call.

"Okay, it sounds like you got it all stowed away there, Dad. I just wanted you to take care with this internet thing. Don't click on any email attachments, or visit any websites you don't regularly go to, or..."

"I'm all over it, boy," his father said, but gently. "Not gonna get fooled twice by some sharpie."

"Okay," James said just as gently. "Things are pretty messed up out here, is all. Didn't want you getting caught up in it. Did Mom say anything about it? Any trouble in town, at the library, the bank? That sort of thing?"

"Didn't mention it, no. And your last transfer dropped into the account yesterday. So, thanks for that. It all helps."

James thought he could hear the slightest change in his father's voice, a hesitant self-consciousness.

"Okay, that's good then," he said quickly. "Maybe it's mostly in the big cities out east."

"Maybe. You want to talk to your Mom?"

"I'll say good night, but then I should go. Big day tomorrow. Big week, really."

"That's good, James. It's good you got the work. You made this business for yourself. You need to tend to it."

"I do," James agreed, carefully not voicing any of the conversation that went unspoken between them.

Tom O'Donnell said goodnight and handed the receiver back to his wife.

"You still there, Jimmy?" she said.

"I am, Mom. I won't stay on. I have to get to bed."

"Okay. You keeping well?"

Here it comes.

"You seeing anyone?"

He smiled.

"Yes, Mom. I'm keeping well. No, I'm not seeing anyone."

"Oh." A pause. Just long enough for her disappointment to fill the space. "Okay then. It's good that you're well and busy, too, but you need to get away from work sometimes, too. And not just to the gym. You need to spend some time on yourself."

She didn't say, 'You need someone special, ' but it was coded into the exchange. His parents had married the first summer after gradua-tion, and most of the kids he'd known in high school were hooked up and popping out their own kids now. He was the stranger in town, the one who got away. But this was an old song, and he knew she was mostly humming it to herself.

"I promise the moment I meet someone good enough to give you grandchildren, I'll get caught up on all that straight away."

"Oh, you. Go on, away with you."

"Goodnight, Mom."

"Goodnight, Jimmy."

He hung up.

They got the money, then. That was a relief.

6

ZERO TOLERANCE POLICY

"Boss wants to see you."

Jonas Murdoch clenched his fists and bit down on the curse he wanted to throw back into Omar's face. He got a leash on his temper, but it was hard knowing he had options now. Or soon would have.

"What's he want?" he asked.

Omar shrugged. "The fuck do I know? Travis wants what he wants, snowflake. Best get your ass moving."

There weren't many people in the warehouse who'd speak to Jonas like that, with such a disrespectful tone. He stood six-three and weighed in at 220 pounds of hard muscle and thick bone, and he would take no man's insult. But Omar topped out the scale at 245, and although he was a little soft around the middle, he was a lifter—and surely a roid monster with it. Those guys always were. Dude was strong, fast, and about ten years ago he'd been picked up by the 49ers as an undrafted free agent. But he'd fucked up his knee in a preseason game, and, long story short, he was running stowage for Amazon these days. Just like Jonas.

Except Omar was the supervisor, and Jonas was there to step 'n' fetch.

They had him on big box electronics this morning, as usual. Six long aisles of monster-ass TV sets. Heavy amplifiers. Speakers as tall as a grown man and just as heavy. All of them a fat bitch to lift and just as awkward to carry. He was already rank with sweat. There was no AC in the warehouse, and the giant, slow-turning ceiling fans—seriously, they were as big as helicopter blades—pushed the hot air around. He didn't mind the work, even though it meant answering to Omar or that shrieky bitch Yolanda when she was on the roster. But man, it was a hard dollar when he knew that thousands, maybe hundreds of thousands of peeps were hitting his podcast right the fuck now.

Yesterday morning's pod, when he dropped the names of Pendleton's victims, took a while to reach anyone – some bullshit problem with the internet. But the pod finally uploaded in the small hours of the morning. Jonas got up super early, hunched over the computer and watched his download count spike up and up and up. He was grinning like a fool when he waved Mikey off to work. He'd picked up another thirty thousand subscribers and a quarter million one-off downloads.

Joe Rogan would be getting down on his creaky old knees to have The Centurion as a full-episode guest on his show now, not just a five-minute audio-only drop-in.

So fuck yeah, it was hard to focus on anything else with all that on Jonas's mind. Even harder to put up with an ass-chewing by Travis Tamoreau. But it would be a blessed relief to get out of the heat for a few minutes, and there was a vending machine in the executive mezzanine where he could grab a few protein bars. He'd missed breakfast with all the excitement, and he was angry-hungry.

"You gotta swipe me off," he said to Omar.

The supervisor looked like he wanted to argue with that, but he waved a smart pen over the chip in Jonas's bracelet, and a small green light flashed twice. He was off the clock.

"You got ten minutes," Omar said.

Murdoch's stomach roiled, and his temper flared again.

"Jesus Christ, Omar. It'll take me that long to get there and back."

"Better get running then. Clock's ticking."

Jonas knew what was happening. Omar was trying to haze him out. Get him to quit, probably so he could bring in a cousin or some homey and set them up with a cushy fucking gig. No hauling 55-inch Samsungs or Sony flatscreens for them. They'd be …

Omar smiled at him, and Jonas realised he'd already wasted precious seconds standing there, seething. He'd have to get Tamoreau to swipe him off the floor again if this took more than a few minutes.

"Asshole," he muttered under his breath, but only after he'd pushed past the supervisor and was far enough gone to be sure he couldn't be heard over the constant rumble and crash of operations in the giant warehouse.

Jonas jogged the half mile through rows of high metal shelves swarming with hundreds of worker drones. He wasn't short of breath when he arrived at the steel staircase that climbed to the small, air-conditioned suite of offices reserved for management. All that cheap, off-brand CrossFit. He'd barely raised his heartbeat with the effort, but he was sweating a lot more, enough that the deodorant he'd put on that morning wouldn't cut it, not after four hours down on the floor.

Well, fuck that anyway. These assholes knew they were running a sweatshop. Let them smell some honest fucking sweat from a hard-working American.

Moisture beaded on his forearms, giving his black tribal tattoos a glistening appearance as if they'd been freshly painted on. His beard, kept short for safety on the floor, itched terribly, and he wiped a hand across his forehead and back through the top thatch of thick red-brown hair he'd inherited from his Irish grandmother. It came away wet, and he wiped the sweat on his jeans before pressing the buzzer outside the entrance to the office suite.

You didn't get in without the right swipe card or a buzz-through from Cindy at the front desk. Jonas wasn't often called upstairs, but he always made sure to charm the shit out of Cindy. She was grossly obese and ugly as a hat full of puckered assholes, but he knew from his time as a lawyer that the front desk bitch was often the true power in any business. You got them on your side, and you had a mighty ally.

"Hey there, Cindysaurus."

His ally wouldn't look at him this morning. She blushed when he used her pet name and muttered that he should go straight through to Mister Tamoreau's office. Jonas's skin tingled in the air conditioning, which felt even cooler than it had just a second ago. An autonomic response, he knew. Blood rushing away from the surface of his body because of a perceived threat. He was annoyed with himself for reacting like that, but he also knew that you couldn't just turn off a couple of million years of evolution. A lot of idiots these days thought you could, but that's why they were idiots.

"Thanks, Cindy," he said, keeping it light and stepping around the reception desk, which guarded the inner sanctum of centre management.

Jonas had no idea what sort of shit was about to go down, but he thought he could smell it coming for him. Travis Tamoreau was a snippy little shit, and nobody ever got called to his office for a compliment. Jonas settled his nerves with a few breaths. He reminded himself that he was twice the size of the shift manager and way more than twice the man. He needed this job for now, but he did not need to grovel for it. He had a voice now. He had options.

Tamoreau's office was an unremarkable plywood box two doors down the hallway from Cindy. The centre manager, Nadine, this Jewish bitch who always gave you the impression that you smelled bad, was up in Seattle, where she spent as much time as possible, leaving ops on the floor to her deputy, Tamoreau. Jonas rapped on his office door and waited to be summoned. Tamoreau was that sort of boss. He looked up from his laptop, saw Jonas, and returned to the screen where Very Important Stuff was obviously happening. He kept typing just long enough for it to become uncomfortable. Jonas was gonna need another swipe off for his bracelet, but Tamoreau didn't care. He kept working that keyboard.

Probably refining his profile on Grindr, Jonas thought, with a private smirk.

The centre's deputy ops manager was a fastidious dresser. French cuffs, Italian silk ties, and Hugo Boss suits always cut so tightly the fabric looked like it could scream. He was fit. Jonas would give him that. But it was the taut and nervy muscle tone of the niche queen spin class addict. Half an hour in the box at CrossFit would probably kill him. Fuck, there were chicks in Jonas' gym who could probably kill him by grabbing a wedgie and tossing Tamoreau around like a human kettlebell.

Jonas, trying not to snicker at the idea, contented himself with imagining this guy trying to flip a truck tire the length of the box. Dude would totally ruin his manicure. He wondered how many new subscribers he had to the pod since he checked it earlier that morning.

Tamoreau finished whatever he was doing on the laptop and gestured to a moulded plastic chair in front of his desk. Except for this guy's outfit and cologne, everything in the office looked like it had been bought at a government auction. Even the laptop was some low-budget shitbox from Dell.

"Sit down, Murdoch," Tamoreau said.

A sit-down meeting? Jonas was definitely gonna need another swipe off for his bracelet.

He took the chair, which was slightly cracked where one of the legs flowed into the plastic seat. It put him on edge, waiting for the thing to collapse under his weight. He leaned forward an inch and casually braced his legs, ready to stand up if the chair suddenly gave way.

"What's up?" he asked.

"I've had a complaint," Tamoreau said. "Sexual harassment."

"Well, maybe you should keep your hands to yourself," Jonas grinned. It was his boyish grin. The one which had been getting him out of trouble all his life.

Tamoreau did not return the smile.

"Two female stowers have complained about you commenting on their appearance. Their supervisor corroborates the accounts."

Time stopped for a whole second before accelerating back into motion.

Jonas was confused and genuinely at a loss. He was always cautious to keep his opinions to himself at work. His opinions, after all, were dangerous. So, as much as he thought Cindy in reception looked like a beached whale or Yolanda had a face like a smashed crab, he would never...

"The stowers claim you were offline when you harassed them."

Jonas felt his scalp prickle, and his balls actually move as though trying to contract into his body. All the triumphs of the morning were forgotten.

This wasn't about him telling his bro Eightball that Yolanda got the super's gig because her ass wouldn't fit between the stacks.

This was about the two Dutch girls hired last week. Purebred smokin' hotties, the pair of them, and fashwave fans with it. Or at least he'd thought so. Coming back from what was laughably called his lunch break, Jonas had diverted to help them move a pallet of *sous vide* machines when they were falling behind on their quota. He'd complimented one of the girls, Anya or Anika or something, on her musical taste. Bitch's tits were really filling out a Xurious tee-shirt.

Was that it?

That was all it took? Being nice to someone?

"Look, I er..." he started, but Tamoreau held up one hand. His cufflinks looked like they'd cost more than Jonas made in a month.

"I'm not interested in reasons, excuses or justifications. The company has a zero-tolerance policy for harassment."

"But I didn't harass anyone," Jonas protested. And he hadn't either. If Jonas Murdoch harassed you, nobody would be in any doubt about it, least of all him. "Is this about those Dutch chicks? Came on last week? All I did was help them keep up and... and... I dunno; one of them had a cool tee shirt. You don't see a lot of Xurious fans in the wild. I told her she looked cool, and she *was* cool. Xurious is awesome, man."

Tamoreau's face took on a baffled expression, but it was fleeting. He shook off his disorientation, literally, blinking a couple of times and shaking his head as if he'd just walked into a spider web. He opened a drawer and took out a manila folder. It was thin. Five or six sheets of paper nestled inside. Jonas saw that three sheets were covered in blocks of text and had been signed. Statements? Two others looked like spreadsheets for a box-ticking exercise.

"Is it the case that you were offline from your assigned sector on

Wednesday last week, at or about thirteen hundred and thirty hours, that's 1.30 PM?"

"I know what thirteen-thirty hours means, *Travis*. And I told you, I was helping the new girls. They were having trouble keeping up. Everyone has trouble when they start. And if they don't pick it up, you fire them. Or the labour-hire firm does."

The fuse on his temper was burning hot now. He couldn't believe they were going to do him this way. It had to be Yolanda and Omar. They cooked this shit up for sure.

"So you can confirm you were offline outside your lunch break?" Tamoreau continued.

"I can confirm I was ahead of my quota. I'm always ahead of my quota."

"We're not here to discuss that," Tamoreau said sharply. "We're talking about your behaviour, attitude and treatment of fellow workers and line management. It has been an ongoing issue. This is not the first complaint."

The fuse burned brighter and faster.

"Oh, so you're suddenly concerned about the workers now, Travis? You gonna stop docking us for the time we gotta stand in line waiting for a full body search to check that we're not stealing some two-dollar Chinese USB cable? Every time we go to the can?"

The fuse was short now.

"You gonna tell that asshole, Omar, to stop bitching out everyone who takes more than ten minutes for their totally fucking unpaid half-hour lunch break?"

The fuse burned down to detonation.

"You should be begging me to work here, not fucking with me so Yolanda can sneak in some bestie as an affirmative action hire."

Jonas stood up so quickly that the cheap plastic chair flew across the room and struck a filing cabinet behind him with a dull, metallic crash.

Tamoreau paled. His vice stammered.

"You... you need to calm down, or I'll have to call security."

"Call 'em," Jonas barked. "See if I care. See if they can get here before I get across that fucking desk to you."

Tamoreau's face was completely drained of colour, and his hand reached for the phone next to his laptop.

He never made it.

Not because of Jonas.

The alarms that went off all over the warehouse stopped him dead.

INTERLUDE

Lu Huang woke, as always, well before dawn. He rekindled the coals in the kitchen hearth, boiled water, and carefully measured a small handful of dry green leaves into the same ceramic pot in which he'd been brewing his morning tea for over thirty years. It was identical to the pot he'd used for twenty years before that, but he had broken the earlier pot after stubbing his toe on a small rock, which had definitely not been sticking up out of the rammed earth floor of his hut when he'd blown out the candle the previous night. Probably, the goat had dug it up, looking for something to eat.

The goat was also long gone. It went into a cooking pot many years after its trickery with the treacherous, toe-stubbing rock in the kitchen. It was an old beast by then, tough and stringy even after many long hours of simmering over the coals in a blood soup, but Lu Huang had savoured every bite. Digging holes in Mr Huang's earthen floor was not the least of that diabolical animal's many sins, and it was good to have revenge at last.

Shuffling about in the deep darkness before the first hint of daybreak, Lu Huang was surprised to find himself missing the animal. But perhaps it was not so surprising. As the end of his life drew near, Lu Huang found himself missing the old ways and things ever more painfully. There was his wife, dead of the wasting sickness before he had even stubbed his toe and dropped that old teapot. His children, moved away to Shenzen. His grandson, a spoiled little dumpling of a boy whom Mr Huang might see but once a year—if his feckless son could be bothered to make the two-day train journey to their home province, far from the bright lights of the seaboard cities. Lu Huang missed the life of the village, which was a good deal smaller than it had once been. He missed his friends who were dying even faster than he or moving away as the river dried up and the soil turned grey.

He missed the soil of his youth.

It had been intensely fertile here on the banks of the river, with almost chocolatey brown earth, suitable for all manner of vegetables and even fruit in the short summer months.

Lu Huang shook his old head, muttering darkly. Summer seemed to get longer each year. Longer, hotter, and less agreeable to the fragile peach trees for which the valley of Lo Pung had been famous since the days of the Yuan Dynasty. Lu Huang did not grow peaches himself. He preferred the steady work of market gardening, raising multiple crops of bok choy and snake beans every year. Unfortunately, the valley's famously rich soil and predictable seasons of rain and flood were not as they had once been. Not nearly so rich. And not at all predictable unless you were to predict that nothing would go well and only the worst of the fates were to be relied upon. Lu Huang wore a pained expression as he brewed his tea.

As the tea steeped, he unwrapped the small rice puddings he had made for himself the previous day. He ate them with his fingers because nobody was watching, and in truth, there was nobody left to care enough for Lu Huang for him to care either. A rooster crowed somewhere nearby, calling forth a reply from a barking dog, but that was the only sound for miles around. He was alone at this hour. He was always alone.

When the tea had drawn its full strength, the old farmer poured a cup for himself and savoured the steam rising from the heavy mug. When you had so little to enjoy in the world, it was essential to take what comfort you could from life's simpler pleasures. A properly brewed cup of tea. A shoulder that was not paining you nearly so much as usual. The quiet hope that things might yet turn for the better.

The merest tincture of grey dawn had crept into the deep blackness of the dead man's hour when Lu Huang finished his meagre breakfast. He rinsed out his tea mug in the bucket of water he'd drawn from the village well late yesterday afternoon. From a peg on the back of the kitchen door, he took down the wide-brimmed straw hat that would protect him from the sun's fierce glare in the coming hours. He stepped into the cheap sandals that waited on the back step. Closed the door behind him and took a deep breath.

He could smell diesel from the small factory which had swallowed up the farms of Xi Peng and Hua Fong two years ago, and beneath that stench, the chickenshit he spread on his garden vegetable patch. But mostly, he smelled diesel. Lu Huang had a considerable walk to the fields where he tended his crop. With there being no sense in delaying the moment, he set off. As a younger man with a beautiful wife and a newborn son to provide for, he had run to those fields every day, covering the distance in less than ten minutes. Now, he shuffled and would be lucky to arrive in less than half an hour.

It did not matter.

The fields were not going anywhere.

The long walk allowed him to gather his thoughts for the day. He had a crop of bok choy planted at the moment. The first shoots came through last week. Lu Huang did not much like the look of them. They had none of the lively green vigour you hoped for in a young plant. The shoots appeared frail to him and speckled brown here and there. He glowered at the lights of the factory as he shuffled past. It made plastic cases for cell phones. Colourfully stupid things they were, made to look like cartoon cats. Thick clouds of foul-smelling fumes poured from the chimney stacks night and day. Pipes, already rusted through, vomited wastewater of the most alarming colours directly into the river at all hours. If he were being honest, Lu Huang would admit that the once lush soil of the valley had thinned out and gone bitter long before the cartoon cat phone-case factory arrived. Still, he was confident his crops had taken a decided turn for the worst as soon as those devils had turned on their machines.

The owners of the factory, who had never set foot in the valley, had paid an artist to paint giant pictures of their ugly phone cats on the side of the factory. Walking past his oversized feline tormentors always put the old man in a foul mood, and he shuffled past this morning with his brows even more deeply furrowed than usual. Lu Huang was very worried about this crop. If it did not come good, he would have trouble paying his bills. The man from the fertiliser factory called every day until Lu Huang's old phone was cut off because he could not pay that bill either.

Soon, the man from the fertiliser factory would be at his door, probably with police officers.

That was how Xi Peng and Hua Fong had lost their farms to the diabolical cat phone people.

These dark thoughts stayed with Lu Huang until he reached the gate of his small holding. The sun was rising, and it looked like another day without clouds or the promise of rain. The cast iron gate creaked on its hinges as he pushed through. The outlines of scarecrows slumped and forlorn against the lightening sky. No birds had yet tried to steal his crop.

Lu Huang's frail and aged heart beat slowly as he neared the first rows of bok choy.

No birds would be foolish enough to make a meal of these plants.

There was enough light now for him to see that the dark spots that had dotted his crop's first shoots were gone. The entire crop was gone. It had turned black and withered away to ruin while he slept.

Lu Huang slowly fell to his knees and wept for all he had lost.

Severino Munoz pushed the small wooden rowboat away from the pier. The boy jumped in at the last minute, holding the rope that had secured them to the rotting timbers of the dock. The boy was still young, with the spindly thinness of an early teen. His eyes twinkled with the adventure of it all, and he moved about the small wooden boat with the surefooted grace of one born to the water.

Severino smiled at him, but it was an effort. They would row for two hours, even with the tide in their favour, to reach the nets off Punta La Madre, and he feared it would all be for naught. The traps caught nothing but plastic bags and bottles these days. The anchovies that once teemed in these waters, which had sustained the families of La Madre and Playa Blanca and Puerto Valero, were all gone, it seemed.

The boy did not care. Not yet.

He was happy to be out on the water with his uncle, even if it meant many hours of hauling an oar, roasting in the sun and dragging himself home with nothing to show for the effort. The boy's father, brother to Severino's wife, had drowned out here under these very waves not three years ago, and it had fallen to Severino to raise his nephew to manhood.

Manhood could wait, thought the fisherman, as he pulled at the oars and watched the boy from under the brim of his old hat.

Manhood was just debt, fear and the struggle not to give up at the end of every godforsaken day. Why did the boy need to rush towards such a future? Severino had more than enough of these sorrows to suffice.

"Uncle, where do the fish go?" the boy asked.

Severino grunted unintelligibly. Often, that was enough. The boy just needed to know he was listening. With an audience, he would babble on for hours about this and that, none of it especially interesting or important. Severino did not mind. It passed the time out here, and increasingly, it felt like time was all he had.

But today, the boy wanted answers.

"The man on the radio said it is El Nino again. He said El Nino chases away the fish."

"Sometimes this is so," Severino agreed and kept rowing. They had passed out through the heads of the tiny bay in which their village nestled between low, scrubby hills. The sun still reflected fiercely off the white render of their homes and places of business, but soon, all that would fall below the horizon.

"But Mama says no," the boy protested. "Mama says there is no El Nino to chase away the fish, and if there was there would still be no fish to chase away."

Severino did not care for this line of talk.

His sister was too smart for her own good sometimes. The boy did not need to bother himself with these things at his age. Why should he be given to worry over such matters? The coming and going of El Nino had shaped the lives of fishermen for as long as anybody remembered. Years, decades before the gringo scientists had arrived to study the waters off Punta La Madre, the men of the district had known that there were times when the ocean grew warmer than usual, and the anchovies disappeared. Usually, it happened just before Christmas. Prayers to the Christ child were always more fervent in those years. But this had been so for centuries, and the fish had always come back.

Not this year, though.

His sister Madelena was correct in that much, at least. The gringo scientists, the government men in Santiago, and the yammering fools on the radio all agreed that El Nino had gone away last year.

The fish should be back.

"Did the fish always come back when you were a boy?" Severino's nephew asked.

"Of course. I would not be here otherwise," the man said, regretting his foolishness as soon as the words left his mouth.

"Then how will I row the boat when you are gone and the fish with you?" the boy asked.

His tone was not sad or scared.

He just wanted to know how his uncle would make everything right.

Severino had made everything right after the boy's father drowned. Severino had even made everything right when Chile fell out of the World Cup.

Severino would surely make this right, too. He would bring back the fish. He would win the World Cup. He would protect the boy and raise him well until the boy was a man, and it was his turn to take out the boat and make everything well.

Severino said nothing.

He pulled on the oars as the sun beat down on them, two specks of life dragging themselves across the vast wasteland of a dead sea.

The nets were still hours away.

Perhaps today would be different.

Timothy Santo marvelled at his cup of coffee. Not because it was unusually good or bad, but because his secretary told him it had cost nearly eight hundred *vatu*. Seven US dollars, more or less. The Foreign Minister of Vanuatu had an MBA from the University of California, and his family exported cocoa to the US, a business that made him sensitive to fluctuations in currency and commodity prices. This morning, he was feeling particularly sensitive and not just about his costly cup of rather ordinary coffee.

Vanuatu was in crisis.

Looking out of Santo's office window over downtown Port Vila, you couldn't tell that. It was still early in the day. Most shops and businesses were closed, and only a few tourists had ventured forth to seek a cheaper and more adventurous breakfast than the fare offered at their hotel buffet. It looked so tranquil, he thought. Palm trees swaying gently in the early morning breeze. The rising sun dappling the blue waters of the Pacific. Boats swaying at anchor in the marina across the street from his office. A paradise, in fact.

But a paradise that could no longer feed itself or pay to import food from anywhere else.

Santo had all the briefings on his desk, but he did not need them. His wife had rung him late the previous day to confirm that the bank was calling in the loan they had taken out two years earlier to expand operations at the main family plantation. The drought had not broken with the change in the Southern Oscillation Index, the measurement of sea surface temperatures in the central and eastern equatorial Pacific that was bound up so closely with weather patterns from South America to India. The drought had not broken. Two crops had failed.

And now Timothy Santo was bankrupt. But that was the least of his problems.

He would have to tender his resignation to the President later today, but first, he had one last duty to perform for the island republic. The drought, which destroyed his family business and, with it, his political career, had also collapsed the island's kava and coconut industries and, unsurprisingly, the businesses of his competitors in the cocoa trade. Vanuatu was as broke as its Foreign Minister.

Worse than that, though, it would soon go hungry if the government could not work a solution.

Fish stocks had declined precipitously around the archipelago, a dire development for a society where ninety-nine per cent of the population still fished by rod and hand line for sustenance an average of three times a week. The small village farms that had once grown foodstuffs like taro, yams and bananas had largely given way to commercial crop plantations.

Just like the one his family owned.

Sorry.

Had owned.

Maybe once upon a time, everybody could have been given seeds and a shovel and told to fend for themselves. But not now.

Keen-eyed observers might have noticed that some shelves in the capital's supermarkets were not being restocked as quickly as usual. The loss of foreign currency earnings had finally flowed through to the local economy, out on the street. It was probably days from seizing up completely.

Santo's heart quickened when he thought about it. He could not bear to read the reports on his desk. The language was dry. The figures were impersonal. But the warning was stark.

Unemployment. Hyper-inflation. Financial collapse.

All of it, coming for them.

The minister jumped so violently at the knock on his door that he spilled half of his very expensive coffee down his shirt, staining it beyond all hope of just dabbing out a few spots.

His secretary, Mary, stood in the doorway, eyes wide, staring at the brown patch on his white shirt.

"The... ambassador is here," she said.

"Damn," Santo cursed. The drink was hot, and it had scalded him a little. More importantly, he was not fit to receive his visitor, and he had no time to change into the clean shirt he kept in his office closet. His suit jacket was draped over the back of his office chair, and Mary gestured at it in desperation.

"Great idea", he mouthed silently, giving her a thumbs-up.

Putting down the rest of the coffee, he quickly pulled on the coat and did up the buttons. It seemed to hide the stain, and he was resolved to ignore the discomfort. The small puddle on his desk he hid by moving an in-tray. The liquid spilled on the carpet behind his desk was not visible to anybody but him.

"Please, Mary," Timothy Santo said with commendable false cheer. "Do show the ambassador in."

A moment later, a tall, well-dressed Chinese man appeared in the doorway, smiling.

Ambassador Yu Wenhao.

"I do hope this is convenient," he said.

"Of course, of course, come in," Santo said, suddenly mortified by the fear that he may have splashed coffee on his pants, too.

The Ambassador did not seem to notice anything awry, not even with the awkward way Santo moved to shake his hand while holding his suit jacket closed.

"Please, Mr. Ambassador, do sit down."

Yu Wenhao took the armchair in front of Santo's desk. Vanuatu's Foreign Minister dropped into his seat with something like blessed relief.

"I am very grateful you could make time to see me at this difficult juncture," Yu said.

Santo's smile faltered just a little bit.

"Difficult?"

The Chinese official nodded but said nothing.

"Well, I don't know that I would characterise things as difficult," Santo said, recovering as best he could. Nobody outside the Cabinet had yet been briefed on the true scope of the looming crisis. Yu had been invited here under the ever-so-slightly false pretence that they were to discuss routine revisions to the structure of the loans - credit that Beijing had advanced the tiny island nation for a host of infrastructure programs that none of the usual Western aid donors would consider.

"Oh," said Yu. "I see. That is good to hear, Minister. I am advised that your country is three days from defaulting on a number of loans and that the government itself will run out of money by Friday."

The words were spoken as though they did not imply the end of the world as Santo knew it. Yu managed to sound both relieved and disbelieving at the same time.

Santo, meanwhile, was reeling.

The room actually seemed to spin around him for a few seconds.

"How could you know..." he started to say before stopping himself.

He had not meant to speak aloud, but in the chaos of his tumbling thoughts and trip-hammering heart, Timothy Santo momentarily lost control of himself.

"The Chinese side always does its due diligence, Minister," Yu said, occasioning another lurch of Santo's heart.

Whenever these people started talking about 'the Chinese side,' you knew you were in trouble.

"The Chinese side is well aware of the fiscal difficulties in which the Republic of Vanuatu finds itself," the ambassador went on. "But the Chinese side requires that compliant with the terms of the loans advanced to the Republic, all payments are to be made on schedule, or failing that, the entirety of the outstanding balance be paid by the close of business in Beijing tomorrow."

Santo opened his mouth to reply, but nothing came out.

Ambassador Yu stared at him, saying nothing.

"But... but..." the Foreign Minister said before running out of words.

Yu smiled.

"But perhaps we might come to an arrangement, he said.

7

THE OAKLAND SHOOT

Jody Sarjanen hated these handovers. She especially hated the need to do them on neutral ground because it forced her to wait for Chad in places like this, the McDonald's off Junipero Serra Boulevard, about a mile southwest of the little Ocean-view bungalow she shared with Ellie and her son, Max.

"The worst house in the best street," Ellie would say, setting up one of their favourite jokes.

"If you're a crack dealer looking for a starter home," Jody would reply with a crooked smile and stagey eye roll.

She wasn't smiling this morning. Chad was late, as usual, and she had to sit inside Micky D's because it was a hundred and six outside, and she couldn't afford to run the AC in the car. The gas tank was super low, and later today, she had to drive to Oakland for a photo-shoot before picking Ellie up from work in Temescal and looping back across the bridge to get home. Maybe there'd be enough gas in the tank... hopefully, there would be.

Anybody sneaking a look at the striking young woman in the booth by the window—and a couple of customers, both male and female, did do just that—would have seen a tall, composed and distantly elegant woman nursing a large, professional-looking camera bag. They might have imagined her a model, waiting on a photographer. Her straight, shoulder-length hair, pulled back into a severe ponytail, was almost shockingly blonde, a natural icy colour that evoked the glaciers and frozen lakes of her Finnish ancestry. If you were bold enough to stare openly at such an exotic beauty, you might have noticed the slight twitching at the corner of one eye, but only if you stared closely. Otherwise, there was no obvious sign of the wild emotional currents that roared within her.

One long leg jigged under the table as she stared vacantly through the dark tangle of electricity poles and wires sagging in the heat. A few storefronts, half of them empty, a gas station, and a Korean corner market seemed to dance in the heat shimmer. A No. 54 bus rumbled past, belching thick oily fumes, adding to the unkempt, defeated appearance of the streetscape.

Mcdonald's was a comparative haven of clean lines and cool air, but there was no escaping the smell of fried meat and hot grease, forcing Jody to breathe through her mouth while trying not to gag. Whenever she attended to the smell of burning flesh, her throat would close up. So she fixed her attention outside, beyond the plate glass window that was hot to the touch despite the air conditioning. There just weren't that many places in Oceanview where she could take custody of her son in a safe and public place. She would have preferred the library on Randolph Street, but Chad was banned from there. He was very loud, no more so than when he was yelling at the 'fatties' and the 'book chodes' that they should get off their lazy butts and burn some 'ass cheddar' at the gym.

With him.

Chad.

Chief executive asskicker of Body By Chad, premium provider of personal training in the Oceanview metropolitan area.

So the library was out.

As was the new playground across from Sheridan Elementary, Max's K-5 school. A gang had claimed it. Not the Vietnamese 5T or the O.G. wannabes in the sad little white homie crew that haunted the failing mall on Sagamore. No. Jody was scared of running into the mothers' group, which had turned on her when she bailed on Chad and hooked up with Ellie. They loved to hang out and brunch under the shade trees in the park. Not that she thought they'd be there today. Their boob jobs would melt in this heat.

She just wanted to get her kid and be gone.

Dinostar Records had commissioned the Oakland shoot, and they were pretty good at paying their invoices on time. But 'on time' meant that their three hundred bucks still wouldn't drop into her PayPal for another week. And Ellie wouldn't get paid until Friday night. El could bring food home from the restaurant, which was great, but you couldn't run a car on leftover tabbouleh.

A black Jeep pulled into the McDonald's car lot, a small supernova of sunlight exploding off polished chrome and forcing Jody to wince and squeeze her eyes shut. Chad drove a Jeep, but it was white and covered in pictures of, well... Chad.

Chad with arms crossed and muscles flexed, veins standing out like purple worms just under his aggressively tangerine-coloured skin.

Chad primal screaming, but looking like he'd never enjoyed himself more than he was at that very moment.

Chad grinning, with almost carnivorous delight, and three cartoon speech bubbles emerging from his vulpine smile.

'Your workout is Chad's warm-up.'

'Nothing tastes as good as Chad feels.'

And Jody's fave, because it was so perfectly, stupidly, incomprehensibly Chad.

'Unless you puke, faint or die, Chad has failed.'

That, right there, was Peak Chad. It seemed impossible she had ever married him, but of course, she'd only done so after falling pregnant. Because she was an idiot.

Not for having Maxy, of course. That little boy was her life now. But marrying Chad? Jesus. She'd been young.

Jody sipped at the bottled water she'd bought and tried not to look at her watch. She knew he was late and by how much. Twelve minutes and counting. When you were playing one of Chad's games, twelve minutes wasn't even getting into extra time. She'd have to be here an hour for that, and she didn't think he'd dare. Chad was already on a warning from the family court that he could lose access rights if he didn't stick to the visitation plan. And one thing she would concede about her asshole ex-husband, he was crazy for little Max.

So crazy he might not give him back one day?

Jody took a sudden swig of the chilled water to shut out that treacherous whisper before it grew into a shout. The water was so cold, and she swallowed so much of it in one gulp that an icy spike shot up through her eyeball and into her head. She squeezed her eyes shut and tried to calm down. Her heart was starting to race.

Deep breaths, Jody. Deep breaths and sane thoughts.

She still had plenty of time to get Max to his playdate and her ass to Oakland and these stupid rappers into the shoot for Dinostar. She was just freaking because it was hot, and she was frazzled, and she had less than twenty dollars to her name in the world. Both credit cards were maxed out. She couldn't afford to fill the Honda's gas tank, and rent was due Saturday.

She was just stressed, was all.

She kept her eyes closed. Breathed in and out deeply. Three times, and opened them again. She imagined Chad's Jeep pulling into the lot.

But it didn't.

Jody caved and checked her watch.

God! He was twenty minutes late.

Now, she did begin to succumb to her fears, to that black rat of anxiety that attended every one of these handovers, quietly gnawing away at her stomach lining. Every. Single. Time.

She did not want to call Chad. She couldn't call him.

He was the sort of asshole who picked up his phone while he was driving.

While he was driving her little Maxy.

She would call Elizeh.

She hated to be so weak, but Ellie was strong enough for both of them. Ellie would know what to do. She would drop bombs and burn bridges and nuke motherfuckers from orbit if that's what it took to make everything right again.

Jody was reaching for her iPhone when it rang.

Ellie's darkly handsome face filled the cracked screen, and Jody felt a wave of cool relief wash through her body. She grabbed up the phone, fumbling and almost dropping it. Her heart missed a beat. Possibly two. It was an old model. She could not afford to replace it.

"Ellie! Oh, babe, I'm so..."

But it was not Ellie. A man's voice answered, speaking in a broad Australian accent she recognised immediately. It was Damien Maloney. Ellie's boss.

"Hey, mate. It's me, Damo," he said. "You better get over here. Maybe bring one of your reporter mates. Your girlfriend's been grabbed up, Jodes. Bunch of floor-shitting Nazis from ICE just kicked down me doors and tried to take away half the fuckin' kitchen. Fuck me raw, it's not a good look just before lunch."

Jody Sarjanen did not hear the last part of whatever Damien had said.

She was already running for the door, trying to text her useless ex as she went.

———

"The fuck is this, Chris? You scrape this shit off the road coming over here?"

Elizeh Jabbarah did not like the look of the super-premium Wagyu beef the distributor was trying to lay off on her. Maybe Chris was trying it on because she wasn't Damo. Perhaps because she wasn't a man. The sous chef at *Fourth Edition* didn't care. She wasn't paying premium dollar for ordinary protein. And this sad-looking tube of bullshit rib eye was very fucking ordinary.

"Ellie, come on, please," Chris said, his tone beseeching. The kitchen space was busy with prep for lunch. It roared with the centuries-old, intimately familiar fusion of rigid discipline and head-spinning chaos that Ellie loved and hated, and could never imagine giving up. Cleavers crunched into bones as second-year apprentices stood over their first-year charges, breaking down a carcass on the butcher's block. Directly behind Ellie, old Sandino muttered obscenely at the giant pot of master stock he had been tending for years, carrying it from one restaurant to the next, whispering pornographically to it every day as though they were lovers and their passion could only be kept aflame with the most profoundly lurid promises and erotic cursing. Pots and pans clattered and crashed together. Blenders whirred. Bones roasted for demi-glace. And dozens of sweating, tattooed kitchen warriors shouted and swore and laughed in half a dozen languages, from the lowliest dishwasher to... well, to her. She carried the rank of sous chef, but the kitchen was really hers, not Damo's. Her crew all laboured with a fierce will to conjure something magical and extra from the produce of the earth.

Unfortunately, there was very little magic to the produce Chris was trying to sell her.

It wasn't his fault. She knew that. The drought was in its fifth year now, and wholesale prices of water-dependent inputs had nearly doubled in that time. The quality, too, had suffered.

Ellie knew that. Everybody in the business knew it.

But giving Chris an even break wasn't her job.

Damien paid her to run his kitchen, to protect his investment, his dream.

And his dream was not to charge a hundred dollars a plate for the sort of meat she could pick up at a fucking Costco fire sale.

"It's not good enough, Chris," Ellie said. "I'm not taking it. I'll rewrite the damn menu if I have to, but before I do that, I'll call the Kasitch brothers and tell them to give me whatever they've got at whatever price they feel like charging."

Chris Kakris winced as though she'd pushed a boning knife in between his ribs. His family had been fighting a wholesale war with Jevon Kasitch and his clan for as long as Ellie had been rattling pans around the Bay. She knew it would hurt Chris to think he could lose *Fourth Edition* to them. That's why she did it.

The sous chef was not just a chef. She was Damo's fixer, his line commander and enforcer. When the *Chronicle* awarded *Fourth Edition* three Michelin stars, it was Damien Maloney as Executive Chef and owner who posed for the photos and sat for two interviews with Michael Bauer, but it was Ellie who gave them the freedom to sit around enjoying their confit of Tasmanian ocean trout with *Do Ferreiro* Albariño while *Edition* served up its usual three hundred lunchtime covers without breaking stride. Damo thoroughly enjoyed the fiction of calling himself the restaurant's master chef, but he could barely burn a piece of toast.

"You know it's the drought," Chris complained. "This is what top-shelf beef looks like now, Ellie. I promise you; this is the best I got. No, it's not A5 or even A4. But you can't get that no more. Not in California. This is the best anyone's got."

Ellie stood back and folded her arms, giving Chris her resting bitch face, but only at about half power. It was enough to undo most men, but Kakris had not survived in the Darwinian cage fight of San Francisco's restaurant industry by wetting his pants every time a chef was mean to him. He doubled down. Offering up his phone.

"You call Jevon. Go on. I got that prick's number in here. I'd like to see what that asshole tries to pass off as A5 Kobe these days because Kasitch wouldn't know his ass from boiled loose meat. You don't even wanna talk to those guys. I know you don't. You want the best, Ellie. Always the best, and it costs," he stabbed his finger at her for emphasis. "It costs you—" *stab* "—it costs me."

Chris jerked a thumb at his chest.

This was costing her time she didn't have. Five more suppliers were due in the next half hour, and one of them, Gannaway, the seafood guys, she actually was gonna deep six. She'd already sourced an alternative supplier for the sea bass, oysters and crab on the menu, and it was gonna get real ugly when she brought the hammer down because she was gonna do it in front of everyone to prove a point. She also had to make sure they had a server coming in to cover Yasmin's shift. She'd twisted her ankle hurrying down to the wine cellar last night. Natalie, the sommelier, had something urgent she needed to clear up, and Ellie was praying it wasn't anything to do with the fake French label scandal that *Table Hopper* had broken wide open last week. The online booking service was down. Of course. Some fucking tapeworm from UberEATS was ringing every goddamned day, trying to convince Damo to let a bunch of stupid kids on motor scooters drive her three-star masterworks of culinary fine art out into the burbs in plastic boxes for assholes who were too fucking lazy to pour themselves into an actual Uber. The tapeworm would not give up, even though the last time he'd called, she had yelled at him so loud, for so long, that the entire kitchen had come to a stop before breaking into wild applause at the hurricane of foul-mouthed abuse she'd roared into the phone.

Ellie shook her head.

"I'm not taking the rib eye, Chris. It's just not good enough. I *will* change the menu before I plate it up. But yeah, okay, the drought. I'm sick of hearing about it. What else you got?"

Chris Kakris's expression was a study in rapid transformation. His shoulders slumped, and his head dipped low when Ellie refused to take the proffered steak. His face went slack and dark when she said she was changing the menu. But a furtive stillness settled over him as she conceded his point about the drought. And it was as though his own personal sunrise had dawned when she asked him what else he had to offer.

He started to say, "I've got some excellent pork belly..." but Ellie never did get to hear the rest of the pitch. The controlled chaos of the kitchen stopped dead as the swing doors that gave onto front-of-house burst open, and half-a-dozen burley men in tactical rigs and baseball caps muscled their way in. Frenetic but directed energy collapsed into mayhem as more agents pushed through the battered flyscreen door that gave out onto the rear alleyway where the kitchenhands typically took their smoke breaks and where Chris Kakris had parked his delivery truck.

"*Chinga la Migra!*"

"Immigration!" one of the men yelled out. "We have a warrant. Everybody stay exactly where you are and have your documents ready for inspection."

A female agent in body armour emblazoned with three white letters, 'ICE', repeated the announcement in Spanish and Arabic, surprising Ellie. Most of her dish pigs and busboys were Spanish speakers, but apart from herself, only the barkeep, Jim Elias, had a passing familiarity with Arabic. Jim's family originally hailed from some valley in the ass-end of Syria—*It's all ass end*, he joked when she'd asked him about it once—but he was third-generation So-Cal. His Arabic didn't reach much further than *jaddati* and *jaddi* for grandma and grandpa. Ellie had a little more, but most of it profane and kitchen-related, picked up in the six months she spent carving meat from the spit roast at her first job, a kebab joint in Rockridge.

At the mention of 'documents', the sudden turmoil in *Fourth Edition's* kitchen boiled over into madness, a genuinely desperate situation in a space that was dangerous at the best of times. Commercial kitchens are full of razor-sharp edges and super-hot things, and the sudden appearance of a fearsome and hated ogre like *la Migra* was not calculated to bring order to Ellie's realm. Kitchen hands attempted to flee. Agents leapt on them in flying tackles. Individual shouts and screams rose and surged together into a savage, incomprehensible din of riot.

Ellie did not try to impose her will on the scene.

She calmly but quickly took her phone out of a back pocket and dialled Damien's number, his private cell known only to a handful of friends, family, and her. Even with the phone pressed hard up against one ear and a finger jammed into the other, she had trouble hearing him over the uproar.

"Yeah, mate. What's... what the fuck, Ellie! What's..."

"Shut up, Damo," Ellie shouted. "It's a fucking ICE raid. Call your lawyers right now. Tell Nick Perriam we need him and any other lawyers he can spare as of five minutes ago. I'll try to sort this out, but it looks pretty fucked up. Forget about opening today."

"I'll sue these cunts," Damien yelled. She had no trouble hearing that. His booming Australian accent fairly thundered out of the phone. "I'll sue the agent in charge. I'll sue the idiot judge who signed the warrant. Wait! Have they even got a fucking warrant?"

"Yes," she shouted, eyeing the asshole waving it around like Willy fucking Wonka's golden ticket.

"Fuck them. I'm gonna sue the judge. I'm gonna..."

"Just get Nick down here, Damo," she yelled over the noise. "Now!"

Ellie cut the call and fixed her radar on the man she assumed to be the agent in charge. Mainly because he was standing, shouting at everyone else, but not risking his own skin by diving into the general melee of scrummaging agents and kitchen hands.

"You," she yelled, pointing at him. "Gimme the warrant, your name and your badge number."

There was no doubt that he heard Ellie's voice, even over the thunderous din. He looked right at her. Then he went back to yelling from the sidelines. Ellie stomped up to him, bottling her rage and fighting fiercely against the desire to punch him in the face because he'd ignored her. She was too smart to lay so much as a finger on one of these assholes.

"You," she shouted. "Warrant. Name. Badge number."

He stopped shouting at his people just long enough to say, in a conversational tone, "Are you Jabbarah? The boss?"

He had a way of speaking that managed to cut through the hurricane-force noise of everyone shouting and fighting with each other.

"I'm Ellie Jabbarah. The sous chef. Damien Maloney is the owner. The boss. And who the fuck do you think you are? Every one of these people is legal. Damien doesn't hire anyone who doesn't have papers. We've got copies in the office for everyone. I would've couriered copies to you. I can show you now if you'll just stand the fuck down."

He looked at her and smiled.

"Nope," he said, and with a nod to one of his deputies, he ordered Elizeh Jabbarah to be arrested too.

8

THE JUNIOR MINTS

James O'Donnell woke at the same time every day.

4.00 AM.

Growing up on a cattle ranch meant beating the sun to work. His parents worked four hundred acres on the fringe of the Gallatin National Forest in south central Montana. Nestled within the folds of an isolated mountain range that punched through the plains sweeping up to the Continental Divide, the ranch was blessed with more than a dozen lakes fed by permanent streams running down from the towering, snow-capped peaks. The providence of good land and water did not guarantee success, of course. You still had to work hard, and James had been tumbled out of bed every day of his young life, first to help his mother cook for the two or three ranch hands his father usually employed and in later years to join those men in the cattle pens and out on the range. The mountains that surrounded them on three sides protected the farm from the hot winds sweeping west off the plains. Still, it did not spare man or beast from the heat of the western summer and gathering the cattle to work them in the pens—branding, vaccinating and castrating the herd, or weaning calves, or pregnancy-testing the cows—was best done before the sun climbed over the high saw-tooth peaks.

Rising early and taking the reins of the day was a habit that had settled deep into James's bones. So deep that he could not shake it even after swapping out blue jeans and leather chaps for tailored suits and a laptop. He didn't set an alarm. He came awake within five minutes of four o'clock, checked his phone on the nightstand by the bed and swung his feet out onto the carpet as he groggily scrolled through the notifications that had come in while he slept. There were dozens, most of them from the previous day. It looked like he was back online.

James flipped open the lid of his MacBook, and the same cascade appeared on screen.

He made an instant coffee from the fixings in his room and drank it down black and sugarless. There was no pleasure to be had from it. He was simply kickstarting his metabolism.

He checked that his newsletter had gone out, which it had just after 2 AM, changed into gym gear, and took himself down to the hotel's small in-house fitness centre. There, he did half an hour of cardio and twenty minutes of resistance training. He was the only guest using the gym at that hour, for which he was glad. It meant he didn't have to compete for the equipment. By the time he'd showered and changed back in his room, he was hungry. He had fifteen minutes to kill before the Marriott's dining room opened to guests, and he used that time to quickly scan the news on his laptop for reports of yesterday's hack.

It was the lead story on all of the national sites he checked, but also in many overseas outlets like the BBC and *Deutsche Welle*.

A crypto worm attack, analysts said, and almost certainly using tools stolen from the NSA. Unlike the Wannacry hijack of 2017, which had been countered by Microsoft releasing emergency patches and the fortuitous discovery of a kill switch that prevented infected computers from further spreading the virus, this latest exploit seemed designed to turn itself off after precisely twelve hours. Many of the compromised systems were still locked up, but the worm had stopped propagating itself at 10.13 PM Eastern.

James had no idea yet what any of it meant beyond the obvious warning that the global economy was acutely vulnerable to disruption by malign actors with weaponised software. He flicked on the TV in his room as the streets outside his windows resolved themselves in the predawn gloom. A minute of channel surfing added nothing to his brief scan of the online news sites other than speculation that the North Korean chiefs in Pyongyang actually weren't to blame. Some analyst on the BBC, a Dr. Cathie Tranent, was adamant that her reading of various ransom demands locking up screens around the world indicated the authors were fluent in Russian and quite proficient in English. The ransomware samples she'd studied in those languages appeared to have been written by one or, at the most, two individuals. In contrast, the notes in the other major languages—Chinese, French, Spanish, German, Japanese and Korean—had very obviously been machine-translated, possibly using Google's technology.

"You can see from metadata in the language files," she said, "that the systems used to create the crypto worm were on a Russian civilian ISP and set to UTC+03:00, which is Moscow's time zone."

The BBC host didn't appear to see that at all, but he plunged on regardless.

"So, this could be the Russian mafia?"

James turned off the television before Dr. Tranent could reply.

The data was valuable. Speculation was not. He could do his own speculating.

TWO HOURS LATER, a guard at the NSC buzzed him through the security gates and gave him a temporary swipe card on a lanyard. He also printed out a visitor pass, which James had to wear stuck to his shirt.

"There's an office arranged for you next to Ms. Nguyen, sir," the guard said, "Just down the hall to your left. The card will give you access."

"Thanks," James said, a little impressed that they'd set him up with access and a workspace so quickly. He wondered how they'd vetted him for a security clearance in such a short time. The swipe card looked like a driver ID from the future, with his name, address, and date of birth printed below a full-face, hi-res picture that had obviously been captured on his arrival the previous day. He recognised the suit and tie he'd worn. An embedded chip and a swirling hologram of the NSC logo hinted at a much greater trove of data buried within, including presumably his clearance level and access codes.

James took off his jacket, applied the visitor pass to his shirt pocket and walked the short distance to the office carrying his briefcase.

It was weird.

He'd never intended to work for anyone other than himself—and his clients, of course. He got a small taste of that when his parents almost lost the ranch, and he had to take over their debts, paying off the second mortgage, the line of credit and three cards they'd used up feeding the herd during the worst years of the last drought. He'd only just got his own business on a stable footing when his dad had reluctantly told him about the troubles back home. Tom O'Donnell hadn't wanted a handout from his son. He'd been calling to tell him in a choked and halting voice that they were being sold up and there'd be no point coming home because there would be no home to come back to. James had refused to accept that. The following two years felt as though he was working solely for the bankers who'd pushed more and more debt onto his old man, right up until the day when they decided to take it all back.

It had been hell.

He'd never told his parents, but at one point, for a few weeks, he'd lived out of his car because he got so far behind on his rent while paying down their loans that he'd had to give up the lease on the apartment he was living in. For James, who'd slept plenty rough out on the range, bunking down in his car was no real hardship. But having to tell his landlord he couldn't make the rent?

That was shameful.

It hurt a hell of a lot more than any stiff neck on the mornings he woke up in the back seat of the Camry.

But here he was, working for the Man again. And not just any

Man either. He suppressed a grin at the idea that he was a civil servant.

At least for a little while.

The pay wasn't great, not by the extortionate measure of the fee he'd charge a private corporation to lay exclusive claim to his time and expertise. But...

But he was surely going to learn things that would be of use to his clients.

And, to be honest, he felt the call of service.

There was no denying it. Just as he could not turn away from his parents when they needed him, James O'Donnell believed he could help his country by turning his mind to the problem Admiral Holloway had asked him to think about. He would put in his best effort here, and perhaps he would sleep a little sounder at night, knowing he had done something other than chase a dollar for a few days.

He was about to unlock the door to his new digs when he heard typing through the open door to Michelle Nguyen's office.

"Hey," he said, putting his head through the door. He held up his swipe card. "This is cool."

"Oh my God, you're such a nerd," she said, looking up from her laptop. She seemed pleased to see him.

James blushed.

"I meant, it's just that I didn't expect..."

She waved his explanation away.

"We started vetting you two weeks ago."

"Oh," he said, feeling a little deflated for no reason he could put his finger on.

She smiled.

"I'm glad you're here. We can grab a cup of coffee before the briefing."

She must've seen the look of mild panic that flashed across his face because she hurried to add, "Don't worry, you won't be saying anything. You'll just be one of the junior minions, or Junior Mints as the admiral calls us, lining the walls while the grown-ups sit at the big table. But it's relevant to your interests. You had breakfast yet? You want to get a coffee on the way?"

James felt a little unbalanced by her rapid-fire delivery.

"Er, yeah, sure. I mean, yes, I've had breakfast, and yes, I could get another coffee."

Michelle told him to leave his laptop in her room, which she locked behind her. They walked deeper into the building, turning a few corners and going downstairs one level to a café that was doing a brisk trade in breakfast rolls and beverages. James didn't actually want coffee. He really just wanted to hang out with Michelle for a little while. Besides Holloway, she was the only person he knew here. And he didn't know her well. They took a booth in the corner of the café, a seat which afforded them a pleasant view over the gardens in front of the Eisenhower building. Sprinklers watered the grass out there, catching the morning sun and throwing off tiny rainbows.

She was frowning.

"What's up?" he asked.

"They didn't have my blueberry muffin," Michelle said. "I had to get a cruller. This is the worst thing that ever happened to anybody."

"No, no, it's not," he said. "I once bought a Roomba to clean up after my cat. I was thinking of cat hair and how much I wouldn't have to vacuum it up by hand anymore. But the cat had other plans, and it laid a big wet poop in front of that Roomba, and that's a thousand bucks I'm never getting back again."

She stared at him, motionless for so long that he wondered if he had said the wrong thing. Perhaps he'd misjudged her. And then she burst out laughing and snorted coffee through her nose and dropped her cruller on the floor and laughed even harder until she started to choke, and James had to lean over and smack her on the back a couple of times.

So that worked out just fine.

When Michelle had recovered and James returned with a fresh cruller to replace the one his Roomba catpoocalypse story had ruined, they chatted for a few minutes about trivialities and each other, which had been the real purpose of coming down here. James was surprised by how much he liked this woman, by how often she blew up his expectations of what an NSC staffer should be. She was obsessed with roller derby and competed every weekend, sometimes driving a three- or four-hundred-mile round trip to make a tournament. She spoke Japanese and had worked briefly in Tokyo as an *Oshiya*, a professional "people-onto-train-pusher". And she had decided two years ago, she told him, to get a new tattoo every month for as long as she had space on her body.

James tried very hard not to stare at the sinuous designs enveloping her like iridescent serpents. He'd never met anybody with so much ink etched into their skin, and he was unsure of the etiquette. Was he supposed to pretend she didn't present as a human canvas? He concentrated so hard on not gawking at the colourful, intricate patterns swirling up and down her arms, disappearing inside her loose black silk top to emerge again at the vee-neck of the shirt, that she finally noticed he was staring with increasingly awkward intensity at her face.

"Have I got cheese bits on my mouth or something?" she asked.

James let go of a breath he hadn't realised he'd been holding. He put up his hands as if to surrender.

"I'm sorry," he said. "It's just that I have never seen anybody with so many tattoos. I mean, they look great, I guess, but I can't help thinking that gee, that must've hurt, and you must have, like, a lot of patience or something..."

He trailed off weakly.

"I wondered if you were going to say anything," she said. "You've been trying desperately not to for at least ten minutes now, haven't you?"

He stared at her and then quickly nodded.

"Yes. Sorry."

She smiled. "You don't have to apologise. If you want to see some peeps totally freaked out by my bitchin' skin art, you should come to Thanksgiving with my family. My grandfather was a colonel in the ARVN. He got his family out of Vietnam on the seventh attempt. Came here, worked as a janitor the rest of his life. His son, my dad, qualified as an accountant. House Nguyen is not known for its free-thinking radicals and artistic visionaries. Except for this hot chick right here."

She jabbed at her chest with a thumb. The one with the bright yellow Tweety Bird tattoo.

"The senior threat assessment analyst with the National Security Council, you mean?" James said with a hint of a teasing smile.

"Yeah. Her," Michelle agreed. "Anyway, come on, the meet-cute scene is over. This movie needs some exposition now."

She took him to a conference room on the third floor. They didn't stop at her office.

"You won't need your laptop," she said. "We're strictly wallflowers for this meeting. Take notes if you want or if you have to, but remember they're classified, and don't speak unless spoken to, which isn't going to happen. It never happens. A few seconds spent listening to some common sense from a lowly Junior Mint like you or me would be a precious opportunity lost for some deputy assistant secretary to show a room full of captive under-secretaries how fucking brilliant they are."

"That sounds very cynical," James said.

"Only about deputy assistant secretaries," she volleyed back. "And don't ask. Once I start rolling on that topic, you'll never get me to stop."

The conference room was half full when they entered. The chairs around the edge of the meeting space were mostly taken. The Junior Mints did not have the luxury of rolling up late. Michelle indicated that James should take a seat next to her in the corner. Admiral Holloway said good morning to them both when he came in a few seconds later, but he was quickly gathered up by more important people and carried away to his esteemed position up near the head of the table.

The meeting opened with a young black woman in an Air Force uniform recapping the previous day's cyber-attack. She'd updated her briefing on the fly as Amazon and other sites were listed as being offline, from Tumblr to Lululemon. James missed some of what she was talking about because she spoke so rapidly in acronyms and government jargon that were a foreign language to him. But he got the gist of it. The intelligence agencies believed that on the balance of probabilities, the attack had originated in China, not North Korea or Russia. It was a state-sponsored operation, not the doing of some freelance criminal organisation or even a front for China's Ministry of State Security.

"It was almost certainly PLA Unit 61398," the Air Force woman said.

This occasioned a lot of nodding and mumbling and general disgruntlement around the table.

James leaned over to Michelle and asked quietly, "Who are these guys?"

"Shush," she scolded him in a low voice before adding, "Very bad guys."

There was some back-and-forth between the important people at the grownup's table about what PLA Unit 61398 had hoped to achieve with a false flag operation designed to look like either a North Korean Bureau 121 operation or a freelance Russian ransomware shakedown. It wasn't like they needed the money.

In the movie, James supposed, this is where he would jump up and stun them with his amazing theories. But he didn't really have any theories, and he didn't want to look like a complete idiot, so he kept his mouth shut. At one point, Michelle patted him on the arm as if she could tell how much trouble he was having just sitting and saying nothing. Following the lead of the meeting chair, yet another retired admiral, James had taken off his jacket and rolled up his shirt-sleeves. The room was hot and stuffy, with so many people crammed into it, and the air-conditioning was struggling as the temperature climbed outside. The unexpected touch of Michelle Nguyen's cool fingers on his forearm jolted him like an electrical charge. He had to cough to cover up his surprise and then dip his face in embarrassment as his loud coughing turned heads all around the room.

Discussion quickly turned to the reason he was there. The trade war.

Now in its third year, it was throwing off a Catherine wheel of unintended consequences. The trillion-dollar hit to the Chinese economy had not brought them to the negotiating table as intended.

Beijing had doubled down on its most egregious violations of international law. Chinese companies were not just openly stealing and copying the intellectual property of American competitors; they were selling them into third-party markets like Europe at prices designed to ravage the margins of companies like Microsoft. James sat forward in his chair as an official from the State Department took them through a briefing based on complaints from Apple, Dell, Intel and Qualcomm about increasingly aggressive demands from the Chinese government for unsustainable investments, technology transfers and straight-up multi-billion-dollar extortion payments.

He made no judgements about the information, which was not out in the market yet, waiting to see whether anybody at this meeting was going to fit it into a wider narrative. A few minutes later, Admiral Holloway did just that.

"We are three years into this shitfight," he said. "Five years into an unprecedented drought which has affected not just the Western and Midwestern food bowls here, but which has also severely affected major grain producers such as Canada and Australia at the same time as it has denuded North Asia, the Middle East and sub-Saharan Africa of arable land. China is rich but starving," Holloway went on. "This would not be a problem if they could buy food from reliable suppliers, but increasingly they cannot. Globally, food supply chains are massively stressed by the Great Drought, the collapse of salt and freshwater fisheries, and aggressive competition for nutrient sources by India, China and the major OPEC economies, none of whom can feed their populations."

Holloway went on for another ten minutes, diving deep into the question of whether or not Thailand and Vietnam would ban exports of rice within a week. It was a story James had been following closely but for other reasons.

"If either country were to do so, it would be an intolerable development for Beijing," he warned. "Unfortunately, my guys don't see any alternative."

James sensed Michelle nodding in agreement next to him.

"Both Hanoi and Bangkok have reached a point where they will feed their people before they export another grain of rice. For them, it's a matter of self-preservation, too. They're not just hungry. There will be more food riots in both countries no matter which course they take, but in Thailand, giving away their last bowl of rice would guarantee a military coup."

James tuned out for the rest of the session, which mainly consisted of military officers detailing the readiness and disposition of various US forces the president could deploy in the event of a crisis in either the Middle East or Asia. Both seemed equally likely to him. But his mind was already racing ahead of that seeming inevitability.

He was thinking about yesterday's cyber-attack. And Michelle's missing blueberry muffin. And his sudden pressing interest in the question of just how long the average American city could feed itself were its food supply to be cut off suddenly.

9

I'D RATHER BE BACK IN FALLUJAH

Rick Boreham stayed and helped out with the rest of Mel's judo class. It was only half an hour, and none of the lost golf balls he might have otherwise policed up were going anywhere. She was a good teacher, he thought. She had a deep well of patience from which to draw. She was also a master delegator, giving him three of the worst knuckleheads to look after while she busied herself with the rest of the kids. They were a pretty good bunch, even the knuckleheads.

"Were you really an Army Ranger?"

"Yep."

"Did you ever kill anyone?"

"Part of the job, son."

"Seriously? Would you ever do it again?"

"Sure. I'm thinking of killing someone right now."

Rick was sweating by the end of the session, although more from the heat of the day than any exertion. He taught the three boys a basic hip throw and a leg sweep. Showed them how to fall to a hard surface without breaking any bones or winding themselves. By the end of the half-hour, they were all sweating. High overhead, a passenger jet traced a white contrail across the vast blue bowl of a cloudless sky.

"Okay, that's it," Mel shouted, clapping her hands. "Bow to your partners and take a minute to stretch everything."

There was a lot of giggling and some playful pushing and shoving as the teenagers sketched out formal bows to end the class. Very few of them did even a moment's stretching. Rick took the time to perform a proper warm-down routine and insisted that all of his knuckleheads do the same. They protested, but it was a pro forma objection. Thirty minutes of training with the former special forces non-com had convinced them he probably knew something about what he was doing.

"Thanks for that," Mel said as the main part of the class dispersed towards the clubhouse and a bus ride back to school. She bowed to him, and after a moment of uncertainty, he returned the gesture, thinking that it was probably second nature to her.

"It was a pretty good workout," Rick said. "Gonna need a nap now, I reckon."

With a whistle, he summoned Nomi from under the shade tree where she'd been dutifully waiting for him, panting and occasionally wagging her tail. She trotted over and sat obediently a few feet away without being asked.

The knuckleheads all thanked him for his time and called him 'sir' before charging off after their classmates. He did not correct them. Mel watched them go with something like bemusement.

"Hey! You three, stop right there," Rick shouted after the retreating figures. It had an effect like the crack of an overseer's whip. They all jolted to a complete halt and turned around nervously.

"Ms Baker was your teacher for today. Not me. You should thank her."

The three boys looked at each other nervously, uncertain of what to do. One of them finally said, "Thanks, Miss," and the other two followed suit. Then they surprised Rick, and Mel for that matter, by awkwardly bowing to her. She smiled and returned the bow.

"You boys hurry back to the bus now," she said, setting them free. They charged away.

"You're pretty good at that," Mel said. "You could do it for a living."

"What? Teach judo?"

She shook her head, "No, just teach. You have a presence. Those guys," she jerked a thumb back over her shoulder at the retreating knuckleheads, "they could really do with some presence in the classroom."

Rick scoffed, "Reckon, I'd rather be back in Fallujah."

"Fair enough," Mel shrugged. "But seriously, thanks. If you'll let me, I'd like to buy you dinner to say thank you properly."

There it was. The moment that'd been coming for five or six weeks now. The moment that probably would have come a lot sooner if he didn't feel as though negotiating even the most straightforward social transaction was something like finding his way through a minefield with a bayonet. He was smiling, but the smile was frozen on his face, and he didn't know how to unfreeze it and...

"You should probably just say yes," Mel said. Her expression was not unreadable. Rick could see in her eyes an awareness of his sudden apprehension and the surprising lack of fucks to give on her part.

"Yes, God, yes," he blurted out, "Oh shit," he added, horrified at his ham-fisted response. "I didn't mean..."

"How about I pick you up at six thirty tonight," Mel said, touching him lightly on the arm. "You look like a steak man. I'll book us a table at Morty's. That way, if it's a disaster, you can bring a doggy bag home for Nomi."

Rick's head was swimming with how fast this was going. For a second, it felt exactly like the moment when she had unbalanced him and flipped him through the air to land on his ass in front of her class.

But it wasn't.

They had been sidling up to each other for weeks now. He could've asked her out on a date at any time in the last month, and she probably would have said yes. But he hadn't, and with each chance that he let slip by, it became easier to let the next one go, too.

"Okay," he said, finding his voice at last. He swallowed. "1830 hours. I'll lock it in."

"Good," Mel said. "It'll be good."

And it was, and it wasn't.

HAVING AGREED TO A DATE – he was pretty sure it was a date – Rick tried very hard not to think about, well, the date. He completed his rounds of the golf course, gathering up fourteen lost balls, which he deposited into a basket at the clubhouse. He patched up half a dozen or so divots on the fairways and made note of a torn net on one of the tennis courts. It would need to be replaced. As much as he was looking forward to meeting Mel for dinner, his anticipation threatened to tip over into anxiety if he gave more than a minute's thought to it.

Instead, he put in earphones and listened to some music. A Foo Fighters playlist of their slower tracks. He threw a stick for Nomi to chase, enjoyed the sun on his back, and generally did his best not to think about something that he'd been thinking about for weeks.

He had first met Melissa when he was shopping for groceries at the Harris Teeter in Darnestown. Rick preferred to do his groceries online, but the site was down, and he was getting short on rations. If he didn't resupply, he'd be tucking into a big bowl of Nomi's venison kibble for dinner.

Like most Labradors, Nomi was hugely sociable. Training constrained that natural friendliness, but her tail set to wagging as soon as she heard Rick grab the car keys from the bowl on his kitchen bench. She rode up front in the cabin. She would've been fine in the tray, but he preferred to have her next to him.

He played Joe Bonamassa's *Redemption* album on the drive down to the market, and they sang along together. Nomi's love of a good blues howl was one of the things Rick most loved about her. The other was that he could trust her.

Being a service dog, Nomi was allowed inside Harris Teeter while your average mutt had to suffer the indignity of being tied to a bench outside. She trotted obediently alongside him, up and down the aisles as he filled his shopping bags, one full of fruit and vegetables and the other with a heavy pork shoulder he would slowly cook down.

The one place she was not allowed was inside the enormous meat locker at the back of the store. Highly trained service dog or not, state law would not countenance the idea.

"Stay," Rick commanded as he ducked into the cold room for his meat. He knew that he could be gone for half an hour, and she would not bark, fret, or leave her assigned post. Only if somebody tried to take her would there be any barking. Some growling and snapping, too, if they didn't get the message. He was inside for less than a minute, quickly gathering the large cut of pork shoulder he needed, before emerging to find a young woman hunkered down and deep in conversation with his dog.

Nomi was soaking up the attention and mugging for a selfie with her new friend.

"Help you, Ma'am?" Rick asked.

She didn't look even a little bit embarrassed to be caught out loving it up with somebody else's dog. The woman stood up and fairly beamed at him, unfolding an impressively athletic-looking body. She was dressed in black lycra and a Nike Run Club tee shirt.

"No, I'm doing just fine," she said, giving Nomi one more head rub. "She is a beautiful dog. How old?"

A little taken aback, Rick drew a blank.

"I, er... I don't..."

"You don't know how old your dog is?" the woman asked, in an unfamiliar accent. It could have been English or maybe Australian.

"I do," he said, feeling himself on the defensive for no good reason. It's just..."

But Mel had lost interest in him, the delinquent dog owner and she was leaning back down and kissing, yes, actually kissing Nomi between the eyes. And Nomi was lapping it up, almost as if she knew how unsettled Rick was by the whole exchange.

"She's three," he said suddenly.

"Sorry?"

"She's three years old," he said, feeling it was important that he say it.

The woman seemed impressed.

"Still a puppy then, really. She is a very good girl. You've trained her well."

"I didn't train her, not entirely anyway," he said. "She's my therapy dog."

The young woman appeared to accept this as a given.

"Were you a soldier?" she asked, but she went on speaking before Rick could answer or try to evade her question, which he sometimes did when people asked him that. "My brother was a Marine. A Royal Marine," she said.

English then.

"He went to Iraq three times. He's all right. Said he loved it, actually. But some of the blokes he went over with, they did it tough, coming home. A couple of them had therapy dogs. I'm Melissa, by the way. Melissa Baker. But just call me Mel."

She held out her hand and smiled at him as if confident that there could be nothing he would want more in the world than to meet her and to just call her Mel. The hell of it was, she was right.

Maybe it was Nomi. If Nomi liked her, she had to be okay, and it was pretty apparent from the lolling tongue and big dopey lovestruck eyes that Nomi was all in on this just-call-me-Mel situation.

Rick shook her hand. Her grip was firm.

He hadn't fallen for her, not then. He hadn't really expected to see her again. It was just a pleasant meeting with a young woman who didn't seem to care about his scars or his history, or the darkness that he sometimes felt as a physical presence gathered around him. But a week later, she'd appeared at the golf course, leading a bunch of high school kids through a self-defence class, and that was when he'd learned that she was an ex-cop. An ex-Bobby, she called herself, two years out of London and the police force and 'well shut of all that rubbish and palaver.' She was a qualified personal trainer now, studying in Baltimore for a high school teaching diploma and paying her way through the degree by doing these classes up and down I-95, anywhere from DC to Philly.

He hadn't offered to help with her classes; she'd insisted.

They got to know each other as she tossed him around like a bag of old laundry, and he had let himself be tossed.

It was maybe the third or fourth week of her picking him up and slamming him down and landing on his chest to pin his arms and mimic beating his face to a bloodied pulp that Rick Boreham had realised that he really, really liked this woman.

He hadn't come out of his cabin for two days after that.

And now, here he was, showered and shaved and pacing the very short distance between his living room and his kitchen, wondering whether he should shower again and change his clothes because he was pacing so much, and he was so nervous that he probably, certainly, almost surely reeked of flop sweat. Nomi was curled up on her old sheepskin rug, tracking his path up and down, back and forth, tilting her head and staring at him as though he had gone mad from a poisoned tick bite.

"This is your fault," he said to her, and she dropped her head to her paws, suitably chastened. "I should have another shower," he said again. He had muttered the same thing to himself three times in the last ten minutes. This time, however, he actually started to head towards the bathroom just before he heard tires on the gravel driveway and squinted as powerful headlights beamed in through the windows of his cabin.

It was her.

Rick cursed under his breath. There was no time for a shower. He would just have to go, reeking of stale sweat and desperation. That's if Mel even agreed to go on with the date now. She'd probably gag and run back to her vehicle as soon as...

He heard bootheels clocking on the wooden steps and three firm knocks on the front door. Keys jingled outside.

It was like the first crack of a rifle shot when the enemy opened contact. None of his uncertainty, his fears and doubts disappeared. But he had stuff to do now, so he did it.

A deep breath. Four strides to the door. Turn the handle, and...

"Hey, Mel. You look great."

Just like a normal person.

She smiled and said hello and walked in without being asked, and then Nomi was bounding over to her, barking and wagging, and Rick took another deep breath and let it go and thought that maybe he could roll through this and perhaps it would be all right.

10

SYSTEM CRASH

The world ended, and the lights didn't even flicker.

Of course, it took a while before Jonas Murdoch or anyone realised that everything they knew had come to an end. Hundreds, hell no, *thousands* of years of Western civilisation had real momentum to it. It'd keep rolling for a while, even after the engines choked out.

The sirens warbling and echoing throughout the giant warehouse cut through his confrontation with Travis Tamoreau like a heavy meat cleaver chopping down between them. The assistant manager, who'd been looking genuinely terrified when Murdoch's anger got away from him, now looked frightened and confused by whatever was happening on his laptop screen. His delicate, manicured fingers danced over the keyboard, but to no effect. Jonas couldn't see what was happening on screen, but the little twink's expression, the panicky bird-like flutter of his eyes, implied nothing good.

Jonas grinned.

He was done here. He didn't need this shit anymore. He had another life waiting for him. Only one thing left for him to sort out. Who'd set him up? He couldn't believe—he didn't want to believe—it was one of the Dutch hotties he'd helped out last week. The answer was sitting on the cheap laminated surface of Tamoreau's desk, in the thin, buff-coloured personnel folder.

Jonas casually leaned forward and picked it up. Tamoreau was so intent on stabbing his fingers uselessly at the keyboard that it took him a moment to realise Jonas had taken the file and was reading it. The violation of the master-servant relationship, of the inherent and accepted power imbalance, was so brazen that it finally pulled him out of his feedback loop with the malfunctioning computer. He almost leapt up out of his chair to grab back the papers.

"Hey! That's confidential, you can't..."

Jonas shoved him back down. It was only a light push, but Tamoreau was only a little guy. Jonas was not. And he was angry. The assistant manager fairly flew through the air, tripping over his office chair and crashing to the floor. Reaching for a handhold, he pulled a landline phone and a cup full of pens down on top of himself. Jonas ignored his outraged squeal. He was already speed-reading the reports in the personnel file with a strange mix of elation and resentment.

He was right.

The hotties hadn't complained about him at all. As if they would. He'd been nothing but a gent to them. No, this was a fucking Yolanda special. She'd complained to Omar that Jonas would not take direction from her without attitude and pushback. That much was true. He'd give her that. But only because pretty much all of her directions were bullshit and sometimes even stupidly dangerous. It'd been Yolanda, after all, who'd ordered the Dutchies to haul those industrial-sized *sous vide* cookers all the way over to dispatch, where the only clear stowage space that day was on a shelf twenty feet off the fucking ground. What were they gonna do? Deadlift the fucking things and levitate up there?

So yeah, Jonas hadn't just cleaned up that mess. He'd let Omar know all about Yolanda's stupidity. But he hadn't sexually harassed her. That was insane. She was an ugly bitch with an ass so big and buttcrack hairy it needed its own crew of fire watchers when the dry summer months came on.

He tossed the report back on the desk. Tamoreau was trying to untangle himself from his chair and the phone line, but he was shaking so much he kept tripping over his spindly limbs. Jonas ignored him. He threw the report back onto the desk and walked out. His reflection in the office window looked calm, but he knew himself. This was the anaesthetic numbness that so often preceded one of his eruptions. He stalked past Cindy at the front desk, who looked like she was quietly freaking out. He ignored her, and she half-waved, half-smiled at him, before going back to her screens, trying to make things happen that obviously didn't want to happen.

Emerging from the offices and back onto the warehouse floor, Jonas was struck by the heat of the day and the blaring alarms. The fulfilment centre sounded as though it had fallen into chaos, but as his boots rang on the metal staircase, Jonas could see the opposite was true. Sirens howled, and red and yellow warning lights flashed, but nothing moved. Most of the workers on the shop floor stood very still, craning their heads back and forth, looking for the source of the alarm. A few managers hurried back and forth, mostly running towards each other, talking excitedly for a few moments, and running off in different directions again. But Jonas could see what was wrong, at least in aggregate.

The entire operation has seized up.

System crash, he thought.

He'd only ever been through one before, but it had looked just like this.

He shrugged and kept walking down the stairs. Apart from the sirens, his boot heels clanging on the metal steps were the only sound he could hear in the vast cavern of Amazon's frozen warehouse. He reached the floor and almost walked straight for the exit. He doubted they'd even pay him for this shift, and he knew he was done in Seattle anyway. He was the Centurion now, for better or worse.

He'd only given Tamoreau a playground push, but that little bitch was sure to file charges, and Jonas already had the assault conviction in Florida. He was also about to add to his criminal record here in Washington state. His limbs felt loose as he walked back to his station. The buzzer in his electronic bracelet went off, helpfully reminding him that he was already overdue. He tore off the tracker and threw it away. A couple of co-workers saw him and called out, asking if he knew what was happening. He forced himself to smile and shrug, and he kept going.

He found Omar and Yolanda deep in conversation, agitated, and so preoccupied with the disruption to operations that they didn't notice him until he was on them.

It happened quickly. His rage always boiled over like that.

He pushed Yolanda out of the way and used the same fist to break Omar's jaw with a fast, looping roundhouse punch. A set of dentures flew out of his mouth, which was pretty fucking funny, and they both went down like bags of wet shit, Yolanda tripping over her fat feet. Omar groaned loudly all the way down until his head hit the concrete floor, and he stopped making any noise at all.

Somebody screamed, but whether it was a man or a woman, Jonas couldn't say.

Couldn't give a shit either. He turned and walked for the exit.

Canada was only a three- or four-hour drive away, a straight shot north on Interstate 5, and he had a third of a tank of gas in his pick-up. He probably didn't want to risk the main crossing at Blaine. Border control had hardened up in the last couple of years. It started after 9/11, of course, but weirdly enough, it got much worse when the stupid cheese tariff war got out of hand.

Whatever.

He'd gas up, head a few miles east, and take one of the quieter, unguarded roads into British Columbia. Jonas had a temper; he knew that. But he was not an irrational man. There'd been nothing to keep him here as soon as Tamoreau pulled out that file. He would go, but he'd be damned if he'd go on their terms. Jonas Murdoch was not some broken soy boy who would be put down without a fight.

People were coming out of their fugue states around him. Some were staring and pointing. Others hadn't seen him hit the two super-visors, and they either ignored him or shrugged in theatrical help-lessness.

Whatcha gonna do?

He was gonna haul ass, was what. He had four hundred bucks on his PayPal from Centurion tee shirt sales and merch and shit, and a couple of hundred more in his Amazon account from affiliate fees and royalties off the manifestos. It would be enough until the podcast paid off, and that couldn't be long now. Not after the epic reveal he'd recorded in yesterday morning's pod. Not with Tucker fucking Carlson and Cernovich sniffing his ass like two dogs checking out the new arrival in the park. He could hold out.

The day was bright and hot outside, but it was a clean heat, not the thermal brutality of broiling alive inside the giant oven of the uncooled warehouse. Jonas stopped just outside the door and took a moment to savour the relative cool and quiet. The sirens were muted out here. Nobody was shouting. The air seemed much fresher and even crisp with the possibilities for redemption.

IT TOOK NEARLY HALF an hour to drive two blocks because the lights were all out, and some idiot had T-boned a Mister Softee van at the intersection of Butte and Third. Cell reception was shitty enough to be useless, so Google Maps could show him he was locked into some monster ass traffic jam but not how to get out of it. The entire grid was red, and it wasn't updating.

Jonas' surprisingly good mood at having quit his terrible job and made a giant fucking bonfire of all the bridges behind him quickly soured as the traffic delay dragged on.

He didn't need long to close down his ops here. He always —*always*—had a go-bag packed and ready. Not because he was some Deep State conspiracy fiend. A man didn't need to believe in a shadowy, unelected government to be wary for his freedom. The government they had was plenty oppressive enough, right out in the open. Having just punched out a couple of fools, he'd be lighting up their threat boards soon enough. He couldn't afford delays.

Jonas rechecked the phone.

No reception.

He thought about mounting the sidewalk and going cross country, but that'd definitely attract the attention of any cops nearby, and besides, even the side roads were heavy with slow-moving or stationary traffic.

Finally, he gave in and turned on the radio.

Jonas never listened to commercial radio if he could avoid it. Most of the FM dial was filthy with rap. Talk radio, even conservative stations, simply served to remind him how lethally fucking stupid most people were. (Especially the conservative stations, if he was being honest). And the incessant consumer babble of advertising enraged him so much he'd once cracked the dashboard by hammering at it in a fury over a thirty-second spot for anti-depressants.

The cure for depression, he knew, was action. Not serotonin reuptake inhibitors.

With great reluctance, he turned on the AM receiver and searched for a news broadcast or traffic update. It didn't take long.

Pretty much every station was live with chatter about some internet outage that had brought the city to a stop. Horns blared around him, and the sun flashed off car windows and metal trim. The pick-up's air-conditioning struggled in the heat as Jonas flipped around the dial, looking for usable information. He finally had to settle for the NPR affiliate, which was starting a run-through of southside traffic conditions before going to a news bulletin about the nationwide outage.

Jonas practised his deep breathing techniques while he sat in the cabin and listened to a bunch of yammering idiots panic about not being able to Uber up a pizza. Amazon Web Services had probably fallen over, he thought, and indeed, one of the NPR cucks confirmed as much a few minutes later. But they went on to say that most of the internet's backbone in the US appeared to have been 'filleted' over the previous twenty-four hours. Eventually, the net had not been able to route around the points of failure and...

"Here we are," Jonas muttered.

Just before the engine of his eighteen-year-old F-100 blew up.

11

MY FIRST DRINK IN A YEAR

Rick had never seen Mel wear anything other than exercise gear before. Dressed for their date – it had to be a date, right? – in boots, a light summer dress, jewellery and make-up, she looked a different person. Stunningly so, to his eye, but less... What?

Capable? No.

Sporty? Butch? No, that was just stupid. Even sweating in leggings and an old T-shirt, there was still no ignoring her very feminine grace.

No, that wasn't it. He understood as he watched her bending over to scratch Nomi behind the ear that she had gone to some effort in prettying herself up. For him. Every other time they'd met, they had met as colleagues, sort of, and she had been dressed for work. But more importantly than that, her entire focus had been on the kids or the other clients she was training. She didn't just do school groups. One self-defence class she'd run in the big function room at the Bretton Woods clubhouse was just for retirees. A club member has asked her to do it after hearing from his granddaughter about the classes Mel had run for her prep school.

Now, as she stood up and gave Nomi a final pat, Rick could see that she had refocused. On him. He felt himself inspected and judged as her eyes scanned up and down his outfit; brown suede boots, pressed khaki drill pants, and a collared shirt in a light blue check. He was suddenly as nervous as a green recruit on his first parade.

"You scrub up all right, don't you," she said. "What are we going to do with Nomi?"

He faltered again, slightly unbalanced by her compliment and noting the way that she had asked what 'we' might do about his dog. It was just a form of words, a simple thing, but he felt that she had somehow drawn a small invisible circle around them. Rick had not often felt himself included in anything since he left the Army. He had not wanted to be included.

Nomi was sitting on her hindquarters, her tail wagging feverishly. She was panting and smiling in that way that dogs do when they anticipate that a caper or a treat might be in the offing.

"She likes to sit out on my front porch at night," Rick said. "She'll wait."

"I brought her a bone if you'll let her have it," Mel said. "It's, like, pretty big. It should keep her amused for a couple of hours."

Rick smiled at his little friend.

"Did you hear that girl? Would you like a bone?"

Nomi's tail wagged even harder.

"I think that's a yes."

She followed them out into the warmth of the early evening. Mel had driven her pickup truck, a battered, dusty-looking Toyota. It was parked just outside the gate to Rick's small front garden. He appreciated that she was careful to close the gate behind her every time she passed through it, even though Nomi was too well-trained to take off on her own. Man and dog waited patiently, both curious to see what came of this. Mel fetched something that looked like a dinosaur femur from the tray in the rear and held it up in offering. Nomi whimpered, but she did not move. She looked up to Rick, who said, "On credit."

Nomi whimpered a little louder.

"On credit."

She started to tremble and looked like she might even bark.

"Paid for!"

The dog barked, which always set Rick's nerves just a little on edge, but he was getting better about it. That was one of the things Nomi was helping him get over. The dog leapt high, turning a full circle in the air before bounding over to Mel, who tossed the bone a few feet away. Nomi fell on it.

"Is that just a cool trick or some sort of super dog training thing?" Mel asked.

"It means she won't take bait from a stranger," Rick explained.

"Did you teach her that?"

"That one was mine, yeah," he said, closing the front door behind him and heading out through the little gate to where Melissa waited on the other side of the fence. He took a small, weatherproof padlock from his pocket and used it to secure the gate as he left.

A cool breeze coming up off the river rustled leaves in the trees overhead. The killing heat of the summer past had eased off a bit in the last week or so, for which Rick was grateful. When the humidity got up like it had been of late, and the mercury hovered in the high 90s at the end of the day, he would sit in his shorts on the front porch and drink gallons of water as the sweat poured out of him. Not quite the look he was going for tonight.

"Is she going to be okay? Like, really?" Mel asked, giving Nomi a worried look as they climbed into her pickup. "She could jump that fence pretty easily, I reckon."

Rick nodded.

"She could, but she'll still be here chewing on that bone when we get back. I guarantee it. She won't eat my tomatoes or dig up the basil plants, either. Nomi," he called out in his command voice. Instantly, the dog attended to him. "Stay and guard."

She barked as if acknowledging the order.

"That is one smart dog," Mel said, turning the key in the ignition. The engine rumbled to life, and they pulled away from the cabin.

MORTY'S WAS an old-fashioned steakhouse about fifteen minutes east on River Road, just before the Stoney Creek turn-off, heading north. The short drive did not take them out of the Virginia countryside, but Rick knew that the edge of the outer suburbs wasn't that far away. If Mel stayed on this road, they would reach Bethesda in half an hour and DC proper a little ways after that. That was plenty close enough for him. The properties out here ran to acreage, and the vehicles parked in the lot outside the steakhouse tended to fall into two categories: expensive SUVs without a droplet of mud to stain their highly polished grillwork and expensive pickup trucks with a few artfully splattered droplets of very expensive designer mud here and there to let everyone know that the owners were serious about their rural pretensions. Parked in among them, Mel's old Toyota stood out like a junkyard dog at Crufts.

She gave no sign of caring or even noticing.

They took turns choosing the music on the way over. Not that there was time for more than three or four songs, but Rick took his choices seriously. He didn't try to impress with his knowledge of what was hot or happening or any of that shit. He had no idea and hadn't for a long time. He just played a couple of his faves. An old blues number by Sonny Terry and Brownie McGee. And Luke Bryan's "Little Boys Grow Up and Dogs Get Old," which made Mel a bit teary. She gave him a backhanded smack on the shoulder for being an asshole and messing up her eyeliner. Except she pronounced it 'arse-hole', which he thought very posh, and she sort of laughed while she was snuffling and hitting him.

He didn't recognise her tunes, but they were okay. A funny one, he thought, about a girl who got in trouble and so ran herself a bubble bath. And some shouty, punchy sort of rock-rap anthem about a girl gang which 'boy, you wish you could join.' He was tapping his suede boots in time to the chorus when they pulled into Morty's. The sun was down now, and the restaurant's parking lot was three-quarters full already. Mel cut the engine and with it the music and the air-conditioning. As they stepped out of the cabin, the lingering heat of the day fell on them like a warm, wet blanket.

She stopped and turned to him as her feet crunched down on the gravel.

"Hey, you're not vegetarian, are you?"

He stared at her.

"Vegan," he said flatly. "I only came along to feel superior. But if there's veal, I might have to get difficult."

He maintained his poker face until she said, "Just for that, you're only getting celery and a wheatgrass juice."

He had the ribeye, medium rare, and a bottle of pale ale from the Caboose Brewing Company. "Because," he explained, "they have a happy hour for dog owners at their brewery, and there's free treats. Also, the beer is good."

He raised his mug in a toast, and Mel clinked her champagne flute against it. Now that he was here and settled in, and he had a cold beer to hand, he had finally started to relax. He'd never eaten at Morty's—couldn't afford it—but he heard folks at Bretton Woods talking about it every now and then. It looked like a secret lair for James Bond villains from the 1960s. It was all exposed rock and rough-hewn timber and groovy-looking furniture like you saw on *Madmen*. The music sounded like old-school lounge classics, but he realised after listening to a vaguely familiar tune that it was all stuff like *Guns & Roses* and *Metallica* played by some soft jazz combo. He thought that was pretty funny. The menu ran to hundred-dollar cuts of rump, and Rick really wanted to try the goose fat fries, but Mel had insisted that she'd be paying, and he didn't want her to think he was taking advantage. He let her choose the fries, and he had a basic T-bone.

Then she chose the goose fat fries anyway; bless her.

"How many of those do you think you can have and still drive?" she asked when their drinks had been served.

"The beer?"

Rick held out his glass and examined it as though it might come with a warning label.

"Don't know for sure, but I do know I can drink a couple of normal beers and blow through a breath test. Why?"

She smiled and held the champagne flute to her lips, taking a sip.

"Because this," she said, "is my first drink in a year."

"Whaaat?" Rick went, his expression comically surprised, and then a little too quickly, he asked, "Are you falling off the wagon tonight?"

Mel laughed loud enough to draw the attention of all the Bond villains and heavy metal jazz fiends at the tables around them.

"No," she smiled, and her eyes sparkled in the candlelight. "No. I broke up with a fella just over a year ago. My husband, actually. A Yank. And it was a pretty bad break-up, but I had to do it. He wasn't good for me. I came out of it a bit of a mess. I was kind of fat..."

"No way!"

"Yep. Like a telly tubby. You get them here? And I was just sort of down on myself and life. So I made a few changes. I needed to lose weight, and a good way to start was to cut all the booze out of my diet. We drank a lot. So, I decided to give myself a year off. And here I am, a year later. Cheers to me. I am Melissa Baker, and this is my story."

They clinked glasses again, and Rick found himself smiling at her easy way with words. She'd just dumped a couple of chapters of her life story on him, and it felt like she was just recalling a funny thing that happened to her on the way to the grocery store. Where they had met, of course.

"You don't look like you've ever been fat," he said. "You look amazing, Mel. Seriously. How'd you do it?"

She leaned forward as if to whisper.

"Top secret," she said. "I ate less shit and burned more calories."

"Whaaat?" Rick said again, purely for comic effect this time.

"And I didn't watch TV. I just read books or worked out. And I didn't date. So I had no arseholes negging me into feeling bad about myself. And then I met a nice fella, and I thought, you know what, I reckon I'm good to go again."

Rick's heart stopped for a second.

"You met someone?"

She laughed, pointing at him.

"You. I met you, Rick. Omigod, the look on your face just then. I like you, mate. That's why we're here, and I'm having a drink again. I know you like me. Girls always know. But we've been getting up close and real personal now for over a month on those practice mats, and you've been a complete gent. You never got bumpy or grindy or even a little bit handsy. So, you want to go out or what?"

He was stunned. Speechless. Not at getting called out like that. She was right. He did like her.

But he had never before been fronted like this by a woman.

A gay guy once tried it on, and Rick had been very courteous but very clear.

No thanks. Not his thing.

"I... I..."

"You should probably say yes," she grinned. "Because you want to, and because I will totally walk out and leave you to pay if you don't. And those goose fat fries you've been inhaling are pretty fucking spendy, darlin'."

He knew that she was joking, and that was all he needed to know.

She was funny. And she got him.

"Yes," he said. "I would like to go out with you, Melissa."

"And here we are," she said, winking at him and taking another sip of her champagne. "Going out."

IT WAS AN ALMOST perfect first date, except for two things. After twelve months of green tea and mineral water, Mel got absolutely hammered on three champagnes and a frozen margarita. That didn't matter so much. As soon as he knew there was a chance he might have to drive, Rick switched to soda. He tried to order a Coke, but the waiter told them they were out. The delivery truck hadn't arrived. Again, no biggie. The only other hitch came as they were leaving. Mel was leaning against Rick, swaying slightly, her arm linked through his for support. She offered up her credit card to pay for the meal, and again, the waiter apologised but said it would not be possible.

"But my card is good," she protested, and Rick felt his anxiety spike. He started desperately calculating whether he had enough money to pay for their meal. The manager, a kindly-looking woman in her fifties, appeared and shooed the waiter off.

"I am sorry," she said. "It's not your card; it's our system. I don't know what's wrong. But we can't seem to get through to the bank. Is it possible that you have cash?"

Mel, who was tipping over the last big dipper on her champagne roller coaster ride, muttered something about nobody having cash these days as she started to search through her handbag.

"No, it's okay," the woman said quickly. "We've got some old card slips in the office. I can do it manually. I'm terribly sorry. It's really not you. It's the bank."

Rick relaxed as he felt the tension run out of the woman beside him. His woman, he thought with a surprise.

He liked that idea. He liked what it said about him that somebody like Mel would even be interested. And he found himself pleased that he was well enough these days to even think about something as normal as dating.

They were a couple of minutes at the front desk, paying for the meal the old-fashioned way, with one of those clunky, noisy slide machines that took an imprint of your card. Rick always imagined his cards getting mangled or shattered in them, but Mel's Visa was fine.

Matter of fact, it was in better shape than she was.

By the time they made it back to her pickup, he had to carry her the last few feet. She was shit-faced, singing and laughing and apologising all at once.

Unsure of what to do, he drove the quarter hour back to his cabin at Bretton Woods, by which time his date had passed out on the seat next to him and was snoring softly. Even bumping and jostling over the rough corrugated dirt track down to his cabin by the river was not enough to shake her awake.

Nomi was precisely where she'd been sitting when they left. Her dinosaur bone looked like it'd been reduced appreciably in size. She waited for the vehicle to stop before bounding over to the fence, jumping and turning in circles.

Worried that he might trip over the dog while he was carrying Mel, Rick told her to sit. Nomi dropped to her butt and waited, quivering with excitement. Rick carried the sleeping woman through to his bedroom. He laid her out on top of the fresh sheets he had replaced a couple of hours earlier. He fetched a jug of water and a glass from the kitchen and left a couple of aspirin next to them. Then he retreated to the couch in the living room, quietly called for Nomi to join him, and flicked on the television, careful to keep the sound down.

He avoided the news channels because they aggravated him, settling instead on a Cubs game.

Nomi lay her head in his lap, and he stroked her ears as he watched Jon Lester strike out a couple of Braves.

All things considered, it was a pretty damn good date night.

INTERLUDE

Gloria limped slowly in the oppressive heat and humidity towards the South Moti Bagh market, having suffered yet another vicious beating by her Ma'am. "You lazy bitch," Ma'am had screamed when Gloria had again failed to return from the market with vegetables.

"Sorry, Ma'am," Gloria had said, "but there were none."

"Then go to another market, you lazy, worthless whore," Ma'am had shrieked, striking Gloria on the hip for emphasis with the flat heel of a broken shoe.

But Gloria had been to three markets, spending her own money on the auto fares, but the truth was simply that the markets were, inexplicably, bare.

She limped on. Her hip aching so badly that she wondered if madam had done something worse than raise another welt there. It was possible she felt terrible simply because of the heat. It was always hot in Delhi, but this monsoon season, coming late and feeble as it had, brought none of the usual relief. The air, while cleaner than in winter, to be sure, was heavy with moisture and as still as a corpse. Gloria reached the top end of the long street that would be teeming with activity on a typical day. Hundreds of Domestics like herself would have been there, haggling for vegetables, dahl, flour, rice. But today, like yesterday and the day before, what buyers remained were outnumbered by sellers, attending their stalls, such as they were, out of habit, but with nothing really to sell. Three Domestics haggled over a soggy bag of flour, the price already way over what Gloria could afford.

Men sat in the dirt, gaunt, bored expressions on their faces. By the water tap, children sat on the rubble of broken hand-made clay bricks, listless. That water was poison at the best of times, only suitable for drinking by untouchables, not civilized people. Certainly not by Sir and Ma'am, who only drank water from plastic bottles, never the tap, not even the filtered water. But now the tap was dry. Two men were urinating against a broken concrete wall. The smell of human waste was overwhelming. Sickening. Autos, the ubiquitous kerosene-burning tuk-tuks whose rattle and constant blaring horns composed the background din of Delhi street life, splashed past, sending mud and shit up the side of Gloria's saree. She would have to change it before she re-entered her Ma'am's house.

Gloria continued slowly down the street. Stray dogs lay in puddles on the road, watching a pair of hungry-looking goats perched on the roof of a car, out of reach. The kids Gloria had seen here for the last few weeks were gone; into some rich man's curry, Gloria supposed. Men lay shirtless on tarpaulins or the bare ground. A man squatted in a concrete hovel amongst a pile of old car parts, smoking and welding something, the flashes momentarily blinding anyone careless enough to look on. A couple of cows, so thin you could see their ribs, stood grazing on a pile of plastic refuse, choking down the chip packet wrappers, curry-smeared plastic bags, and other waste that would soon enough choke up the poor beasts' digestive systems. Gloria felt so sorry for them. Cows are sacred, and no one, even a non-Hindu, would dare eat one. The laws were strict for Hindu and non-Hindu alike, yet everyone seemed happy enough to let them die horribly in the street, choking on trash, their corpses stripped for leather, and the carcasses fed to the dogs.

She passed three children listlessly throwing broken pieces of brick at a cat, which skulked off with a limp as pronounced as her own. To her left, a fight erupted, fists flew, a man accusing a woman, another Domestic, but nobody Gloria knew, of having stolen an onion. Shoved backwards by the man, the woman tripped on the edge of a muddy pothole and fell back into the filth. Three other women started to kick the stranger. The man beat at her with a metal fence-dropper. The beating continued well after the woman had stopped moving. Stopped screaming. Stopped breathing. The onion lay in the mud near Gloria's feet. She was smart enough to leave it untouched.

Tetsuo Yamada spilled out of the bar around the corner from Shinjuku station, staggered a few paces, and vomited into the gutter. He could hear his friends laughing at him over the roar of traffic and the cries of dismay and disgust from the crowds surging around him.

Fuck them.

He was not the only drunk on the streets tonight. His workmates were just as bad, but unlike him, they had not worked through the previous night to settle the contracts for head office. The assistant undermanager of Asahi Legal had personally emailed Tets a thank you for his efforts and told him to get roaring drunk tonight.

Tetsuo Yamada was a good company man, and he would never go against the wishes of the assistant undermanager.

He hung onto a lamp post as the world tilted under his feet, and he heaved and heaved again until his stomach hurt.

He had not eaten a proper meal all day. Indeed, since arriving at work two days earlier, he had not eaten anything but rice crackers and one greasy *imagawayaki* pancake filled with mystery curry from the kerbside vendor outside head office. He had been working that hard on the acquisition. They all had. And now it was time to celebrate. They had secured a vital deal for the company, the freehold purchase of three thousand acres of soybean plantation in Australia, in the south of Western Australia, where the grip of the Great Drought was not as fierce as it was elsewhere. Tets did not fool himself that he was responsible for this coup. The deal had been finalised somewhere in the heavens, so stratospherically far above his lowly head that he could barely imagine the fantastic creatures which abided there. It was not merely a commercial deal, after all. So great and portentous were the auguries attendant on the final disposition of a simple soybean farm that Ministers and even Prime Ministers from both countries had become involved. Even more significantly, the protests from the Chinese Foreign Ministry had grown so shrill and unbalanced that the whole affair was being discussed as a crisis as far away as Europe.

Ha. *Fuck the Chankoro, too*, Tets thought, as he finally stopped dry-heaving and dragged himself upright, using the lamp pole. He staggered as a heavy hand landed on his shoulder. It was his supervisor. Mister Inoue.

"Come, Yamada," he barked. "We must fill you with ramen so you can hurl it up all over again!"

The braying laughter of his colleagues was not hurtful.

He knew they were impressed with how quickly he had settled the fifteen thousand pages of documentation for the sale. He was young, but he was building his legend. One day, he would be the assistant undermanager, and then...

Who knew?

Perhaps he might inhabit those rarefied heights where these deals were negotiated. One day, Tetsuo Yamada might sip French wine with gaijin Prime Ministers, not cheap beer with rowdy salarymen.

"Come along; we will have ramen and katsuo," his boss declared. "And Asahi will pay."

A great cheer arose at that.

The cheap beer they had been drinking.

It was not so cheap anymore.

And the ramen with skipjack tuna at Menya Musashi, while still famous up and down the Shinjuku line, no longer attracted lines of customers twenty deep. Very few people could afford it now. Tuna was worth its weight in gold these days. And gold had been getting more expensive, too.

The small team of lawyers from Asahi's Legal Affairs Division did not have to line up at the vending machines by the entrance to the restaurant. There was no crowd waiting to get in. In fact, Tets could not remember the last time he had seen one here. Although he could hardly afford the eye-watering prices on his salary, so he did not come by very often. He mainly worked until ten and caught the train home to Naoko.

He flushed with momentary shame at the thought of his young wife.

He had not seen her in two days.

Had not spoken to her either.

They had worked so hard for the soybean farm.

Naoko would understand.

She was as hopeful for his career as Tets was ambitious for advancement. And besides, when he had to work these long days and even overnight at the office, it meant their grocery bill was that much smaller. He was well paid, and their rent was quite reasonable, living so far outside the centre of the city. But even so, he knew that Naoko struggled with her duties at home. Everything was just so expensive these days.

He took his ticket from the vending machine and presented it to the young woman by the entrance to the restaurant.

"Kotteri," he told her before she could ask.

He wanted his ramen done in the heavy style. And he wanted an extra egg. And pork.

Despite having just thrown up all over the street—and himself, he realised, looking down at the stains on his suit jacket and shirt— he was starving.

The waitress did not so much as glance down at the disgusting mess he had made of himself. She had six rowdy customers wanting to spend money. Inside the darkened eating house, Tets could see three cooks in the open kitchen. He recalled the nights when he had just started as a young lawyer, when seven or eight noodle chefs worked the pans, yelling and performing for the crowd as they hauled steaming ramen from boiling water. There was no crowd tonight.

But still... they were here now, and so it would be as great a day

for Menya Musashi ramen shop as it had been for the corporate
warriors of Asahi's Legal Affairs Division.

They all piled in one after the other.

Everybody was hungry.

Mayor Andy woke into a furnace. The same furnace they'd all been
living in for nearly five years. The Great Drought had scorched the
red soil bare for a thousand miles around the town of Walcott. The
wheat and soy crops that had sustained generations of farmers and
townies were just memories now. The leaves were gone from every
tree in the town's Memorial Gardens. The drought had even burned
the grass from the greens at the local bowling club. And now it had
finally taken the last drop of water.

Andy's phone started buzzing in the hot, still hour before dawn.

It was Pete Barraclough, the Shire Council's chief engineer.

Filtration plant is gone, Pete texted him. *Control board failure
overnight. Pumps seized up. We're dry.*

In his mind, groggy and sleep-deprived, Andy heard the bad news
in Pete's broad, flat Australia drawl, with all the cursing.

Farkin' plant's gaawn, mate. We're farkin' dry.

Andy's wife, Sarah, rolled over in bed, turning away from the light
of his phone screen. She half-mumbled a question, asking if everything was okay. Andy turned off the screen and tip-toed out of their
bedroom. Nothing was okay, and there wasn't much he could do
about it until the water trucks arrived from the Snowy Mountains
depot, two full days drive to the east.

He padded toward the kitchen out of habit, intending to put the
kettle on for a pot of tea. He couldn't do that, of course, and when he
remembered that he couldn't, he swore quietly, still not wanting to
wake his wife.

The bore water the town had been living off the last three years
was brown and flinty and made for a diabolical brew. If you put
enough condensed milk and sugar in it, you could almost pretend
you weren't drinking something that tasted like some old bastard's

fetid piss strained through a pair of unwashed football socks. He took a bottle of store-bought water from the fridge. Ten bucks a pop it cost, but it was clean and sweet, and he made do with a single swig. It was cold, too. Beautifully cold. They were running low on everything but heat and dust.

Andy checked the time on his phone. 4.47 AM.

Jeez, Pete must have slept out at the plant.

Or not slept, more likely. The engineer had been obsessively monitoring the town's only source of drinking water since a lightning strike during a dry storm last week had fried the circuits on the number two pump's control board. The Council had voted to buy in a couple of tankers of drinking water, but they had to wait at the back of a very long queue. There were more than a hundred towns west of the mountains who'd gone dry even earlier than Walcott.

Andy pushed through the screen door, keeping the flies out of the kitchen, and stepped out on his back veranda. The sky was still a deep, obsidian black, awash with the hard brilliance of a billion stars. He felt the wooden floorboards underfoot, still warm from yesterday's heat. A pair of old folding chairs bathed in the glowing blue status light of the big Tesla Powerwall they'd installed with the government subsidy a couple of years ago. At least there was that, he thought. With all of the solar cells on the roof and the batteries every second homeowner and business had put in lately, they could at least run the air-conditioning without feeling like they were adding to the problem.

"Shit," Andy cursed as he realised he was wrong about that, too.

Just like he had been about the tea.

With the whole filtration plant down and the tankers at least two days out, they'd have to go to Stage 7 water restrictions, and that meant turning off any water-cooled plant and machinery. Like the older air-conditioning units over at the base hospital and the 'swamp-ies' that a lot of the older folks about town tended to use because they were cheaper.

He cursed again, turning around to hurry back inside.

Mayor Andrew Old needed to get out to the plant and see Pete Barraclough as soon as he could. People were going to start dying if they couldn't run those units, but there was literally no water left to keep them going. Unless Pete could work a miracle, they would have to start moving people around, rehousing them wherever they could stay cool.

It was going to be a long two days.

12

YOU DIDN'T DO NOTHING WRONG

Jody's car ran out of gas two miles short of Temescal. She made it over the Bay Bridge and down the Webster Street exit, heading for Broadway-Auto Row, but her little Civic started coughing and bunny-jumping as she came up on the Walgreens.

"Noooo," Jody cried, punching the steering wheel.

She wanted to scream and wail. Instead, she sent up a prayer to the patron saint of single mothers, and she steered the spluttering Honda into the car park at the pharmacy. It died half-in, half-out of a parking bay. She cursed herself for running the AC. It must have guzzled the last few drops in her gas tank. But she had no choice. The midday heat was scorching. She felt the interior of the car begin to heat up like a pizza oven as soon as the engine and the air-conditioning cut out. Opening the door and stepping out into the day was like getting fried by a massive bank of Klieg lights. It seemed impossibly hotter.

"Yo bitch, learn to drive!"

The voice was harsh, male, and so San Fernando stupid that it could've been Chad. Jody couldn't help turning around towards whoever had shouted at her. It wasn't Chad. This asshole, striding through the parking lot toward her, was about half the size of her ex-husband. His most striking feature was a head full of improbably long, greasy red dreadlocks. He was a multitasker, too. Ogling her butt as he abused and insulted her driving technique. Jody gave him the finger. Slammed the door. Stormed away.

Her angry Valkyrie act was ruined by having to turn around and stomp back to the car to retrieve her camera bag. If she left it behind, there was no way it would still be there when she got back. She was already sweating as she retrieved the bag, slung it over her shoulder and locked the car again. She thought about calling an Uber. Her last twenty bucks was sitting in her PayPal account, which made it pretty much useless for anything out here in the real world, except maybe for catching a ride the last couple of blocks to *Fourth Edition*.

"You run out of gas?"

It was the same guy. In the stress of the moment, Jody had almost forgotten him, but he hadn't forgotten her. She jumped at the close-ness of his voice. He had moved to within a few feet of her, and she could see that although he was smaller than Chad, he was still lean and ropey with muscle. His arms filled out the sleeves of a faded, moth-eaten Metallica tee shirt. He looked younger than her, but only by a couple of years. Early 20s, maybe. His face was pockmarked with acne scars, but his skin was otherwise clear. He was staring at her intently. Half grinning.

"Yes," she said, moving past him. "I ran out of gas. Excuse me, please."

He reached out and took her arm.

"I can help, baby. I got some gas at my place. Just around the corner if you want to come," he said. He leaned into the word 'come'.

"No, thank you," Jody replied as pleasantly as she could, but her face was a rubber mask of sick and sudden dread. She had been here before.

Metallica's grip on her arm tightened painfully.

"Nearest gas is miles away," he grinned, wider. The expression was carnivorous.

She tried to shake her arm out of his grasp.

"I need to go," she said as firmly as she could. Her voice was shaky, and that made her feel even more frightened.

"Nah, you should come with me," he said. His voice didn't change. He didn't snarl or hiss or do anything to threaten her, but the threat was real. Jody felt her heart race away, and her head began to spin. Her vision started to grey out on the edges, and she stumbled on legs that felt unexpectedly numb and strange.

"No," she shouted and pulled away as hard as she could.

Her camera bag swung around and hit the man in the arm, slipping off her shoulder and falling to the asphalt between them. Even though it was a good bag and heavily padded, she freaked. All of her equipment was in there. She couldn't afford to repair any breakages. Jody lunged forward to grab her stuff back, but the man laughed and hip-checked her so hard she fell into the side of the little Honda. She struck the car with a hollow metallic thump. Stars filled her head, and her legs buckled underneath her. Jody watched, dumbstruck and paralysed, as he grabbed up her camera gear and ran. He was halfway out of the parking lot before she recovered her wits enough to yell to nobody in particular.

"Help! Help me please."

High overhead, fourteen lanes of traffic roared by on the MacArthur Freeway. Down at ground level, Jody felt stupid and feeble and...

Humiliated.

A hot flush of shame reddened her face as she realised she'd just been robbed and she had done nothing, exactly fucking nothing, to defend herself. She couldn't even see the guy anymore. He was already in the wind.

"Miss? You okay, Miss?"

Another voice. Male. But older, kinder. She still flinched away from it, feeling tears welling up and hysteria not far behind them.

"I could chase him for you, but my heart, it ain't what it was. I got his picture, though. Filmed the whole thing on my phone."

A shadow fell across Jody's face as the man shuffled in front of the sun. She raised a hand to shade her eyes, realised that was a bit dumb since he was already blocking out the sun, and wiped away her tears instead. He made no further move toward her.

"Mister Burés, he's the pharmacist, he called the police," he said. "You should probably get up if you can. You're sitting in an oil patch."

He was right. Jody was wearing her favourite pair of vintage white denim jeans, and she had planted her ass deep in the middle of an oil slick.

"Oh God," she said quietly. Her voice trembled and cracked.

The tears came for real, then. Not for her ruined jeans, although that was super fuckin' upsetting, but for everything that had gone bad; not just today, but it seemed like every fucking day since she'd moved out here with Chad. The parking lot blurred, and her goodly Samaritan dissolved into a watercolour wash as she gave up, shaking with deep body tremors and succumbing to a full-blown seizure of racking sobs and moans that arrived on a freight train of wild grief. The intensity of her emotional wipe-out was a little frightening. She didn't realise at first that the kindly, older man had squatted down beside her to gingerly pat her shoulder and say, "There, there," over and over again. She didn't really notice him until he'd been doing it for a minute or more and had been joined in his vigil by another man in a white smock decorated with a small WALGREENS logo. Mister Burés, she presumed. Or would have if she was capable of rational thought.

"The police will be here soon," the newly arrived man said. "That guy, I know him, he's trouble."

No shit, Walgreen? Jody thought bitterly, but she was at least able to put the thought together, and then she registered the presence of her... what, rescuer? That wasn't exactly accurate, was it? After all, she was sitting in a puddle of motor oil, bawling her eyes out, and she had lost her camera gear.

But the white squall of hysteria had passed, and she made an effort not to be a complete bitch.

"I'm sorry," she said, and her nose was so full of snot that she sneezed and blew the whole, repulsive mess out onto her shirt, ruining it too. "Oh God, I'm sorry."

"You didn't do nothing wrong," the man crouched down next to her said. "Here. Take this. It's clean. I got more, and you need it."

Jody blinked away the last of her tears and took the small white square of Kleenex he held towards her, using it to dab at her eyes before blowing her nose again. She felt marginally better until she remembered that all of her equipment had been stolen, and she had a photoshoot to do, *and* she wasn't going to get to the shoot anyway because something terrible had happened to Ellie, *and* Max was missing, possibly taken by Chad and...

The tears came flooding back.

"Hey, come on now, we'll get your stuff back."

The old man was gripping Jody's shoulder, his hand not far from where the mugger had grabbed her. She flinched away as a siren whooped once, and she heard car tyres crunching over loose pebbles and small trash in the car lot. The police had arrived, but that didn't give Jody any sense of relief. Not with Ellie in some sort of trouble. Things happened quickly, then. A young woman appeared from the pharmacy with a bottle of still water and a couple of painkillers. The pharmacist took them from her and offered them to Jody. She drank most of the water before remembering to take the pills.

Her rescuer—she supposed she could call him that because things could have gone worse, much worse, if he hadn't turned up—introduced himself as Karl Valentine, and having possibly interrupted her kidnapping and assault, and God only knew what, he took it upon himself to deal with the police.

"I saw it all," he told them. "I'll testify, don't you worry about that. And I got film too. I filmed it all on my phone."

She could see now that he wasn't an old man, just older than her attacker, possibly twice his age. Karl was somewhere in his forties and had the pleasant, unthreatening air that some men carried with them their whole lives, not as camouflage or a mask, but simply because they really were no threat to anyone.

The pharmacist, Mr Burés and his assistant, a young Blasian girl wearing the name tag 'Aliyah', helped her into the Walgreens, where a female police officer asked her about 'the attack'.

Jody had her very own 'attack' now.

That was weird.

She'd have to tell Ellie as soon as she could.

If she could find Ellie.

"Ma'am? Ma'am?"

Jody shook her head and dropped back into reality. She'd been spiralling away from the here and now since that Metallica jerk had knocked her down, and she'd bumped her head, falling over. The lady policeman—no, the lady police *officer*—was leaning over her, looking at her closely. Jody was sitting down inside, where it was cool and so much nicer than out in that car lot. But when had she sat down? She didn't recall. The cop's eyebrows were knitted closely together, and deep frown lines creased her forehead between her eyes.

She would have to stop doing that, Jody thought.

Or she would get wrinkles.

"Ma'am, is there anyone who can pick you up? You shouldn't be driving," the policewoman said.

"Can't drive," Jody said absently, slightly annoyed that people didn't seem to understand that a car needed gas in the tank to go anywhere.

"Is there anyone who can come and get you?" the cop asked.

"Ellie," she answered.

"Ellie? Is that your friend? Your roommate?"

"My girlfriend."

"Can you call Ellie? Or would you like me to call her? Is her number in your phone?"

Jody stared at the woman. Her name tag read VANDENBERGH.

"I don't know where she is."

"Okay," Officer Vandenbergh said, standing up straight. She turned to Mr Burés, who was still hovering nearby, talking to Mr Valentine, who had rescued her. Jody thought she liked Mr. Valentine. He was kind.

"She's in shock," the policewoman said. "We might need an ambulance. Get her checked out for real."

"An ambulance would be very expensive," Mr. Valentine said. "If she doesn't have insurance."

Oh, he was thoughtful too. Jody could not afford an ambulance. No way.

They all turned to look at her.

"Ma'am, I think you need an ambulance," Officer Vandenbergh said.

"No, I need my camera bag," Jody replied with absolute conviction but not complete certainty. She knew she needed her cameras, but... she'd forgotten why.

"Do you have insurance, dear?" Mr Burés asked. "For the ambulance?"

"Ellie," Jody said, a little critically.

"Ellie has insurance?" Mr Burés asked.

She nodded. "Ellie's a chef. At a restaurant."

"Which restaurant?" Vandenbergh asked.

For a strange, dizzying second, she could not remember, but then it came back to her.

"It's called Fourth Edition!"

"I know that place," Mr. Valentine said. "It's just around the corner from my apartment. I can drive her there if you like. It would save me a walk home."

Officer Vandenbergh looked doubtful, but her friend, the other policeman, hurried in through the pharmacy door and shouted, "Vasquez got him! Three blocks over at the bus stop on Telegraph."

Officer Vandenbergh beamed at her.

"Looks like we got lucky with this guy, and we're going to get your things back, Ms Sarjanen."

She turned to Mr Valentine. "Sir. Can you send me a copy of that video you shot? Of the assault? Right now? So we know for certain we have it."

"Sure. I can do that. And I can testify," Mr. Valentine said. "I want to."

Officer Vandenbergh turned her attention back to Jody.

"Ms Sarjanen, I have to go with Officer Stafford and grab up your perp. Sounds like an off-duty colleague caught him trying to catch a bus. We need to take him to the station for processing. And we'll need a statement from you later. Are you comfortable with Mr.

Valentine here driving you to Ellie's restaurant? We have all of his details."

Everything was happening in such a rush.

"No gas," Jody said.

Vandenbergh frowned.

"Your car has no gas?"

She shook her head.

"I keep a spare can in my pickup," Mr Burés said. "You're welcome to it. I am very sorry for all your trouble, miss."

"Okay," Jody said, feeling as though events were carrying her along, but at least now they seemed to be carrying her toward Ellie.

"Can you drive my car?" she asked Mr. Valentine. "I feel woozy."

"I can drive pretty much anything," he said. "I used to drive big rigs for a living."

The police officers left, anxious to lay hands on their perp. He was theirs now, as well as Jody's. Mr Burés and Mr Valentine agreed that it had been a very exciting morning and that it was a good thing that Mr Valentine had picked up a new bottle of heart pills. They filled Jody's tank from a small red can of gas that Mr Burés produced from the back of his pick-up. Jody got back into her little Civic, feeling as though this was just about the weirdest day of her life so far, and Mr Valentine drove her the rest of the way to Ellie's restaurant.

ELLIE DID NOT RESIST. She wasn't that stupid. Even when a female agent slammed a hammerlock on her and painfully wrenched her arm halfway up her back, she bit down on her need to cry out and fight back. Another agent, a male, grabbed her neck and together, the two officers frogmarched *Fourth Edition's* sous chef out of her kitchen and over to a black SUV. The sun was high overhead and uncomfortably hot. Ellie could feel warm sweat running down her back and sides. Sandino was already half-in the vehicle, sitting awkwardly on his hands, which had been cuffed behind his back. The *saucier's* eyes were wide with shock. His lips were moving, but no words came out.

Ellie wasn't cuffed yet, and she reached for the old man to hug him. The grip on her neck tightened, and she felt herself rammed forward. Her forehead hit the side of the car, and stars filled her eyes.

"Ow!" she cried out.

The grip on her neck and the hammerlock both disappeared as the female agent forced Ellie to assume the position while she patted her down.

"I'm not carrying any knives," Ellie said.

"Just shut up," the woman replied, briskly searching her up and down.

Ellie twisted around to peer back past the agent at her crew, who were all being forced into the other vehicles, a mix of SUVs and plain, unmarked vans. She saw Chris Kakris arguing loudly with the agent in charge, and she felt bad for the hard time she'd given him over his shitty Kobe beef. Chris was all up in that guy's grill, yelling into his face, gesturing wildly with both hands.

"Turn around," the female agent ordered, pulling on Ellie's shoulder to reinforce the direction.

"What the hell are you guys even doing?" Ellie said as she came around. A male agent stood behind the woman. His face was unreadable, obscured by mirror shades and a baseball cap. "Everyone you just grabbed up is legit," Ellie went on. "Half of them are citizens. Like, born here. Everyone else has a green card. Damo doesn't hire..."

"Shut up," the woman said. "It doesn't matter."

"Fascists," Sandino muttered to himself.

"Shut up," the male agent said. "You heard her. It doesn't matter."

Ellie craned around again to see past the agents blocking her view of the alley out back of the restaurant. It was quite a sight, all of those kitchen hands and chefs and apprentices climbing out in their white double-breasted coats and houndstooth pants. Someone in the centre of the small crowd was even wearing a toque blanche, the traditional chef's hat, but Ellie couldn't see who.

The woman elbowed her in the ribs, winding her.

"Stop moving," she said.

Ellie grunted but stood up and faced her squarely. She'd worked some pretty tough kitchens. These guys thought they were hard. They weren't.

"How about taking Sandino's cuffs off?" she said. "He's an old man, and he's got a heart murmur. He makes sauce and stock, not trouble."

"Just shut up, you mouthy bitch," the male agent said.

"Fuck you," she said. "You been told now. You been warned. We're both natural born Americans. You got no jurisdiction over us. You hurt him, and our boss will sue your agency for sure, but he'll sue you personally, too. And he'll win. And he'll take your house, your pension, everything. It's a high price to pay for the momentary pleasure of being an asshole. So take his fucking cuffs off. I'm not wearing any, and believe me, I'm way more trouble."

No reply this time.

Ellie moved quickly to one side and shouted at her crew.

"Don't worry. You're all good. Damo will look after you..."

Ellie didn't doubt that Damien Maloney would pay for every minute his people were detained, just as she did not doubt that every last one of them was legitimately employed and legally in the country. Damo was a bit of an old-school socialist for a millionaire businessman.

"You're all on the clock," she called out. "You're all getting paid..."

The female agent punched Ellie in the side, just above her kidneys. She wasn't ready for that. It drove the air out of her and sent shockwaves down her spine and into her legs, which nearly buckled beneath her. Ellie stumbled but didn't fall.

Her people cheered her on. Some yelled abuse in Spanish at the woman who'd struck her.

But mostly, they cheered when Ellie clawed her way back up to her feet.

13

DEMONSTRABLE STUPIDITY

U n-fucking-believable.

Smoke poured through a small hole punched in the hood of Jonas Murdoch's pick-up by something that looked like a crowbar. Had he thrown a rod? He'd only bought the truck three months ago. It was a piece of shit, to be sure, but the mechanic he bought it from had certified it as roadworthy.

The engine smoke got thicker.

Horns blared in the traffic jam around him. His stomach fluttered and his limbs felt like they might float away. Shock, Jonas knew. Nothing to be embarrassed about. That's just how the human body reacts to violent discontinuity.

He saw flames starting to lick at the edges of the puncture wound in the hood, and he scrambled to get out of the vehicle. His legs almost folded up underneath him as his boots crunched down on the tarmac. He stared dumbly at the burning engine block, unsure of what to do. Before he could take action, another motorist appeared with a small fire extinguisher.

"Get out of the way, man!" he shouted before hosing down the engine fire with a few discreet bursts of dry white powder. He moved in quickly, shooting two solid volleys directly into the rupture in the F-100's hood. The fire inside appeared to be extinguished.

"Thanks, man," Jonas said, still not sure what to do. The guy who had helped him looked to be in his 40s, a little fat but strong with it. A dude who worked hard every day rather than working out.

"It's okay," the man said. "I got another two bottles if we need them. But we better get your rig off the road, son. It's not gonna help with this mess."

The dude gestured at the traffic jam, which had seemingly metastasised around them. Jonas could see evidence of gridlock blocks away now. The blaring of horns was an unholy racket. Drivers in the vehicles around his dead pickup had abandoned their cars at the first sight of the flames. He could see some of them running, actually running, down the street. Idiots.

The guy with the fire extinguisher was wearing some sort of uniform, a sweat-stained grey shirt emblazoned with the logo of a propane gas company and a name tag: SAM. Probably explained why he seemed to be packing so many fire extinguishers. Jonas would've left the car there, but this dude was already getting set to push it out of traffic.

A couple of drivers who'd left their cars but not run away approached warily. Some were filming with their smartphones.

"Come on, you guys," Propane Sam shouted to nobody in particular. "Let's get this thing off the road."

Nobody came any closer.

"It's safe," he assured them. "But we gotta get it moved, so come on. Everyone pitch in."

"You want me to steer?" Jonas asked.

"Hell no," Propane Sam said. "You look like you could pick this thing up and carry it home. You push. Hey you! Lady!"

A young Asian woman tried to pretend she hadn't heard him, but this propane-powered hero was having none of it.

"Just pop up in the cabin there and steer us over to the pavement," Sam ordered, and much to Jonas's surprise, she did as she was told. Her obedience seemed to influence the others, and within a few seconds, half a dozen men and women had surrounded his pickup. A minute later, they'd muscled it out of the jam and onto the verge. They even gave themselves a round of applause when it was all done. The woman who'd steered for them handed Jonas his keys.

"Sorry about your car," she said, but she looked like this had been the highlight of her day. She was gonna be pissed if she couldn't get on Twitter to tell everyone about it later.

Propane Sam popped the hood and gave the engine block a scep- tical once-over. He scowled at whatever he found in there, gave it another taste of the dry powder and nodded as though satisfied at last. His small crowd of 'volunteers' was already breaking up, heading back to their vehicles where they would undoubtedly sit with the windows rolled up and the cold air blasting until the jam cleared itself.

Sam ran a thick, callused hand through his thinning blond hair.

"I'd offer you a lift, man, but you know..." he gestured helplessly at the stalled traffic, which now appeared to be spreading in all directions.

"Thanks anyway," Jonas said. "But I live nearby." He patted the passenger side door of the F-100 ruefully. "And nobody's gonna be stealing this useless bitch. I can get it towed tomorrow."

Sam nodded sagely.

"Reckon you'll be the first one of us home and out of this crap then," he said. He extended his hand to shake, and Jonas took it. They both gripped firmly and pumped up and down, once, twice, three times.

"Good job, Sam," Jonas said. "Nice working with you."

WALKING home confirmed the extent of the traffic jam. It was a monster snarl. Jonas expected to see traffic lights out everywhere, but instead they all seemed functional. Or dysfunctional. At nearly every major intersection he passed, three or four vehicles, sometimes more, had collided at speed. It was as though the lights had tricked dozens of drivers into accelerating when they should have been slowing down. Some of the pile-ups were obviously fatal. Some were burning, and Jonas closed his mind to the screams. He heard sirens in the distance, but none of the emergency services could get through to the worst of the accidents. At one point, he saw a couple of paramedics running at full tilt with an old-fashioned canvas stretcher held between them. They were both struggling in the heat, sweating torrents, their faces as red as fresh split watermelon.

This shit was starting to look a little gnarlier than Amazon Web Services crashing and taking down a bunch of stupid Instagram influencers. Jonas felt his gorge rising a little at the chance that he wouldn't be able to access his funds. He needed money. He needed to get gone.

Traffic had backed up all the way home, but the side street in which he lived was clear except for a couple of cars at the intersection with Algona Boulevard. They were waiting, with seemingly endless patience and demonstrable stupidity, to merge into the static river of hot steel clogging up the main stem. Jonas shook his head. People were idiots.

Mikey, his roommate. He was an idiot. A well-intentioned and occasionally useful idiot but a mouth breather, nonetheless. Mikey's ambitions in life reached no further than one day owning his own Burger King franchise, and if that happened to be at the Supermall and he didn't have to change anything about his life besides working harder, that would suit Mikey just fine.

Jonas checked his watch, a Swiss analogue model he'd stolen from the fulfilment centre. It amused him to wear it to work.

2:42 PM.

It seemed like the entire population of the city was trapped in their cars. The blare of horns and warbling sirens was loud enough to follow him through the front door when he got home. It was marginally cooler inside the house, thanks to all of the asbestos in the walls and roof. Dark, too, and he stood in the vestibule while his eyes adjusted. When Jonas could see where he was going, he closed the door on the chaos behind him. He could still hear it, slightly muted, in the distance.

Not really expecting success, he tried logging onto the Internet.

Mikey's PC took up half of the table where they ate the infrequent meals they shared. The machine was asleep—Mikey was obsessed about never actually turning it off—and it woke up fine, but as Jonas expected, he could not get online. He turned the modem off for 30 seconds, sweating in the dark, stuffy closeness of the empty house. Turned it back on and tried again. Nothing.

Looked like he wouldn't be checking on his website and podcast then.

He checked his phone, but cell reception had always been shit here. He wasn't surprised to see he had no service.

The import of what he'd done earlier started to creep up on him. Knocking Tamoreau on his ass. Assaulting Yolanda and Omar. And not just in front of witnesses but on CCTV.

Fuck, what had he been thinking?

Truth was, he hadn't been thinking at all. He'd just let his temper off the leash, the same way he had back in Miami.

A thought occurred. A hopeful thought.

Perhaps the security systems were down. Everything else seems to be out.

Following a hunch, he tried the television. Mikey had cable.

It was out, too.

For some reason, that made Jonas feel better. Witnesses he could deal with. But there was no arguing with cold, recorded video. Shit, they'd probably throw his ass in jail for this. And if anybody found out about his podcast, it was a laydown fucking certainty that some asshole prosecutor would try and ramp up his sentence by juicing it with a racial hatred angle.

He had to get out of town.

It was too hot to think. He could feel his thoughts running away from him. He had to move quick, sure, but he had to do so with deliberation. Hasten slowly, as they said. He knew that most felons got picked up as soon as they tried to run. They didn't think it through. They didn't plan. They just ran.

He had to do more than just strike out for the horizon. He had to get away clean *and* somehow plug into his newfound but anonymous fame to make some scratch.

He figured he had at least a few hours. There were cops everywhere at the moment, but like the rest of the city, they were stuck in traffic. Nobody was coming for him. Not while everything was locked up like this. Jonas took a bottle of cold tap water from the fridge, poured himself a glass, and drank slowly. No sense in getting a headache now. He had a second glass and started to calm down as he cooled down.

He would need to change clothes.

He showered and he shaved off his beard, and when he dressed, he did so in the best disguise he could think of: a pair of Mikey's bike shorts and a racing top.

His roommate was not just a cyclist. He was a mad fucking cyclist, like, really political about it. It was pretty much the only thing the otherwise mild-mannered idiot ever got worked up over. Jonas had seen him punch cars in traffic. He smiled at the memory. And at the idea that it gave him.

He'd waved Mikey off to work on his racing bike that morning while he was checking on the pod's boner-inducing download stats.

But his roomie had a second bike that he kept in his room. A heavier, ruggedised model that he rode on the rough dirt tracks in the remnant forest over the highway to the west. It could go all sorts of places the racer could not.

Jonas collected his go-bag from the cupboard in his bedroom. He didn't need to check it. He knew what was in there, and only he knew the combination of the two padlocks that secured it. Clothes, weapons, some energy-dense foodstuffs and a few camping items. More than enough to get him out of the city and over the state line. He was annoyed that he couldn't transfer his PayPal balance to the debit card he'd set up for just such a flight, but he could try that again from an Internet café on the road. He would even take the precaution of pedalling half a day out of his way to throw the cops off his heading. But that was all for the future.

He did have a solution to his immediate cash flow problem. Mikey Summers had an unusual life hack. He never carried five-dollar notes. Whenever he came into possession of one, he put it into a small wooden box on the bookshelf by his bed. He told Jonas that over a year, he could save enough that way to pay for a two-week road trip. On his bike, of course. He was planning on riding all the way down to Corvallis later this year.

"Sorry, buddy," Jonas said, taking the locked box and smashing it open. "But Corvallis sucks anyway. All those fucking college students. I'm doing you a favour."

Mikey did Jonas the favour of $865 in five-dollar notes.

He took his roommate's money, riding gear, and bike. The spandex was uncomfortably tight on him. But spandex did stretch, and if Jonas bulged out of the skin-tight costume, he figured that would serve as a distraction and, in a pinch, even a disguise. Witnesses would be too busy staring at his rock-hard ass and over-sized genitalia to give the police a helpful description of his actual appearance.

His preparations done, Jonas wheeled the bike out to the footpath less than forty minutes after getting home. The day was still scorching hot, and the later afternoon sun blazed fiercely from the metal and glass of the cars jammed up at the end of his street. Nothing had changed out here. But everything had changed for him. Again.

He climbed onto the bike and rode away from the house without a backward glance.

14

YOU'RE ROLLING WITH THE DEEP STATE NOW

James didn't wait when the conference broke up. Telling Michelle he'd meet her back at her office, he hurried downstairs to the little cafe where they'd bought lattes and a cheese cruller — because Michele's favourite muffin had been unavailable. The early morning crowd had dispersed, and James had only one other customer to wait behind. She grabbed a takeaway coffee with raisin toast and hurried off after paying with her watch.

A transaction that went off without a hitch, he noted.

The server, a young woman, smiled as he approached the counter.

"Back again?"

"Uh, yeah," he said, surprised to be recognised. "That was good coffee. I'll have another to go."

He used his Apple Watch to pay for the purchase, and again, it went through without a problem.

"Still no muffins?" James asked.

The girl shook her head.

"No, sorry. They just didn't turn up."

He nodded.

"Weird question, but could you give me the name of the distributor?"

"Dude, you must really be hurting for a muffin."

"When are we ever not hurting for a muffin?" James smiled as winningly as he could. "Seriously though, it's like a matter of national security." He paused. "I've always wanted to say that."

The serving girl looked at him as if uncertain of his sanity.

"Is it really national security?"

He shrugged. "I don't know yet, but could you check?"

She disappeared into a supply room that was more of a closet, reappearing a minute later with a Post-it note, which she handed to him. Written on the small yellow square were two words: *US Foodservice.*

"Thanks," James said and started to hurry away.

"Hey, you forgot your coffee," she called after him.

He pulled up just short of the exit. Caught between waiting for the young woman to make up his order and getting back to Michelle.

"You know what, just pay it forward. Give it to the next person who comes through in need of caffeine. Be the highlight of their day."

She smiled. "That's so nice."

He returned her smile but hurried away without his drink.

Michelle Nguyen was already back in her office, and she met him with an inquiring tilt of the head.

"'Sup, Corn-fed?"

James pulled up a chair in front of her desk. He had trouble stopping his legs from jigging up and down.

"Is there like some spreadsheet or briefing paper or something detailing which companies and government departments got hacked yesterday?"

He knew it was a grossly inappropriate use of the term 'hacked', but he didn't care. He just needed what he needed.

"I imagine so," Michelle said. "Probably half a dozen of them floating around by now. The NSA's will be the best, though. You want that?"

He looked at her with wide eyes.

"You can get that?"

"Dude, you're rolling with the deep state now. We can get anything. Just give me a second."

She pulled a trackpad a little closer, woke up the screen on her computer, and started to type. The computer was a big iMac, but she used a crazy ergonomic keyboard that was so ugly it had to be Microsoft. Within a minute, she turned the screen around to face him. It was dense with information.

James shook his head slowly.

"Okay, this'll go a lot quicker if I just tell you what I'm thinking, and you tell me whether I'm crazy or not."

"Oh, I can totally do that."

He sat back in the chair, took a breath and composed his thoughts. How best to phrase what he was thinking? What did they need to know to know what they needed? He decided to plunge in at the deep end of the crazy pool.

"Most of the food in America," he said, "is distributed by four companies. Did you know that?"

Michelle leaned back in her chair, nodding.

"I write the food security briefings that nobody reads," she said. "I'd have said six companies, but I know where the number four is coming from. Sysco. US Foodservice. Performance Food Group. And Gordon Food Services."

"Yeah, okay, you're right," James conceded. There are six of them if you include Food Services of America and Reinhart. Between them, they control 280 of the 298 food distribution centres in the continental US. Your missing muffin? It was supposed to come from one of those warehouses this morning. And it didn't."

Michelle looked at him as if waiting for the next clue.

"Well, a lot of things got messed up yesterday, James. They're still sorting out traffic jams in half a dozen cities."

"Yeah, I know," he said. "I had the same trouble as everybody else. Couldn't pay for my gas. Couldn't pay for my hotel room..."

Michelle interrupted him. "But we're paying for your hotel room. Including room service."

"Yeah, but they still hit you with that scammy holding fee, or resort charge or whatever they call it," he said.

"Ugh, I hate that."

"The Marriot was only a buck," James said. "But they still had to use one of the old mechanical slides to get an impression of my personal card."

Michelle shrugged. "Sorry, dude."

James mirrored the gesture.

"It's fine. A buck is fine. But what I'm saying is, yes, I know everything melted down yesterday. What I would like to know..." He pointed at the screen sitting between them. "... Is whether those food service companies got hit differently to everybody else. Can you look into that data and tell me whether anything stands out?"

Michelle narrowed her eyes at the screen, shaking her head.

"I can't, or at least I can't do it off the top of my head," she admitted. "But we got some data nerds who could. You want me to hit them up?"

"That'd be awesome," James said.

"Okay," she said, primarily to herself, as her fingers flew over the weird-looking keyboard again. "I've sent it to the mavens and flagged it as priority ultra. If there's anything there, like anything really obvious, they'll get back to us pretty quickly. Where are you going with this, James? It's not what Holloway asked you to look at."

"I know," he said. "And I've already done some work on his brief. I promise I'll double down on it as soon as I close out this hunch. And it is just a hunch, but I got to thinking in that briefing this morning that if you really wanted to kick the legs out from under any American response to..."

He waved his hands in the air, not quite sure of the words he needed to use. Michelle finished the thought for him.

"Any American response to Chinese aggression in Southeast Asia? Is that what you mean?"

His leg stopped jigging up and down.

"Yeah, I guess I do. I mean, how desperate are the Chinese? Is it worse than it looks?" he asked. "Because it looks pretty bad already."

Michelle's expression was blank. She sat across the desk from him, staring through him as though weighing something up. Her appearance, the severely cut clothes, the bright tattoos, the punk revival haircut, it all served to unsettle James, to make him feel as though he'd fallen through the looking glass.

"It's bad enough," she said, "that if they don't get what they need, they could definitely go to war and take it."

"But that's..."

A notification pinged on her computer, interrupting him.

"Jesus, that was quick," Michelle said.

She stared at the computer screen for a moment.

"We better go see Holloway," she said at last.

THE ADMIRAL WAS UNAVAILABLE.

He wasn't in his office, and he didn't have a secretary to run interference. He was simply missing in action. When they couldn't raise him, James followed Michelle back to her room, where a couple of seconds of high-speed typing on her misshapen keyboard brought up a new window.

"Huh," she said. "OfficeLink says he's in transit to the White House. It's an unscheduled meeting."

"I'm gonna guess that doesn't happen every day," James said.

"You'd be surprised, especially with this president. But we need to take this up the line now. You'd better get your story straight."

James felt as though he was falling after missing a step going down into an unlit basement.

"What? Wait. No. I don't really have a story, Michelle. I just..."

"You just discovered a point of critical failure that was probed yesterday by a hostile foreign power, probably the Chinese, who have both motivation and means to effect a fundamental discontinuity in the national infrastructure and who tried to cover up their reconnaissance with a broad-spectrum cyber-attack that brushes right up against the definition of an act of war. So, you have a story, James. And you're gonna tell it."

The magical tattooed alterna-babe had disappeared.

In her place, a cold and deeply serious Michelle Nguyen all but frog-marched him down the corridor into a section of the building he had not yet seen.

James recognised the atmosphere, however. He was almost certainly entering the governmental equivalent of C-suite territory. Deputy secretaries or under-secretaries or whatever Uncle Sam called his chief operating ass-kickers in the national security business. Pulled along in Michelle's wake by the forceful change of her personality as much as anything else, he glanced into those offices where the doors stood open. He saw waiting rooms as big as the lounge in his apartment and ferocious-looking personal assistants who glared at him as he passed. James O'Donnell tucked his head in and tried to gather his thoughts. What the hell had he just done?

He needed to figure it out quickly because Michelle had just barged into a corner office with expansive views in two directions over the gardens surrounding the building. She was demanding to see a General Somebody-or-other and muscling her way past the PA who tried to stop her. James expected armed marines to appear, but instead a surprisingly diminutive, grey-haired man who reminded him of Colonel Potter from the TV series MASH (his dad's favourite) stuck his head out from behind the double doors of an inner sanctum.

"What on earth is going on out here?" Colonel Potter demanded to know.

"General Panozzo, this is James. He's doing some consultancy for Admiral Holloway. I think he found something in the margins of yesterday's cyber-attack, sir."

General Panozzo emerged from his office and thanked his secretary, Denise, for attempting to defend his redoubt. He looked James up and down with a sceptical expression furrowing his brows.

"Well, son, what is it? And don't try to bamboozle me with any of those ten-dollar buzzwords you consulting types love so much. What have you got?"

James's heart was pounding in his chest. He didn't know what to say, so he just said it.

"It's Pearl Harbour, sir. But with muffins."

15

THE FOLLY OF WISER HEADS

L ike all great cities, Shanghai did not sleep. If anything, General Chu Jianguo thought, the city of twenty-five million seemed to gather itself as darkness fell, like a dragon drawing in breath to burn away the night with one long monstrous blast of fire and light. Chu stood so close to the highly polished glass of the double-height floor-to-ceiling window on the top floor of the skyscraper that his breath fogged up the windowpane, obscuring his view of the scene below. It was well after one in the morning, but the vast electric landscape was alive with movement and energy. Millions of vehicles turned thousands of roads and streets and even tiny back alleys into a boundless web of streaming light. Fantastic towers reached towards the heavens, their forms so various, so unpredictable that even knowing the city as well as he did, Chu was often surprised and sometimes even shocked by some new and wondrous architectural marvel that had seemingly sprung into being as his eye had lingered briefly upon some older, more familiar sight. How could anyone behold such a vista and doubt the power, the undeniable, uncontainable power and glory of the reborn Middle Kingdom?

Chu could.

Because he knew the truth.

He chewed an antacid tablet as he waited for the order which he knew was coming. The attack would proceed because it had to. They had no choice. He and his comrades were responsible for the lives of the millions of souls he could see before him and beyond them to one billion more. He was even responsible, he acknowledged, to humanity as a whole. He could not allow the current crisis to spiral out of control into the insensate slaughter of a conventional world war. Or worse.

"I will wager you did not imagine yourself here when you joined the army as a sent-down youth, eh Chu?"

"I did not imagine anything other than filling my rice bowl a couple of times a day," Chu grunted, but not unkindly. He turned to the man standing next to him, a true comrade. "And what of you, Song Jiasheng? I will double your wager and hazard my pension that you did not imagine when we survived the battle at Laoshan that we would fight our next war from a hotel suite with room service."

His old friend laughed.

"No, I did not. But I will take this over that Vietnamese shitting hole any day. And there will be no war. The Central Committee has said so."

Both men chuckled, each in their way. Chu snorted at the arrogance implied by the Committee's decree. When they had sent him down this path, they had indeed ordered him to ensure that the plan did not result in armed conflict with the United States and its allies. As if wishing for something could make it so. General Song Jiasheng chuckled more to himself. Unlike his old comrade, Song was still able to take some pleasure and even amusement, however doubtful, in the folly of supposedly wiser heads.

"Perhaps if they had been at the Laoshan Front with us?" Song said. He did not need to finish the thought. Chu understood perfectly. Between them, they were the only members of the army's general staff with actual battle experience, and they had earned that many decades ago as lowly riflemen in an infantry platoon surrounded by hundreds of Vietnamese. It was a wonder they were alive to draw breath, let alone that they had risen through the ranks to their current stations. An experience like Laoshan, however, that stayed with you forever. Perhaps, Chu conceded, it made him conservative. Perhaps, despite its present crisis, China had grown far beyond the constraints of ordinary powers. The Americans, after all, and the British before them, had not felt themselves constrained at the heights of their power.

But as he stood high above the vast and spectacular panorama of Shanghai at night, General Chu Jianguo could not shake the feeling he recalled from the morning they had marched into battle at Laoshan.

They were all going to die.

THE GENERALS ATE SIMPLY. Not combat rations, of course. There was no sense in being perverse, but nor did either one feel it appropriate to gorge themselves. General Chu Jianguo and General Song Jiasheng of the 2nd Bureau, Third Department of the People's Liberation Army General Staff, slurped up hot bowls of fat rice noodles with pickled radish and slivers of pork. They drank jasmine tea, and they waited, talking as old soldiers will of their younger days.

Three minutes after one in the morning, Chu heard the soft rapping of knuckles on the door of their hotel suite. He and Song exchanged a glance. With each other, they could let their true feelings show, and what they felt was a deep anxiety about what might happen next. Chu had no special insight or information about the tough diplomatic talks underway with the governments of Thailand and Vietnam to guarantee China's food security for at least the medium term. But he did know what would happen if either of those negotiations failed to literally put food on the table in Beijing.

"Your luck was always better than mine, Chu," Song Jiasheng said quietly, almost smiling as if to apologise for something. "You should answer."

Chu Jianguo replied with a rueful grin of his own.

"This is not mah-jong, old friend."

Nonetheless, he put aside his noodle bowl and padded over to the door. Chu did not look through the spyhole or ask who was there.

The 2nd Bureau had quietly claimed this entire floor of the hotel, a Business Club level with its own lounge and conference facilities.

"Come in please, Colonel," he said as he opened the door for himself.

Colonel Tsien was used to his superior's simple ways. He undoubtedly imagined Chu's good manners and care for the feelings of his underlings as the persistent humility of a born peasant. The ambitious son of a Central Committee member, Tsien was not excessively favoured with manners or humility. As he entered and saluted, however, his unusually rigid formality struck Chu as a mask the man had pulled over his true concerns and creeping dread. Were this bold course to lead them into disaster, many, many powerful figures and great families would perish there.

"We have orders to proceed," Tsien said, his voice tight.

Chu nodded to himself. He had been afraid of this. For a moment, he did nothing, said nothing. Like a tiger with its jaws clamped around his head, a treacherous memory had taken him. Chu cowered in the red soil of Laoshan. The earth beneath him turned to mud with the piss soaking through his fatigues, adding his water to all the blood that cursed valley had already drunk of so deeply.

"General Chu? Sir?"

"Very well, Colonel," Chu said, coming back from the past with a jolt. "Prepare the unit. General Song and I will join you presently."

Tsien snapped out a stiff salute and turned on his heel, closing the door behind him with a slightly too forceful pull.

"It is happening," Chu said, having trouble believing it himself. His voice was shaking, and he took a breath to centre himself and regain control. "It is actually happening," he said less anxiously. More in wonderment.

"The Thais or the *Yuenán houzǐ* said no, I presume," Song ventured.

Chu threw up his hands, but more in resignation than anything else.

"What does it matter?" he said. "A bad beginning makes a bad ending, and I fear no matter how well we think this will go, it cannot help but end badly."

"Come now, Chu," Song chided him. "All things are difficult at the start."

The general gathered himself. His friend was right. They were on this path now; there was nothing but to walk it until the end. Chu Jianguo put on his jacket and fastened the buttons. He indulged himself in one last look over the city. It remained a boundless, brilliant swirl of electric colour, a billion moving points of light, alive with energy even in this darkest hour. Chu thought of all of the millions of souls he could see down there, and he hoped he was about to secure their futures, not destroy them.

The generals departed their suite, returning the salutes of the soldiers standing guard in the hallway immediately outside. Heavily armed men lined the wide corridor, two commandos standing opposite each other every ten metres. They all wore the black combat fatigues of the PLA Navy's Sea Dragon special forces. Unit 61398 of the 2nd Bureau was not a traditional combat force and could not provide for its own physical security. It was the target of ceaseless, full spectrum surveillance and harassment by China's enemies, most especially by the Americans and their so-called Five Eyes partners in the English-speaking democracies. Like the Sea Dragons, it was an elite unit, but its members carried laptops, not assault rifles, and those on duty tonight had gradually infiltrated the hotel as guests in parties of one and two over the previous week. Hundreds more remained in the unit's four major data warfare centres in Shanghai, where they would cover for the absence of their comrades.

As Chu strode down the plush carpeted hallway, past stern-faced commandos and the occasional bowl of complimentary fruit—quite an extravagance given the current difficulties—he worried that some CIA drone was orbiting overhead or that NSA 'tailored access' operators were already sitting on his networks, watching everything in real-time. Despite the assurances of his network security people, he suspected there was no way to truly make these things, these damned computers, impregnable. And now the whole world ran on them. Such abject foolishness.

"Attention!"

As Chu and Song entered the largest of the conference rooms, dozens of programmers came to attention while sitting in their chairs; spines ramrod stiff, arms held straight down by their sides. Chu, who was not himself technically minded, was quietly proud of having foreseen the potential for disaster with a room full of operators suddenly leaping to the feet to salute a superior officer. He imagined the entire mission failing because somebody pulled out a plug or knocked a laptop to the floor.

"At ease," he ordered. "Continue preparations."

The room returned to the quiet, focused diligence he and Song had interrupted with their arrival. Screens glowed, fingers clicked on keyboards, and the only talk he heard was the low voices of the supervising officers, carefully walking the floor between the conference tables, which had been laid out in a grid pattern that a Roman legionnaire or Shang Dynasty general would instantly recognise as the outward form of a disciplined military unit.

What would they make of his war? Chu thought.

They might not understand the arsenal, but the principles of warfare did not change. The opportunity of defeating the enemy was always provided by the enemy himself.

Colonel Tsien broke away from conferring with two of his officers to shepherd Song and Chu to the nest of screens where they would watch the opening salvos of the war. Now that the moment was upon them, Tsien appeared to have found his spirit. His colour was high with excitement, and a thin sheen of sweat glowed on his forehead. He led them through a break in the wall of curved monitors, stacked three high, to create a digital fortress within which Chu could not see his cyber-warriors at their stations. Whether by design or happenstance, he was content with this arrangement. Although the generals and Colonel Tsien wore the uniform of the People's Liberation Army, none of the programmers here did so. They had arrived at the hotel in various guises, most often posing as businessmen and women, and even now, they maintained the ruse, performing their duties in a frankly disgraceful mix of civilian garb. Chu would prefer not to look upon the strangeness of that sight.

Within the bastion of giant, curving screens—all of them made by Chinese firms, naturally—he was finally able to put aside his unease.

Here, with his old comrade and attended by Tsien and two majors of the Central Military Commission, General Chu could feel as though he was playing his role in a more conventional battle. Some of the screens displayed news feeds from both Chinese and Western sources, all with the volume turned down and the latter featuring real-time translation scrolling as text across the bottom of the screen. CNN reported on the enormous traffic jam, which still paralyzed much of Los Angeles and which had occasioned serious outbreaks of looting and riots when the city's criminal underclasses realised the authorities were as hindered in their movements as everyone else. He was about to gift the barbarian *yáng lājī* running wild in that city a great and terrible favour.

On Bloomberg, a bald man explained how much money had been lost to the disruption of the previous twenty-four hours, while a panel on Fox News were in furious agreement with each other that blame for the disaster lay squarely upon the Democrats in Congress.

"When the enemy is relaxed, make them toil. When full, starve them. When settled, make them move," General Song said, quoting the great Sun Tzu. "This enemy thinks it is starving, but we will soon show them otherwise," he went on.

Chu kept his own counsel as he watched video feeds from the PLA's closed networks. Thousands of men from the 15th Airborne Corps hustled into their transport planes at three separate airbases as the Peoples Liberation Army Air Force prepared to drop six brigades of paratroopers onto critical targets in Thailand and Vietnam. In deep bunkers on the Mischief Reef base in the South China Sea, troops of the PLA's Rocket Force hurried to ready sixteen 12x12 erector launchers with DF-26 'East Wind' ballistic missiles, while on Fiery Cross the rocketeers fussed over another two dozen launchers laden with the shorter-range DF-21s. These, Chu understood, were a mix of land attack and anti-ship variants tasked with servicing counterforce targets in Singapore, Malaysia and throughout the Indonesian archipelago. With a reach of up to four thousand kilometres, the East Wind 26s would soon punch into targets in the Bay of Bengal and northern Australia, delivering tonnes of conventional payload to the naval and air bases of hostile powers without the ability to hit back like the United States. One monitor appeared to cycle through live cams looking over the decks of a container ship, although Chu understood that the imagery was being fed from three separate vessels.

General Chu Jianguo had his favourite lesson from Sun Tzu's *Art of War*, but he muttered only the first half to himself now.

"Victorious warriors win first and then go to war."

He did not think it prudent to finish the aphorism.

While defeated warriors go to war first and then seek to win.

On a satellite display, Chu watched the South Sea Fleet, ostensibly on a training cruise east of Hainan, begin the long swing to the southwest, heading for the southern coastline of Vietnam. On the screen immediately next to it was a computer-generated infographic map. Chu watched the map show the East Sea Fleet heading out from Ningbo and Shanghai to secure the eastern approaches against the South Korean and Japanese navies.

It was time.

Alarms would already be ringing in the Pentagon and throughout the capitols of allied powers. Chu knew it to be most unlikely that the Americans had penetrated his operational security, no matter how much he might worry about NSA hackers and the CIA's counterintelligence division. But there could be no hiding the sudden movement of so much military power out in the open. He accepted that somewhere across the Pacific, other men stood in grander facilities than his temporary war room and pointed their fingers at satellite or computer-generated imagery of the PLA's mobilisation. They would right now be making their first calls, interrupting the luncheons of other American generals and admirals and senators, and possibly even the President himself.

It was time to put out their eyes.

Time to win first and then go to war.

"All is ready, Colonel?" Chu asked.

"Of course, sir," Tsien replied. "You can release the first package here."

Colonel Tsien indicated a keyboard resting in front of a desktop computer. A single bright red key, labelled ENTER, stood out from the other black keys.

Chu had not prepared any words for such a momentous occasion, and it was not in his nature to grandstand anyway. In the end, he was a simple soldier, and he knew how to pull a trigger.

Or, in this case, to press an ENTER key.

He glanced at his oldest surviving friend. Song Jiasheng nodded once, his face the unreadable clay mask of a terracotta warrior. They both knew what this meant.

General Chu Jianguo pulled the trigger.

PENTAGON WAR PLANNERS had long prepared for a digital Pearl Harbor. USCYBERCOM was created in 2009, initially with a defensive mission to secure the US military from the sort of devastating 'assassin's mace' attacks that the NSA had long prepared to unleash on America's rivals. When Cyber Command envisaged full-spectrum online warfare, it imagined GPS satellites raked from the heavens, datalinks severed between sensors and shooters, firewalls breached, and soft civilian targets compromised by brute force DDOS attacks. It did not expect weaponised porn. Or hostile Facebook status ops. Or the SWATting of the Secretary of Defence.

The Central Military Commission had tasked General Chu with a very delicate balancing operation. He had not been ordered to take the mace to the US military, striking it down with one mortal blow. To do so was to invite massive retaliation from a foe that remained an existential threat to the PLA and to the People's Republic itself. Chu had instead been told to prepare an operation that would merely cripple the American giant, removing it from the coming fight just long enough for the Chinese side to effect a complete transformation of the strategic and political reality in its immediate neighbourhood. To this end, Unit 61398 of the 2nd Bureau had made ready a most unusual strike package.

When General Chu Jianguo pressed ENTER on the keyboard, as indicated by Colonel Tsien, he released a barrage of malign code that triggered consequences varying in effect from annoying and inconvenient to utterly disastrous, at least for the individuals on the receiving end. One packet of black scripts altered the Facebook relationship status of a randomised selection of married US military personnel to 'it's complicated'. Another revealed to FBI agents investigating paedophile rings the presence of thousands of child porn images carefully planted on the personal computers of senior State Department officials. In Washington DC, heavily armed police officers stormed the family home of the US Defence Secretary, responding— they thought—to an alert that a violent schizophrenic with a knife had broken in and attacked the Secretary's wife. At the same time, a Secret Service tactical response group raced to the same address after receiving a credible report that DefSec's family had been targeted by terrorists wearing stolen police SWAT uniforms.

Launched from compromised machines in Iran, Iraq, Venezuela and North Korea, thousands of singular attacks affected individuals identified as critical actors in US government emergency management processes. These small, bespoke ambushes, tailored over many years, exploited the earlier theft of tens of millions of records from the US Office of Personnel Management. They effectively constituted a bloodless decapitation strike. The Secretary of Homeland Security, for instance, found herself suddenly locked out of both of her phones, her laptop and even her office. While she was attempting to deal with that inconvenience, her husband arrived at the front gate of the DHS Complex on Nebraska Avenue, red-faced and out of breath. He had ridden their son's bicycle over because his car had been impounded for late lease payments, and the sheriff's office had sent two deputies to evict him from their family home after the bank had foreclosed on their mortgage.

The Secretary of Homeland Security was a former drug company executive. Her husband owned sixteen Chik-fil-A franchises. Their home was fully owned, unencumbered by any mortgage. Her husband's car was indeed leased for tax purposes, but his food service company paid that lease, and it was more than solvent. People did like their Chik-fil-A, after all.

At least they weren't arrested by IRS agents for tax evasion, like the head of FEMA.

Or forcefully quarantined by the CDC, like the Administrator and deputy administrator of the TSA, who were attending a conference in Houston at a hotel that was suddenly red-flagged as a hot spot for a bird flu outbreak a few minutes before their respective spouses received emails containing explicit videos—deep fakes, as it happened—of the FEMA boss and his second-in-charge enjoying a vigorous sexual encounter in the rooftop pool of the same hotel.

These thousands of individually targeted civil servants were dwarfed in number by the millions of serving military personnel who found themselves in arrears on credit cards and personal loans they had not opened. Their personal accounts were frozen by the auto-mated systems at banks, S&Ls, and credit unions. Partners and dependents called in panic when they couldn't buy gas or groceries.

Islamic State pages on the dark web released statements claiming responsibility for the attack.

Wikileaks dumped a cache of documents into the wild that 'revealed' plans by the CIA to effect a coup in Thailand.

The hacker collective Anonymous released the President's tax returns to the *Washington Post* and *New York Times*.

Thousands of businesses, small and large, were paralyzed by ransomware, widely recognised to have come from North Korea, using tools stolen from the NSA by Edward Snowden.

Half of the officers in the LAPD received text messages telling them they had been put on administrative leave pending an Internal Affairs investigation into credible allegations of corruption and brutality.

And there was more, much more.

However, given the porous, interconnected nature of the online world, some of the effects spread rapidly to Europe and throughout the Asia Pacific, leading to increased disruption. Some effects, the general knew, would even manifest themselves here in China. Indeed, there was another unit of the 2nd Bureau busily faking reports of massive disruptions to the PRC from 'criminal internet gangsters'. And all of it was merely a distraction for the assassin's mace.

A few seconds after General Chu unleashed digital hell on the

United States, the IT systems of nine food distribution companies melted down.

The tens of thousands of employees who worked for those companies found themselves individually subject to a plague of cyber assaults that replicated the attacks on more significant and nominally powerful figures such as the Secretary of Homeland Security, the administrators of the TSA and the frankly dumbfounded boss of FEMA. He was, at that very moment, standing in the foyer of his Houston hotel, wondering what the hell his wife was screaming about so hysterically on FaceTime and why a bunch of guys in moon suits had just rushed the concierge desk.

16

THIS IS NOT HOW IT WORKED IN ALL THOSE TOM CLANCY BOOKS

T he email from Michelle's data mavens satisfied General Panozzo that the Chinese had targeted the IT systems of the leading food distribution companies in the continental US. Panozzo's hot take? So fucking what? James was half an hour convincing him that it was any more serious than the other cyberattacks that had caused so much chaos yesterday and which, thankfully, seemed to have eased off overnight.

"Everyone's got back-ups," Panozzo grumbled in a thick New Jersey accent. He sounded like a Harley Davidson on a cold morning. "So what? You saying 'dese guys don't back up some muffin orders so I gotta tell the president to call out the marines? Because I'm telling you, Mishy," he said, ignoring James and talking directly to Nguyen, "that's gonna be a helluva hard sell given the mess we're cleaning up this morning. You read the morning brief? We got hospitals lost all their patient records until they pay some Nigerian asshole a Bitcoin ransom to give 'em back. There's a permanent traffic jam in LA now, and people are shooting each other from their cars. My kids are ringing me because the Xbox ain't working no more. And you seriously want me to escalate your breakfast issue?"

"General, it's not the muffins, okay," James said, pushing back into their exchange.

Panozzo glared at him.

"It's everything. It's..." he had a lightbulb moment. "It's logistics. That's what you guys always say, right? Armchair generals talk about tactics. Professionals are all about logistics or something?"

He snagged Panozzo's interest with that.

"Something like that, yeah." The general sighed. "Go on."

James rubbed his hands together like an anxious conjurer trying to coax the magic into his fingertips before he plunged into the top hat, looking for a rabbit that might not be there.

"Look," he said. "A modern city usually has enough food on the shelves to keep everyone fed for about a week and a half. Perishable food is, you know, perishable, and a grocery chain or a supermarket starts to lose money when a non-perishable or a long-life item, like, say, a tin of beans and franks, sits on the shelf unsold for too long. The shelf space has to earn its way, right? Their own sales data lets them run just-in-time ordering software so that the shelves are always packed with stuff that always sells very quickly..."

James had Panozzo's attention, but he stopped, suddenly realising something he hadn't thought of earlier.

"Jesus," he said, turning to Michelle Nguyen. "I'll bet it's not just the distributors. I'll bet if you check with your NSA guys, they'll tell you that Krogers and Walmart and Safeway and all the big grocery chains all got probed yesterday, too. Can you do that now? Can you check?"

Michelle, who looked like she might be regretting having even asked Panozzo to see them, looked to the general for permission. He nodded, like what-the-hell, and she flipped open the lid of her laptop and ripped out a quick email query.

"Anyway," James went on, "you take out those systems at the source, the food source. You take out the distribution and re-ordering systems, and a modern city *runs out of food a week later*." He paused for a second, then added. "Unless there's panic buying. Then it's maybe a couple of days. And when people can't feed themselves and their families? Like in New Orleans after Katrina? You know, after the hurricane..."

He waved in frustration as if the conclusion should be evident to anyone. Mostly, however, James was frustrated with himself for yammering on so incoherently. He'd have been embarrassed to stand in front of a room full of investors with such a poorly expressed argument. It seemed to be getting through to Panozzo, though. His brow was furrowed, and he worked his jaw like he was chewing on gristle.

"Mishy," he said at last. "Make sure them little weasels at the Fort know your last query got the highest priority. Right?"

Her computer pinged as she was about to reply.

"They got it," she said, reading whatever had just come up on screen. "And... yes, the fifteen largest grocery chains all reported minor IT issues yesterday, but no major disruption to ops. I can ask Fort Meade to do a forensic sweep of their systems if you..."

"Do it," Panozzo said.

When the NSA confirmed five minutes later that they had detected evidence of intrusion into the inventory control system of each of the businesses, Panozzo agreed to get them a ride over to the White House, where Admiral Holloway was briefing a meeting of the NSC.

———

DC's ROAD net was still glitching, with traffic lights out across most of the inner beltway districts. Cops in white gloves worked the intersections with whistles and bright orange batons that reminded James of the toy lightsabres he'd played with as a kid. Michelle agreed they'd be better off walking, even in the brutal heat and humidity. He carried his jacket over his arm, and they hastened along 17th Street without breaking into a run. It would've been intolerable in the hundred-plus weather and as likely to get them shot by security as hospitalised with heatstroke. Even so, he was sweating like a wheel of bright yellow cheese when they reached the first barrier and presented their credentials.

"Ms Nguyen, Mister O'Donnell, we were told to expect you in a cab," the uniformed guard said, as though not arriving in a taxi was some terrible breach of protocol. Maybe, given James's sweating pits of doom, it was. "If you'll come with me, ma'am, sir," the guard said before leading them to a golf cart and indicating that they should climb onto the rear seat. James almost rolled off the back when they took off way faster than he was expecting, causing Michelle to snort at the panicked expression on his face.

He wasn't sure how the hell he was supposed to convince anybody that he was worth listening to or what he seriously expected them to do if they did listen. He was red-faced. He smelled bad, and the breeze from their passage up the driveway to the rear of the West Wing made a mess of his hair. This was not how it worked in all those Tom Clancy books his dad liked so much.

They passed through two more checkpoints; the first at a sort of service entrance, where a truck driver delivering fresh flowers was given priority, and an inner entrance hall where James had to take off his shoes and belt after he tripped an alarm on the metal detectors.

"Sit here," a page instructed them, "Somebody will be out to get you soon."

Half an hour later, they were still waiting when more alarms went off all around them. These were not the annoying ping of the metal detector. They were full-blown sirens. Marines and Secret Service agents ran past in tight phalanxes – or at least James assumed the men and women wearing earpieces and suits to be Secret Service agents. In the shouting tumult and sudden disorder, it was hard to be sure of anything.

"What's going on?" he asked Michelle, who was no better informed than him. But what the hell? Maybe she did this all the time.

Turns out, no, she didn't.

"No fucking idea," she said, raising her voice to be heard over the uproar.

She got to her feet. James stood up, sat down and got up again, unsure of what to do or where to go. Surely this was not the standard White House reaction to crisis? A recorded message boomed out over the public address system, a soothing female voice that was weirdly at odds with the mayhem breaking loose all around them.

"All visitors are advised that due to unforeseen circumstances, tours of the White House have been cancelled for the day. Visitors must stay in their groups and follow the instructions of their guides as they evacuate the building."

"Evacuate?" James said.

"All visitors are advised that..." the woman's voice started again.

"Come on," Michelle said. "We have to get out of here."

"But nobody's seen us."

"And they're not going to. Come on, right now."

She took James by the wrist, like a misbehaving schoolboy, and dragged him into the throng of people heading for the entrance they'd negotiated half an hour earlier. He wasn't sure whether there was a separate channel for exiting the building, and a crowd was quickly building at the chokepoint of the metal detectors. James was about to ask if there was a bomb or something, but his common sense kicked in before he opened his mouth and made everything much worse. Less than a minute later, somebody yelled out that there was an attack. Some other panicky idiot shouted something about terrorists as James was trying to squeeze through the metal detector with the heaving crowd. His head hit the heavy frame, and stars filled his eyes as he was suddenly pushed from behind. He did his best to create a safe space for Michelle, who was much smaller than him and in danger of being crushed or knocked down and trampled.

There was half a minute or so of genuine fear when he thought they might be trapped by the surging numbers of people jammed up behind them. It was every bit as bad as the time he'd come off his horse in the middle of a cattle herd back home on the ranch, but somebody smashed open a double door somewhere up ahead, and it was like pulling a plug. The crowd surged forward and carried them along a short hallway and through the service entrance out into the fresh air. James kept an arm around Michelle and, at one point, had to elbow a guy he later recalled as the flower delivery man from before. He was trying to scramble over her. Outside, under a cupola, it was still hot, but the rank and sickly fug of body odour and fear sweat dissipated as they cleared the press of bodies.

James heard a dull thudding sound that grew to a roar.

"Marine One!" Michelle shouted over the din. "They're evacuating the President. Come on, we gotta get back to the office."

It sounded a genuinely insane thing to say, but of course, he was on the government's dollar now, and Michelle's office was the National Security Council. She really did need to get back there. They hurried away from the White House, part of a larger group of a hundred or more people, some wearing expensive business attire and multiple ID cards on coloured lanyards, some tourists in summer leisure wear, and some folks who obviously worked as gardeners or cooks or service staff of some kind.

"We'll walk. It'll be quicker," Michelle announced when they cleared the outermost checkpoint, where the security guard had given them the ride in the golf cart.

"Damn!" James said.

"What?"

"I left my jacket hanging on the chair back in there," he said and suffered a cascade of emotions as he realised his wallet was in the breast pocket and he was never getting that jacket back.

"Jesus Christ, James," Michelle shouted over the din. "We're well beyond dress code issues here. Forget your fucking jacket."

She was pissed, and he wasn't inclined to tell her that he'd lost his wallet too. At least his ID card was still flapping from the lanyard around his neck.

It took only a few minutes to get back to the front entrance of the Eisenhower Building. They turned left at Lafayette Square and cut through the manicured gardens James had admired while they'd eaten breakfast about a million years ago. It took longer to get back into the executive wing than it had to walk there. Soldiers or marines —he wasn't sure which—now guarded the entrance and exhaustively checked everyone's identification before allowing them past. He was sure his own very temporary credentials had probably been revoked and was surprised when a sergeant waved him on through.

The chilled air inside the vestibule was a sweet kiss after a long exile in Hell, and he risked Michelle's ire to stop and take a few mouthfuls from the water bubbler at the end of the hallway where she had her office. He needn't have worried. She was just as hot and flustered as him, and she took a few seconds to splash cold water over her face. The corridors of the NSC were heaving with severe-looking people hurrying about their very serious-looking business. Having escaped the chaotic crush and headlong dash back to work, James realised his phone was ringing in his pants pocket. He pulled it out and saw that it wasn't ringing but buzzing with dozens of notifications.

"Hey, Michelle," he said. His stomach felt like he'd just plunged over a sickening rollercoaster drop. "You'd better see this."

He held up his iPhone, but she shook her head as she hurried away down the corridor.

"Just tell me. No time."

"It's a run on the banks."

She stopped dead.

"Shit."

Michelle turned around and hurried back to him. He passed her the phone, but the screen turned dark as it went back to sleep, and it refused to open when his Face ID didn't recognise her.

"Oh, for fucks sake," she said. "Forget it. Come on."

A few seconds later, they were sliding into chairs on either side of her desk as she woke up the screen on her computer. Hundreds of notifications slid down the right-hand side of the display, and she swore quietly as she clicked on one, seemingly at random.

"Jesus Christ," she said softly.

"What? What's going on?"

"It's the Chinese. They moved on Vietnam, Thailand, Malaysia and... fuck, I dunno yet. It's going to take hours to digest all this. Here, look."

She angled the screen around to give James a better view. Dozens of windows were open, but one stood to the fore. It wasn't framed in red or flashing with alerts. It was a simple text document headed FLASH TRAFFIC CINCPACCOM.

James had trouble deciphering the content. It was dense with acronyms and jargon.

"Sorry," he said, "what does it all mean?"

Michelle shook her head but not at him. He could see she was just as overwhelmed by the torrent of data flooding her screen. She stabbed a button on the keyboard to cut off the pinging alerts for more notifications. They were pouring in at the rate of three or four every second. He felt a little calmer as soon as she restored some relative quiet. It was still bedlam outside, though.

"They've hammered Vietnam's air defence net and fighter bases with cruise missiles," she said, scanning and simultaneously translating the document from the original DOD jargon. "Cam Ranh Bay is a fucking dumpster fire. Biên Hòa air base, Hòa Lạc and Thanh Son are all smoking fucking craters. PLA naval air strikes have wrecked everything south of Hanoi, and the South Sea Fleet is closing in on the coast."

She went quiet for a few seconds, losing herself in the text. James sat quietly and waited for her to return.

"The Vietnamese air force is... gone. The Navy, too. Nine frigates and corvettes sunk, three Kilo-class submarines with them, two of them at anchor. The army is mobilising, but cruise missiles have targeted most of the major barracks."

"Most?"

Michelle's eyebrows knitted together; whether in concentration or disapproval, James couldn't say. He was struck by the sudden comprehension that this was more than just a professional crisis for her. Michelle Nguyen's family had come as refugees from Vietnam. She would have more family back there.

"Chinese bombers refuelled by inflight tankers are hitting the naval base at Phu Quoc right now. That's... Jesus Christ. They hit Tindal air base in Australia with a bunch of DF-26s! That's like... we've got... we have a fucking alliance with them! Like, an actual alliance. Holy shit, these guys are not..."

She fell silent, and James felt his balls trying to crawl up into his body when he saw the expression on her face. There was something else.

He said nothing. He didn't want to know.

When she spoke, it was in a tiny voice.

"They hit Pearl, Guam and Okinawa," she said.

17

THE GRAND BALLET OF STEEL

S tanding squarely in the centre of the bridge on the carrier *Liaoning*, Admiral Feng Danyu maintained his severest glower and stern disposition as the South Sea Fleet altered course. The two Philippine Navy corvettes, which had been 'escorting' the task force south to war games off the island of Luzon, appeared for all the world as though their helmsmen had suddenly taken to liquor. They heaved to, tacked aback, and for a brief period described a confused, chaotic track which broadly kept them in contact with Feng's command. They abandoned that effort when electronic warfare officers from the Type 52 destroyer *Yinchuan* blinded the corvette's primitive sensor arrays and cut their commlinks to Manila. Watching through powerful binoculars, Feng Danyu's forbidding expression did not change as first one corvette, then the other, poured on steam and ran south for home, throwing up great white fantails of water. They did not get very far before anti-ship missiles fired from two J-15 fighters of the *Liaoning's* own Combat Air Patrol speared into their flanks and ripped the flimsy little vessels apart in twin explosions of shredded steel and oily fire.

Below him, on the *Liaoning's* flight deck, three helicopters lifted off and banked away toward the burning wreckage of the Filipino ships. The *Liaoning* was the oldest carrier in the People's Liberation Army Navy, a former Soviet flattop laid down in 1985. It had been extensively refurbished in the dry docks in Dalian, but it had none of the amenities of China's modern carriers, constructed by Chinese workers from Chinese blueprints. The clattering roar of the choppers was loud enough to make conversation difficult in the *Liaoning's* bridge. Not that anybody had much to say. The three aircraft racing in toward the sinking corvettes were not tasked with Search and Rescue. They were dark grey and waspish in appearance. Z-10ME gunships. Feng lowered the binoculars from his eyes and rolled the stiffness out of his shoulders, turning away from the industrial hammering roar of the choppers' miniguns raking the seas free of any survivors.

He took no pleasure in the necessity of such tactics.

Tactics served strategy, and China's current strategies provided not for glory but for her very survival. This could not be realised without forceful measures and the most dreadful resolve. Feng took nothing, not even grim satisfaction, from drawing first blood. He did not doubt that many of his sailors would give their lives in service of the republic and her people in the coming struggle. He might yet join them in their sacrifice.

"Prepare the first strike," he ordered, and with that, the bridge crew of the fleet carrier erupted into activity around him. Dozens of officers began issuing orders down their lines of authority. Out on the flight deck, he saw the first step in the grand ballet of steel and blood as hundreds of crewmen in a rainbow assortment of brightly coloured hi-vis shirts burst into activity, clearing and stowing the gear from the rotary wing launch moments earlier. Far below him – in a hostile, howling maelstrom of piercing noise, hot exhausts, whining air vents and a buffeting sea breeze – deck crew swarmed the remaining fighters of the *Liaoning's* J-15 attack squadron as pilots in green Nomex flight suits and bulbous white helmets completed their pre-op checklists.

Raising his binoculars again, Feng looked across the foam-flecked waters to the *Shandong*, the newer of the South Sea Fleet's two aircraft carriers. Like his beloved *Liaoning*, its flight deck curved up at the bow in a prominent ski ramp. Feng swallowed his resentment of the slight done to the Fleet by the assignment of the three newer, more advanced platforms to Admiral Wen and the East Sea Fleet. Feng's task force would soon enough likely engage the Japanese and Koreans and perhaps even the US 7th Fleet should things go wrong, and he thought it was only sensible that they should ride into battle on the strongest horses carrying the longest bows.

The gunships detailed to police the wreckage of the two corvettes finished raking over the last drifting remains of the wryly named *Armada de Filipinas* and cross-decked to a pair of Type 55 destroyers, saving crucial minutes for *Liaoning's* flight deck. Everything was so tightly scheduled that Feng could not help but worry. He had argued strenuously back at Zhanjiang HQ that for any military plan to have a hope of success, there needed to be robust margins built in for error, ill fortune and, naturally, for enemy action. Who was to say there was not some American or Australian submarine plotting firing solutions on his fleet right now or a wing of Japanese F-35s locking missiles onto Admiral Wen Bo Xi's fleet?

Feng dropped the spyglasses and finally returned to his command chair, grateful to take the weight off his feet after two hours of standing and forever adjusting his balance against the roll of the ocean swell. He had not prevailed in his arguments, and perhaps that was for the best. Whether setting one army against another or one man onto one opponent, when the moment to fight was upon you, it was better to let your plans be dark and as impenetrable as night and when you did move, to fall like a lightning bolt.

The thunder of the first flight of J-15s arrested his self-indulgent moping, jolting Feng back into the moment. Having given his order, he had nothing to do but let the *Liaoning's* officers fight the battle. Flurries of orders, queries, answers and acknowledgments flew around him as the great ship of war adjusted course to put her ski ramp into the wind. Admiral Feng Danyu felt his pulse quickening as the first planes roared away, and his heart seemed to fall into his stomach with the inevitable dip of the heavily laden J-15 as it threw itself from the launch ramp six hundred feet away. And then the deadly grey hawk soared up and into the skies, which rippled behind it, distorted by the plane's powerful jet engines. Feng Danyu's heart flew away with it.

They were committed now.

THE STATE-OWNED China Ocean Shipping Group boasted of a great many vessels in its huge commercial fleet. More than a thousand on the day the container ship COSCO *Vancouver* left the port of Guangzhou under the command of Captain Bei Zhihui, fully two weeks before Admiral Feng's battlegroup steamed from Zhanjiang. Bei, a thirty-eight-year-old mariner and native of Guangzhou, looked every inch the grizzled and veteran sea dog as he sat in the captain's chair in the bridge high over the container ship's main deck. As well he should. Bei Zhihui had gone down to the sea as a gangly, awkward sixteen-year-old, and most of the following twenty-two years had seen him crewing and eventually commanding a line of increasingly important ships.

Not for the masters of the China Ocean Shipping Group, however.

Bei Zhihui was not a captain of the merchant marine. He was a decorated and well-connected officer of the People's Liberation Army Navy.

Nearly six thousand miles east of Feng and forty minutes out of Honolulu Harbor, Captain Bei Zhihui received his final orders via an encrypted satellite phone at 0703 hours local. Bei had no idea what was happening at home, only that the time to do his duty had arrived. He was dressed in the uniform of a PLA Navy captain. All of the bridge crew wore naval fatigues, but those who had reason to go out on deck still disguised themselves in the workaday coveralls of merchant seamen. Bei regretted the necessity of that. They had discussed it on the long voyage across the Pacific. His men would have preferred to die as warriors, facing the enemy arrayed for battle, rather than skulking and sneaking and striking like hidden vipers.

It was...

He hesitated, his eyes squinting into the morning sun.

It was not... dishonourable, as such. After all, deception was a time-honoured weapon of war. Twenty-four hours before they had departed Guangzhou, engineers swapped out thirty shipping containers for thirty more, which arrived on trucks in the dead of night. The ship's automatic ID system, a tracking beacon carried by all large commercial vessels no matter their homeport or national flag, showed the *Vancouver* as still being moored to the wharf near Gate 33. Shortly after Captain Bei and his crew departed, another COSCO ship of the same class did indeed take up that berth. It even loaded out with the same configuration of containers on the main deck. A curious photo analyst at the CIA or DIO could compare the colour palate and even the item numbers painted onto those containers and not find one point of difference.

Thousands of miles away, on the real *Vancouver*, Bei ordered Lieutenant Tu, the drone specialist, to deploy the weapons.

The lieutenant, who had graduated first in his engineering class at Beijing Polytech and who might have gone on to found some great company had history run differently, flipped open his ruggedised laptop, a Huawei Matebook X Pro, and bent to the task. The *Vancouver* – now emitting a transponder signal identifying itself to US customs and port authorities as a New Zealand-flagged container ship, the *MV Dunedin* – maintained station just outside the US territorial limit of twelve nautical miles. She was scheduled to enter port late in the afternoon. The nearest vessel, another container ship, was three thousand metres to starboard.

Like Admiral Feng, so far away to the east, there was little for Bei to do, having delivered his ship to the launch point for the mission. Like Feng, he too sat back and watched the opening moves of the attack. The other officers and enlisted men on the bridge were quiet, the atmosphere palpably tense as Lieutenant Tu worked his computer. For a while, the click-clack of keys was the loudest sound, save for the occasional report over the ship's tannoy from the engineering and deck divisions. After a quietly fraught couple of minutes, Tu looked up and nodded to Captain Bei, his eyes asking an unspoken question.

"Proceed," Bei said with a nod.

The young officer breathed in and out as though preparing to lift some large weight in the gymnasium. He also nodded, but only to himself, as if assuring his conscience that there was nothing unusual happening here. A single keystroke followed, and the course of human affairs was turned from a hopeless but knowable future towards ... another fate, perhaps more promising but ultimately inscrutable to everyone who would now await its judgment.

Bei sat slightly higher in the captain's chair as sirens sounded down on the main deck. He saw movement on the uppermost layer of shipping containers. Thirty of the long metal boxes cracked open, hydraulic pistons lifting the heavy slabs of ribbed steel like the opening of a child's music box. The mechanisms were powerful and custom-designed for this one task. The profile of *Vancouver's* container stack changed rapidly. Another siren sounded, and dozens of dark oblong canisters shot out of the shadowed interiors of the open containers, launched a hundred metres into the air by magnetic catapults. The outer carapace of the massive projectiles popped open just before they reached the apogee of their short, almost vertical flight paths, and the sky around the ship was suddenly filled with hundreds of drones.

Some were larger than the others, and these boosted themselves away from the flock as stubby winglets unfolded and small jet engines spooled up. They sped off under full power, dropping down to a few metres above the waves and engaging terrain following sensors stolen and aggressively adapted from the True Depth camera system in Apple's iPhones. Behind them, hundreds of smaller drones began their flight towards Pearl Harbor and the US Air Force bases Hickam and Bellows. All of the drones were cloaked by radar-absorbent meta-plastics developed in the laboratories of the PLA's prosaically named 'science and technology committee'—otherwise known as the Chinese DARPA. Powered by miniaturised scram jets, they accelerated to hypersonic speeds in less than a minute, closing with their targets before any of the US military's early warning systems could detect or respond to the attack.

The development team at the science and technology committee had been given a challenging brief. The drones were to avoid the

American defences, naturally, but when servicing their targets, loss of
life was also to be kept to a minimum. The Party did not seek a war
with the US. Its grand strategy was entirely bent toward avoiding one.

With this admonition foremost in their thinking, the Committee
had armed the drone swarm with shaped charges and directed EMPs
to strike at the most vulnerable points of the US military's undeni-
ably powerful war-fighting machine. The swarm arrowed in so
quickly that human eyes could not detect them as anything but a
rippling blur in the sky and an eerie, humming whipcrack as they
passed overhead. On land, the smart warheads guided by machine-
learning algorithms fell upon USAF airfields and onshore naval facilities with a thunderous uproar, belied by a lack of breathtaking cine-
matic eruptions of fire and devastation. Instead, the almost
supernaturally imperceptible kinetic hurricane swept over and
chewed up aircraft wings and engine housings, shredded satellite
dishes and fried communication hubs. For many long seconds, the
fifteen ships and submarines resting at anchor in Pearl Harbor rang
to the tiny hammer blows of thousands of micro-munitions as
though some malign hailstorm had fallen only upon the most delicate components of the vessel's external sensor arrays.

Very few aircraft and no warships were actually destroyed at Pearl
Harbor or in the three other drone missions to the 7th Fleet's home
port at Yokosuka in Japan and the naval and air bases on Guam.
However, the damage to such sophisticated, technology-dependent
platforms was such that American military power in the Pacific was
reduced to a merely modest variable in the calculations of the PLA's
war planners.

There were some human casualties.

A Petty Officer First Class and two seamen on the USS O'Kane, an
Arleigh Burke-class destroyer tied up at the Safeguard Street dock,
were all killed while touching up the paint on the forward 5-inch gun.
The guidance chip in a packet of tungsten penetrators meant to
disable the steering works of the submarine USS Santa Fe was faulty,
and instead of fragmenting the intricate machinery at the stern of the
sub, they passed cleanly through the hull, Seaman Derek Hanson,

and the box of cantaloupes he was carrying to cut up for breakfast in the officers' wardroom.

All up, twenty-three Americans and one British naval officer on secondment died in the attack, a casualty count that the planners at the Central Military Commission had determined was below the threshold likely to prompt a declaration of war. Especially not given the chaos consuming the mainland US as the full effects of General Chu's cyber strike unfolded across the continent, from sea to shining sea.

Captain Bei Zhihui knew none of this.

He only knew that his mission was successful and it was time, if possible, to escape.

He ordered the helmsman to put back out to sea and lay in a course to the rendezvous with the submarine *Yuan*. There was no urgency to his instructions or to the crew's efforts as they made ready to withdraw. Bei had been nominally briefed on the effects of the strike he had just launched. He knew it would land as a heavy but not lethal blow on the enemy, and he waited now for them to reply.

There was an excellent chance, he understood, that he would not even realise when he was about to die. Anti-ship missiles fired from over the horizon would tear *Vancouver* apart between one heartbeat and the next. He might experience a split second of blinding white light and searing heat before everything went dark. Or he might not.

"I will have another cup of tea," he said to Lieutenant Tu, who now found himself with little to do but to wait on the consequences of what they had just done. "Make one for yourself, Lieutenant, if you wish, and tell the men that they have my permission to drink to the success of our mission and the People's Republic. A real drink, for them and you. There are two bottles of Baijiu in my cabin. Break them out for the crew. But I will have tea."

The bridge crew cheered, and Captain Bei smiled.

Much to his surprise, he did not die then or at any point before rendezvousing with the *Yuan*. He would die later, at home with his family. Like a billion of his countrymen.

INTERLUDE

Karletta had another three hours to go on her shift when the computerised despatch went down. The little unit attached to the dashboard of the taxi just up and died on her. She still hadn't earned back her buy-in for the shift. She needed another eighty-three bucks to break even and a whole helluva lot more than that to cover the dentist's bill for her kid's wisdom tooth. It was impacted for sure and possibly even rotting way down deep in his gums. Poor little Kevin was a trooper, but Karletta could see how much pain that kid was in. She needed to finish this shift in the black and back up for another one. And she probably needed to do that at least six times this week.

She had just bid on a solid fifty-buck fare from downtown KC to the airport when the unit crapped out on her. Everything just froze. She swore loudly and smacked the treacherous little box upside the head. It did nothing. Still swearing but under her breath now, she pulled into a loading zone out front of the Crown Centre complex to use her radio. She rarely touched the thing these days and didn't trust herself to use it without rear-ending somebody in the stop-start traffic clogging the city centre.

Soon as she turned up the volume Karletta could hear every other driver in Kansas City hammering on the dispatchers via their own radio sets. The airwaves were a hurricane squall of angry voices and static feedback. Most peeps weren't looking for work. They wanted tech support on their despatch units. She replaced the handset and turned down the volume. A headache was building behind her eyeballs, and she could feel her pulse racing into the red zone. Karletta took in a deep breath, let it out, and took another one. Time was when she'd have been frantically trying to get a bid in over the air, desperate to replace that lost fifty-buck gig as quickly as possible. Now she knew it was time to do some real old-school cab driving. If despatch was down, then for sure there would be hundreds of passengers needing transport just wandering the streets. Some of them would try Uber or Lyft or even one of those stupid electric scooter things. But plenty would flag down the first cab they laid eyes on. She could pick up her fares the old-fashioned way by rolling right up on them. Those assholes at Uber hadn't figured out how to hijack that part of the business yet.

Before she'd even pulled away from the front of the Hallmark building, Karletta had to jam on the brakes as her peripheral vision caught a flash of movement to her left; a white lady in business clothes running down the steps, waving frantically to her. She paused half in and half out of the loading zone to let the woman climb in.

"Oh God, thank you so much," she said as she threw a shoulder bag on the back seat and all but dived in after it. "I've got to get my daughter. Quickly."

"Strap in, ma'am," Karletta advised, but the woman was already pulling on her seat belt. Karletta had no trouble keeping her voice calm and level. She was used to passengers thinking it'd mean the end of the world if they didn't get where they thought they needed to be. "Where's your kid at?" Karletta asked.

"Gordon Parks Elementary, the woman said. "Do you know it? I think the internet is down. There's no maps or anything."

"I know it," Karletta said, careful to keep the sour tone out of her voice. She had tried to get Kevin in there, but the admissions staff had made it pretty obvious that his learning difficulties would be all a bit too complicated for the school to cope with. Perhaps she might try her local public school. Non-charter. The city did have some excellent programs for slower children. Karletta ground her teeth at the memory. Still, this woman wasn't one of them. She just needed to get to her kid.

"You got a sick little one?" Karletta asked as they pulled out into traffic. She would pick the kid up, of course, but she wanted to prepare herself for the possibility of puke in the back seat and the warning she'd have to give this already hysterical lady about the cleaning fee.

The woman just looked at her as though she was mad.

"Haven't you heard?"

Karletta allowed a city bus and a garbage truck to get past her before she slipped into the traffic stream.

"Been working since before sunup, ma'am," she answered. "And I can't stand the radio, especially not the news these days. Something wrong at school?"

The woman caught her eyes in the rear-view mirror.

"Oh. You don't know. The Chinese have attacked. They're saying they've dropped bombs and missiles all over. Schools are being evacuated."

Karletta felt her stomach do a forward roll. She almost pointed the car in the direction of Kevin's school across the other side of town. But her sudden panic abated when she remembered that he was at home with his grandmother, full of kid's aspirin for his bad tooth. Still, sounded like she would need to get back there as soon as she could.

"I'm sorry I hadn't heard that, no," Karletta said, feeding the accelerator a taste of her old shoe leather. She had a good flow of green lights ahead. "The Chinese? You sure? That sounds kind of crazy. I know about the trade thing and all, but that ain't worth killing over."

The woman looked pissed off to be questioned.

"I got a text message from the school," she said. "And an email from Emily's homeroom teacher. It's a genuine evacuation. We're not just pulling her out of school; we're getting out of town. Chinese missiles could be on their way."

Karletta couldn't keep the disbelief out of her tone.

"Missiles? I don't think so, ma'am. That's crazy talk. But if you don't mind, I might put on the news radio. Maybe find out what's what."

Her passenger didn't object. She was already stabbing at the screen of her cell phone, trying to make a connection that obviously wasn't going through. Karletta fiddled with the controls for the car stereo, trying to find a talk news station. There was a lot of crazy talk, she would admit, but not just about China. There was a whole heap of other craziness, too. Mainly about some big computer hack or internet thing and something about a bad accident at a warehouse just outside of KC. Four or five workers killed, she heard, before flipping the dial again in search of a bulletin that might make sense of the whole thing for her.

Many thoughts tussled for attention inside Karletta Abianac's head. She was worried about Kevin and her mom, sitting at home and freaking the hell out if they'd heard anything about this China business. She was concerned about Kevin's wisdom teeth. About whether she had the staying power to keep driving for as long as it would take to get him seen by the dentist. She worried about covering the rent next week even if she did make enough to pay for the tooth doctor. And, to be honest, she was a little freaked out by her passenger, who was now arguing loudly in the back seat with someone, possibly her husband, about needing to get out of the city as soon as they could.

Perhaps if Karletta had not had so many things on her mind, she would have noticed the sudden strangeness of the traffic flow around her.

But she didn't notice and instead, distracted by half a dozen competing fears and thoughts, Karletta Abianac drove her cab into the four-way intersection, rolling at speed through the green light.

The delivery van that T-boned them was moving at almost the same speed, as were the other eight cars that speared into that crossroad where every light burned a bright, steady green.

Dillonvale was a railroad town that hadn't seen a train in twenty-five years. Tammy Kolchar had lived her entire life in sight of the tracks on Rice Street. She could only vaguely recollect the last of the trains, heavy with black coal dug out of the surrounding hills. Tammy grew up in Dillonvale, fell in love there and began her working life there. That love soured and went bad, leaving her with two little ones to feed. Not an easy thing on a cashier's wage at the Dollar General. Especially not when Gutterson, the manager, wouldn't never give her more'n six hours in a shift because that'd put her over the top into full-time pay. With benefits.

Nobody working at Dollar General got the benefits except for Mister Gutterson, of course.

So Tammy made do with child support, ten cents an hour over the legal minimum wage and an Oldsmobile she'd inherited when her dad died from the black lung fifteen years past. Sometimes she thought her ex-husband had married that damn car instead of her. Lord knows he'd fought like a pit bull to hold onto it when he went away to the fracking in Ohio. Hell of a lot harder than he fought to hold onto their marriage. Bobby was hooked up with some waitress now, and Tammy's roommate Roxarne was home watching all of their kids and the Kardashians. Roxy didn't have much else to do since the Blockbuster in Hermantown went under and took her job down with it. They pooled what little they had and made do. It worked after its own fashion, as her dad used to say.

This morning though, jeez. Tammy Kolchar sorely wished it was her at home keeping up with Kardashians and Roxy in here, riding herd on the tweekers and junkies and the never-ending parade of Dillonvale's finest.

The customers just wouldn't quit coming, and the delivery truck hadn't arrived from Hermantown. Her register wasn't working right. Mister Gutterson had told her "cash only for the duration of the outage", whatever the hell that meant. And then, of course, he promptly disappeared, leaving Tammy and Wynette O'Farrell to deal with increasing numbers of increasingly pissed-off shoppers.

Right now, for instance, Tammy was trying to talk a thin man with meth mouth and prison tats down off the edge of going absolutely

postal 'cause he couldn't get his favourite brand of cigarette. Pyramids. Which, to Tammy's mind, was the preferred choice of those
who could not afford more than to suck on a burning stick of floor
sweepings and dog hair.

"What d'ya mean I can't get my pack of Pyramids?" the no-good
waste of human skin was complaining while Tammy was trying to
put through Mrs Puller's weekly mountain of cat food.

She wanted to run and hide in the cold room.

Instead, she said, "I'm sorry, sir, but the machine isn't doing debit
payments today. We're cash only till the machines are back on."

"Bitch I need my smokes!" He whined.

Tammy's eyebrows furrowed around the front end of the monster
headache she had coming on. "I'm sorry," she said, swiping through
tins of cat meat and pitching her voice to carry to Wynette at the next
register over.

For a wonder, the prison tatt guy simply spun around and left.
Tammy let out a breath. Mrs Puller took it all in, her eyes sparking
like a squirrel with a secret store of nuts for the winter.

"I have cash, my dear," she said. "I listen to the news and I got the
government warnings. I took out extra cash."

Tammy bagged her cat food. She was sure the old biddy was
eating just as much of it as her army of strays.

"Thank you, ma'am," she said automatically as she rang her up.
"Have a nice day."

Mrs Puller paid with a few crumpled notes that looked as if they
hadn't been unfolded in the light of day since the 1900s. It didn't
matter. They were legal tender, so into the drawer they went, and the
old lady with the wide mouth shark's grin got to feed her cats and
maybe herself for another week.

She was lucky.

The store's shelves were emptying at such an alarming rate that
Tammy was having to tell every second customer they didn't have
nothing in stock for them. Not Mac 'N' Cheese. That was long gone.
About twelve boxes walked out with Laverne Walters half an hour
ago. Not Hamburger Helper. Mrs Ekner loaded up on a whole damn
pallet of that and a ton of cheap loose meat from the butchery. Had

her simpleton son Erik carry it out to the car for her. And most mysterious of all, leastways to Tammy, they had run out of the bright orange government cheese you could only get with food stamps — and could possibly only want if your station in life had fallen so far that you was living off food stamps, with a little supplemental dumpster diving on the side.

Her cash drawer was filling up, too. She'd have to get Mister Gutterson to put the extra cash in the safe soon. All that paper money made her nervous. Three years ago she had been in the store during an armed robbery attempt, and this day felt a lot like that. People were edgy and weird.

As Tammy rang up the next customer, who complained there was no Mac 'n Cheese left, her hands started to shake. She looked around. The food aisles were packed with people, and they were taking everything. Like, everything. Even the stuff that never sold, like cocktail-smoked oysters and Larry the Cable Guy's beer bread in a box.

Even more people were starting to push into the store. They raised their voices. They argued over who had dibs on the canned German potato salad. Tammy's eyes cast about. Where was the manager? She rang up a young woman she didn't know, some out-of-towner, who had somehow scored a whole case of pork and beans. Tammy was pretty sure they had none of that on the floor yet. It was sitting out back, waiting to be unpacked. But she rang it up anyway, and the woman left the store hugging the cans in a protective embrace.

Tammy hadn't been a good student at school, but she wasn't stupid. There was something going on here. She couldn't talk to Wynette about it. She was flat-out busy with the unusual rush, too. But when Mister Darramore from the hardware place turned up in front of her with an armful of beef-flavoured rice and Vienna franks, she had to ask as she was ringing up his order.

"Mister Darramore, what is going on this morning? Why is everyone shopping so damned hard?"

Mister Darramore was a nice man. Tammy had been at school with his son Roger, who got killed in Iraq. He looked at her with something like pity.

"You been working all morning, Tam?"

"Yes, sir."

"You should check the news. We're at war now. With China. Or maybe Russia. Nobody's really sure. Either way, news says they did a sneak attack. Bombed a bunch of food warehouses and wholesalers. Really made a mess of things. People are stocking up while they can. Some folks are getting out of town, but I don't see Beijing bothering with anywhere as small as Dillonvale, do you?"

Well, that didn't make a lick of sense. How could you not know whether you were fighting a war with someone?

What Tammy did know was that she and Roxarne had very little food at home. And about thirty-eight dollars between them. Payday was at the end of the week; she planned on a big shop for Saturday. But looking around the crush of people backed up at the registers here, Tammy Kolchar knew that she'd never make that trip. This place would be stripped bare in an hour or two.

And she knew the truck wasn't coming.

Mister Gutterson had said so.

When a man entered the store cradling a shotgun, Tammy made a snap decision. She rang the button for the manager one last time, waited, rang up another angry customer, and emptied the twenties tray when the drawer slid open. One smooth, unnoticed motion was all it took to commit grand larceny. She closed her drawer and spoke up.

"Sorry folks, I'm going to take a break. Be back in five."

Wynette glared at her with axes in her eyes.

The crowd groaned, and a few people protested, yelling at her to stay and serve them. Tammy ignored them all.

With a pounding heart and a pocket full of cash, she left the Dollar General, pushing through the close-packed crowd and out of the sliding doors. She walked directly to her Olds, fired the pig up, and drove away.

She was going to get Roxarne and the kids and pile them into the car, and drive west for her brother's place. He had a farm.

Tammy wasn't smart.

She wasn't a deep thinker.

But for some reason, it seemed vital that they get on the road and away to Michael's place as quickly as possible.

She never returned to the Dollar General or Dillonvale. A small food riot started soon afterwards when the guy with the shotgun couldn't get what he wanted and loosed a round into the asbestos roof tiles to emphasize his disgruntlement with the service. The Sheriff never did show up.

No one missed those twenties she swiped, either.

18

A CARNIVORE IN SILVERTON

There was no run on the US banking system until there was. The three cell phone notifications that caught James O'Donnell's attention in the hallway of the Eisenhower Building were spam texts spoofed up as news alerts from *The Wall Street Journal*, *Bloomberg* and *The New York Times*. They contained links to dark-mirror sites, which almost perfectly reproduced the content of the legitimate news services, updated every thirty seconds, but with one significant difference. The dark-mirror sites all reported as their lead story a run on six major US banks. They even had 'live' video of customers waiting in long lines to withdraw their cash. (General Chu's merry pranksters used archival footage from the 2008 financial crisis and a Spanish bank collapse in 2014, and although the ruse was called out on a Reddit thread within forty minutes and *The New York Times* itself an hour later, the correction made little difference. All the clicks went to the hotter links, and the collapse of America's banking system was white-hot clickbait.)

The spam text, blasted out of a server in eastern Europe, which had previously been used for Russian mafia phishing scams, arrived within seconds on more than a hundred and sixty million cell phones in North America alone, including the thousands of employees of the three targeted media companies. The alarm within The Journal, The Times and Bloomberg was immediate, but management soon determined that their servers remained secure. All three refreshed their home pages to publish stark, unmissable warnings about the spoofed text messages and phantom websites.

It made very little difference.

If any.

Within five minutes, a Google news query would return more than five thousand hits on search strings built around phases such as "US banking collapse" and "run on the banks". Most of those stories cut and pasted the text from the mirrors. Within half an hour, there were more than ten million new results for the same Google search. By late afternoon, when Jonas Murdoch peddled his roommate's stolen bicycle into the small town of Silverton, on Woods Creek Road, about eighty miles northeast of Seattle, long lines were snaking outside the Wells Fargo branch and a local savings and loan called Farmers Mutual Provident. Smaller groups clustered here and there at cash machines, and it was one of those crowds that brought him to a halt when two men got into a fight, which spilled out onto the road directly in front of him.

Jonas had been riding hard all day.

He was fit, strong and, most importantly, he was young. He worked out. He'd worked hard in that goddamn warehouse, and he had the spectre of the law on his heels to keep him peddling when his thigh muscles started to burn on the long, uphill stretches of road reaching into the heavily wooded hills outside of the city. There was another three or four hours of good daylight ahead, another forty or fifty miles he could put between himself and what he'd done back in Seattle as he enjoyed a gentle, curving glide down into the main street of Silverton. He was tempted to lay up there for the night. Spend some of Mikey's money on a room and a hot bath because he was sure enough gonna need the rest and a long soak before he put his ass on the road again in the morning. But Jonas was no dummy. The cops would not prioritise his simple assault and robbery, but if by some bizarre fluke they decided he was public enemy number one, it wouldn't take them long to work out how far he could get on Mikey's wheels. Best answer to that was to go further in another direction. He'd already laid a few breadcrumbs heading south, paying for a bottle of water with his credit card in a gas station back in the city—they'd had to use one of those old slide machines to take an imprint—and buying protein bars at a Whole Foods a few miles further south. He made sure the security cams got a good look at him there; in a collared business shirt and jeans he took off in a blind alley a few minutes later.

Then he turned the bike around and headed north past miles of gridlocked traffic.

Jonas had never intended to stop in the small logging town. He judged it way too close to the scene of his crimes. The map apps on his phone had all frozen, but he had a pretty good Rand McNally road map of Washington State folded up into his go-bag. He'd already circled a conspicuous tourist trap village near a lake with a bunch of camping grounds another two hours further on. This time of year, there'd be a lot of traffic through the place. A lot of new faces and transients like him every day. Probably a lot of sweaty guys in spandex, rocking $3,000 road bikes, too. That was a crowd he could blend in with. Unfortunately, the crowd outside The Farmers Mutual had other ideas.

There was only one road into Silverton, two lanes of blacktop hugging the side of a steep, thickly forested hill that fell away hard on the downslope. With his core temperature raised by hours of cardio and some real tests of strength through the steeper climbs into the foothills of the National Forest, Jonas was grateful to be able to coast down the dip in the road and let the relatively cool, pine-scented mountain air wash over his face and exposed arms. It was such a pleasure that he even thought about stripping off the slightly too-small riding vest and letting the breeze of his passage play over his upper body. Would have been nice. Didn't happen, though.

What did happen in rapid succession was that he passed a hand-carved timber sign at the town limits, announcing he was about to enter SILVERTON, POPULATION 485; he realised he was going way too fast coming into a built-up area, and he applied the brakes just a little too hard; the front wheel started to wobble as he lost his balance; the gentle curve of the road shortened into a much tighter turn; and he suddenly found his path blocked by dozens of pedestrians who'd spilled onto the tarmac from the pavement in front of a two-storey brick building to which even more people appeared to be laying siege.

Jonas barely avoided crashing into them by veering left and mounting the grass verge on the other side of the road in front of a vacant lot. His front wheel hit the gutter and almost threw him over the handlebars. He managed, but only just, to effect a complete stop without coming off, and shaking a little from his second shock of the day, he climbed off the bike.

It took one look for him, like everyone else, to be transfixed by the sight of two men fighting. Or rather, the sight of one guy beating the hell out of another. Unlike everyone else, however, he didn't remain spellbound by the violence. The guy doing all the punching, some kicking, and a little bit of elbow work (Muay Thai-style, to spice things up) was easily as young and fit as Jonas. He was also pretty obviously some gang banger. He wore jeans, motorcycle boots, and a white wife-beater singlet that was soaked with sweat and splattered here and there with dollops of blood. Not his own. He was covered in tattoos, but not with sleeves of nicely inked Celtic designs or tribal motifs, or even old-school conventional skin work. His arms and shoulders and neck and face crawled with crude designs in blue-black prison ink. Jonas had no idea what sort of crew this asshole ran with, but he recognised the species. He'd been a lawyer in Miami, after all, the major US entrepot for the Mexican cartels.

And the guy this dude was beating on? Well, he didn't look like he was quite ready to retire to Miami, but he wasn't far off. An older guy, overweight, balding, and clutching a plastic shopping bag to his chest like a kitten he was trying to rescue from a house fire. He probably wouldn't have been able to defend himself anyway. Still, by holding onto that bag, by curling around it like it was more important to him than his own life, the old guy made it ridiculously easy for the carnivore to go wild on him.

All of this, Jonas took in between one thumping heartbeat and the next. Already angry and looking to punish someone, he was off his bike and charging – literally charging – at the gang banger before his heart had a chance to beat again or before his common sense told him to ride on. Jonas wasn't a hero. He was not a white knight. Jonas Murdoch was pissed at nearly crashing his bike and almost breaking his neck. But more than, oh so much more than that, he purely and simply hated those taco-eating motherfuckers.

His boss in Miami? Fucking Hondo? The reason he'd been disbarred and barely escaped doing time? The reason his wife had left him, and he couldn't see his kids anymore? A greasy fucking beaner.

The cop who came after him? Same thing.

Both of them as crooked as a dog's back leg.

Subscriptions to his pod always surged whenever he unloaded on these assholes. Not like they'd spiked this week, of course. But he'd have wailed on them anyway, even if nobody was listening. Same way he'd have charged in like a raging bull if he'd come around the corner and seen the same jacked-up Mexican beating on someone's old grandpa.

It was the right thing to do.

Jonas closed the distance between himself and the two men in about four or five strides, a long enough run up to really put some speed behind his considerable mass. Everything seemed to move impossibly slowly. He felt as though his senses were both heightened and dulled in different ways. Sounds reached him as though through a thick blanket, and the edge of his vision greyed out, even as the colours popped vividly in the centre. He'd played a lot of football in high school. Been good enough for a half-scholarship, too. Not to a great law school, no, but to an affordable college because of his football. And it all came back to him ten years later. He had no training in the martial arts. Had never done so much as a single boxercise class. But he stood six-three and topped out the scales as a heavyweight. Less than twelve per cent of his body mass was fat. Jonas Murdoch was a solid fucking wedge of hard-packed American beef, and when he hit that loose meat tortilla, he blew through the motherfucker like a hurricane through a trailer park.

Dude didn't even see him coming. Not many did, except for a couple of kids who captured his whole thunder run and head-high tackle on their phone cams. The rest of the crowd was still frozen with bystander paralysis, but they reared back as though struck by a shockwave when Jonas smashed into the perp and knocked him flying clean through the air and into a lamp post. He heard a sort of sympathetic 'ooh' as everyone heard the sick, wet crack of bones breaking against the cast iron pole. Barely slowing in his forward momentum, he drove on, legs pumping, fists clenched, and he connected a second time, smashing his knee into the gang banger's upper torso.

If he were being honest with himself, Jonas would admit that he hadn't been much of a lawyer. He lost most of the cases he fought and defaulted to talking his clients into pleading out most of the time. Truth was, they were either guilty as charged, or they were guilty of something they hadn't been charged with. None of them were a loss to polite society when they disappeared inside America's gigantic correctional labyrinth. One thing he did learn from reading hundreds of briefs of evidence, though, street violence was Hobbesian. When it happened, it was always short, nasty, and brutish. Most criminals, especially drug addicts, were animals. If you got into a fight with one of them, you either put them down or you suffered for your weakness.

Jonas was not weak.

He drove another knee into the gangsta's face and rained a windmilling frenzy of blows down on his head and neck until something broke the spell hanging over the crowd and a couple of men found they still had a pair on them and pulled him off the limp, unconscious form of the...

What? What was he? A Mexican. A Colombian? Did it matter?

As Jonas passed through the red rage that had taken hold of him, he became aware of his surroundings again. Panting for breath, his eyes stinging with sweat that blurred his vision, he could hear cheering. And clapping, and he flinched away a little, expecting to be tackled to the ground himself by the local sheriff who must have just turned up.

But somebody pressed a bottle of cold water into his hand, and someone else had an arm around his shoulder and was leading him away from the bloodied ruin he'd made of another man, and the cheering got louder, and he realised at last that the cheers were for him.

He was the hero.

A POLICE SIREN WHOOPED, and Jonas almost ran. He was still jittery from the near accident on the bike, his head roaring and his blood singing with the madness of real violence. He was not thinking straight. But the adrenalin backwash also robbed him of strength, and when he took a step, his legs folded up underneath him. He was quickly surrounded and held up by onlookers.

"Whoa there, big fella, take it easy."

"Sit him down and give him some air."

"Over here, give him water. We got some water."

A little dazed, he let himself be led to a wooden bench and lowered onto the seat where somebody fanned him with a magazine and someone else splashed cold water over his face. He realised he was still wearing the bike helmet, and he tried to take it off, but again he was overwhelmed by helpers. He let his hands drop, and somebody undid the plastic latch on the chin strap. The helmet came off, and his head felt as though it might float right off his shoulders.

More cold water came, this time poured directly on top of his head, and it was glorious.

Gradually, his wits returned, and he got his breathing under control, and the crowd parted as a great round barrel of a man in a brown sheriff's uniform came at him, but with his hand out as if to shake, and a smile creasing the corners of his eyes.

"Thank you, son, thank you very much," the man with the sheriff's badge said, and Jonas wondered if he'd come off the bike and hit his head. Perhaps he was lying on the road, hallucinating all this, as his brains leaked out of his shattered skull.

But the crowd, which had closed in around him, parted again, and a second man, the old guy he'd...

Well, Jonas had saved him, he guessed.

More helpers half-carried the old guy over to the wooden bench. They gently lowered him to the seat, and someone splashed him with cold water. A woman in a doctor's coat, like a for-real white lab coat, kneeled in front of him, shined a torch in his eyes and waved a finger in front of his face, asking the guy to follow it. All while Jonas watched on dumbly before she did the same thing to him.

"This one is fine," she pronounced of Jonas, "But Al's a hell of a mess. Concussion, for sure, maybe some broken ribs, and I really don't like that swelling in his face. Where's the other one?"

The sheriff snorted at some joke she'd just made.

"He's cuffed in back of my cruiser, Doc. Mac is looking him over."

"Yeah, well," the doctor shot back, "as thorough as I'm sure Deputy McFarland will be, Dave, I'll thank you to let me do my job with him, too. You can hang him later."

Sheriff Dave didn't look too happy with that idea. Looked like he wanted to sort out a hanging right now, but he didn't object, and the woman in the doctor's coat said she'd be right back. She pushed through the press of people still crowding around the bench, none of them really proving to be of any more help than they'd been during the fight.

Jonas felt a hand squeeze his arm. It was his neighbour on the bench. His grip was weak and shaky.

"Thanks, big fella," the old guy said, although now that things had calmed down some and he could get a good look at the dude, Jonas guessed him to be somewhere in his fifties. So not that old. He looked a lot closer to death because he'd just had twenty years punched out of him.

"What the hell was that about?" Jonas asked. His voice was croaky, and he gestured for a drink to a young woman holding a bottle of water. She gave him the bottle and said, "You keep it, dude. You were awesome."

"I was taking my money…" the man on the bench said, but he got no further.

"'Fraid I'm gonna have to ask you to put a cork in it, Al."

It was the sheriff. What had that lady doctor called him? Jonas couldn't remember. He was still buzzing from the fight, and his thoughts zipped around crazily like fireflies in a bottle.

"Fella saved my life, I reckon Dave…"

That was it. Sheriff Dave.

"And you can buy him a steak dinner for his troubles later, Al," the sheriff went on. "But you all are witnesses now, and that asshole that Doc Cornwell's checking over in my squad car looks like he's seen the inside of a courtroom before. Let's not give him a chance to walk out of the next one because you two compared notes."

"What's… going on, Sheriff?" Jonas asked. He was over his initial fear of arrest. He'd obviously walked into something here, but he couldn't say what. Only that it had nothing to do with him.

The crowd wasn't breaking up, but it was moving away, a short distance down the street, where a line had formed at another cash machine.

"I was just taking my money…" Al repeated to himself.

"That's fine, Al," Sheriff Dave said. "The doc'll be back to tend you presently. You just sit quietly there, okay?"

"Okay," Al said, almost childlike.

The two kids who'd shot the whole thing on their phones were part of the reduced huddle of people now hovering around the bench.

"We got it all, Sheriff," one of them said, holding up his phone.

"Is there a reward?" the other one asked.

"An ice cream sundae at Al's, I'm sure," Sheriff Dave replied. "After the trial. And I'm gonna need your phones before you put those videos on to the damned Instagram or whatever."

"Too late," the older one smiled. "YouTubed it."

"Goddamn it, Liam."

"But we still get a free sundae, right, Al?" the kid asked.

"Sure, sure," Al nodded, then groaned and put his head in his hands. He was still holding his plastic shopping bag, and Jonas gaped at what looked like thousands of dollars in there. No wonder the con had mugged him. For that kind of scratch, Jonas would've turned the guy over himself if he thought he could get away with it. Not fucking likely, though, with Sheriff Dave and the YouTube twins and half a dozen rubberneckers still standing in a half-circle around the bench. He'd regained enough presence of mind to look up and down the main street. First, he needed to check his bike hadn't been stolen, but it was still lying on the grassy verge across the road in front of the vacant lot. Some local dad type was very obviously standing guard over it for him.

Good for you, Dad.

The main drag, which honest to God was called Main Street, was still unusually busy with foot traffic and the pedestrians were all lined up outside the local bank and some dinky S&L. A sizeable crowd of people milled around a public park, which sat like a long island in the middle of the main stem, with eastbound traffic to one side and westbound to the other. A couple more lines of customers snaked away from cash machines in front of a cafe, a bar and a druggist. Lot of cash machines for such a pissant little town, but as the fog cleared in his head, Jonas started to note a few details. The number of coffee shops. Antique shops. Bed and breakfast places.

Silverton wasn't a real town. Not a logging town anyway.

It made sense. The national forest had probably put an end to that line of honest work, and Silverton had remade itself as a tourist trap. A few more details gelled for him.

The blood-stained bag of cash this Al guy was nursing. The one he'd almost been killed for.

The tense, nervous looks on the faces of the people in line to withdraw money up and down the street.

The way Sheriff Dave kept worrying at the big crowd in front of the Wells Fargo.

"Is there a problem with the banks?" Jonas asked.

The Sheriff looked at him as though he might be a little bit dense.

It was a sympathetic look, though.

"You been riding your push bike all day, son?"

"Yeah," Jonas said. "I'm... on vacation. Why?"

The lawman looked ill.

"Hell of day, son. Hell of a day. Looks like war with China and a stock market crash and a bunch of pure damn craziness all decided to break out at once."

"The banks have crashed," Al said next to him on the bench. "It's all over the news. You should go get your money out while you can."

19

THE SECRETS HIS FLESH
MIGHT BEAR

el Baker did not remember drinking the huge tumbler of tap water by the bed or washing down a couple of aspirin with it. Still, she must have because the glass was mostly empty when she woke with the sun, and her hangover was a bitch, but only a little bitch, and morning-after Mel was so fucking grateful to drunken idiot Mel that she could've kissed her.

Speaking of which...

She sat up. Carefully. With the briefest moment of disorientation. It was more like she was getting ready to think, "Where-the-hell-am-I?" rather than actually thinking it because she saw Nomi the Labrador at the foot of the bed, thumping her tail on the mattress.

Rick Boreham's bed.

Melissa breathed in suddenly and whipped her head left and right, looking for him. That was a poor choice. Her head did start pounding then, and her neck ached badly. She needed to pee. God, she'd had so many mornings like this—okay, much worse than this, but, you know, kinda like this—when she'd been with Gary. Maybe she should think about having another year off the piss?

Mel heard snoring from the other room.

Nomi's tail wagged so hard she looked like she might take flight.

The smiling lab quivered with excitement but did not move to come any closer while Mel checked out the room. It was clean but spare. No open drawers or cupboard doors. No photos on the wall, but two on the bedside table. An older lady with a family resemblance to Rick. Mother? Grandmother? And some army guys on a dusty, six-wheeled Land Rover. They all wore beards of varying lengths and chocolate chip desert camouflage, and they were all of them grinning and mugging for the camera. She thought she recognised Rick or at least his smile. He looked much younger and thinner, if it was him. But happier, too. He was heavily armed. They all were.

Mel didn't remember picking the photo frame up, but she had, and now she carefully put it back on the little table by the bed. Her brother was in a lot of photographs like that. It was possible, she thought, that Andy and Rick might even have crossed paths. Possible, but not likely. The war was a big place, and a lot of people got lost there.

Outside, the sun was well up and streaming in through the windows, which had no curtains. She squinted out at the view. Rick's vegetable patch, tomatoes on the vine blazing red in the morning light, bright green herb bushes that might be basil, a wooden fence that looked freshly painted, the woods falling away to the river.

He was still snoring somewhere in the cabin.

She took a few breaths and tested her head again. She could move it without significant pain or discomfort. She just had to be careful. It'd been a year since she'd had a drink, and she had absolutely no piss fitness. Her mouth was dry and tasted like some scary desert lizard might have taken a dusty shit in there overnight. Mel reached for the water tumbler and drank the last inch in the bottom. It was warm but still a blessed relief.

A few more breaths. She thought about another aspirin but decided she didn't need one.

She wasn't wearing her boots. They were neatly stood up under the window next to Rick's. She was wearing her dress. She held her breath and checked her underwear.

Yep. Still there.

She had no bite marks or bruises, or beard rash that she could find or feel.

Apart from the hangover, which wasn't going to kill her, she felt pretty good. Rested even.

Rick snored again. Nomi's tail thumped loudly on the mattress. Mel lowered her bare feet to the wooden floorboards. She could feel the grain of the lumber under her toes, but although coarse, it had been buffed by years of use and cleaning. No splinters.

She took the glass, intending to get some more water, and tip-toed quietly out of the bedroom. Rick's snoring eased a little, and she stopped where she stood, but his breathing was regular, and he didn't sit up or even move much at all. She could see his feet hanging over the end of the couch. Tiptoeing to the kitchenette, Mel poured herself some more water and sipped it while looking over the garden. Her pick-up was parked outside the gate. She didn't remember getting back there and had to take another sip of water to distract herself from the embarrassment she felt. God, what a total wally she'd been. A two-pint screamer.

She still had to pee and had no idea where the toilet might be. The cabin was pretty simple, though. The tiny kitchen was part of the main living room, which wasn't big. Rick's bedroom sat at one end; a doorway onto a hall stood open at the other. Not wanting to disturb him—and to be honest, not wanting to face him yet because she was going to have to apologise for last night—Mel ghosted through the little cabin, finding a simple laundry and bathroom arrangement through the doorway at the far end.

A few moments later, greatly relieved, she sat in the single tub chair opposite the couch where Rick Boreham lay sleeping, a low table between them. She recognised the furniture, old worn-out loungers from the Bretton Woods clubhouse. The three-seater he'd slept on was big. It dominated the room, but Rick was bigger. His stockinged feet stuck out at one end. He would not have had a comfortable night's sleep.

His wallet and keys lay on the cheap, pinewood coffee table.

And a weapon of some sort. A curved, short-bladed fighting knife.

There was no mistaking it for anything else. It was not a woodsman's tool.

Mel regarded him in silence.

Andy was another one for always going armed, but you couldn't do that as freely at home as you could here. Mel wondered why Rick carried a knife and not a handgun. She assumed he could get a license.

Perhaps he'd had enough of guns.

Fuck knows she had.

Mel stood and quietly padded over to the sink to refill her glass with water. She didn't need to. The glass was half full. She just felt the need to move. Nomi watched her from the bedroom, smiling a big, wide, doggy smile when she returned to sit opposite Rick.

She'd made it very clear she was interested in him, and he'd agreed to go out with her. From what she remembered of the night before, they'd got along easily, with a real connection sparking between them. Why hadn't he...

What? Taken advantage?

Why was she even asking herself that?

Had Gary fucked her up so badly that she couldn't recognise a decent bloke doing the decent thing and not just suiting himself? Mel leaned back in the tub chair, her eyes sweeping over the sleeping man with lazy enjoyment. He was stacked; there was no denying it. His shirt had ridden up, exposing some proper tasty abs and a tan line where his pants had slipped down a little. She saw white cross-hatching of old scars and one pink, fist-sized patch of skin puckered by a fading burn mark. Mel wondered at what other secrets his flesh might bear.

No blatant tattoos, which wasn't merely odd for a soldier; it was just plain unusual for anyone these days. Rick turned a little ways toward her, and his thighs bunched powerfully inside the taut fabric of the pants he still wore. He had undone his belt and the top button of his fly, and Mel found herself mouth breathing and staring openly.

Jesus Christ, she wanted this man.

She was about to stand up, step out of her dress and join him on the couch when a memory resurfaced, a warning her brother, the Royal Marine, had once given her.

Never wake a sleeping killer. Not even with a cup of tea.

Shit. What could she do?

The rapid thumping of Nomi's tail on the mattress in the bedroom, as she stood gave her the solution. Mel smiled.

She carefully moved Rick's everyday carry – his wallet, keys and knife – out of reach. Then she grinned at Nomi and said, "Good morning, young lady."

The dog barked happily at the invitation and leapt from the bed, charging into the lounge room. Rick grunted and blinked his eyes drowsily. Mel winked at the happy Labrador, led her over to the front door, and let her out.

"Stay," she said. "Guard."

Outside, Nomi barked just once. Like last night, as if acknowledging the order.

When Mel returned, Rick was half awake, and gathering his wits, he'd raised himself on one elbow and was looking around. He smiled at her, still fogged with sleep but with the natural ease of an innocent man.

"You were quite the gentleman last night," Mel said, moving to stand directly in front of him.

"Huh," he went, still not quite sure what was happening.

"But that'll be enough of that, then," she said.

Mel reached up, undid the string bow at the back of her summer dress, and let it fall to the bare wooden floor.

She joined him on the couch.

AFTER MAKING LOVE TWICE, they made waffles and coffee. They showered together and dressed, and Rick Boreham floated through the easiest morning of what felt like the best day of his life. He had some leave owed and figured he might even take a whole day. Bretton Woods was super chill about that stuff. Probably all of the Europeans on the management board. They even made him take paid leave if it built up past a certain number of days. He was elbow-deep in warm suds, cleaning up the waffle mess, listening to Mel sing as she dried her hair, and thinking she had a really sweet voice when he remembered the VA.

He had an appointment with his counsellor in two hours.

"Goddamn it," he said loudly enough that Mel stuck her head around the corner, looking worried.

"You okay?"

Rick shook his head.

"I'm sorry," he said. "I got a doctor's appointment at eleven-thirty this morning. I gotta go. I can't... I never miss them. It's just..."

He could feel all of the bolts and wires in his head tightening up. He didn't want to drag his ass into the VA. Not today. He wanted to spend the day with Mel. They'd talked about driving upstate and letting Nomi swim in Little Seneca Lake. Mel knew of a cheap place they could stay overnight if they wanted. Rick cursed himself for having forgotten the counselling session. He had never missed one and had promised himself he never would because they were important.

"Baby, what's up?" Mel asked, wrapping herself in a bath towel and hastening across the room to him, but carefully. Her feet were wet. "You got your doctor's appointment? Go see your doctor. It's important, right?"

"Yeah, it is. We never miss one. Nomi too. We're part of a trial, a program."

"And you won't miss this one either. I've gotta stop by my apartment anyway. You know, do the walk of shame? Change my clothes." She tilted her head and smiled a question, "And maybe pack an overnight bag?"

The wires and cranks in his head eased off a little. The fires in the dark engine dimmed. Her brother was a soldier. She understood.

"Sure," he said, and it felt like letting go of a breath held just a little too long. "Sure. Sorry. I get too wrapped up in stuff sometimes. That's why I'm out here. In the woods. Picking up golf balls for a living."

"Hey," Mel said, "It brought us together. Can you get tomorrow off work, too?"

"I think so. This place is, well, it's not like some places you work. They're not screwing the world for every dime they can take."

"I know. They pay my invoices on time, too. So, go to your appointment, get the extra day off if you can, and we'll have an adventure."

As USUAL, finding a parking spot at the VA was a chore. Rick sat in his car and tried not to fume as he tailed the line of cars into the dark maw of the underground garage. Nomi, wearing a blue vest emblazoned with the red letters "Service Dog," butted her head into his shoulder, sensing his distress. He scratched her behind the ear, eliciting a happy pant. It helped. By the clock on his dash, which was four or five minutes fast, his appointment was in half an hour. If he could get parked, they should make it... of course, Veterans Affairs being what it was, he'd left plenty of wiggle room in the schedule.

He needed to see the docs. Specifically, Doctor Cairns. As good as it felt with Mel, and she was awesome, some things were bothering him, some stuff he needed to let out, and it was not appropriate to drop that load on her. Not if he expected her to stick. She'd been a cop in London, sure. Her brother was an English marine or something. No doubt she knew the deal better than most. But he was not such a fool as to think she was ready to carry his load. Or that she ever would be.

The VA was where he shucked off that weight. And if he couldn't get parked, he was gonna miss his session. Rick's fingers drummed upon the steering wheel, and he inched forward. A car pulled out, and the vehicle in front of him took the spot, of course. But now he was clear. He idled forward, turned up the ramp on the green level and saw his chance. An elderly veteran with a walker was easing into a red Buick, his wife helping him into the passenger side seat. Rick waited while the couple got settled. They were a while talking before she keyed on the engine, and he did his best not to get riled, even as the driver behind him leaned into the horn. Everyone here was here with good reason. Finally, the vehicle's reversing lights came on. The Buick backed out and pulled away in a cough of oily exhaust smoke. Rick turned into the vacant spot. Nomi's tail thumped on the seat.

Rick was careful to leave behind the talon blade he always carried. He pulled the sheathed weapon from his pocket and carefully placed it in the glove box. There were signs everywhere. No weapons—firearms, knives, pepper spray, anything—none of it was allowed inside the VA facility. The only time he went without some sort of weapon was when he came here. Even at dinner with Mel last night, he'd carried this blade in a pocket. He got out of the car, and Nomi followed him in her Service Dog vest. Clipping the leash to her harness, Rick glanced about, double-checked his door locks, and headed toward the stairs to the blue level, the main entrance.

Negotiating flights of steps and a few metal doors, the pair reached the main hall. It was brightly lit, and as usual there were dozens of veterans headed toward their various destinations. Rick went straight for the kiosks, where he had to swipe for pre-registration. He fumbled out his wallet and produced his white VA card. It had his mugshot with the tiny letters "Service Connected" beneath it and an Army Star for his former branch of service. He slid it into the tray, and a green light danced over it.

The kiosk lit up. It asked for the year of his birth, and he started plugging in answers to the prompts that followed. When he was done with pre-registration, a printed white slip of paper spat out of the kiosk. He glanced at it. It read 'CSRC 1300 Room 1E55'. He crumpled up the slip and threw it in the trash. Rick knew where to go.

He idly scoped out his fellow vets as he crossed the main hall. An ancient gentleman in a wheelchair with an Iwo Jima hat sat next to a much younger woman, who patted his hand. Rick guessed it was his daughter or maybe even a granddaughter. The family resemblance was strong. Another man lurched toward Physical Therapy, short of one leg. Somebody was playing a piano next to a table set up with a sign "Cookies For Our Heroes."

Rick snorted at that. The cookies were genuine, but he knew that actual storybook heroes were few and far between. He was just getting through the day.

Nomi, who was just as familiar with the VA as Rick, led them toward a set of double doors from which hung a brown and white placard, "CTAD/CSRC". As they walked through, Rick glanced at the VA motto on the wall above and to his left, a quote from Abraham Lincoln. "To Care For Him Who Shall Have Borne The Battle."

Battle, he thought. It was always there, never far from his thoughts. He pushed through the swinging doors, being careful not to clip his dog. They emerged into a sunny hallway with a series of doors to the left. Rick made a brief stop by the restroom before continuing to room 1E55 of the CSRC, or the "Combat Stress Recovery Clinic."

Rick went through the doors and walked into a wall of silence. There were a dozen men and women seated in the room, which was painted light brown. As usual, no one spoke. Rick knew that everyone present was a confirmed combat trauma case; he could hear the fluorescents hum. He walked over to the reception desk. The person closest to him, a middle-aged woman, looked up and spoke.

"Name and last four?"

"Boreham, 5088."

The receptionist typed something into her computer, frowning. She sighed and tried again.

"Problem?" Rick asked.

"Not for you, sir," she said. "Systems been glitchy since yesterday, is all. There, you're good, Mister Boreham. Doctor Cairns knows you're here. Please have a seat and fill out this survey." She handed Rick a clipboard with an attached government-issue black Skilcraft pen. Rick disliked the surveys but did as he was told. He found a chair facing the door with room for Nomi at his feet.

He sighed and shook his head as he filled out the questionnaire.

"How often do you have intrusive thoughts?"

"On a scale from one to five..."

He forced himself through, answering as best as he could, but how do you quantify the personal aftermath of war? He didn't know, and he knew the VA couldn't either. These surveys were the best they could do to assign a number, "from one to five," to pain and loss and the creeping horror that clung to them.

A second door in the room, directly opposite the entrance Rick and Nomi had come through, opened with a click and whoosh. It was the door to the wards. His counsellor came out, Doctor Alan Cairns.

"Mister Boreham? Nomi. Come on in."

Rick stood. He gave a slight tug to his dog's leash. A Vietnam guy glanced at Rick, nodded, and then returned to studying his hands.

He returned the nod. Rick, Nomi and the doc went through the door, followed by ghosts.

20

JUST LIKE THE CROCODILE HUNTER

Somebody finally got smart, and the ICE agents removed Sandino's cuffs. The bitch who'd kidney-punched Ellie disappeared too, replaced by some black guy who was all tooled up and body-armoured like the rest of the agents, but he didn't seem to have as much of a hard-on. He politely asked her to sit in the car.

"Because it's cooler," he explained.

And it was. They had the AC running at full arctic power and even sitting half-in, half-out with the door open so she could keep an eye on this pig circus, Ellie had to admit it was more pleasant than standing out in the hot sun taking random kidney shots.

And random seemed to be the organising principle at work here.

The ICE guys put her people into the vehicles.

They took them out.

They put them back in again, but they never actually drove away. This went on for nearly two hours. There was no way they'd be open for lunch.

She saw the guy in charge, the one she'd spoken to inside, taking calls on a tactical radio and two mobile phones. Somebody was kicking his ass. She'd had enough of those conversations to recognise when things weren't going well.

"Hey, Sandino," she said to her saucier when the agent threw one of the phones away. "You seeing this?"

Ellie half expected the new guy to tell her, or at least ask her, to shut up. But the agent seemed remarkably chill. Like he was more of an observer than a participant.

"Am I seeing what?" Sandino asked.

Ellie pointed at the dish pigs climbing out of the van they'd just been loaded into.

"Pah," scoffed Sandino. "They don't know what they're doing. Or somebody is stopping them. Perhaps Damien's lawyers, no?"

"Perhaps," she said, frowning.

The ranking fed looked pissed.

"Agent?" she said to the black guy watching over them.

"Yes, ma'am?" he answered, surprising her a little.

"Is something wrong? What's happening?"

He snorted.

"Your guess is as good as mine, ma'am."

He turned away from whatever was happening or not happening and looked at Sandino.

"Are you doing okay, sir? Can I get you some cold water?"

"You can let me get back to my work," Sandino said. "My master stock, it will be ruined."

"I'll get you some water," the man said. He waved another agent over and spoke to him. The second man nodded and ran back inside the restaurant.

None of this seemed right to Ellie.

Not just the raid itself. That was an obvious fuck up, and she didn't doubt that Damo's lawyers had been firing off injunctions and restraining orders and all sorts of legal high explosives. But she didn't imagine that it would make much difference either. *La Migra* was feared with good reason by everyone in the restaurant trade. These motherfuckers were true believers. And in their way, Ellie would admit, they were utterly fearless. A lawyer's letter or even some uppity judge telling them to stand down wouldn't usually knock them off course.

But two hours after they'd stormed her kitchen, they still hadn't taken anybody away. And their arrogance had given way to uncertainty and something approaching apologetic disquiet.

The agent who'd been despatched to fetch water returned with two bottles, but he brought with him something even better.

Word that they had been set free.

KARL VALENTINE WAS a man of his word. The retired trucker drove her the last couple of blocks to Temescal, managing the little Honda in difficult traffic as easily as Jody might handle a disposable camera at a kid's birthday party. It took more than the five minutes he'd promised, but that wasn't his fault. A string of lights was out along Telegraph Avenue, and the cops weren't policing the intersections yet. *They're all busy with my attacker*, Jody thought. As they crawled past the old blue church on the corner of 41st, Mister Valentine asked if she wanted him to try a different route, a workaround, but the side streets were already jammed up with cars trying the same.

"No, thanks," she said in a small voice. "This is fine."

They managed little better than a walking pace most of the way to *Fourth Edition*, but Jody was just glad not to be out in the heat or tied up in some rapey Metallica fan's murder basement. Mister Valentine had a kindly manner, and he seemed to know not to ask her too many questions. With somebody else's gas in the tank, they could afford to run the AC at max, too. Valentine talked about being a truck driver. First for the Army back in the Gulf War and then for some big transport company out of Kansas City. Jody faded in and out of the conversation. She wasn't bored or uninterested. She just had trouble holding a thought. Twice on the way over, she jumped when she remembered that she didn't have her camera bag with her before getting annoyed with her own foolishness. How could she forget that?

"That's just the shock," Mister Valentine told her the second time she apologised for suddenly freaking out on him. "Seen it a lot in the Army. In Iraq. That's why I can't drive the big rigs now. Doctors said my nerves was no good, not from the shock but. Mine was from the chemicals and meds, and the army had to pay me my compensation, but they said I couldn't drive trucks for anyone after that."

"You seem like a good driver to me, Mister Valentine," Jody said absently. "Thank you."

"I am a good driver, Miss. And please, call me Karl," he said, pushing the bill of his baseball cap up an inch and peering at the tangle of traffic ahead as though looking for a secret passage through. "I ain't complaining none," he went on. "Bought me a little place with that compensation money. Before the housing got crazy round here with all the hipsters and the computer people. Couldn't afford to buy here now of course. So I ain't complaining. Figure I made me a tidy profit on getting poisoned by Uncle Sam."

Another two minutes saw them past the place Ellie liked to get a cup of tea before work, a cafe called the Hawk and Pony, and ten minutes after that Karl nursed the Civic past the tofu place and the Second Half cocktail bar where they'd gone for Ellie's birthday drinks. It didn't help Jody's mood to remember those things. She distracted herself for a minute, sending a long text to Chad, apologising for not waiting at the pick-up...

(Even though he was already half an hour late.)

... And telling him she would get Maxy this evening.

(Even though she had no idea how the rest of this day would turn out.)

It felt better to send it. Like she was taking control of something.

"Nearly there," Karl announced a few minutes later as the Angel Rose massage parlour slowly—very slowly—receded in the rear-view mirror. Jody's heartbeat quickened when she saw Ellie's boss standing out front of the restaurant, waving his arms around, making people do things.

Damo was good at that, Ellie said. His big Australian voice frightened the hell out of everyone, especially when he got very angry and super loud, and nobody could quite understand what he was shouting at them, just that he was swearing a lot. It was best to do all the things when that happened, Ellie said, and hope you got the right one done. Her girlfriend didn't seem the least bit intimated by the big, shouty Australian, which was probably why he hired her. Ellie could match him word for word when it came to potty-mouthed abuse, too. That was perhaps another reason Damo liked her.

"Thank you," Jody said, turning slightly to look at Mister Valentine. "I don't know what I would've done if I hadn't met you this morning, Karl. You've been so kind." She squeezed his arm and felt like crying again.

"You'd-a been okay, miss. You're tough. I can tell. You just had a bad scare is all, and a knock on the head, and you're worried about your little boy. I can wait if you like. Got nothing else to do. You might need some more driving done, and I'd be happy to help out, you know if you need the help."

His offer of help was almost apologetic, making Jody feel guilty for even needing the support. She was about to say no, reflexively, when she realised she might need him after all. She was having trouble turning her head. That Metallica asshole had wrenched something in her neck when he pushed her over and grabbed her camera bag. She didn't think she could turn her head to check the lanes when she was merging.

"Okay," she said. "I'd appreciate it, Karl. You should meet Mister Maloney. I mean, Damien. He's Ellie's boss. He's a bit scary, but she likes him. He's Australian."

"Like the crocodile hunter?"

"Just like, yeah. He even wears the shorts," she said and wondered why she found that funny. Today of all days.

Probably because you're losing your mind, girl, she thought.

And Damo was indeed dressed in his usual outfit of a white linen shirt and knee-length khaki shorts. He wore a Panama hat and sunglasses, too, and he kept taking them off and putting them back on as he shouted at some people she didn't recognise.

Jody shaded her eyes and peered into the fierce white light. She had to squint hard when the sun burst off the chrome on Damo's Lexus. The SUV had a lot of chrome. She could see he was furious. One of the men with him was in a suit, and he was nodding along no matter how much Damo flapped his arms around. The other two looked like some weird mash-up of cops and soldiers. One of them was a woman. She had her arms folded, a scowl twisting her face.

The other one stood with his hands on his hips, and his jaw jutted out at Damo, no matter how much the Australian raged and ranted at him.

"This doesn't look good," Karl said as they pulled off the main drag and into the tiny car lot next to Damo's Lexus.

But Jody didn't really hear what he said.

She had just seen Ellie emerge from the front of the restaurant with a small group of *Fourth Edition* kitchen staff. Jody almost cried out in relief.

She didn't wait for Karl to turn off the engine as they pulled up. She threw open the door and ran across the parking lot, past Damo and the people he was yelling at, racing toward Ellie, who was very surprised to see her. The kitchen hands saw her coming and parted, making a space for her to run through and into her partner's wide-open arms. She almost knocked Ellie down, she was moving so fast.

"Whoa, baby, slow down, be cool," her girlfriend said, even as Jody hugged her fiercely and kissed her, just to know that she was real, that nothing could keep them apart. Pain spiked through her neck and into her eyeballs, but Jody would not let go. Pain she could deal with. Losing Ellie or Max, she could not.

"Jody, you're hurt," another voice said. It was Mister Sandino, the old chef, who did all of Damo's soups and sauces. He was a lovely man. He gently took her arm from around Ellie's neck, and Jody winced a little. Her wrist hurt, and she realised for the first time that it was swollen and her forearm was bruised.

"Baby, what happened?" Ellie Jabbarah asked, her voice growing dark. "Aren't you supposed to be at your photo shoot? How did you get hurt?"

"I'm okay, I'm fine," Jody said. "I just fell over," she explained, wincing as she turned her head, and the pain of sudden movement set her teeth on edge. "Mister Valentine...he helped me get my cameras back?"

"Who?" Ellie said. "Jody, what happened?"

"Nothing. It's not important. I can tell you all about it later. I have to get Maxy from Chad and... and... Oh God, what a morning."

Damo's voice rolled over the top of her own, loud as always but not angry like before.

"Maaaate, what's up?" he boomed. Damo swept both Ellie and Jody into his embrace and launched into a rapid-fire barrage of dialogue in his flat, nasal accent. He was hard enough to understand even when he wasn't roaring strange antipodean swear words. This was almost a foreign language. "Jeez, you look as crook as a fucking dog, Jodes. But don't worry, young Nick here, he's gonna sue these pricks and they're gonna pay your girlfriend a massive fucking settlement, and they're gonna give me a genuine reach around, but you guys, with the payday you got coming from this fucking teddy bears' picnic you're gonna be able to buy a house and a boat that's so fucking big it'll have its own little baby boats hanging off the arse end of it, just like mine."

Damo was loud and unstoppable, and he never seemed to draw breath. He made absolutely no sense at all. But there was something elemental and comforting about being wrapped in his massive hamhock arms while he roared like a gigantic meat-eating Qantas bear about the shit storm of biblical retribution he was going to rain down on his enemies. Jody felt herself safe for the first time in hours.

"And who the fuck are you, mate?"

She pushed out of his bear hug, realising he was talking to Karl.

"This is Karl," she said quickly. "Mister Valentine. He's a good guy. A friend. He helped me when... Oh, Damo, Ellie, I was mugged."

"Honey, no!" Ellie exclaimed.

"Oh, for fuck's sake," said the Australian. "What a cunt of a day. All right then, Karl, right? That's your name?"

"Yes," the trucker said, as though he wasn't quite sure anymore. "Miss Jody got mugged. They got the fella what done it. And I gave her a lift over here."

"The fuck is all this about?" Ellie said. "You got mugged?"

"And you got arrested!" Jody replied as if that made them even. She looked for the other people Damo had been shouting at, standing by a black SUV.

"Damo told me you'd been arrested," she said to Ellie, not sure of anything anymore. "What happened?"

Damo answered first.

"Jodes," he said, pointing to the man in the suit. "This bloke here is Nick Perriam. He's my lawyer. I keep his firm on a frankly fucking extortionate retainer, and they're gonna earn their feed today, let me tell you."

The lawyer, who was anonymously handsome in a TV lawyer kind of way, smiled and shook her hand. He was the man who'd been nodding at everything Damo had been shouting earlier, when they pulled into the lot. He looked so cool and unruffled that she wondered if his expensive suit was somehow air-conditioned.

"Ms Sarjanen," he said, shaking her hand. His palm was cool and dry. "Please do not worry about your partner, Ms Jabbarah. For her, this will soon enough be a minor inconvenience and an excellent story for your next dinner party. For the government, however, and for the agents responsible for this mess, it is about to become a truly horrifying legal nightmare."

Everyone turned at that.

Jody was surprised to see the two people Damo had been shouting at standing just a few feet away. The woman was looking at her feet. The man had pressed his lips together, and his jawline was working as though chewing through a thick and bitter root.

"Mister Maloney," he said.

"Yeah, what do you fucking want?" Damo said.

Nick Perriam stepped between them, holding up one hand.

"Damien," he said. "I should handle this." He turned to the suits. "You can't talk to Mister Maloney anymore or to any of his staff. My firm has commenced proceedings against your agency. All correspondence must now go through your in-house counsel or the Justice Department if they decide to get involved."

The agent sneered at Perriam. "Whatever." He turned and spoke to Damo. "I'm directed by my superiors to apologise for any inconvenience."

"Any inconvenience!" Ellie blurted out. "Are you fucking serious?"

"I am informed that a malicious breach of our database resulted in your business being incorrectly targeted for enforcement action. I am not authorised to offer further comment. You are all free to go. Have a nice day."

The two agents turned around and stalked off, chased by abuse shouted in Spanish and English and one roaring torrent of thunderous Australian swear words.

21

THE CITIES WILL STARVE

"We're up," Michelle said.

"Wait. What?" James said.

He was still trying to navigate the information blizzard on her computer screen while also chasing down the story of the banking collapse. It was weird. When he clicked the link on his phone, the *New York Times* piece came up with the latest update ("Federal Reserve Chairman Describes a Market in Meltdown"), but when he opened a browser on his laptop and called up the *Times,* he could find no trace of the banking run.

"What do you mean we're up?" he said, abandoning his attempt to reconcile the news sources on his computer with those on his phone.

"General Panozzo got us a three-minute slot at the NSC pre-con. You're gonna explain your muffin theory to a room full of angry spooks and generals."

"But it's not just about muffins," he protested. "The muffins are a metaphor."

"Then find a better one," she said without much sympathy. "This is a red meat crowd. And we're up."

Michelle grabbed her phone and hurried out the door as though she fully intended to leave him behind. Dazed and more than a little confused, James sat for a moment, wondering what the hell an 'NSC pre-con' might be. Michelle stuck her head back into the room as though reading his mind.

"It's a pre-conference hook-up of all the principals who'll have to brief the President at a full meeting in the situation room later. Or wherever they've stashed him now the White House has been flagged as a target."

"A target for what?"

She rolled her eyes as if that was answer enough.

"Hurry up, James, clock's ticking."

James tried to gather his thoughts while he grabbed his laptop and briefcase. Everything was moving so quickly. Part of him marvelled at the speed of it all. People in business often thought of bureaucrats as lazy and diffident, but this whole building seemed to have exploded into tightly controlled mania. People were hurrying up and down the halls, some of them running, but they all seemed focused and goal-directed. Unlike him.

He had no idea what he was doing.

Dozens of soldiers clad in body armour and carrying weapons had appeared as if by magic and stationed themselves at seemingly random checkpoints throughout the building.

He was sure the points weren't random, but their meaning was a mystery to him, at least until two of the soldiers barred their passage into a conference room to scan their ID tags with handheld readers. The device pinged as a green light came on.

"Good to go, folks," said the one in sergeant's stripes as he unlocked and held open the door for them.

James followed closely on Michelle's boot heels, half expecting to be dragged back out of the room by the scruff of his neck. The door closed firmly behind him.

The conference room was twice the size of the one they'd visited earlier in the day and contained nearly three times as many people. There were many more military uniforms than he'd seen this morning, and the men and women wearing them looked collectively older and way more senior. James had no idea what all of the decorations on their chests and shirt collars and shoulder tabs meant, but the density of the display immediately struck him. The civilians were likewise represented by an expanded phalanx of power players in the sort of bespoke, hand-tailored suits he'd expect to see on Wall Street. Having lost his suit jacket, he was acutely aware of how underdressed he looked in his rolled-up shirtsleeves.

A woman in a red cardigan and pearls was stepping down from the podium at the head of the long, crowded table as they entered. *Why a cardigan in this heat,* James wondered fretfully, pointlessly. Maybe she worked with a planet-sized CIA supercomputer that needed to be kept super-chilled. He never found out.

General Panozzo half-stood and hurriedly waved them both forward as if to catch a departing train. James's heart, which was already hammering away in his chest, beat even faster. What the hell was he supposed to say to these people? He'd barely been able to make his case to Panozzo earlier. And he hadn't been given a chance to refine the message at any White House briefing. It had been cancelled.

Stumbling along in Michelle's wake, fearful of tripping over his own feet, let alone the tangle of legs and briefcases barring their way to the podium, James was terrified of face-planting into some admiral's crotch before he had a chance to humiliate himself more conventionally. Michelle did not even wait for him to catch up before she addressed the room.

"Good morning," she said. "I am Michelle Nguyen, Division 6, National Security Council. This is James O'Donnell, one of our consultants. He identified a threat vector in yesterday's cyber-attack, which hasn't yet been featured in public or classified reports. James?"

And she yielded the floor to him.

Shit!

"You have two minutes, max," she whispered as he half staggered past her. Dark sweat stains stood out on his shirt, and he was pretty sure he was the worst-smelling guy in the room.

"Uh... hi," he said, only stopping himself from nervously tapping the microphone by sheer force of will. "Uh, yeah."

And he froze.

He had no idea where to start, no idea of where to go. Panozzo was frowning at him. Michelle nodded encouragingly. The whole room waited.

Muffins weren't going to cut it.

James took a deep breath, let it out and said a little too loudly, "Our cities are going to starve."

That got a reaction. A rippling movement ran around the table and the room like a series of competing, overlapping Mexican waves at a football stadium. He heard grunts and mutters, and somebody distinctly asked, "What did he just say?"

James wasn't sure who asked that, but he turned in the general direction of the voice he'd heard.

"I said our cities are going to starve. The cyber-attack yesterday was significant in itself, but it was more significant as a distraction..."

No, that wasn't the right word for these people.

"... As a diversion," he added, "from a focussed... *attack* on the country's food distribution network."

"How?"

The question came from an Air Force general a few seats down the table on James's left. Or at least he assumed it was an Air Force general. He wore a blue uniform, like on *Stargate*, which his Dad had always loved. And the room was full of generals and admirals.

"Hackers got into the servers, the computers, of all the main food distribution companies in the continental US. If they take those systems down, like really smash them, it would be like..."

He reached for a better metaphor and drew a blank. James was hideously aware of how exposed he looked and felt in front of a room full of really fucking serious people. He found the words just as his search for the correct phrase was becoming uncomfortable, with some of his audience beginning to shift in their seats.

"It'd be just like bombing and completely destroying a railway network in a war," he blurted out. "And taking out roads, ports, everything all at the same time. The food that should have moved from the farm gate to your dinner table or the TV dinner factory to your lap, it'll just sit and rot where it is because the way you normally move it, the transport and distribution network, it's gone."

He made a little explosion noise and mimed something blowing up before he had a chance to regret it.

More murmuring, more movement around the table.

Michelle winked at him, which was weird, given the circumstances. Panozzo nodded brusquely once and said, "Thank you, Mister O'Donnell."

And he was done. A younger officer in a tan-brown uniform appeared from off-stage to escort them to an exit in the nearest corner of the conference room. He heard Panozzo talking about "getting Homeland and NSC on it ASAP." Then they were through the door and standing in a smaller room, where half a dozen aides and functionaries typed frantically on laptops, ignoring their arrival. Michelle turned and punched him on the shoulder.

"Boom! Nailed it," she said.

Still struggling to understand how all of the moving parts worked together, James shook his head.

"But I just... we didn't really..."

"We're just the messengers," Michelle explained and pointed at the door that had just closed behind them. "They decide what to do with the information."

"And what are they going to do?" James asked.

She shrugged.

"Under normal circumstances, it'd get kicked across to the Cyber Response Group. They'd work up an attribution memo, and then stakeholders, US agencies, allies and partner nations would confer on defense and response and..."

"Jesus Christ," James said. "We'll all be dead of hunger before then."

"I said under normal circumstances, James. Chances are they're ordering a bunch of lethal drone strikes on every hacker in the CIA's Hostile Disposition Matrix and a compulsory hold and secure over the IT assets of the food distributors."

"Wait. What? Every hacker?" James said, not quite believing her. "But isn't... isn't this the Chinese? Who else would they go after?"

Michelle said nothing.

James stared at her, feeling as though he was teetering on the edge of a vast abyss that had just opened up inside his head.

"What have I done?"

Michelle Nguyen smiled. It was not a reassuring expression.

THERE WERE DRONE STRIKES. Eighty-three of them. And extraordinary renditions. Twelve of those. And even three very messy, old-fashioned hands-on killings by wet-work teams put together under CIA control and despatched to lay the vengeance of the Republic upon its enemies.

All too late and often misdirected.

The assassination teams would not even leave the US for another three days, and all of their targets were in Eastern Europe. None had anything to do with the PLA.

As Chinese drones serviced US military targets across the Asia-Pacific region and the great fleets of the People's Liberation Army Navy sortied into the South China Sea, a lieutenant of Unit 61398 received authorisation to proceed with the attack on America's food distribution network. Four seconds after he hit the Enter key on his laptop, the IT systems of nine American food wholesalers melted down into unusable slag. In a small irony, some of the malware he unleashed was adapted from the Stuxnet worm written by the US, with Israeli help, originally programmed to destroy thousands of centrifuges used in Iran's secret nuclear weapons program. Rewritten by Unit 61398, it caused more than a hundred automated warehouses of five of the larger food distributors to violently dismantle themselves in a collective fit of robot madness. Mostly, however, six different types of malicious software infiltrated the companies' various stock control systems. Rather than deleting the data, the malware aggressively randomized it before locking up the databases with military-grade encryption.

The severity of the attack and the enormity of its consequences explained the lethality of the US response. In addition to all of the drone missions, snatch teams and hit squads, the President authorised cruise missile strikes on the known locations of Unit 61398 facilities.

But that would not come for another week.

Well, after the food riots in dozens of American cities turned deadly.

22

THE REVELS OF THE CONDEMNED

The bar was busy. Crowded and noisy. But Jonas kept hearing the same things over and over again.

"Cash only."

"No plastic."

"I said we're only doing cash sales, Pete."

Big Al's had stepped back in time. No credit cards. No swipe and pay. No contactless. Just good old-fashioned greenola.

"Not for you, sir," the waitress told him, when he tried to pay for his beer with one of Mikey's five-dollar notes. "Al said everything's on the house for you. Drink up."

It was tempting, an open bar, a magical tab that would never need paying off, but Jonas restrained himself. He needed to keep his wits about him. Shit was getting out of hand, and not just in Silverton. The crowd at Big Al's was roaring so loud that he couldn't hear a word coming from the TV screen over the bar. But it was tuned into a local news show, and the news ticker crawling across the bottom of the screen read like the subtitles to a disaster movie.

DOLLAR IN FREEFALL

TRADING ON WALL STREET SUSPENDED

NATIONAL GUARD CALLED OUT IN TWENTY-THREE

STATES

6 POLICE AMBUSHED AND KILLED IN DALLAS

Oh, and something about a fucking WAR WITH CHINA?

He noted the question mark. That was a helluva thing. Not knowing whether you were in a war or not. How fucking soft in the cock had this country gone?

Needless to say, there was no reporting anywhere of his big reveal on the pod. Nobody cared who'd fucked whom in Hollywood anymore. Jonas gave up trying to follow the dozen chaotic threads on the TV. The images told him enough. It was like something from one of his crazier podcasts. A prophecy of collapse, war and an unholy bloodswarm of chaos and revolt, all rolled into one convenient bulletin. Most telling of all? For him, at least? Nobody even looked sideways at a stranger in town carrying hundreds of dollars in a bag full of cash.

Everyone was cashed up. Like Germany in 1930.

Jonas tried to keep to himself, sitting at the end of the bar, nursing a locally brewed pale ale, and carving into the monstrously large T-bone the kitchen had sent out on Big Al's say-so. Al himself was nowhere to be seen, having been sent to bed under doctor's orders. But the staff had their own orders to make sure Mister Murdoch was made to feel at home. He couldn't go more than a minute without some local sidling up to shake his hand, pat him on the back or offer to buy him a drink for "saving poor Al", "takin' care of business," or "wiping that shit stain clean off of the streets." Jonas made an effort to remember the names of his kind of people. So far, he'd committed three to his mental contact app. Brad Rausch from the auto shop. ("Damn, but you fucking showed that wetback.") Dale Juntii, an ex-Marine. ("If we'd built a fuckin' wall, we wouldn't have to keep stomping these roaches.") And Tomi Yates, a design student who looked like a Fox News hottie, who leaned in close to breathe gin fumes and cigarette smoke into his ear while she told him that in the olden days, "a real sheriff would've hung that fucking wetback from a tree."

Jonas wasn't sure whether it was Tomi's breasts rubbing up against his arm, her casual out-loud statement of racial truth, or the unexpected feel of her hand on his thigh under the bar, but he found himself suddenly dizzy with lust.

Not stupid with it, though.

He'd grown up in a small town, and he knew women like this. Knew the sort of assholes who usually claimed them as their own, too. Somewhere in town, if not in this bar, there'd be a two-hundred-and-forty-pound slab of football hero or wannabe outlaw and his fucking posse, and no matter what Jonas had done to put himself in the town's good graces today, those boys would kick him to actual pieces for laying hands on Tomi Yates. Indeed, Jonas knew they'd be looking for an excuse. Small-town heroes didn't like to share the spotlight.

He kept his hands in plain sight, holding his knife and fork to either side of his dinner.

"Then maybe I should run for sheriff," he smiled at her, ignoring the discomfort of his growing erection.

Her smile did nothing to cool him down.

"You think you'll hang around then?"

Jonas shrugged but held her gaze.

"I could be tempted."

"I'll bet you could," she grinned, turning a few inches to block the sight of her hand sliding onto his crotch and squeezing gently before she laughed throatily and wandered off to rejoin her friends. She would totally have a table of friends somewhere in this heaving crowd. All the hottest bitches in town.

Jonas breathed in and out. On TV, images of talking heads, politicians mainly, cut away to scenes from a military base where fire crews fought a blaze burning in the conning tower of a submarine. He shared pleasantries and accepted thanks from another half dozen locals while finishing his steak. He'd relaxed considerably about the prospects of any legal trouble following him out of Seattle. From what he could see of the news, the cops were gonna be tied up with the end of the fucking world for at least a week. It'd be a while before things calmed long enough for anybody to follow up on reports of simple assault and theft.

The black and brown slums of LA were already burning with

riots.

Jonas allowed himself a brief, quiet snort of laughter at that.

If he was gonna fuck up—and he could admit that losing his shit at work and stealing Mikey's beloved bike and vacation money was a fantastically stupid fuck up—today was undoubtedly the day to have done it.

He'd even fallen ass-backwards into a free cot. Al Barrett had not only comped him a steak dinner and all the beer he could drink; he'd told Jonas he had a bunk in one of the guest rooms for as long as he wanted it. Big Al's operation ran to more than food and drink. He had sixteen rooms for rent out back, and they were larger and more comfortable than the dump Jonas had been living in with Mikey. The main bar and restaurant ran to tourist kitsch, with a lot of artfully rusted old sawmill shit on the walls and an eight-foot-tall stuffed grizzly in one corner. But the accommodation was clean and comfortable and surprisingly upmarket. The sheets on his double bed felt like expensive cotton, and somebody had left him a picnic basket full of preserves, smoked meats and local sweet treats. A handwritten note said, 'With thanks from Silverton'. Still, Jonas didn't imagine he'd stay around more than a day or so, even with the dangerous temptation of Tomi Yates to consider. He'd made a clean break, and he needed to keep going. The news would calm down the way it always did, and he could take another run at Disney and Pendleton. His zen cool was so chill that when Sheriff Dave sidled up to him a few minutes later, Jonas waved at the barstool next door and invited the lawman to sit down and have a drink.

"If you're off duty, of course," he teased.

"I am," the Sheriff confirmed. He held up two fingers. Jonas assumed for two beers, but the waitress produced a single shot glass from beneath the bar and poured out a double bourbon.

"Another pale ale, stranger?" she asked Jonas.

"Sure," he said. It didn't seem like Sheriff... Muller. His name tag read MULLER, and it didn't seem like he was here to give Jonas any grief. He could take that second beer, but it would be his last tonight. He was still a fugitive, and he could *not* trust these people. Especially not one wearing a badge.

"I know Albert has paid for your dinner, Mister Murdoch," Sheriff Dave said, holding his bourbon up as if to contemplate it for a while. "But I'm gonna insist the Sheriff's Office picks up the tab. Wouldn't do to have Mister Morena's attorney make a meal of the fact that Al paid for your dinner tonight."

"Morena?" Jonas said. "That's the... dude who attacked Big Al?"

Muller scoffed, confusing him a little.

"Ain't nobody calls him Big Al," he explained. "That's just the name of the bar. He's Albert to us, and I am personally grateful for your intervention today, son. I had my hands full with all this other nonsense. I fear things could have gone poorly if you had not stepped up. Turns out Mister Morena has a long and colourful record."

"No doubt," Jonas said, committing nothing more to the conversation. Somebody plugged a dollar into the jukebox, and Bob Seger struggled manfully to be heard over the uproar.

"Before you head out of town," Muller said, "I'll need your particulars so we can get you back for the trial. That gonna be a problem?"

"Nope," Jonas replied as innocently as he could. He was a practised liar, and that was more than innocent enough for this backwoods rube.

"Good to hear," Muller nodded, finally taking a sip of his liquor. "Hell of a day, son. I could do with fewer complications in my life."

"Couldn't we all, Sheriff."

"Indeed. If it helps motivate you to stay in touch, it turns out there was a reward for the capture of Mister Morena. I hope you don't mind the liberty, but I've put your name forward. Morena was on the run from the marshals for skipping bail on a heavy drug charge down in Texas. You could be in line for twenty-five grand."

"Whoa, seriously?" Jonas said, unable to stop himself from doing a double take. He'd never had that much money to his name, never once in his life. Not even when he was still working as a lawyer. But his initial surprise and delight didn't last more than a single heartbeat. He was a fugitive now. Lawmen didn't come looking for the likes of him to hand over a reward.

"The Texas Rangers?" Jonas asked, playing for time to think. He had to raise his voice over the music and the noise.

"No. United States Marshals Service. It's good federal money you're after. Get some of your taxes back."

Jonas lifted his chin towards the TV behind the bar. Long lines snaked out of a bank in a big city.

"Don't suppose I could get that reward in gold bars."

"Oh, this'll pass," Muller said, but he frowned as he did so.

"Pass quicker if they locked up a couple of bankers this time," Jonas countered. His mind was already turning over what little of use he recalled from his brief career in Florida, most often repping for guys like Morena. Was there any case law on criminals claiming rewards for the capture of other criminals? There had to be, surely. Probably hundreds of cases. Guys like Morena might die rather than give up their own, but they'd turn on a rival without a second thought.

Oblivious to Jonas's sudden anguish, Muller went on, his frown deepening, "Ain't like the last time. Back in '08. From what I hear, this was the Russians or maybe the Chinese playing games on the internet."

He lifted his shot glass to the screen, and a small amount slopped over the rim. His hand was shaking.

"So you're serious. About the reward money?" Jonas asked. He had to shout to be heard.

"Hell yes," Muller said, finishing his drink in one swallow and raising two fingers for another round. The barmaid nodded but held up her hand to indicate she'd be a moment fixing his order. Half the town seemed to have crammed into Big Al's, and the serving staff were run ragged trying to keep up with the demand for hot food and cold drinks. Jonas marvelled at the scene, wondering if he was the only one who thought it resembled the frantic revels of the condemned. He'd read a Stalin bio for a history class when he was at college. The only thing that stuck with him from that class was a memory of the orgies of the Russian oligarchs when they knew their doom was near.

He sipped at his ale and pushed the thought away. No doubt a stolid, unimaginative normie like Sheriff Dave would put it down to folks needing some company at the end of a hard day. And it wasn't important. Not like the sudden prospect of twenty-five grand dropping into his lap.

"I've already put the paperwork into the marshal's offices in Seattle," Muller said as his second drink arrived. He had a way of projecting his voice so that Jonas had no trouble hearing him over the crowd. "Just wanted you to know is all. I was mighty grateful today. Got my re-election coming up later this year. Wouldn't have done to let a hoodlum like Morena have the run of the streets. Not with all this going on."

He raised his glass to the TV screen again, where an infographic screamed of massive losses on the stock market. Apple had lost nearly half of its value at the close of trading. Dozens of banks had sought government protection, but the government seemed to be crippled as much by the evacuation of the Executive to 'a secure and secret location' as it was by a massive cyber-attack.

Jonas grunted non-committally.

Twenty-five grand was a hell of a payday. Enough to give him pause in his headlong flight. Certainly enough to get him set up in his new digs when he stopped running. He could buy a computer, a microphone, all sorts of cool shit.

But how was he ever going to collect without getting jammed up for what he'd done back in Seattle?

Jesus!

This was so fucking typical. He finally got a break, and he might've already fucked himself right out of it.

He downed all of his second beer before realising he'd been necking it to cool his mounting fury at the injustice of it all.

He ordered another beer, and remembering Muller, asked if the sheriff wanted a nightcap.

"Nope. Figure tomorrow will be just as bad," he said. "Remember, we'll need a forwarding address if you're taking off again. Do drop by the station, Mister Murdoch."

"No problem," he said. "Call me Jonas. I'll come by before I leave."

But Jonas Murdoch wasn't going anywhere until he figured out how to get his hands on that twenty-five grand without having to answer for any bullshit back in the city.

INTERLUDE

At sixty years old, hawk-faced and rake thin, Sebastian Yuriev did not much look like anybody's idea of a computer hacker. Nor did he present as a 'glue machine tube repairist', the occupation listed on his current identity card.

His name was not Sebastian Yuriev either, but as a former US Defence Secretary once famously observed, you go to war with what you have, and what the Main Directorate of the General Staff of the Armed Forces of the Russian Federation had this morning, was the loyal service of a man calling himself Sebastian Yuriev.

The glue machine repairman, currently known as Yuriev, hastened down Savushkina Street in the exclusive Olgina district of Saint Petersburg, once upon a time a dacha village where the likes of lowly tube repairists might fear to tread. Even though summers had been growing noticeably longer and warmer the last few years, summer in Saint Petersburg was all too short. This morning the weather was glorious and the menace of winter far removed. Yuriev wanted to enjoy the brief pleasure of the sun on his face and a chance to breathe in the sweet fragrance of the rose bushes and the bright white flowers of the wayfaring trees that so beautifully ornamented this block of Savushkina Street. It might be some time before he was able to enjoy them again. Perhaps not until next year. Winter would come, as it always did, and to be honest, that was no bad thing in Yuriev's opinion. The Russian soul, after all, was hard and frozen.

He was early, but it would not do to delay his business for the indulgence of personal comfort. Working for an ostensibly private company known as Glavset or, in Western media reporting, the Internet Research Agency, Sebastian Yuriev had before him the prospect of a great and terrible responsibility. Glavset had come to unfortunate and unwanted prominence as 'the trolls from Olgina' who had interfered in the so-called democratic processes of the West. American presidential contests, British referenda, French and German parliamentary elections, Glavset had done its best to subvert them all. But today, the trolls had another mission.

Yuriev paused for a moment to contemplate the exquisite perfume of a mock cherry tree. He closed his eyes, inhaled deeply, and allowed his thoughts to stray, just momentarily, from duty and service. The two heavyset men trailing him a discrete distance away also stopped and waited for their principal to resume his morning walk.

Yuriev sighed.

He could not abstract himself from the dire necessity of what must come next. He had but a minor role, yet it was vital. Putting aside all indulgence, he turned on his heel and marched the few final steps to the bright yellow dacha converted some years ago to a bespoke data management centre by his engineers. The bodyguards followed. Most of Glavset's thousand-plus employees—most of its trolls, for in truth that's what they were—laboured at their computers another mile further on, at the company's headquarters in a modern, four-storey building of steel and glass. But the two dozen specialists employed here at 198 Savushkina Street were men and women of a different ilk. They were true engineers, and although employed by the Agency, they all held officers' ranks within the reserve military forces of the Russian Federation.

Yuriev did not have to present his thumb to the digital reader embedded in the doorbell of number 198. The blue-painted oak door clicked and swung open as he climbed the front steps. The young, conservatively dressed man who held open the door bowed his head ever so slightly but with apparent deference to the newcomer. His nod to the trailing bodyguards was more perfunctory. They nodded not at all, but they followed their charge into the dacha.

"You are early, General," the young man said. "But everybody is here and awaiting your direction."

He helped Yuriev out of his expensive suit coat, carefully placed it on a wooden hanger and hung the jacket in a hallway cupboard. As he reached up into the closet, his suit jacket fell open to reveal a Makarov pistol in a shoulder holster. Yuriev released his two bodyguards to the kitchen. Like him, they had been up since early morning, and he knew they had not eaten. The men thanked him and excused themselves.

The young man led Yuriev along the main hallway into the suite of offices at the rear of the building. The dacha had been extensively remodelled inside, and they turned left into a large, open space where more than a dozen men and women, most of them decades younger than Yuriev, worked diligently at three long, common tables.

"Attention!" Yuriev's escort shouted. Everyone in the room sprang to their feet and snapped out rigid salutes.

Yuriev straightened his own back and returned the salute.

"Good morning," he said. "It gladdens me to see the finest of the Rodina ready to serve her in this the hour of our peril. Do your duty to the motherland, and she will always remember you."

He nodded, and they sat down with a sound of scraping of chairs and a few scattered mumbles of 'thank you' and 'yes, General.'

They all had work in preparation for the mission.

All except Yuriev.

He had but to wait.

The market in Rezekne, a small Latvian town forty miles from the Russian border, was already busy when Svetlana Bykov pushed her bicycle past old man Degtyarev's turnip stand. He had the best position, as always, the old bastard, and his baskets of dirty, misshapen tubers spilled out into the common paths blocking her way.

"Degtyarev, you fool! I will kick your worthless turnips into the river if you do not move them. They are as shrivelled and useless as the nasty little turnip in your pants!"

"Witch!" Degtyarev shouted back at Svetlana. "You should pray I never let you taste my turnip, you repugnant crone."

But he whipped his nephew, the gormless Rafik, into movement, and the idiot boy created a path for Svetlana into the crowded chaos of the marketplace.

Her bicycle, nearly as old and as creaky as her, was not easy to manoeuvre through the heaving crush of sellers and buyers. A handbag merchant, she had hundreds of pocketbooks, satchels and old leather pouches all bundled up in a giant hessian net, which she balanced precariously on a makeshift wire frame fixed to her bike instead of a seat. Svetlana never rode the bike. There was never anywhere for her to sit.

Her usual place in the market, next to Nazar Bazhenov's salvaged tractor parts carrel, remained unoccupied an hour after the first stall holders had begun to set up. Nobody would dare usurp her claim on the spot. Ruslan Alekseyeva had tried that once, some nine years ago, and still the whole of Rezekne whispered of the grim fate that had befallen his prized flock of long-haired goats.

Svetlana untied her giant collection of old handbags and dragged the load from the back of her bicycle like a fisherman hauling in a giant catch of herring. Bazhenov barked at his mongoloid child Simyan to help her, but she shooed the imbecile away. His help was more trouble than it was worth. She unfolded her dusty, mottled tarpaulin and painstakingly laid out each bag and a dozen pairs of shoes she had acquired cheaply from Tibor, the Armenian over in Griskani. Setting up her display was the slow work of a long hour. There was no guarantee she would sell a thing. It was rare now for the Latvians or the Latgalians to show themselves and their money in the overcrowded labyrinth of the town's Russian market. Unfortunately, they were the only ones who had any money. Rezekne's Russian speakers, stateless ghosts since the break-up of the old Soviet

Union, grubbed along selling old clothes or car parts or patched-up household appliances. They lived in a shadow state.

Not all of them, naturally. Old man Degtyarev was lucky. Everyone needed turnips, and with the weather having grown so much warmer these last few years, the dirty devil had more turnips than one man could hope to eat or even sell in a lifetime. Oh, what wealth he lorded over them, and none of it earned by anything more than dumb luck. The injustice and despair of it was a greater pain to Svetlana than the grievous cramps and spasms in her back as she laid out her wares.

It was a rare day when she went home from the market with more coins in her purse at the close of business.

No Russian Мамка would be so stupid as to loosen her family's purse strings for a bag she did not need, and it was many weeks since any foolish tourist had journeyed all the way from Riga to waste their money on Svetlana's 'genuine Soviet accoutrements'.

She laid out the final pieces of her display, a time-worn female Red Army officer's purse and a genuine medic's bag from the emergency at Chernobyl. Simyan, the mongoloid boy, seeing she was finished, hurried over with the wooden crate on which she daily sat while waiting in vain for custom, and Svetlana lowered herself onto it with a groan of relief. She thanked the boy, of course, for it was only good manners that cost her nothing and might yet offer an improving example to him. She would have to get up again soon enough, lest her legs fall asleep and refuse ever to wake up, but for now, she could rest.

Svetlana Bykov unscrewed the cap of her battered stainless-steel flask and poured out a long, hot measure of steaming black tea. Some of the younger ones, like the idiot child Rafik, whined for cold drinks and sugar water in the summer, but Svetlana knew what all Russians knew: that hot tea was a nigh magical elixir that warmed the body in winter for sure but cooled it too in these increasingly warm and beastly summers by the simple trick of opening the pores to sweat.

She sipped her tea and sat, watching the life of the market around her.

It was a shame, she thought, how things had gone between people here. Rezekne had been a better place for everyone when Russians and Latvians and even the difficult Latgalians had all mucked into together. Now it was the same tired faces, all of them Russian, every day.

She sighed and took the last sip of tea she would ever enjoy.

The huge improvised explosive device that had been hidden in a box of broken carburettors at the back of Nazar Bazhenov's tractor parts stall exploded, and hungry crimson light, searing and strangely silent, enveloped Svetlana, her handbags, and the whole of the world that she knew.

The man known for now as Sebastian Yuriev received notice of the terrorist attack he had ordered a minute after the IED detonated, killing more than two hundred Russian-speaking occupants of the former Soviet republic of Latvia. He did nothing.

Captain Evseyev, the respectful young man who had greeted him at the door of the dacha at 198 Savushkina, brought tea with a slice of lemon and a small heel of black bread with hard sausage. Yuriev reviewed the status of his little task group and waited for his orders.

They arrived an hour after confirmation of the attack on the ethnic Russian enclave in Rezekne and a declaration by the President in Moscow that he had authorised Russian special forces to secure the safety of the town's orthodox Christian minority.

Rezekne was less than half an hour's drive from the western border of the Rodina, but it was a crucial half hour that would put Russian military forces well within the borders of a full member of NATO. Sebastian Yuriev knew that the Main Directorate of the General Staff had determined that America was not likely to speed to the defense of Latvia. It had been unlikely to do so for a number of years, and now that the failing superpower was assailed by enemies both known and unknown, the chances of Washington honouring its treaty obligations were judged even less likely.

Yuriev knew this because he had sat on the very committee of the General Staff which had made that determination. His orders now arrived by safe hands, a courier from the chairman of that committee, General Anatoly Yefremov.

Sitting in his private office, a small annexe of the main room at the rear of the dacha, Yuriev heard the courier by motorcycle. He listened for the crunch of heavy boots on the stone steps and the urgent knock on the solid oaken doors.

Captain Evseyev was courteous but quiet in answering the knock and did not converse with the courier. He took a small, somewhat crumpled envelope, sealed with wax and stamped with the famous star of the Red Army, and hurried it through to Yuriev, who opened it.

A note with a single word lay nestled inside.

Yuriev teased out the piece of paper and read his instructions.

PROCEED.

He filed the paper away in the envelope. It would be worth something one day, he was sure. He did not take a final sip of his tea or delay in any way for a single moment in doing his duty.

Sebastian Yuriev, executive vice president of Glavset, but always and forever a general of the army of the Russian Federation, marched out of his office and into the control room where his systems engineers and operators awaited their orders.

He did not disappoint them.

"Operation Molodi is commenced," he said. "The Rodina demands that we do our duty."

This time, nobody came to attention. A chorus of voices bellowed, "Yes, sir!" Everybody went immediately to their workstations and began typing furiously.

Yuriev watched for a few moments but eventually returned to his small personal space.

It was odd, this new form of so-called hybrid warfare, he thought.

So quiet and even banal on the surface, but with a few words he had unleashed upon western Europe a cyber-storm to make the attack on America seem a schoolboy's prank.

Nobody from the degenerate West would be coming to the aid of Latvia now.

23

FOUR LARGE BY MIDNIGHT

W ar is always ironic in ways big and small. Some of the ironies that attended the attack on America and her allies were obvious. General Chu Jianguo thought it only fitting that the critical strike, which would save the Chinese people from starvation, would expose and possibly even doom many in the United States to the same fate. That was a great and terrible irony, in his opinion. The use of the American-developed Stuxnet program to destroy the enemy's food distribution network was a lesser irony but just as proper in its way.

One of the arbitrary and unremarked coincidences of Chu's master plan, one of which he remained unaware, even at the end, connected the fate of a software engineer at a booming Californian FinTech start-up to a semi-retired mining executive who had gone into the food business in the hipster village of Temsescal, San Francisco.

Just as General Chu's team of militarised programmers could not provide for its own physical security, instead having to call on the services of a naval special forces group, Unit 61398 had no capacity to work on the ground in enemy territory. For that, they called on the services of Bureau 13 of the Ministry of State Security. In this instance, the Bureau provided a deep cover agent who had been placed inside the US college system some eight years earlier. The agent, since graduated with first-class honours and employed in America's civilian tech sector, was activated when General Chu convinced his counterpart at 13 of the strategic leverage which could be effected at just the right moment by one very talented, trusted engineer sitting at the right screen in a California-based financial technology company.

Twenty-six hours before James O'Donnell realised something was wrong with Texaco's payment processing architecture, the Bureau 13 agent, known to his colleagues as Benny Wong, received his activation code via Instagram: a picture of the village in which he had been born in the province of Ningxia. Another picture followed thirty minutes later: a broken wooden tablet engraved with characters in Gwoyeu Romatzyh, the Romanised lettering system used in pre-Communist China. Decoding the inscription by way of a key he had memorised many years ago, Benny unpacked a web address to a one-time downloadable file, which he read on his phone while sitting in the chill-out zone at the headquarters of The Scratch App, eating a breakfast burrito.

He almost vomited when he saw what they had ordered him to do.

His queasiness did not deflect him from the path, however. Benny Wong was a patriot, and he had prepared for this moment all of his adult life. He returned to his desk, downloaded the code he needed from the address he'd been given on GitHub, and used his executive-level access privileges to inject the new programming into the app, which had made his employer one of the hottest, fastest-growing FinTechs in the US. Benny had stock in the company, due to vest in six months. He knew that in following his orders, he was destroying more than two million dollars worth of personal equity.

The new code pulsed out to millions of subscribers over the following day.

When Benny received another Instagram pic of the village in Ningxia, he opened his laptop, tapped a few lines of instructions into a program written by the very best code warriors of Unit 61398, and with a slightly trembling hand, he hit ENTER.

What happened next was very complicated in its technical details but devastatingly simple in effect. Tens of billions of dollars disappeared from the accounts of The Scratch App's millions of subscribers.

Benny, who everyone said had been looking off-colour for a day or so, left the office early. He had a booking for lunch with two colleagues at a restaurant called Fourth Edition, about ten minute's walk from the Scratch app HQ.

He did not make the lunch.

DAMIEN MALONEY DID NOT GET the fake news alerts that stopped James O'Donnell in his tracks two and a half thousand miles to the east. He routinely kept most of the notifications on his phone turned off, save for three exceptions: text messages and calls from his chef, Ellie Jabbarah; phone calls and iMessages from his mother in Broken Hill and his son in LA (but not you will note, from his ex-wife, who was also in LA); and alerts from Scratch, his financial management app. This last piece of software, used by three and a half million other subscribers, almost all of them high-wealth individuals like Damo, had access to all of his personal and company accounts and had been invaluable during a tax audit last financial year. The company behind the Scratch app had also been targeted for penetration by Unit 61398, working closely with Bureau 13 of the Ministry of State Security.

This made Damo an unlucky but by no means unique two-time loser on the first day of the first and last war fought in cyberspace.

"What the fuck?" he muttered as his phone buzzed and the screen lit up with an alert from the Scratch app that he had insufficient funds in any of his accounts to cover a recurring subscription to Bob Parker's private newsletter. The wine writer charged ten dollars a month for a subscription to his weekly bailout.

Damo, who'd retired three years earlier from his first career as a broker specialising in coal and natural gas, had a lot more than ten bucks sitting in his various accounts. He was worth a little over two hundred and thirty million dollars, and he'd opened *Fourth Edition* as a hobby. He got his first job in the mining industry as a camp cook on the gold fields of Western Australia, and it pleased him greatly to now fashion himself as the executive chef of one of the best restaurants in America. Knowing the abysmal truth of his culinary skills, this deeply amused Ellie Jabbarah, where it might offend and even infuriate other culinary professionals.

"Fuck me purple. What now?" Damo said as everyone moved back into the restaurant to salvage what they could of the day.

Ellie had already returned to the kitchen, insisting that Jody and Karl stay and have something to eat and drink in the cool. Jody wanted more than anything to get back in the car and drive straight over to Chad's place to pick up Maxy, but Ellie, Karl and old Sandino combined to forestall that choice.

"Miss Jody, you are hurt badly and very confused with it," Sandino said. "I will make you chicken soup, yes, and pour you and your friend a glass of prosecco, and you will get better before you go anywhere, no?"

It was not really a question.

"I like chicken soup," Karl confirmed. "But I don't know about that other thing."

They were almost inside when Jody heard Damo swearing again.

He kept his voice low at first, but he spoke with such intensity that he drew her attention to him. His jaw muscles bunched and his lips barely moved, but he was holding his phone so tightly that his fingers turned white as he stabbed a number into the screen.

Nick Perriam, the lawyer, was frowning at the screen of his phone, too.

"Nick!" Damo growled. "I think these cunts have frozen my bank accounts."

"It's not just you, Mister Maloney," Nick said. His voice was strangely thin. "And I don't think it's the government this time. It's not ICE or Treasury and the accounts aren't frozen. They're... empty."

Jody was sick with the heat of the sun and the stress of the morning. She just wanted to get into a cool, air-conditioned car, drive as fast as the traffic would allow, and gather up her son. She wanted to get her little boy home and close the doors on the world and this terrible day. She could pick up her camera gear later, unless of course...

Shit. Would the cops want to keep it as evidence?

Car horns blared out on Telegraph Avenue and sirens started up somewhere in the distance, but she couldn't say whether that was the police or not. She might have tipped over another emotional cliff at that point, obsessing about her cameras. That equipment was her livelihood and she needed it.

Just like she'd needed that photoshoot job today.

But Jody Sarjanen angrily shook her head. That hurt like hell, but it also chased off the self-pity that wanted to take hold. She had to be here for Ellie and Max.

And maybe for Damo, too, by the look of him.

The restaurant owner had closed up like the fist of an angry giant. He was stalking through the front doors of *Fourth Edition*, barking questions, orders and Australian profanities into his phone.

"What do you fucking mean there's no money?" he shouted at whoever was on the other end of the call. "Are you telling me you lost it? You gave it away? You wiped your arse with it or what?"

For no reason she could put her finger on, nausea slowly filled all of Jody's hollow spaces.

Nick, the lawyer, was having a phone conversation of his own. Quieter than Damo's, but just as intense in its way. He did not look cool and self-assured anymore. He looked like a man whose doctor just gave him some awful test results.

"What's going on?" Karl asked. He was looking around the interior of the restaurant, marvelling at the expensive fit-out.

"I don't know," she said.

Jody and Karl stood helplessly in the cool reception area at the front of the restaurant, waiting for either Damo or Nick to let them know what was happening. The other staff had all hurried away to the kitchen where Ellie was yelling orders and almost as many swear words as Damo. Jody heard the sound of breaking glass outside— something big like a window smashed by a rock, not just a bottle dropped on the pavement—but she wasn't sure where. The blaring din of car horns seemed to be getting louder, and she saw through the dark-tinted glass of the foyer that two drivers had jumped out of the vehicles right in front of the restaurant and were advancing on each other with fists raised.

What the hell was up with people today?

Nick finished his phone call quietly, cut the connection and put the handset away in the breast pocket of his suit. He was sweating now, red-faced, but he waited for Damien Maloney to finish up. Damo did so by smashing his iPhone – one of the new, super-expensive models – into the heavy granite reception desk where diners checked in for the reservations. It shattered in his hand.

"Fuck!" he shouted.

Jody flinched.

Outside on the street, the two men who'd climbed out of their vehicles to shout at each other were now trading blows.

Damo pulled his lawyer aside and they conferred in private for a minute.

"I think something else has gone wrong," Jody said softly to Karl.

"Reckon so," he nodded, watching the fight out on the main road. A big Italian-looking feller and a more diminutive Chinese guy. The Chinaman was fast and seemed to know all sorts of moves, but the Italian was a brawler and had a lot of mass to absorb all the kicks and punches.

Damo looked very worried when he re-joined them with Perriam at his elbow.

"Look, I dunno what's going on today, Jodes," he said, "but I gotta get to my bank. Can you tell Ellie I had to fuck off? I'll call her later. Tell her to forget about opening today at all. Just clean up and close for now. Can you tell her that, darlin'?"

"Sure," she said. "Is everything all right? I mean, with you guys?"

Nick Perriam shook his head.

"It's just this app," he said cryptically. "It's... I dunno. It's just bad data or something."

"Fuckin' hope so," Damo said. "Or else you're going to be suing those arse-clowns at Scratch and fuckin' Chase Morgan, too."

"You got that right," Nick Perriam agreed.

. . .

KARL VALENTINE DID NOT CARE much for prosecco when he found out
it was Italian champagne. He very much liked Sandino's chicken
soup, however, and the Italian beer they fetched up for him from the
kitchen was pronounced more than agreeable. Jody had two glasses
of the bubbly wine, which went straight to her head. Karl insisted it
would not be a good idea to have any more in her condition, and she
was happy to do as he suggested.

Ellie and her crew spent another two hours cleaning up and shut-
ting down for the day. Before they left, Damo rang the front desk
from his bank and Jody answered it, a little tipsy.

"Fourth Edition," she said.

"Jodes, is that you? It's Damo. Is your girlfriend there, mate?"

"She's in the kitchen, Damo," Jody said. "Do you want me to get
her?"

"No, mate. She'll be busy. Can you tell her to pay everyone in cash
from the safe? She'll know what to do. But make sure she knows. Are
you feeling better? You gonna remember that?"

"I'm good, Damo," Jody said. "Cash from the safe."

"Yeah, all of it," Damo said. "Just tell her to top everyone up.
Herself included. Don't leave anything behind, all right? You got that?"

Jody was pretty sure she had it but repeated the instructions back
to him just in case. She was still finding it hard to concentrate.

"Do it now, mate," Damo said. "And tell Ellie that I'll see her at
your place later tonight. Tell her it's important."

"Okay, Damo," Jody said. "I will."

She wanted to ask him if he found his money, but she was too
scared. Instead, she said goodbye and hung up.

Karl was mopping up the last puddles of chicken soup with a
fresh bread roll.

"Can you drive us again later, Karl?" Jody asked as she headed
toward the kitchen.

"Sure," he said. "Only had the one beer. But won't Ellie want to
drive you home?"

Jody stopped. It was awkward, what she had to say, but there was no avoiding it.

"We have to see my ex-husband," she said. "And he doesn't like her. And he's like this angry weightlifter and…"

She trailed off and Karl waved off her concerns with the last of his bread roll.

"Don't you worry none, Miss Jody," he said. "Like I said, I'd be happy to."

Jody beamed.

She was starting to feel better for the first time since she'd been attacked.

What a freaky day.

She went through to the kitchen to pass on Damo's message. Everyone in there was talking about the Chinese attacking Pearl Harbour, which was super weird. Jody was pretty sure it was the Japanese who'd done that.

ONE OF THE two men who got into a fistfight in front of Damien Moloney's restaurant was Tommy 'The Tripod' Podesta, a debt collector for the Milano organised crime family; a family business, it must be admitted, that had fallen on hard times since Jimmy 'The Weasel' Fratianno had flipped on the LA mob all the way back in the late 1970s.

These days, the mob was strictly about the small-time rackets. A bit of loan sharking, some hookers, and money laundering. Lots of money laundering for their bigger and much better-resourced cousins over the state line in Nevada. Tommy Podesta, who was not even a made guy, struggled to pay his rent most weeks. The cash he had from collecting debts for Paulie 'the Mooch' Milano wasn't nothing. If he'd been careful with his outgoings, he could've made his rent, his alimony, and his kids' murderous fucking school fees.

But Tommy 'The Tripod' Podesta was not careful.

The Tripod was the sort of guy more likely to drop every fucking dollar he had on a 300-1 shot at the track out at Los Alamitos than he was to be careful about his fuckin' outgoings.

Thus it was that a two hundred and forty pound, broke-ass, clinically depressed but violently anti-social, third-rate standover man was trapped in his shitty, rusted-out Camaro in gridlocked traffic in front of Damien Maloney's Temescal restaurant on the morning that General Chu ordered Unit 61398 into battle.

Being a guy who was deeply invested in the cash economy, the Tripod was not much affected by the opening salvos of the cyber war between his country and the Middle Kingdom.

But he was affected—he was fucking homicidally enraged, to be perfectly honest about it—when some slanty-eyed gimp in a Nissan Leaf ran right up his ass while he was trapped in the motionless hell of this monster fucking traffic jam. That was bad enough. But while thus trapped, the Tripod had not been wasting his time. He had been busily, and somewhat desperately, trying to nut out a way to explain to Paulie Milano how the four grand he was supposed to be bringing back from San Francisco had literally disappeared while in the strictly temporary possession of licensed bookmakers out at Golden Gate Fields.

He had won, for once. That was the hell of it.

Tommy had chanced a few dollars...okay, four thousand of them... on Dufflecoat Supreme, a six-to-one prospect at the Golden Gate. And he had fucking won. Twenty-four fucking grand.

His horse had come in — about a minute before the stewards had shut down all business at the track for the duration because of a problem in the computerised tabulating computers or some shit.

Tommy had won, and they hadn't paid him because their fucking computer was on the fritz.

Oh, they promised to honour his ticket once everything was sorted out, but that could take days, and he had to be back in LA with Paulie's four large by midnight.

Was Paulie likely to buy this story?

No. This was the sort of story that got a guy buried in the desert halfway to Vegas.

The Tripod sat in his overheating Camaro and despaired. He was nothing but a degenerate fucking bum who couldn't be trusted not to fuck himself in the ass first and every chance he got. Deep down, he knew it.

A six-to-one payday, and before he even leaves the track, he gets rolled by fucking computer gremlins?

So, you can see why Tommy Podesta got out of his Camaro, ready to throw down, when some rice-eating asshole banged into his rear fender, interrupting the flow of his thoughts.

Even worse, the little Chinese faggot gets out of the Leaf and starts yelling at him, for fucks sake. At the Tripod! Like all of this was his fault. The guy obviously had some issues in his life.

That's when the Tripod gives him a slap for his disrespect, and you wouldn't fucking believe it, but this diminutive fucking hero squares up with all this Kung Fu and shit.

Well, at that point, Tommy Podesta has had enough. He straight up hauls off and punches this guy in the face, and the guy falls down and cracks his head on the gutter.

Is that Tommy Podesta's fault?

Seriously, is it?

Nobody can say, and it doesn't really matter. Because the man Tommy Podesta knocked down and killed in a traffic jam outside of Fourth Edition was not the first or the last to die in the city that day.

But he was an agent of Bureau 13 of China's Ministry of State Security. His colleagues knew him as Benny Wong.

Benny never did get to lunch.

24

POWER DOWN IN CRAZY TOWN

M el Baker lived in a townhouse complex that had been fashionable a few minutes before hyper-colour t-shirts took over as the new hotness. The mock Melrose Place bungalows sat back off the shoulder of State Route 112 through Darnestown, maybe ten- or fifteen minutes drive from Rick's place, depending on traffic. They weren't set all that far back from the road, though, and a thin line of dying Sycamores didn't do much these days to screen out the noise of passing cars and trucks. Still, her small one-room studio was cheap because it overlooked the driveway, and at night, as cars rolled into the parking garage downstairs, the head-lamps speared into her apartment. The walls were thin, and it sounded at times as though she was trying to sleep in a 24-hour parking garage. It was not a great place to live, but it had been better than staying with her ex-husband.

She expected to find the block quiet and deserted when she returned. The odd hours Mel worked, she was used to coming and going day and night. Mid-morning was always a dead zone, with almost everyone else in the townhouse complex away at work. Not this morning, however. She pulled her pickup into the driveway, meaning to take one of the two visitor parking slots. Her little studio didn't rate a space of its own, another inconvenience that made it affordable. Surprised to find both of the visitor bays occupied, she had to reverse back out onto the main drag. The kerbside parking was also tight, with half a dozen vehicles stacked on the side of the road as though nobody had gone to work this morning. Mel finally found a space to pull into around the corner, wondering what the hell was going on. Walking back to the main entrance, she could hear radios and the sound of arguments. That was odd. Most people kept their places buttoned pretty tight and ran the AC through summer. The traffic noise really was hard to take otherwise. Walking down the driveway, she saw most of her neighbours had their doors and windows open, letting in the hot air and car fumes.

Crazytown.

"Power's out, Mel."

She stopped and craned her head back, shading her eyes against the fierce late morning sun. As she feared, it was Mrs Comino up on the third floor.

Bugger.

She totally didn't want to be taken as a conversational hostage this morning, and Marie Comino was one of those old jabbertooth tigers who latched on and never let go.

"In a hurry, Marie," she shouted back. "Sorry! Late for work."

Doubling her pace across the baking concrete of the driveway, Mel put her head down and almost ran into the doublewide figure of George Neary emerging from the stairwell up to the first floor. Neary, a retired Coast Guard veteran, rarely got his arse out of the armchair he'd parked in front of *Fox News* about ten years ago, not even to answer the door for UberEATS. He left his door unlatched and tipped a little extra to have his Wendy's and Chik-fil-A delivered right to his lap. Marie Comino said he had a loaded handgun in one of the TV remote holsters hanging from the arm of his recliner, just in case somebody other than his food guy came through the door.

George had always been pleasant enough the few times Mel had run into him, but he looked angry and fit to burst when he came stomping out of the shadows of the stairwell.

"Goddamn cable's out!"

"What?"

"Cable's out," he barked as though to an idiot. "Power, too. But the cable went first. I saw it. And now this piece a crap too."

He held up his cell phone, looking as though he might throw it across the street.

"Sorry," Mel said, performing a rather neat *irime senkai* as she slipped past him and tossed the apology back over her shoulder. It was cooler in the darkened stairwell. Still hot, of course, but nothing like the open furnace out in the car lot.

God.

She just wanted to get out of here and back to Rick. Part of her, a large part actually, wanted to get out of here and never, ever come back. But she was pretty sure her new boyfriend would run halfway across the continent if she tried to move in with him just an hour or two after they'd first bonked.

Boyfriend?

Was he?

She paused, ever so briefly, on the first stairwell landing and considered it.

Yes, Mel decided. He probably was. They knew each other very well after all of those training sessions he'd helped her with at Bretton Woods. It wasn't like they'd met in some bar, got drunk, and bumped uglies.

God. Was it?

No. Mel scolded herself for second-guessing her thoughts and feelings. She knew her own mind. Always had. That's what'd given her the strength to leave Gary. And she knew in both heart and mind that Rick could be good for her and she for him. Resuming her climb up the stairs, she turned left on the first floor and started searching for her keys.

The door to Mister Gilmartin's place, the one next to hers, was open like so many others in the complex. Henry Gilmartin lay face down on the bare wooden boards of the short entry hall. A small white dog, his Maltese terrier Frankie, trembled and whined near his head. It started barking when Mel passed by. She had been so intent on getting her stuff and pissing off as quickly as possible that she hadn't noticed poor old Henry collapsed on the floor.

"Shit," she said when she saw him, hesitating for the briefest moment before her years of training and experience as a London copper kicked in. She rushed into the apartment, shooing Frankie away when he started yapping and barking in protest or perhaps in excited relief. His little claws skittered on the floorboards as he darted forward to lick Mister Gilmartin's ear.

The man groaned, and Mel felt the smallest measure of relief. He wasn't dead yet.

The heat was stifling inside the townhouse, and his face was dry and a bright shade of red. His breathing was rapid and noisy, his pulse racing.

Heat exhaustion.

She'd seen a surprising number of cases in London as the summers grew longer and hotter, especially in the council towers where old folk were bottled up in small, airless flats. Mel reached for her phone, suspecting it would be useless, and finding that George Neary spoke true. Cell reception was down. She had a quick look for a landline in Gilmartin's kitchenette but found nothing. She plugged the small sink, threw in a couple of tea towels and pulled open the refrigerator door, looking for ice water. If she tried to use the cold-water faucet, it would doubtless run hot from the pipes. The power was down, as Neary had complained, and there was only half a pint of cold water in the fridge, stored in an old Coke bottle. Mel tipped it out over the towels, soaking them while she searched the small freezer compartment. She had better luck there.

Gilmartin groaned, and Frankie whimpered as Mel pulled out a packet of frozen peas, now half defrosted, and a tray of ice cubes – mostly melted. The ice cubes went into the sink. She knelt in the narrow hallway, pushing Frankie away as she quickly undid Gilmartin's belt and fly buttons.

For a mad half-second, she flashed back to her morning with Rick, to the rush they'd been in to get all their clothes off.

This wasn't that.

Mel almost tumbled over when she unbalanced, tugging down

Gilmartin's threadbare brown corduroys. His underpants went next, exposing grey pubic hairs and wrinkled, flabby genitals. Her face ashen and lips pressed firmly together, she quickly jammed the frozen peas into his groin. Gilmartin gasped.

A voice cried out behind her.

"Oh my word, what are you doing?"

It was the jabbertooth tiger.

"He's dying!" Mel shouted at Mrs Comino. "Heat exhaustion. I need towels and cold water. Bring me anything you've got. Check the other neighbours, too. Go! Hurry!"

For once, words failed Marie Comino, but action did not. She disappeared, crying out to the complex, "Help, someone. Henry is dying. Help."

Working quickly, Mel retrieved the three cold, wet tea towels from the sink. Two of them she packed into Gilmartin's armpits, the third she used to pat down his head, checking the pulse in his throat as she did so. It seemed a little less volcanic, a little less as though his heart might explode out through his ribcage, but she couldn't be sure. Frankie yipped, skittered and turned in tight little circles on the wooden floor, his tiny paws finding no purchase and frequently slipping out from underneath him. Mel returned twice to the diminishing store of cold water and rapidly melting ice cubes in the sink before Marie Comino came back with two jugs of cold water and fresh towels, with George Neary bringing up the rear.

"Water in the sink," Mel ordered, and Marie hurried to comply.

Neary took up so much space he had to turn slightly sideways in the harrow entry hall, but he moved with purpose and surety, and he was carrying a first aid kit. He placed it on the kitchenette's breakfast bench as he squeezed past and motioned for Mel to give him some space.

She did.

He had all those years of service in the Coastguard, and he was friendly with Gilmartin. They liked to get together and complain about 'young people these days'. Neary gave him the same once-over that Mel had performed, checking all of his vital signs. His expression was grim, but he kept muttering, "Good, good work."

Marie Comino appeared behind Neary with a placemat, which she used to fan them all.

"Thanks," Mel said.

"You get a heart rate?" Neary asked.

"No," Mel confessed. "I took his pulse, which was running wild, but I wanted to get him cooled. I didn't do a proper count."

"I had him at 134 bpm," Neary said. "We'll get him turned over. Recovery position, and we'll recheck it."

George had to move his considerable bulk back to create enough room to manoeuvre Gilmartin onto his side, with arms and legs crossed to stabilise the position. Squatting at Gilmartin's head, Mel made sure his mouth was pointed down so that any vomit or bile could drain but that his chin was up to keep the epiglottis clear. Marie ran to and from the sink to deliver cold, wet towels.

"One thirteen," Neary announced, measuring Henry's pulse against the old steel wristwatch he wore. "I think he's gonna pull through, but we gotta get him to the ER."

"An ambulance?" Mel suggested.

"I tried," Neary said. "No cell cover. And my landline is down, too. We'll have to drive him ourselves."

Mel cursed inwardly. She had a couple of hours before she was supposed to hook up with Rick again, but this looked like it was going to knock her well off course. If the phones were down, she had no way of contacting him.

Nothing for it, though. The poor old man needed more care than they could give him. Even getting him into the chilled air of a hospital, which would surely have a backup power supply, would help.

"I can drive him," she said, "but my truck's pretty basic."

"I don't have a vehicle," Neary said. It sounded like a confession.

Mel knew that Marie Comino didn't either. She'd had to drive her to the grocery store and the pharmacy more than once.

"All right," she said, accepting the inevitable. "My pick-up can sit three across if you can come with us and look after him while I drive."

George Neary nodded.

"I can do that. Cable's out."

THE HOSPITAL WAS A SHIT SHOW. Traffic was gridlocked in the surrounding streets, and Mel only got through the snarl by mounting the kerb and driving over a line of orange cones meant to secure a break in the fence line around the Holy Cross hospital.

"What the bloody hell is all this?" she asked, mostly just thinking out loud.

"They'd have a lotta traffic accidents because of all the lights being out," Neary answered. "And heat stress. Like Hank." He had one big, meaty arm around Henry Gilmartin's shoulders, like a drunken friend he was nursing home from a big night out. Mister Gilmartin drifted in and out of consciousness but never made it to complete lucidity.

"You just hold on there, Hank," Neary said when it sounded like Gilmartin was protesting weakly. "You've had a hard fall, buddy. Miss Baker is driving you to the Holy Cross in Germantown. You're gonna be fine. You hold on."

He had to hold on for more than an hour.

The hospital had backup power, but the computers had glitched out. Admitting Gilmartin meant fighting through a crowded ER and straight-up bullshitting the admissions nurse about his health insurance. Or at least Mel thought Neary was bullshitting her. She found the American health system almost impossible to understand. The few times she'd brushed up against it, it had given her a powerful longing to flee home into the waiting arms of Britain's moribund and decaying National Health Service.

Ninety minutes after they'd parked in a no-parking zone and carried Gilmartin through the sliding doors of the Holy Cross ER, he disappeared around a corner on a trolley with a nurse hooking up an IV line to his arm and a doctor hurrying alongside, making notes on an old-fashioned clipboard.

Mel checked her phone.

No service. Neary saw her peeking at the screen.

"You should go if you got somewhere to be," he said. "I'm gonna stay and wait on Henry. They got cool air and television here. More than I got at home."

He held out one giant paw, and Mel took it, her small brown hand disappearing inside Neary's enormous and calloused but surprisingly gentle grip. The heaving crowd parted and swirled around them, thanks mainly to Neary, who was big enough to break up the surging tides of hot, angry people.

"That was a good thing you did for Henry, Miss Baker," he said over the racket. "You used to be a cop, right? Back home?"

"In London," she said.

He nodded as though pleased to be proven right.

"Well, this is a helluva mess," Neary grumbled. "Worse than that business yesterday by a long mile. Guess I don't need to tell you to look out for yourself. People go crazy when the power goes down."

"Thanks. I'll be fine," she said, letting his hand go. "I was heading out of town anyway. Upstate...with my boyfriend."

She hesitated ever so slightly before calling Rick that, but Neary didn't seem to notice.

"Nice," he smiled. "And smart." He swept a hand around to take in the chaos of the ER. "Looks like it might be worth hunkering down a while in a nice cabin somewhere. I'd pack an extra big picnic basket if I was you."

She returned his smile, feeling a little ashamed that she had always written him off as the angry old white man who watched too much Fox News. He seemed perfectly lovely once you got to know him, and he'd been a godsend with Henry Gilmartin. They said their goodbyes, and Mel headed for the exit.

She checked her watch and cursed.

She was already running two hours late, and she had no way of contacting Rick.

RICK WAS an hour in session with Doctor Cairns. Nomi too, of course. The first thirty minutes, he unloaded all of the shit he couldn't possibly dump on somebody else, especially not Mel. Not if he wanted her to stick. For another twenty minutes, the two men discussed specific actions Rick could take to deal with his feelings of powerlessness and the occasional terror it inspired. Cairns was a good counsellor. Probably because he'd done two tours of the sandbox as a corpsman, way back in '03 and '04, before spending his GI benefits on med school tuition, Rick could talk to him as a fellow combat vet, not just a headshrinker. For the final ten minutes, they discussed Nomi and the support dog program, all while the black Labrador happily wagged her tail at his feet, fully aware that she was the subject of their conversation. Cairns' office was quiet and enjoyed a view over the gardens that was only slightly marred by the intrusion of a staff parking lot. As always, Rick Boreham left the session feeling like a heavy pack had been quietly lifted from his shoulders while he sat and talked with the psychiatrist.

Outside of Cairns' office, everything had gone sideways.

"What's going on?" Cairns asked as Rick paused at the door.

The hallway leading back to Combat Stress Recovery was eerily dark, and Rick wondered if he'd somehow lost track of time until he realised that half the lights were off.

"Not sure," Rick said. "Looks like a brownout or something."

Cairns came up behind him and stuck his head out into the corridor.

"Hmm? That's weird. I'd say we're running the genny. You're my last appointment this morning, Rick. I'll come with you. See what's what."

The two men and the dog walked through the CSRC, which was even quieter than before because it was empty. The Combat Stress Recovery Clinic had never been empty on any of Rick's previous visits. This wing of the facility was always hushed. Tranquillised rather than tranquil, Rick thought, but now it was wholly empty. Even the ghosts had fled.

They could hear voices in the distance, however, and found a heavy crush of visitors and staff in the general admissions area where Rick had earlier seen the old guy in the Iwo Jima hat. Neither the vet nor his young carer were still there, but more than a hundred people were jostling for position around a single television suspended from the ceiling. Somebody turned the volume up just as Rick and Doctor Cairns came in, allowing them to hear news of the attack on US Naval facilities over the growing ferment of the gathered onlookers.

"... Casualties are said to be light, but damage to ships and aircraft is extensive according to reports from the scene..."

The room stirred, and the ruckus rose to drown out whatever the news anchor said next. Nomi pushed her head into Rick's side, sensing his anxiety. Doctor Cairns placed a hand on his shoulder and squeezed.

"It's a long way from here, Rick. And not your concern anymore. You've done your part. Now breathe."

As if responding to an actor's cue, Rick performed the breathing exercise Cairns had taught him when they first met. It helped. But he was the only one in the room who calmed down. People started shouting for everyone to shut up so they could hear the news. The screen cut to vision of what looked like a riot at the White House, or maybe a rout, with Marine One taking off from the lawn and popping countermeasures as it went.

"Holy shit," Rick muttered. "That's not good."

The crowd of vets only got rowdier, and he felt Cairns tugging at his elbow.

"Come on, let's go."

Rick allowed himself to be led back into the VA facility, where the shrink led him two floors down in a stairwell marked 'Staff Only'. They emerged in the parking garage. It was just as crowded as earlier, but now everyone was trying to get out rather than in.

"Can't help with the traffic, Rick," Cairns said apologetically. "But you'll get home sooner if you go now. You look after him, girl," he added for Nomi's sake, giving her a quick pat and a scratch behind the ear, which she took as being entirely her due.

"Thanks, Doc," Rick said uncertainly. "What are you gonna do?"

"Go back to work, I guess," he shrugged. "I can see my schedule filling up fast."

They shook hands, and Cairns told him again to go home and chill out.

"Don't watch the news. Don't be checking Facebook or anything.

See if that new girlfriend of yours wants to binge-watch Netflix."

Rick tried to smile, but he was already worrying about Mel.

It took him fifteen minutes to clear the underground car lot, and as soon as they made the open road, he checked his phone.

He had one bar of AT&T, and that dropped out as soon as he tried to call her.

Damn.

Rick stopped himself reaching for the button to turn on the radio.

Cairns was right. There was nothing to be gained by plugging into rolling news coverage of whatever had happened or was happening right now. It would only aggravate him and fuel his anxiety, which had come roaring back.

Instead, he popped a CD in the player—his truck was that old—and let Kenny Wayne Shepherd soothe his ragged nerves. Thunderheads were slowly piling up on the horizon, big purple suckers tinged with green, but the sky above the road was still a hard cerulean blue. He tried calling Mel again.

No luck.

"Okay, girl," he said to Nomi, who sat in her harness on the passenger seat up front next to him. She panted happily as the black ribbon spooled beneath their wheels. "The doc is right. Right? This changes nothing. There's always some shit in the news, and it's never good. That's what makes it the news. I say we grab Melissa and get us some quiet time by a lake somewhere. That sound good to you?"

She seemed to smile wider.

"Me too, then. Let's go."

He fed some boot leather to the accelerator, hoping to get ahead of the storm.

He had Mel's address in his phone and written down in the notebook he carried with him because his memory had not always been reliable after getting mortared in Anbar province. He would drive to Mel's place. Pick her up as arranged. And if the traffic meant driving to the lake without stopping at home to grab his bags, then so be it. He would bathe in the lake and get around the cabin buck-naked.

It was warm enough, and after this morning, he didn't think Mel would object.

25

A KILLING IN THE OUTER MISSION

"All of it?" Ellie asked. "No fucking way."

"I think so," Jody said, and it felt strangely like a confession.

Karl was driving. He wore his baseball cap and his zip-up jacket. Ellie insisted Jody sit up front next to him. Her neck and back were so sore she could barely turn around to talk with her girlfriend in the back of the Honda, and when she did, Ellie waved at her to turn back and face forward. Ellie had climbed in behind Karl on the driver's side to let Jody push her seat all the way back.

"It sounded like the bank lost their money," Jody explained.

"Sounds like the banks lost everyone's money," Karl put in. Late afternoon traffic on Alemany was slow, but at least it was moving, unlike the solid ribbon of rubber and steel seized up both ways on the 280. Karl had no trouble turning his head to address Ellie. At that moment, they were stopped outside the Shell on the corner of Alemany and Geneva. They hadn't moved in three minutes.

Still better than the 280, though.

"Maybe we should pull in and get some gas," Jody said. Her thoughts had been flitting around like that, like the path of a butterfly through an open field, except that rather than dancing from buttercup to daffodil, her imagination ran from a violent rape in some metalhead's torture basement to wild, runaway fears of Chad driving off with Maxy and disappearing forever.

"I'm gonna call Damo," Ellie said. "You might be right about gas. We've been stuck in this traffic for three hours. We're gonna empty the tank just running the AC."

"On it," Karl said, and without waiting for further instructions, he pulled the wheel over and eased them out of the near-frozen traffic and onto the tarmac of the filling station. "Er, how will I pay?" he asked as they pulled up at the pump, but Ellie had already passed a twenty-dollar note over the back of the driver's seat. She also ignored all of the warning signs about using cell phones while fuelling up, and Karl said nothing about it.

Karl was a professional driver, Jody thought. If Karl thinks it's okay to use the phone here, it must be. And then her butterfly mind lit on the giant red and yellow logo for Shell, and she remembered the time they had taken Maxy hunting for seashells at the beach, and she imagined Chad walking into the ocean with Max and walking and...

"Jodes! You good?"

It was Ellie. She was back, and they were moving, but not towards Alemany Boulevard.

"Got a break on Geneva," Karl explained cryptically. "We can get through to your ex and your little boy quicker this way. I don't trust the GPS. Reckon the Chinese or the Russians put a big spoon in and gave it a stir. They been giving plenty of things a touch-up, it seems."

It was scary, Jody thought. All of this craziness. And now people were talking about war. She'd started the day with a nice photographic job to do and Max to look forward to when he came back from his visit to Chad. And now? Everything had turned to shit.

They proceeded down Geneva Avenue at a walking pace, and Jody stared at all the people out on the street. It was still ferociously hot outside. That's why they were running the air in the car so cold, and even so, it was struggling with the three of them in there. It was lucky she'd met Karl, she thought because she couldn't drive after...

"Shit."

Jody Sarjanen cursed herself for being so weak-minded. She couldn't hold a thought for more than a second. Maybe she shouldn't have had those bubbly wines.

"Why is everyone out in this heat?" she asked.

Karl frowned at the question, and she saw him looking for Ellie in the rear-view mirror.

"Busy day, babe," she said. "For everyone. Let's get Maxy and get you home. There's no work tonight. We're not open."

"I know that," Jody said, a little peeved. "I already told you that."

She stared out of the window. She couldn't help but think that all of the people out there, and the guy who'd stolen her cameras, and the trouble at Ellie's work, that it was all somehow part of the same thing. But she couldn't piece it together.

"Oh," she said. "Did you talk to Damo? Did he find his money?"

Ellie reached forward and squeezed her shoulder as Karl eased the Civic around the corner onto Cayuga Avenue. It looked like a carnival. So many people out on the sidewalk with all of their things. It was like a street party. People had moved furniture and clothes and TVs and everything out there and were piling it into the cars and onto trucks, but Karl was a very good driver, and he somehow picked a way through all of them.

"Damo's gonna come over, babe," Ellie said. "He's paid everyone in cash from the safe at work. But he's coming by our place after that to pay me and talk about some things."

For some reason, that information seemed familiar to Jody.

"Damo's nice," Jody said. "He swears a lot. And he shouts. But he's Australian."

"Baby, I think we need to get you to a doctor."

"I'm good," Jody said, as Mister Valentine actually drove up onto the footpath for a little ways to avoid some people who started pushing and shoving each other when some other people dropped a big TV set on the road. Jody heard it crash to the ground, and the shattering of the screen, and it did not sound good at all. A lot of things were getting broken today.

The Honda bumped down off the gutter on the other side of the argument, and Karl was able to speed up for a short distance because so many people were running towards the fight that it actually cleared the road ahead of them.

"I saw a doctor, didn't I, Karl?"

Mister Valentine shook his head, but not unkindly. Not like he was scolding her for getting it wrong.

"No. That was Mister Burés, Jody," Karl explained. "He's a pharmacist, not a doctor."

"Oh."

"I think you might have some concussion," he said. "I seen plenty of that in the war. You got a headache at all? Double vision?"

"A bit," she admitted.

"Yep. Concussion. I knew you shouldn't have had them drinks."

"Did Damo get his money back?"

Karl looked for Ellie in the rear-view mirror again. "What do you want me to do, Miss Ellie?" he asked.

Jody was about to protest that they were going to get Maxy because nothing else mattered, but Ellie went on to say, "We'll get Max first, and then get Jodes home to rest," and Jody loved her more fiercely at that moment than she ever had before.

"You should just lay back a ways and close your eyes, Miss Jody," Karl said. "We won't be long now. Best you not be staring into the sunset anyway. It'll make your headache worse."

"Okay," Jody agreed, and she laid her head back.

She felt Ellie's hand on her shoulder, and she fell asleep.

WHEN VALENTINE PULLED up outside of Chad Moffat's place, Ellie thought about letting Jodes sleep through the handover. She was in a bad way, and they were going to have to get her to a doctor, which was probably going to cost every fucking dollar that Damo had promised to drop by later that evening. Ellie was seriously fucking freaked out by where this day was headed.

It had already swirled down the toilet, but the toilet seemed to be hooked up to the cesspits in one of the lower levels of Hell. She'd thought things couldn't get any worse than the fucked-up ICE raid this morning, and then someone had turned on a radio while cleaning up the kitchen, and the bullshit had really piled up. She'd ordered one of the dishpigs to find a music station or throw the fucking radio in the bin. Fucking banks collapsing and war in the Pacific. It was insane. She could understand why people were getting out of the city while they could.

"You want me to come in with you or stay here and keep an eye on her," Valentine whispered.

Ellie managed a small, faltering smile for him.

If they were in Hell, they'd picked this guy up as some sort of angelic travelling companion along the way. Jody was like that. Always attracting stray dogs and lost souls. It could be annoying, but having spent the better part of the day with Valentine now, Ellie was grateful for his presence.

"Thanks, man," she said. "I can handle this asshole on my own. She's had a worse day, and she's messed up. I don't want her waking up on her own in the car. And she needs the rest, so maybe if you stay with her for now."

"Roger that," Valentine said.

She almost expected him to salute, but he didn't.

Chad lived in a dead-end street that ran right up against the rail line tracking alongside the freeway that formed the northern boundary of the Outer Mission. The traffic noise was a constant snarl, drowned out every ten minutes by the roar of goods trains. It was a garbage dump for a garbage human, and she hated that Jody's kid had to spend any time here at all. But the law said he did, and so she climbed out of the hatchback, thanked Valentine again for his help and patience, and steeled herself for an encounter with Chad.

There was no doubt the asshole was home.

His stupid van, covered in more Chad than any sane human would ever need or want, was parked outside of the rundown, single-storey bungalow he shared with two other 'health professionals'. Some crazy fucking lap dancer turned 'tantric therapist' and a

CrossFit mental case who rarely ever got to the Box because of all the injuries he did himself every fucking time he turned up there.

Ellie stalked past the grinning oversized image of Chad on the rear of the van— *'Nothing tastes as good as Chad feels'*— and pushed through the open gate onto the overgrown, weed-choked front yard. She could already hear the thrashing music and automatic gunfire of whatever stupid Xbox game this douchenozzle was playing with Max. It didn't surprise her at all that, unlike the rest of the city, Chad Moffat wasn't throwing a change of clothes and bag full of tinned food into his car and heading for somewhere, anywhere, less likely to get nuked by the Chinese.

Most times, Chad barely knew what day of the week it was, and then only because some app told him to "SMASH IT OUT FOR GLUTES DAY BRO!"

He was not a keen student of current affairs.

Ellie marvelled at the noise of so many honking car horns and sirens drifting down from the freeway, loud enough to be heard over the racket from inside Moffat's place. She climbed the front stairs, a weird one-and-a-half step arrangement that always wrong-footed her. The front porch was so crowded with garbage bags and rusting pieces of gym equipment that there was only room for one person at a time up there. She didn't bother ringing the doorbell. It didn't work.

She hammered at the door.

"Moffat!" she yelled. "It's Elizeh Jabbarah. I'm here for Max."

Nothing.

She hammered at the door again.

Still nothing.

The late afternoon sun, still murderously hot, slanted in from the west, baking her on the stoop. The garbage bags, some of them untied, some split and spilling their contents, smelled worse than the back alley behind the worst restaurant she'd ever worked in. Thick black clouds of flies buzzed loudly around them.

"Motherfucker," she muttered.

She was about to take a short weight bar to cut a path through the bushes that grew wild down the side of the house when the door opened, and a small boy looked up and said, "Hi, Ellie."

Max. She barely heard him over the music.

Ellie didn't bother calling out for Moffat or one of his asshole roommates again. She took the little boy by the hand and said, "Your mom's here to pick you up, Max. Come on."

"But my bag," he protested.

"Not important. We'll get..."

He tugged against her grip and pulled away.

"It's got my stuff in it! It's all packed."

He ran back into the darkness, and Ellie, feeling her temper slip the leash, followed him in. It smelled even worse inside than it had on the front porch. The flies were louder, too. It was hard to see, coming from the bright afternoon into the gloom of a house with all the curtains pulled closed, but she didn't need much light to know what a fucking mess the kid had been sitting in for two days.

"Jesus Christ, Moffat. You fucking animal," she said quietly.

She bunched her fists and stepped around a bicycle, leaning up against the wall. It was missing a wheel, and she just knew it was stolen. It would have been chained by its wheel to a pole or something, and one of these douchebags had undone the bolts fixing the wheel to the frame so they could take the rest of the bike.

She couldn't prove it.

She didn't have to.

She just knew.

Ellie's hands were bunched into painfully tight fists as she started looking for Chad, desperate to rip him a new one. Not because he was a fucking deadbeat and a loser, and he should never have been given joint custody of Max. But because she needed to wail on somebody or something, and he was the nearest available human piñata. Who deserved it, as it happened. But before she could get any further into this dive, the music cut out, and Maxy came running back up the hallway carrying his Captain America backpack.

"Come on," he said. "I've got to tell Mom."

He dodged around Ellie with ease and was nearly out the door when she called out after him.

"Wait, hang on, Max. Where's your dad? I have to tell him you're with us."

Max stopped in the doorway, his tiny form silhouetted by the fierce afternoon light.

"Oh, Dad's not here. He and Troy went to get guns."

"What?"

"There's going to be a war," Max said, as though it was the most obvious thing in the world. "Come on. I have to tell Mom."

Shit.

He ran down the front path.

Ellie heard him calling out to Jody as soon as he saw the car. She hurried out after him, closing the door behind her, wondering how long Moffat had left him alone in the house.

Jesus fucking Christ. What a waste of skin he was.

She saw Maxy pull up short of the Honda and do a double take when he discovered Karl behind the wheel, but Jody was awake, if groggy, and she was already climbing out to gather him up in her arms. Ellie squinted into the sun, shading her eyes against the glare.

Perhaps if she'd seen Chad Moffat a few seconds earlier, things might have gone differently. They might have driven away without trouble. But she didn't. And there was trouble.

Jody was down on her knees, unsteady but hugging her little boy, who was excitedly telling her all about how there was going to be a war, and Chad and Troy were pumped to kill some Chinese, and they'd had to hurry to the gun shop in case it was all over before they could get some, and Jody looked very confused. Ellie was getting angrier and angrier, and she was so lost in her rage – and, to be honest, in her fear – that she didn't see Moffat and his dumbass CrossFit Nazi sidekick until it was too late.

"The fuck d'you think you're doing, bitch?"

Ellie's heart jumped. She squinted into the sun.

Jody tried to turn and stand, but Max was holding onto her, and she was in pain from her injuries. She fell over and took the boy down with her.

We're just picking up Max...

Is what Ellie should have said, in a calm and reasonable tone. But...

"Back the fuck off, asshole," is what she yelled at him because she'd had a hell of a day, and she might be out of a job, and it didn't matter anyway because it seemed like the world might actually end before rent was due this week.

They were the only people on the street. Unlike the circus out on Cayuga, the short, dead-end road where Chad Moffat's miserable life had fetched up was deserted. Jody's ex was dressed, as he always was, in bicycle shorts a size too small and a singlet a size too large, which meant it was a very large singlet indeed. Chad was huge. His offsider, Troy, was less of a hairless mammoth, but not by much. They were both carrying shotguns from which dangled small paper price tags on white string.

Chad appeared to have equipped himself with a samurai sword, too. He wore it on a strap, angled across his back. The handle poked out over his shoulder.

"Shut up, dyke," Troy said, and his voice sounded high and strained.

She knew both of these idiots were 'roid monsters, and in the heat and hysteria of the day, she didn't doubt they could flip over into real madness.

"We're just picking up Max," she said, but it was too late for that. She shaded her eyes and saw two jacked-up fuckwits who'd talked themselves into an apocalyptic wank fantasy. It was a wonder they'd made it home without starting a lethal free-for-all back on Cayuga Avenue.

"No, you're not," Chad replied. "It's dangerous now. Shit's getting real. Max needs to stay with me."

Jody half-climbed back up on her feet, but dizziness got the better of her, and she fell over.

"Mom!" Max cried out.

Chad hefted his shotgun.

"She can't even look after herself," he said. "Never could. Shit's going down, and she's falling over. Probably from doing coke and lesbian shit. Come 'ere, Max."

Chad gestured with the shotgun for his boy to join him. The little tag flapped around at the end of the barrel.

"No," Jody cried out, wrapping her arms around Max to keep him close.

Troy laughed.

Ellie took one faltering step towards them on legs that had gone numb. She almost tripped over her own feet.

"Shit. You've both been doing drugs," Chad said. He raised his voice. "Max! Now!"

The boy burrowed himself deeper into his mother's arms.

Ellie couldn't believe this was happening.

She'd been arguing with Chris Kakris about his shitty, bogus wagyu, and then everything, like the whole fucking world, had gone sideways. Hard.

She took another step down the cracked, baking tarmac towards Chad and Troy, intending to put herself between them and Jody and Max. She didn't really want to because she could see where this was going. She had trouble making her legs work. But she slowly, awkwardly, put one foot in front of the other.

She was still wearing her chef's uniform.

She had helped build up one of the best restaurants on the West Coast.

And she was going to get shot by a mouth-breathing roid monkey.

Unless you puke, faint or die, Chad has failed.

How did that happen?

A man's voice cut through the madness of the moment.

"That'll be enough, gentlemen."

Everybody turned to the new actor in this deranged piece of theatre.

Karl Valentine had exited the car without being noticed.

Seriously, Ellie thought. *How did that happen?*

He stood on the other side of the Honda, holding a gun in a practised shooter's stance. Or what Ellie assumed was a practised shooter's stance. Both hands on the grip, the muzzle pointed at Troy, both eyes open, breathing normally.

"Holy fuck!" Troy squealed, and he swung the tube of his shotgun up towards Valentine.

Ellie considered it all in super slow motion.

It was weird the way things slowed down like that, but they did. She had all the time in the world to watch Troy attempt to raise his weapon and lay the sights on Karl Valentine. She actually gaped in wonder as Chad dropped his shotgun and reached for the hilt of the Japanese sword poking out over his shoulder.

But was it really a Japanese sword?

And why not use his shotgun?

She heard Jody crying out, wailing in protest, *"Noooo,"* as she wrapped herself even more tightly around her little boy. And she marvelled at the fact, the inexplicable but undeniable fact, that she was *still* walking towards these two men. *Still* trying to put her own body between them and her lover.

Was she crazy now?

But mostly, what she marvelled at was the small round hole that appeared in the middle of Troy's forehead with a clap of thunder. And the extravagant eruption of red, white and grey matter that small wound occasioned from the back of his head.

Although, she thought idly—as if she'd had many hours to consider the question before deciding on it—the bullet didn't really emerge from the back of his head. It was more like the rear half of his skull disappeared and rushed away on a bright river of ruin.

She observed the smooth, almost machine-like way the smoking muzzle of the pistol traversed just an inch or two. In her weirdly abstracted, hyper-accelerated state of mind, Ellie did a very compli-cated mathematical calculation which, she was sure, proved that the next small red hole was about to appear in Chad Moffat's forehead as he ran towards them with his shiny new Samurai sword raised on high.

Except it didn't, and he didn't.

Chad kept running all right, but in a bizarre, almost cartoonish trick, he performed a perfect U-Turn and ran away.

Up the street.

As fast as his oversized legs in those undersized bike shorts would carry him.

Ellie had stopped moving.

Jody and Max had started crying.

And Karl Valentine had put his pistol away in the holster he wore under his zipper jacket before everything sped back up to normal again.

26

THE PLAN JERICHO OUTCOMES

The storm broke over Rick as he pulled into Mel's place, a small townhouse development, early Reagan-era, judging by the faded *Miami Vice* aesthetic. There were two visitor parking slots, both occupied, forcing him back out on the main road, where he pulled up onto the kerb a two-minute walk back down Route 112. Traffic was heavy and slow for a place like Darnestown in the mid-afternoon. Rick felt the first drops of cold, heavy rain plop down as he and Nomi climbed out of the cabin. They started to jog back to Mel's place as the rain intensified. By the time they turned in through the driveway, it was pouring. Rick was running hard, Nomi keeping pace beside him, but when they reached cover, he was already drenched. Nomi panted and grinned as though she had been given the most fabulous treat of all: the gift of wet dog hair.

The rain stopped abruptly, but within less than a minute, hail was falling. Small slushy pellets at first but ramping up into a storm of murderous hailstones as big as golf balls. Rick cursed. He imagined the damage his car was taking under hundreds of icy hammer blows. It had been a long time since he'd had to run from a storm. You didn't see them that often these days.

After an explosive arrival, the hail petered out within a few minutes. Thunder rumbled in the distance, and a light rain fell in patches, but the tempest had passed. Steam rose from the road surface, and Rick could feel the humidity pressing in like a damp, heavy blanket. He checked Mel's apartment number in his notebook, guessed it would be upstairs, and carefully took the steps with Nomi. A lot of rain had come in through the open breezeway.

At least half of the residents appeared to be home. Not Melissa, though. Her door was closed when he arrived, and nobody answered his knock. Rick checked the car lot for her pickup but didn't see it. He knocked again.

"Excuse me. Are you Richard? Are you looking for Melissa?"

A woman was approaching from the stairwell. An older-looking woman. Greek or Italian background.

"Yeah, I'm her friend, Rick. We were supposed to meet up here, but I think..."

"She is at the hospital," the woman said, giving Rick a start. Before he could ask what had happened, she went on.

"Poor Mr Gilmartin had a fall, and Melissa took him to the hospital with Mr Neary. He lives downstairs. He used to be in the Coast Guard. She said you might come by."

His heart stopped racing. Melissa was okay. She was helping out a neighbour.

"Do you know how long she'll be gone?" Rick asked. "I can't reach her on the phone."

That was all the invite the old woman needed. She threw up her hands.

"Oh, I know. It's terrible. The cable is out. The phone is out. I have my old landline, the one plugged into the wall. But nobody answers their old phones anymore. It's always the telemarketers, you see. They ring every afternoon from India. Every afternoon they ring to tell me about the virus on my computer. Well, I don't have a computer, but I sometimes pretend that I do, and we talk until they realise I don't and..."

Rick could see himself getting trapped for hours with this old chatterbox. He tried to move away from the door to Mel's place.

"What a lovely dog you have," she said. "There's no dogs in this complex, of course. It is a great pity. I would love to have a little dog to talk to or even a cat. Although there is no talking to cats, is there? They never listen; they only pretend to."

She had to draw breath at some point, and when she did pause for the merest second, Rick jumped in.

"Do you know which hospital she went to, ma'am?"

The woman thought about it for a moment.

Thunder rumbled overhead. Traffic hissed by on the wet, steaming tarmac of Route 112.

"Now let me see," she said. "I think it was probably Holy Cross. Melissa didn't say where they were going, but Holy Cross is the closest emergency room. It's where I go when the vertigo comes on and..."

"And I'd better get to her before she leaves," Rick said. "Thank you," he added, gently tugging at Nomi's lead to get her moving. She hadn't been trained to break contact with an indefatigable motor-mouth, but she was a good dog, and she knew it was time to go.

"Oh, you're going," the woman said. "Should I say you called if she comes home?"

Rick had to admit that the chances of passing Mel in transit were pretty good. He paused at the edge of the stairwell.

"Tell her Rick called in and that I was heading towards the hospital to try and find her. Could you ask her to stay here? Tell her I'll circle back if I miss her at the ER."

The old woman laughed as if he had told the funniest joke she'd heard since Johnny Carson was on air.

"I can ask her, Richard. But you can't tell these young women anything these days, can you?"

That stopped him for just a moment. She was smiling at him almost devilishly.

"No, ma'am," he said, not bothering to hide his grin. "No, you cannot."

R ICK DIDN'T FIND Mel at the hospital. He'd forgotten the name of the neighbour she had helped, so he didn't know who to ask for at the admissions desk. The ER looked like a Baghdad market during bombing season. Road accidents, he imagined. The lights had been out on the way over, and he'd almost been T-boned at one intersection. The brief hailstorm wouldn't have helped either.

He circled back after a fruitless hour haunting the hospital and its car park, returning to Mel's apartment in Darnestown just as the late afternoon rush hour was pouring even more traffic into the difficult conditions. He parked further away this time, but at least he and Nomi didn't have to run through a storm. Some of Mel's neighbours were loading up cars with camping gear and boxes of food when he arrived. He ignored them, heading upstairs to the first floor. They evinced no interest in him.

Her door was open.

"Mel, are you home? It's me, Rick," he called out.

Her face appeared from around the corner down the corridor. It was dim inside the apartment. She had no lights on, but he could see the smile that lit up her face. She beamed at him and hurried down the corridor, throwing her arms around him as they met.

"Oh man," she said. "I've had a day. I'm sorry, really sorry, Rick. But we had a bit of a thing here, and I had to..."

He eased her away, giving Nomi room to nuzzle in with her snout, looking for a scratch behind the ears.

"It's okay," he said. "Not a problem. And not your fault at all. I talked to some old girl who..."

"That would be Mrs Comino. What you probably meant to say was she talked at you."

He grinned, "Yeah, something like that. Anyway, she told me what happened with your neighbour. It's good that you were here for him."

Rather than asking him inside, Mel joined them outside on the narrow walkway.

"Electricity went off," she said. "It's stuffy as Hell in there."

They leaned against the safety rail, looking out over the main road, where outbound traffic was moving slowly.

"What do you want to do?" Rick asked. "It's a bit late to try and get to the lake tonight. Looks like the traffic's gonna be grim."

"Can you get the day off tomorrow?" Mel asked.

"Shouldn't be a problem," he said. "The resort is closing for a few days because of everything happening. I got a text from my boss before the network fell over. You want to try again tomorrow?"

She smiled at him. Her teeth were very white, and her eyes sparkled with mischief.

"I think we should try, yes," she said. "Everything's a bit of a mess right now. It'd be nice to get away from it all for a few days. I'll grab my stuff, and we should go back to your place. We can head out from there in the morning. Or maybe the afternoon."

He gave her a puzzled look.

"Why the afternoon?" Rick asked.

Melissa's smile was a promise.

"You're going to want to sleep in," she said.

WHILE RICK BOREHAM searched without luck for Mel Baker at the Holy Cross Hospital, twenty miles away, Michelle Nguyen left James O'Donnell buried in his laptop while she went looking for Admiral Holloway. Her division head hadn't returned following the emergency evacuation of the White House, and she wanted his permission to re-task James away from researching the trade war with Beijing. They were beyond worrying about trade talks now, with actual fucking missiles and shit flying around, and James had proven himself to be something of a boss-level savant at threat detection. She wanted to bring him in, to let him start working some of the darker scenarios they had for a showdown with the Chinese. But that would mean clearing him well above his current level and possibly exposing him to the threat of hard sanction if he couldn't deal with what he was about to learn.

If she could find Holloway, of course.

Towering thunderheads rumbled in the distance as she stalked the halls of the Eisenhower Building, her progress slowed by multiple checkpoints guarded by Marines in full battle rattle. Her clearance level was not Triple-A, but it was close enough, giving her access to most areas. After twenty minutes of floor walking and door knocking, she'd determined that Holloway wasn't even in DC anymore. He'd been evacuated to an alpha site and probably wouldn't be back online until later in the evening. She did get a number for the site, though. It was in Colorado.

She was heading back to O'Donnell when she heard a gruff, familiar voice calling her from the stairwell to the executive level.

"Ms Nguyen, a word?"

It was Panozzo, released back into the wild from the briefing she'd taken James to earlier. He looked drawn but pleased to see her.

"General?" she said, "Can I help you?" She realised as she said it that he could help her.

"Your boy wonder back there; he dropped a real turd in the hot tub."

"Yes, sir. He's quite the performance artist in that way. Very transgressive."

Panozzo snorted.

"Yeah, well, whatever Holloway's paying him, you got your money's worth. Turns out he had the Chinese plan totally fuckin' nailed. It's a damn shame he was too late. They hit us just like he said they would. Trashed our whole food supply chain."

Michelle felt a cold, clammy wave roll down her back.

"Jesus, seriously?"

Panozzo nodded.

"Yeah. FEMA is looking at critical response using the Army and the Guard, but it's bad. Real bad. Just thought you'd wanna know. You should probably tell your boy he had a bright future in threat detection if he'd been a bit quicker off the mark."

Michelle bristled at that.

"Hey, James only came on board this morning, you know. And he figured out what was happening within an hour, and that wasn't even his job. It was a fucking side project for him."

She came on more fiercely than intended, surprising both of them, and Panozzo threw up his hands in defence.

"Okay," he said, "I'm not criticisin'. At least we know where to lay the crosshairs, thanks to him. Chinese are gonna pay for this, and the butcher's bill is gonna be fuckin' steep, I'll tell you that."

They had met on the landing between the second and third floors. Big picture windows afforded a view of the gardens and the Renwick Gallery. The light outside was a sick, almost malarial yellow, washed through the filter of the storm clouds. Gusting winds picked up litter and fallen leaves, blowing them across the cut grass.

"I'm sorry," Michelle said. "I was out of line, but I really believe James did good work for us."

"He did great work," Panozzo conceded. "Just, you know, too late."

"I'd like him to do more," she said, seeing her chance and ignoring the jab. "Admiral Holloway's got him preparing a briefing to Cabinet on trade talks. With Beijing. It's not the best use of his time."

Panozzo laughed at that but without any real humour.

"No," he said. "I guess not."

"I was wondering if we could re-task him?" Michelle asked, lowering her voice and checking that they could not be overheard. The hallways were busy with foot traffic, but nobody was close enough to listen in on them. "We should put him onto the Plan Jericho outcomes."

Panozzo shook his head, and Michelle got ready to argue her case, but the general's demeanour was not dismissive as much as defeated.

"No point," he said. "You haven't heard?"

"No," she said. "Heard what?"

"All non-essential federal staff are being stood down..."

"What!"

"On full pay. It's not a shutdown, but the White House, on Home-land and FEMA's say-so, wants everyone to sit tight while they sort out the food supply issue, the transport grid, and, well, this whole stir-fried clusterfuck. If you're not essential to the immediate emer-gency response, you're either stood down or being re-classed as a remote asset. You should have an email by now. You'll be remote, for sure."

"Jesus, I've got like five thousand unread emails since this morning."

Panozzo stared out at the storm in the distance.

"Bottom line is there's no point bringing your new guy in. We're all headed out for the duration. There'll be curfews, too. And they will be enforced, so I suggest that if you need to get to the grocer and stock up, that you do so. Quickly. The President's gonna do an address this evening and recommend the states and private employers follow our lead. Homeland thinks the best way to get through this is to dig in and hunker down."

"Jesus," Michelle said quietly, and mostly to herself. "People are gonna lose their shit."

She stared at him. He looked haunted.

"What do you think, General?"

Panozzo turned away from the storm, but he couldn't quite bring himself to look her in the eye.

After a long moment, he said, "I think we already lost this one."

27

REMINDERS OF THE FALL

"Jesus, Karl," Ellie said, still not believing it. "You killed him."

"Yep," said Valentine. He came around the car and helped Jody to her feet. She was sobbing and trembling. Maxy stared at this new man with eyes like dinner plates. Valentine leaned forward and held out a hand.

"I'm sorry to make your acquaintance like this, son," he said. "My name is Karl. I hope I didn't just shoot your old man."

Maxy gaped at him but slowly held out his tiny hand. He said nothing as they shook.

"That wasn't Chad," Ellie said shakily. "That was his roommate."

The enormity of what just happened rolled over her. She had to turn away and take a couple of deep breaths to stop herself throwing up.

"Shit!" she breathed when she had her stomach under control again. "What are we going to do?"

Karl spoke first to Max.

"Can you help your mom into the car, son? She's hurting, and she needs you to look after her."

The young boy nodded, still seemingly unable to speak. He took his mother's arm and pulled her toward the open door of the Honda

Civic. Jody went without protest, checking Max all over for wounds and injuries.

Karl edged up to Ellie. He didn't appear nervous, but he was subdued.

"It was self-defence, Ms Ellie," he said. "Or close enough. Looked like he was gonna shoot you with that damned elephant gun. So, I shot him. That how you saw it?"

Ellie was shaking. Hot flushes and cold sweats raced up and down her body. She felt giddy and sick in the relentless heat. But she bobbed her head up and down.

"That was how I saw it, Karl. Troy was going to shoot me, and probably Jody and Max, too. And Chad was running at us with his stupid sword..."

Her voice trailed off. It sounded flat and weird in her ears.

"... But. But what are we..."?

She was lost for answers. This was so far removed from the stuff she usually dealt with. She had no idea where even to begin sorting this shit out. A low-flying aircraft temporarily drowned out the constant blare of car horns. The airplane looked military, a fat grey transport of some sort.

"C-130" Karl said when it passed over. "Got a pencil, some paper?" The black clouds of flies buzzing so loudly around the garbage on Chad's front porch were now buzzing even more thickly around his dead roomie.

Ellie almost protested that she wasn't a damn waitress, but she caught herself. She did have a notebook and a little pencil. She always carried one in the pocket of her chef's pyjama pants. It helped her keep track of the dozens of things she had to stay on top of through a typical day at *Fourth Edition*. She fumbled it out and opened it to a new page.

She had scribbled the last entry earlier that day.

Talk to Natalie re table hopper!!

What the fuck was a table hopper? And why would Damo's sommelier...

The scattered pieces of her former life clicked into place. She'd meant to find five minutes to talk to Natalie Ong about the fake

French label wine story in Table Hopper magazine. But that was a fucking long time ago in a galaxy far, far away. She gave Karl the notebook. Her hand was shaking violently. So was his, she saw. Just a little. Otherwise, he seemed calm.

He took her hand in both of his. She let him. His hands were hard and calloused, but his grip was gentle.

"Still feel a pulse in here," he smiled. Karl squeezed, but not hard, and let her hand go, taking the notebook and pencil.

"Your heart is still beating, Ms Ellie. You can still see the world. Feel it, because you're in it."

He turned toward the dead man.

"He can't. But you can. That's what matters."

His voice was steady, reassuring.

"We're not staying here," he said. "And we're not leaving the scene of a crime. This wasn't a crime, and I'm writing out a statement for the cops and details of how to contact me. I'm telling them we have a woman in need of medical attention, and her child, and we cannot stay here. I'd be grateful if you would add your contacts."

"Of course," Ellie said quietly.

The pencil scratched on the notepaper as Karl went on.

"To be honest with you, Ms Ellie, I don't think the police will be here any time soon, and I don't imagine they will care much what happened if and when they do turn up. I think we're a good way past that now."

He stopped writing for a moment and raised his face to look past her as though surveying the whole of the city.

"This reminds me of Iraq," he said. "When everything was falling apart."

He returned to scribbling momentarily before signing whatever he'd written with a flourish. He handed the notepad back to Ellie.

"Your name and address will be enough. But you can sign it if you like. Leave a phone number, and place of work."

She did. It felt important to do so.

Valentine's statement ran over three pages. She carefully tore them out and gave them back to him. He folded the note over twice and tucked it into the waistband of the dead man's shorts.

"Blood won't get on it there," Karl said. "Come on. We'll get you home. After that, I don't know."

THEY TOOK two hours to get back to Ellie and Jody's place in Oceanview. Two hours of grinding, stop-start traffic to travel a couple of blocks that would usually have taken five or six minutes to drive. They could have walked if Jody weren't in such poor shape. Ellie sat up front this time while Jody and Max slept in each other's arms in the back. Twice Karl had to pull over and let the boy take a piss by the side of the road.

Ellie turned on the radio, keeping it low and scanning the news stations.

"Why is this happening?" she asked as a panel discussion on NPR struggled to bring coherence to the shape of all the terrors that had escaped into the world. While they had been collecting Maxy and murdering Troy, it seemed that Europe had suffered attacks and weird collapses every bit as severe as the chaos in America. And Indian warplanes had attacked military bases all over Pakistan.

Karl shrugged.

"Why does anything happen? Not because people like you and me say so."

"But Karl, this is so stupid. Why would anyone do this? To us?"

"I don't know, Ms Ellie. I'm just a driver. And they won't even let me do that these days. Not that there's much driving to be done right now."

Outside the car, vast rivers of red and yellow tail lights snaked away in every direction. They finally got back to their little bungalow in Oceanview at a quarter past eight. Ellie could see that many of her neighbours had packed up and fled or were busy doing so. Minerva Street, usually filled with parked cars by this time, was half empty of vehicles but busy with people looking as if they'd all decided to move out or take a road trip. Having just struggled through hours of hell traffic, she didn't know why they bothered. Nobody was going anywhere. She saw Damo's Lexus pulled over a little way up.

"Which one's your place?" Karl asked.

"Pull up behind that big black SUV," she said. "That's my boss."

"I remember him. Big shouty Australian guy."

"Yeah, that's Damo."

Karl pulled over, careful to avoid the Guttierez family loading two mattresses into the back of a pick-up. Their youngest kids ran in circles as if this was the most excellent adventure they would ever have. The older four, all teens and tweens, were merely resentful and sullen as they ferried suitcases and boxes out to the street. Raymon and Julia Guttierez looked haunted and exhausted.

"Karl," Ellie said as he shut off the engine. "I don't see how you can get home to Temescal tonight. I think you should crash at our place. It's not much, but I can make up the couch for you. And I can promise to cook you something great."

He smiled.

"That's kind, Ms Ellie. And I won't pretend I was looking forward to getting myself home through this mess. I will gladly take you up on that."

Hard to believe he'd just blown a man's brains out.

"Thank you," Ellie said. "For everything."

It was surreal.

Everything was weird and eerie.

She reached back and gently squeezed Jody's leg.

"Hey babe. We're home. Damo's here. And Karl is gonna stay over."

Jody came awake slowly, groggily.

She suddenly gasped.

She had remembered.

Maxy hugged her, and Ellie rubbed a hand on her leg.

"It's okay, baby. It's all good. We're home. Let's get you inside. Get some ice on your head."

She turned to Karl.

"Can you help her in? Front door key's on the ring there with the car key."

"Sure."

Ellie left him to help Jody out of the car and up the front path.

Maxy carried his backpack over one shoulder and wrapped his free arm around his mom's waist. She heard Karl telling him what a good boy he was.

Julia Guttierez hurried over as soon as Ellie alighted from the car. Dark half-moons lay in the hollows under her eyes.

"Are you getting out, Elizeh?" she asked. "Is your Jody all right? Are you going too? You should go while you can. The Chinese are coming."

Ellie smiled and squeezed her arm as she walked past, but she didn't stop.

"Jody is okay, Mrs G," she said. "She's had a fall, is all. She'll be fine. Excuse me, I have to go. My boss is here."

Ellie didn't hear whatever the woman said next. She was already moving away. She found Damo sitting in the driver's seat of his Lexus, listening to shitty old white guy music. It was deafening, and she had to rap on the window to get his attention. Damo stabbed at a button, and the music cut off. He opened the door and climbed out, looking thoroughly beaten down by the day.

"Sorry, boss. You been here long?"

"Nah, mate," he said, sounding as tired as he looked. "Only just got here. Took fucking hours, but. You mind if I come in? Have a drink? It's been a cunt of a day."

"Sure," Ellie said. "Come on, come in. You wanna get that stuff out the back?"

The luggage compartment of the Lexus was crammed full of boxes. She recognised them from the storeroom at the restaurant.

"They'll keep," he said.

Damo leaned back into the Lexus and took a buff-coloured envelope from the centre console. Then he slid a small, black pistol from the cup holder into the envelope. He said nothing, and neither did Ellie. Damo closed the door firmly and keyed the lock.

They stepped around the smallest Guttierez children, still running wild on the sidewalk, and trudged up the path to Ellie and Jody's front door.

There was no power in the house.

Ellie cursed as she tried and failed to flick on the lights in the entry hall.

"Yeah. Power's out all over the place," Damo said. "I think that's what's fucking the traffic up. That and a bunch of fucking Teslas gone rogue."

"What?"

He waved the question away.

"We can still drink. Don't need a stovetop for that."

"We're on gas, Damo. I can cook you dinner. And I probably should if the power's gonna be off for long. All the stuff in the fridge will go bad."

She paused.

"And my phone is getting low on battery."

It was dark inside, and they moved cautiously up the hallway towards the kitchen at the back of the house, where candles already burned with a soft, flickering glow. Ellie took the phone from her back pocket and used the flash as a torch.

She found Karl in the kitchen alone, sitting at the small table where they usually ate breakfast.

"Hope you don't mind," he said. "Ms Jody showed me where to find the candles. She and her boy are lying down. I wrapped a pack of frozen peas in a tea towel. For her swollen wrist. Got her some ibuprofen for the headaches and made her drink a glass of water. I think she'll be fine. Reckon the shock was worse than the knock."

Elle surprised him by bending over, throwing her arms around his neck and squeezing hard.

"Thank you, thank you, Karl. I don't know where she found you, but we're not giving you back."

He chuckled and awkwardly returned the embrace with one arm. Damo opened the fridge, cursed at the lack of light and borrowed Ellie's phone for a torch. He took three cans of beer, ripped off the tops and handed one to Karl Valentine.

"Still owe you a feed, mate," he said. "For today."

Karl took the beer, a Grolsch Ellie had brought home from work. He seemed grateful for an excuse to escape the unexpected embrace.

"There's a steak in every can," he said, lifting the brew.

Ellie let him go and sat down to drink her own. Only when she'd finished half the can did she realise her hands had stopped shaking.

"Before I forget," Damo said. "I got your pay. I'm gonna advance you the next two months."

"What?"

"Don't be a silly bitch, just take it."

He tipped the contents of the envelope onto the Formica-topped table. Thousands of dollars in cash spilled out. The small black pistol thumped down on top of it. "'Scuse me," he said, standing to put the weapon away in a pocket. Ellie felt Karl's eyes suddenly locking on hers, but she smiled and shook her head.

"It's cool," she said.

Damo caught the exchange between them.

"Sorry, mate," he said to Karl. "I worked copper mines in New Guinea and Africa. Had to carry a weapon a lot of the time. And always when we moved money around. I fucking hate 'em. But they're a tool, and sometimes you gotta use them."

"Amen to that, brother," Karl said.

Ellie wondered if he would say anything about shooting Chad's roommate, but he didn't. And she didn't feel that she could or should. She hadn't pulled the trigger.

Damo counted out her wages for work she feared she would never do.

He smiled, and the candlelight softened his features.

"When I was a kid," he said, "I watched my parents count out their pay packets every Friday night. They got paid in cash in those days."

"I remember," Karl said. "Happy days."

"For some," Damo agreed. "Every Friday night, they'd build these little piles of money. Mortgage here. Groceries there. Bills, and so on. Used to make my brother and me watch and count along. Gave me a real sense of how tight things were. Used to be about fifteen, twenty bucks a week left over when they'd paid all the bills."

He slid over a stack of twenties and fifties.

Ellie didn't bother to count it.

"Thanks, Damo," she said. "Jody told me there was a problem with the bank?"

Damo shook his head.

"Nick Perriam reckons it's all part of this shit," he said, waving his hand around the darkened kitchen, drawing in the city beyond. "It's not just me. It's everyone who used this fucking app. Even Nick and his mates. You should've seen his fuckin' face," Damo said with a wry Aussie chuckle. "Anyway, I'm not as freaked out as this morning. Those lawyers are a bunch of fucking hammerheads. They'll get every dollar back, and if they don't... shit... my bank balance would be the least of our problems."

"What do you mean, Damo?" Ellie asked.

He leaned forward and lowered his voice.

"I mean, I'm a bit fucking worried about where this shit's going, mate. I had a lot of time to twiddle my thumbs today. I was bingeing on the news when I could get it. Fucking Twitter when I couldn't. Although that's flaked out now, too. I think the whole of the fucking internet's offline or something."

Ellie drained the last of her beer. She was starving, and she knew the alcohol would hit her in a minute, but she took another three from the fridge. Passed two around. Sirens wailed in the night outside.

"We saw some pretty gnarly shit today," she said, her eyes flicking to Karl.

Was he gonna talk about it?

"Yeah, me too," Damo said. "I put my kid on a flight to Sydney. Told him to get out to LAX with his passport and a spare pair of undies. Just piss off home, you know. He caught one of the last flights before the airport shut down. Dunno why it closed, and I can't find out why. But soon as he was gone, I read the fucking Chinese had tossed a couple of missiles at Darwin. The fuck is that about?"

"It wasn't Darwin," Karl said, sipping at his Grolsch. "It was one of your airbases nearby. The Marines would have staged out of there. They got a whole expeditionary unit based in Darwin. Never went there myself, but I knew some who did. Your boy will be fine, Mister Maloney. Sydney's a long way from Darwin, isn't it?"

"Fuck yeah," Damo said, opening his second beer. "Hope you're right, Karl. I felt like a fucking idiot sending him back there when I heard. But... I dunno. Still feels smarter than having him here."

"It was," Karl said. "Nobody should be in Los Angeles now if they can get out."

"You don't seriously think the Chinese would attack LA, do you?" Ellie said. "That'd be crazy."

"They already attacked it," he said. His tone was mild. "That's why we're sitting here in the dark. It's the same all over."

"But why?" she asked for the second time that evening. She did not sound mild. Not like Karl.

He smiled and shrugged.

"You would have to ask the Chinese, ma'am. They might not tell you, but I'm sure they'd have their reasons. People always do."

"Food," Damo said. "They've been running short of food for years because of the drought when the clouds started disappearing. And I mean running really short. Beijing's fucking grocery bill is not to be sniffed at, mate. I've been looking to get into exports because of it. Aquaculture, you know, up in Canada. It would've made coal and copper mining look like small change. Guess it's not gonna happen now, but."

They sat in silence for a few moments.

Beyond the walls of Ellie's home, the usual hum of the city at night sounded louder, harsher. More sirens. More horns. More shouting.

A couple of times, Ellie heard cars backfiring or guns discharging. She couldn't be sure which.

"I'm going to check on Jodes," she said.

"You got eggs?" Damo asked. "I can make an omelette."

"Sit the fuck down," she shot back at him. "You can't even make toast, Damo. Just give me a second."

She left the two men in the kitchen, talking in low voices while she looked in on Jody and Max. They were both asleep on his single bed, and she stood quietly watching over them for a minute or so, her heart swelling uncomfortably but not unpleasantly. When she returned to the kitchen, Karl was telling Damo about the shooting at

Chad's place. Her boss was listening quietly. She knew that look on his face. He was weighing up decisions, making judgments. But not about Karl.

"I left my details in a note for the police, but I don't expect to hear from them."

"No," Damo agreed. "Maybe not... Probably not."

He saw her come in.

"Ellie, sit down," he said. "I'll get you to make us a feed in a minute, but I need to talk something through with you. You're always calm when things get crazy in the kitchen. I need you to tell me if I'm being crazy now."

Her head was spinning a little from the beer buzz, and she thought about opening a bottle of Pinot Gris she knew they had stashed at the back of the vegetable crisper where it was coldest. But Damo's sombre expression gave her pause. She sat down again at the small table. Her money was neatly bundled up and held down by a coffee mug. Damo's gun sat on the envelope with the remaining cash from the restaurant safe. Karl's gun was also on the table.

"Karl told me about those fucking idiots with the shotties this arvo," Damo said.

"He had to do it," Ellie said quickly. "You've got no idea, Damo..."

He held up one meaty paw.

"I got a pretty good idea, mate. I saw three blokes kick a cop half to death on my way over here. Fired a few shots from my Roscoe to see them off."

She frowned before realising he meant his pistol.

"Saw another bloke in front of a Korean grocer abso-fucking-lutely pissing bullets up the street after another bunch of blokes. A gang of some sort. Looked like he had a fucking Kalashnikov or something. Saw enough of them in Africa. Figured they'd tried to rob him. No sign of cops anywhere. No sign they were ever coming. And it's not just the city. The whole fucking country's going bananas, mate. I dunno whether you had time to follow it today but this fucking cyber-bullshit or whatever it is, it's done some real fucking damage to the supply chains in our business."

"What, restaurants?" Ellie wondered why anybody, let alone a hostile foreign country, would attack the San Francisco dining sector.

"No," Damo said. "Food. Before everything went down, I was in a Slack channel with Chris Kakris and some other suppliers. They reckoned Sysco, Performance Group, US Foodservice, they all got fucking smashed by these hackers. Bottom line, the food distribution system within the continental United States no longer exists. It's gone, mate. Fucking dead. It is an ex-parrot."

Ellie sat quiet and still for a few seconds.

She wanted to run back to Jody and Max and climb into bed with them, pulling the covers over their heads until this madness passed.

She looked to Karl Valentine. He was a level-headed sort. He'd know what to make of this. Karl stared back. Shrugged.

"I heard something on the news. But you can't trust that. Your boss here probably knows better. He's in the business."

"Shit," she said at last. "What's going to happen? What can we do? Should we provide free meals at the restaurant or something?"

Damo smiled.

"You're a good kid, Ellie. Tough, but your heart is true, as my mum used to say. No, we won't be providing free meals. We won't be opening again, I reckon. Ever. I'm going to get up to the yacht club and take my cruiser upriver. Up the Sacramento. I got a place in Canada, near the fish farm. I figure it should be a good enough bolt-hole until things blow over. Or they don't."

He paused, and when she didn't speak, he went on.

"You and Jodes and Maxy, you're welcome to come along. It's not gonna be safe here. I think it's gonna get really fucking medieval if you want the truth."

"I don't think I do," she said, trying to smile. Failing.

"Your old mate Karl here, he told me about putting that animal down this arvo. I got this gun," he said, "but I don't know that I could ever do what he did. Just as likely to shoot myself in the dick, I reckon. So I've told him he's welcome to tag along, too. He can come as far upriver as he feels he needs to. All the way to Canada, if he wants. I think you should come too. Seriously."

Ellie looked at Karl again.

He nodded.

"Mister Maloney is..."

"Call me Damo, Karl."

"Okay...," Karl said. "Damo is right, Ms Ellie. I've seen countries fall apart. It looks like this."

"Like what," she asked, sounding slightly desperate, even to herself.

"Like people killing each other in the streets."

28

DEFCON 2

"They're evacuating the capital," Michelle said.

"What?" James mouthed, barely paying attention to her. For the last hour, he'd been neck-deep in the accelerating collapse of the banking system, and he finally thought he had a handle on it. The Chinese, or the Russians, or some three-hundred-pound troll on 4chan, they hadn't hacked the banking system.

They'd done something much easier.

They'd hacked the news media and public opinion. James had no real idea how safe the core IT systems at Citigroup or Bank of America would be in the face of a state-sponsored cyber-attack, but the Russians had already proven that people's fears, hatreds and baseline irrationality were very easily exploited to tip an election one way or another. As he mined the web and worked the landline in Michelle Nguyen's office—cell reception was non-existent—he could trace the outlines of a fiendishly simple plan to tip the US financial system into free fall.

Some elements of the scheme appeared to be highly sophisticated black operations of a sort he imagined only state actors could pull off or even dare to attempt. This hack of the Scratch app looked increasingly like that. From Michelle and her direct line to the intelligence agencies, he knew the FBI was hunting for an employee they suspected of the exploit. (And, damn, how he wished he had access to this sort of inside data for his investment newsletter. It was gold). Other elements, like the fake news-bombing of reports about a run on the banks, were intricate and hi-tech in execution—setting up those mirror sites wasn't a hobbyist project—but they worked like brute force multipliers.

"They're. Evacuating. The capital," Michelle said, breaking his reverie.

"What?"

Michelle touched his shoulder and pulled him around in the swivel chair.

"James. We have to go. The president has ordered the government to evacuate."

"Wait. What?" He frowned. Sounding stupid even to himself. "We're leaving?"

She sketched a half-shrug that was both a concession and a rejection at the same time. She did not look happy.

"Not us, no. We're surplus to core function."

She smiled. It was an apology.

"Sorry bud. The president thanks you for your service, but your services are no longer required. Mine either. At least not here. I'm a threat analyst. I'm supposed to see the threats coming around the corner. But they're here now, all of them in a rush, so..."

Michelle shrugged.

"Game over for me. Parts of NSC are going with the Executive, but we must make our own arrangements."

James's face must have given away his bewilderment far more eloquently than his monosyllabic grunting. Michelle, who was stuffing items from her desk into a backpack, paused long enough to explain.

"The military's gone to Defcon 2. A nuclear strike on national command is factored into the planning. So they're bugging out."

James' mouth hung open. He almost strangled on his next words.

"Jesus Christ, they're launching nukes?"

Michelle shook her head.

"Nobody has launched. Nobody is launching. Or at least they weren't as of two minutes ago. But the *possibility* is judged real, and the government is evacuating all essential personnel to secure and classified hold-out locations."

She paused. He still didn't get it.

"We're not essential," Michelle explained before jamming a small photo frame in her bag.

"But... but..." James started.

"But you did so well figuring out the attack on the food distribution network?" she said. "Yes. You really did. But too late. I just heard it from Panozzo. All nine companies got hit this morning, just as you predicted. Same time as the attack in Asia. They're pretty much gone. Getting the systems back online will take weeks, and half the warehouses are scrap. Like, literally. The automated systems and stock management robots tore themselves apart."

James felt his balls contract.

"Holy shit. But what are we going to do?"

He wasn't sure whether he was talking about him and Michelle or the entire United States. A blizzard of half-formed thoughts and vertiginous panic blew through his head. Outside, it was late afternoon, and the sun was setting, throwing long shadows and shafts of golden light into Michelle's office. He'd lost track of time. Picking loose the tangled knot of the attack on the banks had so completely absorbed him that he'd forgotten this wasn't just an intellectual exercise. The country was at war, even if Congress had not met and declared it so.

"What about... Congress?" he croaked. Still finding it hard to express himself in more than one word at a time. His mind was already racing toward what an 'evacuation' would entail. Was it just a few hundred or a couple of thousand people? High-ranking military and administration types? Or had the whole city been told to get out?

His skin prickled as he looked out of the window, expecting to see crowds fleeing on foot. Why did everything look so normal? Hot flushes and cold, clammy waves rolled over his skin in quick succession.

"Congress isn't in session, James. But yes, it will now convene in emergency session somewhere else. Somewhere secure," Michelle added impatiently.

Traffic on the roads immediately around the Eisenhower Building was light, but he remembered that the capital police had been blocking off roads hours earlier. Perhaps things were gridlocked just a few blocks away. He looked at Michelle, unsure of what to say.

"Should I... er, invoice or something?"

Her face was blank for a second, and then she laughed.

"Yeah. Do that. And triple your fee, if you like. I'll sign the approval."

He looked at the screen of his laptop. He had multiple images of *The New York Times* home page open and over them, more windows with emails from contacts in the private sector—financial analysts, IT consultants, and some media types. He could see how the hackers had done it. He could also see that it didn't matter. The contagion was loose. Fear was driving the market. He closed the MacBook and stood up, collecting his stuff. He tried to remember whether he needed to pick anything up from the temporary office he'd been assigned a geological age ago.

All he could think of was his missing jacket and wallet.

"What are we... I mean, what are you going to do?" he asked.

Michelle finished packing her bag, a soft brown leather backpack that looked like it had given long service. It had been sewn with colourful patches and was adorned with small keepsakes she'd picked up on travels around the world.

"Buy some groceries, I imagine," she said. "Hunker down."

A couple of soldiers in combat gear jogged past her open door. Their boots thumping rhythmically on the tiles receded down the hallway.

"Ah, do you mind if I make a suggestion?"

"Sure. As long as it's not creepy or anything."

"Huh?"

"I don't think we're gonna get nuked, James. So I'm not up for drinking twenty espresso martinis and getting my freak on if that's what you're thinking."

James stared at her. That hadn't been where he was going at all.

"You were about to say something very different and immensely sensible, weren't you?" Michelle conceded.

"Yes," he said, still unable to stop himself from blushing at the idea of Michelle Nguyen getting her drunken apocalypse freak on. "I think you should get out of the city, too," he said quickly to escape the embarrassing moment. "Like, right out. Forget nukes. The Chinese are trying to save themselves, not commit suicide. They won't nuke anyone who can strike back ten times as hard."

Michelle turned off her computer, closed the top drawer of her desk and locked it.

"Figured as much myself, but go on," she said.

"What I said this morning," James said. "About our cities starving. I meant it. I wasn't exaggerating. I mean, maybe the army and the National Guard can maintain order and, I dunno, distribute emergency rations or something. But..."

He trailed off.

"But you don't think so, do you?" Michelle finished for him.

He shook his head.

"Not for three hundred million people, no."

"Three hundred and forty-two million is our current estimate," Michelle said flatly. "There's millions of visitors in-country on any given day. Undocumented migrants too, of course."

"Exactly," James said. "And they all have to be fed. Every day. I think that was China's plan. Tie up the military here at home, dealing with a serious crisis, but not an existential threat. Nothing that would give us reason to burn their cities to ash. And a crisis they could deny causing. Plausibly deny it, too. Giving them time to..."

He looked for the words to explain what he meant. It all sounded so unreal in his head.

"To change the reality on the ground," Michelle supplied. "That's one of our favourites around here. The reality on the ground. And I think you're probably right. That was their plan. Is their plan. But the reality where we stand isn't what they see or expect to see."

James shook his head.

"No. They're a dictatorship. They're used to smothering dissent, crushing it if necessary. They'll kill millions to save a billion without breaking a sweat. I don't think... I don't know if we can do the same thing. I think it's all gonna fall apart, Michelle. I think they've miscalculated badly. And I'm pretty sure that when those guys we spoke to this morning, when they realise what's going down, they will bring the hammer down on Beijing. Hard. Not *even* if it's the last thing they do, but *because* it's the last thing they'll do. Ever. We need to get out of this place. Everyone does."

"We?" she said, tilting her head a little.

James took a breath and let it go with a nervous sigh.

"I'm going to go to my parents' place," he said. "They have a farm in Montana. It's a long way from anywhere. Pretty good water, too, despite the drought. They won't go hungry. They..."

He stopped. She was looking at him as though he had indeed suggested twenty or thirty espresso martinis and some desktop humping before the air raid sirens started screaming.

"Er... sorry," James said. "You must have someone who..."

She shook her head.

"No, I don't. I'm just wondering whether to trust you."

Again, his expression gave him away. In this case, the offence he took at the suggestion that he was being anything other than honourable.

Michelle snorted.

"Cool your jets, maverick. I think you're a nice guy. But you forget, my specialty is threat assessment. I'm just running the numbers on you. Wondering whether you're a potential threat. Specifically, I'm trying to figure out whether you're a bedwetter."

"What?" James spluttered.

This time, she smiled. He'd never met anybody who was so wholly unreadable, so reliably disconcerting. Michelle shook her head. The blue tints in her long black hair caught the setting sun and turned a striking shade of opalescent golden green.

"I was assessing whether you might be a panic merchant or a prophet," she said. "I have no one here. My family is in LA. When I leave the building today, in a few minutes, I'm officially re-designated as a remote asset. I have to be available but not present."

She held up her phone.

"This is good enough for that. A landline would be better, given the network problems. But what I'm wondering, James, is whether you're right. Whether we need to get the fuck outta Dodge as well."

James looked out the window. It seemed perversely quiet out there.

"Tell you what," he said. "Walk me back to my hotel. Or I can walk you home if you want, I mean if you're close. Maybe just check some stuff out. Make your own call. But I'm gonna go home. You're welcome to come along. If it's nothing, if I'm wrong, I'll make sure you get back here as soon as you can. If I'm right..."

He trailed off again.

Michelle Nguyen furrowed her brow. A small vertical line appeared between her eyes.

"If you're right, I need to call my parents," she said. She stared at the phone on her desk. "Do you mind?"

It took him a moment, but James realised she wanted the room.

"Oh sure, sorry. I'll get my stuff."

He took his gear back to the office they'd assigned him. It had less of a view than Michelle's. He waited. The hallway was busy with NSC staffers hurrying to and fro. They all seemed to be carrying something. Files, laptops and tablets, boxes full of documents. He fretted about his jacket and wallet. NSC still had reliable net access, allowing him to transfer money onto the credit card linked to his Apple Pay, so he had access to funds. Maybe. But he felt keenly the loss of the suit jacket. It was such a dumbass thing to do. And losing his wallet. Shit, what a nightmare. He was going to have to cancel everything.

But was he? Really?

Not if he believed what he'd just told Michelle. If he genuinely thought it was all going sideways, what was the point of administrivia? He would be better off getting hold of a gun and a backpack full of dried foods.

Michelle was ten minutes coming back to him, and when she did, he could see she'd been crying. Her eyes were red, but she gave no other sign of distress.

"They're good," she said. "They're leaving for my uncle's place in Washington state tomorrow. He's a fisherman."

She explained no further, and James did not ask.

He turned in his visitor's pass at the front desk. The civilian guard inspected Michelle's bag and his backpack but waved them off.

"Good luck," he said.

APPLE PAY WAS NOT WORKING. No credit cards or point-of-sale systems were functional. And cash was getting hard to find.

"Okay, this sucks," Michelle conceded as they humped their bags another block, looking for an ATM that hadn't been emptied or which wasn't about to dry up with a long, long line of agitated customers still waiting to grab whatever they could get from it.

They crossed 18th Street to avoid a fight that broke out at the cash machine in front of a Subway restaurant at the intersection with G Street. Vehicular traffic was light and mostly official, but foot traffic was heavy and concentrated around cash points, although the local bars were doing a brisk trade as well.

The heat had eased off some, but it was still punishing, and James offered to carry Michelle's bag for her. She said no. She was one-strapping it, and James noted she clutched that single strap tightly with both hands. His eyes flitted left and right. The city had an ominous feel to it. News of the government evacuating had crowded everything else out of the headlines and appeared to be stoking wide-spread alarm that could quickly flash into something much worse.

"I think we've got a couple of hours before this shit explodes," Michelle said as they hurried past a CVS pharmacy with its own line out the door. "Just gimme a second, would you?"

She trotted over to the long queue and spoke to a few people at the rear before returning to James.

"They're not lined up to cash out," she said. "They're stockpiling medicine."

"Great."

"Yeah. James, where are you parked?"

"The hotel. I moved my car out of the short-term lot yesterday. I'm gassed up, too."

"Let's get there. Now."

They picked up the pace, turning left at 20th and hurrying through the hot dusk and the surprisingly dense crowds of people who seemed to be wandering around with no discernible intent beyond obsessively checking their phones and randomly piling into those businesses that were still open despite the problems with electronic payment. It was a relief to get into the chilled air of the Marriot and recognise the faces of the two women behind the front desk. Wendy... No, she was *Wendi*, he recalled. And Dee, or something. James smiled and waved to them.

They looked even more stressed out than yesterday, but each managed a wan smile in return for him. Their manager, the douchebag, was nowhere to be seen, but James had that guy flagged as a lurker. He'd be around somewhere. Or he'd be a hundred miles gone by now.

"Mister O'Donnell," Wendi said. "Welcome back, sir. It's so nice to see you."

And the sad thing was, he believed her. Wendi looked like she'd had a day from hell, and even a vaguely familiar and friendly face was a blessed relief.

"Computers still out?" he asked as they approached the desk. He tried to make it sound sympathetic rather than demanding.

Wendi checked over her shoulder—so yeah, the lurker was still around—and nodded furtively.

"It's been a day," she said, and her colleague—Deonie, that was her name—bobbed her head in agreement. "Have you been watching the news?"

"That's our job," James said, indicating Michelle standing next to him.

The front desk women took in his companion and her fiercely outré style without blinking.

"Hi," Michelle said. "You just starting your shifts?"

"No," Wendi answered. "Thankfully, we're just about done. Night shift is coming on soon."

"Get home quick then. And safe," Michelle said. Her voice was flat, almost threatening.

Wendi and Deonie exchanged a look.

"Do you work with Mister O'Donnell? At the National Security?" Deonie asked as if it might be a state secret.

"Yes," Michelle confirmed in the same affectless voice. She stared into their faces, one after the other. "Get home quick. And safe. You understand me?"

They did.

"I'm going to check out," James told them.

"NSC will cover everything," Michelle added. "As per the booking arrangements."

That same worried glance from Wendi before she leaned forward, lowering her voice.

"But the government is leaving."

"No. Some assholes are leaving. The government isn't going anywhere," Michelle assured her. "And if it was, you'd have bigger problems to worry about than chasing down the Marriot's invoice, wouldn't you, Wendi? You have a family? I strongly suggest you get home to them."

Even under all of the makeup Deonie wore, James could see the colour blanch from her face.

"I'll just get my stuff from the room," he said. "I'll get changed too, into some road clothes. Can you sign for the bill?" he asked Michelle.

She waved the ID card hanging from the lanyard around her neck.

"That's just one of my superpowers. But hurry up."

He hesitated, then asked, "Should we eat? Before we head out? Might be a while, you know..."

Before Michelle could reply, Wendi interrupted.

"I'm sorry, Mr. O'Donnell, but the restaurant is closed. None of our deliveries arrived today. Nobody's did. They're saying it's an internet thing. Some problem with the stock system."

"Okay," James said. "Thanks anyway."

Michelle grabbed his elbow before he could leave.

"Clean out the minibar," she said. "The food anyway. Uncle Sam is paying."

They had a reasonably clear run along the Potomac to the beltway, passing through two checkpoints where soldiers informed them they might not be allowed to return to the inner city with their car until the emergency declaration was lifted. Michelle surfed the news radio channels while James navigated traffic that was no worse than any usual peak hour, except that it never ended.

By the time they made the I-495 interchange, heading north for Maryland and beyond for the long haul west on I-80, James's usual route home to Montana, it was becoming apparent they might need a new plan. The soft summer evening was riven by vast electric rivers of ruby-red taillights. Hundreds of horns blared, and some drivers had already given up and pulled over to the shoulder, abandoning their vehicles to walk. They had more than two and a half thousand miles ahead of them, and they'd already eaten all the chocolate bars and potato chips he'd taken from the room.

Michelle had not even stopped at her apartment to pick up extra clothes or belongings. Having committed to their own personal bug-out, she reasoned she could pick up a bag and whatever she needed once they cleared the city. It seemed more important to get out of DC as quickly as possible.

"Jesus Christ," she said. "Look at this fucking traffic. It probably goes all the way out to Rockville."

James was listening to a report about the Chinese attacks in Southeast Asia. Having struck so decisively at US facilities, the PLA had focused almost the entirety of its expeditionary combat forces on Vietnam, Thailand and Malaysia. Japan, Korea, Indonesia and Australia had all been warned to stand down their forces or face 'the fury of the Chinese people'.

He turned down the volume as Anthony Kuhn reported from Seoul that the North Korean military had fully mobilised, and all roads out of the southern capital were gridlocked.

"I think this traffic is probably worse," James said in response to the radio, not really meaning it.

"Jesus, James! There's like twelve or thirteen thousand artillery pieces buried in caves and pointed at Seoul," Michelle said. "It's that close to the border. Time-on-target from a long-range gun in the north to a residential high rise in the middle of Seoul is about forty-five seconds. That city could be gone a minute from now."

He turned off the radio. It wasn't helping. None of their mapping apps worked, and he didn't need traffic reports to tell him they were caught in a stationary parking lot that stretched away over the horizon.

"Are you fit?" he asked. "You carrying any injuries?"

She stared at him before answering. A police officer on a motor-cycle roared past in the breakdown lane, his siren wailing.

"I do some Zumba," she said.

"Your boots, are they comfortable?"

"They're Docs."

As if that was all she needed to say.

"So you can walk?" James went on.

"You want to leave the car?" Michelle asked.

"We need to leave the car," he volleyed back. "This is a bad invest-ment. We need to cut our losses and get out now."

"And what happens after we get out?" Michelle asked. She wasn't anxious or pleading. She was assessing their odds.

James looked out over the miles of stalled traffic. It snaked away and over the world's edge in the darkness, somewhere far ahead.

"We walk."

"To Montana? Are you fucking serious?"

He snorted.

"No. To Germantown. Walking a standard four miles an hour, that's where we'll be by tomorrow morning. I'm going to buy another car. Something better suited to dealing with this sort of thing."

He waved a hand out of the window.

"You can't just buy a hover car, future boy. You lost your wallet, remember?"

"I still have money. For now. And I have clients up that way. I've made them some money. I can do them another favour. Warn them to get the hell away from any major population centre before it's too late. And I'll ask a favour in return. A shower, some food. A lift to a branch of my bank. I don't need cash. A letter of credit for a car dealer will do. I don't know how long people will keep taking cash once they go hungry anyway. We need a vehicle and gas. Enough to get to Montana. If we have to hunt for food and live off the land along the way, I can do that. I grew up country, you know."

He saw her do that thing. Her threat assessment thing.

He saw her make a choice.

"Okay," she said. Let's go. But you must promise you'll never again say anything like 'I grew up country, you know'."

"Yeah. Okay. It did feel a bit weird as it came out," James conceded.

"That's because it was weird. Stick to investment metaphors."

"Done deal," he agreed.

"There you go," she nodded.

James pulled the car into the breakdown lane and turned off the engine. He almost left the keys in the ignition. After all, what was the point of taking them? But if he was wrong about all this, and he had to make an insurance claim on the car, no way would they pay him out for leaving the keys behind.

They stepped out into the close, hot night. The noise of the traffic jam rolled over them; the blaring horns, the shouts and the music and clashing talk radio stations drifting through the open windows of so many stationary cars. He smelled rubber and exhaust and fried foods. James left his suitcase in the trunk. It had nothing they could use. They started walking, heading for the next exit onto the 117.

He still carried a backpack to haul his laptop along with him. When he ditched that, he knew it would mean the end of the world.

29

THE CITY BURNS ON WATER

Jody Sarjanen emerged from a deep sleep in a disorienting tumble of memories and thoughts and a half-remembered dream. It didn't matter because the first real thing she knew was Maxy curled up in her arms. She lay on her side in his bedroom, spooned around him, as though all she need do to keep him safe from the world was lie there, quietly.

"We have to go."

The foggy tendrils of sleep started to drift apart. Was that Ellie she could hear through them?

"Babe, I'm sorry, but we have to go."

It was. It was Ellie. She was home. For the briefest time, Jody enjoyed the warm comfort of knowing everything was right in her world. And then the day's jagged edges pierced that moment, and everything fell apart.

"What?" she said. "Where?"

Ellie sat down on the bed next to her. She was holding her phone, using it as a torch. Ellie had it pointed down at the floor, but enough of the beam leaked up to light the curves of her face.

"Baby, we're going to go to Damo's boat. You've been there before.

At the yacht club. Things are a bit crazy and we'll get away for a couple of days. Until they calm down."

Jody eased herself up. The painkillers she'd taken earlier had backed off the headache and a lot of the muscle and joint pain from her mugging that morning.

Or was it yesterday? Wait. What?

She was mugged!

How could she forget that? And then everything she'd forgotten came back in a rush.

"Omigod, Ellie! That guy. Troy. We... he..."

"Karl shot him, yes. He's dead, Jody. He had to,"

"And Chad, what happened to Chad?"

Ellie looked almost annoyed to be asked. She got that line between her eyes. The one Jody called her 'Fuck you' line when she was in a mood to tease her.

"Chad ran away," Ellie said. "He's fine. Or, you know, as good as it ever gets for Chad. But we need to go, Jodes."

Jody whispered, worried about waking Maxy. Especially to hear this.

"Because Mister Valentine shot Troy?"

"No. Because Mister Valentine's gonna have to shoot a lot of other people if we don't go now. It's serious, babe. We've been talking about it for hours. Damo's here. He's been checking the radio in his car. It's the only news we can get. There's riots and everything."

Jody started to shake her head but stopped at the spike of pain that caused. She breathed in carefully.

"There's riots cos of Troy?"

She was having real trouble following this. Her thoughts went around in circles like the little paper planes on the mobile she'd made for Max and hung over his bed.

"No," Ellie said, forcing herself to be patient. Jody recognised the tone of voice. "The city is fucked up. The radio said there's going to be a military curfew tomorrow. Like for reals. They'll shoot people for breaking it. We've gotta get out now while we can."

None of it made sense. Jody squeezed her eyes shut for a second.

Everything was the same when she opened them. Her camera bag had been stolen.

No. Those cops got it back.

She hurt all over, but not as much.

The paper planes still turned in the dark over Maxy's bed.

"Shouldn't we just stay here then?" she said, thinking it sounded like the smartest thing she'd heard all week.

"Jodes, we've got almost no food in the house. The grocery stores are going to be empty by tomorrow. For sure. There's like food restrictions and rationing already. And people are just ignoring them. Fucking motorcycle gangs have been robbing 7-Elevens and shit. But for groceries, not money. We gotta go. It's just for a while. Until shit calms down."

Ellie played her winning card then.

"It'll be safer for Max on the boat. If Chad comes here, he'll have that fucking shotgun with him, and he'll be full of 'roids. And probably waving that stupid sword around."

That did it.

"I need to pack," Jody said.

"You don't. I did it all while you were sleeping. Maxy's stuff and yours. We need to go. Damo and Karl are in the car. His car. It can go cross country if needed."

"Cross country?"

"Parks and shit. Come on. I can take Maxy. He's too heavy for you. You're hurt."

Jody conceded that, at least. She didn't know how long she'd been out of it. Hours, it felt like. And the sleep had helped. Having Maxy had helped. But she was still hurting, and she didn't trust herself to carry the little boy anywhere. Ellie gave her the phone to hold and scooped Maxy up without waking him. She was very strong. Jody had once seen her carry a whole side of beef.

Jody led the way because she had the phone with the torchlight.

It felt wrong, sneaking out of the house like this, but she couldn't be here if Chad came around. Thinking of her ex-husband meant thinking about the moment his roommate's brains had splashed all over the street. Jody turned away from those thoughts.

Instead, she wondered at the fireworks she saw as they left the house. And then she realised it wasn't fireworks. It was an actual fire. A big one, nearby, sending great orange tongues of sparks into the night sky.

The sky over the city was a dense and vivid black, seemingly darker than normal but also lit with stars that were luminous, diamond-hard points of brilliance. It took her a moment, but she realised she could see so much more of the night sky because the city was largely blacked out, except for those fires.

Now they were out of the house, she could make out at least five separate blazes.

Ellie closed the front door and gently steered her down the path towards Damo's car. Fewer cars were parked in the street tonight, and she wondered briefly why. Had they left town, too?

Karl appeared from around the other side of Damo's Lexus and opened the rear door. He was such a lovely man, she thought.

And her mind's eye filled again with the image of Troy's brains exploding out the back of his head.

She shivered.

Max stirred in Ellie's arms as she lifted him into the middle seat in the rear of the SUV. Karl climbed back into the front next to Damo. He had the radio on but turned down low.

"Hey Jodes," he said. "Long day, mate."

"Very long," she agreed, taking her place next to Max. Ellie sat in the back, on the other side of the car. They pulled the doors closed, and Damo drove away.

"I'm gonna steer clear of the main routes," he said. "We can take residential streets most of the way there."

And they could, but they still had to cross a dozen or more major roads as Damo slowly hauled north towards the Golden Gate. Every time they hit a major crossroad, they struck cars piled bumper to bumper. Damo waited ten minutes at the first intersection, where Jules crossed Ocean near the Target they sometimes shopped at. Finally, muttering lots of Australian curse words, he pushed into the traffic, flashing his headlights and leaning into the horn, which woke

Maxy, but not for long. He burrowed his face deep into Jody's arm and went back to sleep.

Damo scraped against another car as he forced his way through the tangle, and Jody flinched, expecting him to start shouting. But he just ploughed on, reaching the other side and the relative quiet of a dead-end street. Jody wondered if they were stopping or picking somebody else up, but no. Damo drove to the end of the street, turned left, mounted the gutter and smashed through a small picket fence. Karl chuckled. Ellie swore quietly. And Damo drove through another fence a few seconds later before emerging onto a tranquil street lined with dark, expensive-looking townhouses.

Jody saw a few torch beams and candles through the windows but no flickering TV screens or other lights. They were deep inside a very wealthy-looking suburb, and over the next few minutes, Damo followed Karl's directions as they wound through curving avenues, avoided cul de sacs, and swerved around some cars that had been abandoned in the middle of the road. Unlike in the afternoon, there were very few people out here, and Jody wondered if they had left or shut themselves inside their homes.

It would typically take about twenty minutes to drive from their home to the Golden Gate. Maybe another four or five to get to the marina where Damo kept his boat. Three hours after leaving Ocean-view, they finally pulled into the parking lot at the yacht club. Two men in uniform stopped them at the front gate, but Damo showed them a membership card, and they waved him through.

"Were they soldiers?" Jody asked.

"Nope. Private security," Damo replied. "Looks like we weren't the only ones with this idea. I'll bet those blokes are earning triple time and cash in hand."

The parking lot was full of cars just like his. Big and expensive. Most were locked up, but a few people here and there unloaded boxes and coolers from their vehicles, carrying them down to where the boats were moored. Jody had no idea how many yachts and cruisers normally stayed here. This was not her world. But she could see that two-thirds of the berths were empty. The marina's offices were lit up, and staff worked inside. She'd bet that didn't normally happen. They'd be people like her. Ordinary people, not rich. Nobody was going to pay them to work at four in the morning. Not normally.

But this was not a normal night.

Ellie took Max again. He woke briefly, cried for a while, and went back to sleep, snoring softly against her shoulder.

Karl helped Damo unload half a dozen big boxes from the rear of the Lexus.

"I hit up the storeroom at work," he told Ellie quietly. "Gave Sandino all the keys and codes and said the staff could take what they needed, too."

She mulled that over.

"We're not opening again, are we?" Ellie said at last.

"Don't reckon so, mate. Come on. Let's get aboard and get moving."

Nobody asked Jody to carry anything, and she felt a bit useless and left out, but there wasn't much she could do. Those boxes Damo had loaded were huge, and it took both him and Karl working together to hump most of them down the jetty and onto the boat.

Jody had been on this boat once before. At a Christmas party for the restaurant.

To her, it looked huge and ridiculously opulent. There were four bedrooms. More than she and Ellie had at home. The kitchen was bigger than they had too, and the lounge, or the chill-out pit or whatever you called the main living space on a yacht, was full of white leather lounges. It filled her with dread at the possibility of Max getting loose in here with a Magic Marker.

She put him to bed in the room Damo showed her, the biggest one on the boat.

When Jody objected, he said, "I got nobody to share with, so it makes sense for you guys to take this one. Besides, I'm gonna be driving the boat for a bit, showing Karl how it's done so I can eventually take a rest."

Jody didn't object too hard. There was a massive television and a separate bathroom with an actual tub. Ellie appeared at one point with two backpacks. She lowered them to the foot of the bed, smiled at Jody and turned to leave again. She stopped. Turned back, hurried over and threw her arms around Jody, but gently. They hugged even more gently, and Ellie kissed her neck.

"I've got to help get us out of here, babe," she said. "But I'll be back."

"It's okay. Go. I'll look after Max. Make sure he's down. Do you think I could have a shower?"

"You should totally do that. You smell real bad," Ellie teased. That 'Fuck You' line between her eyes was gone.

Ellie kissed her once more, deeply this time, and hurried back to the upper deck. Jody's heart swelled again, watching her go.

She tucked Max in under the covers and took a shower with the door open so she could keep an eye on him. He didn't move.

The water was hot and came out of the shower head under pressure. This boat was like the hotel Ellie had sprung for on their first anniversary. Jody wondered if they would ever get to live like this, but it was a silly thought. Damien Maloney did not make his money from the restaurant. That was how he spent his money. Running a restaurant and owning a boat.

She remembered then that all his money had disappeared, and her heart lurched to think of it. She stayed under the shower for another minute to calm down. Damo didn't seem fussed about the problem with his bank anymore, though. Maybe he'd sorted it out. Or perhaps he'd found other things to worry about.

She finished showering, towelled off and opened one of the backpacks. She got dressed in a pair of cargo pants and a white shirt. Max snored behind her. As she was pulling on the shirt, the boat engines started, and a minute later she felt the deck shift under her feet as they backed out into the bay.

Jody couldn't find the light switch and decided it would be better to leave them on anyway. If Maxy woke up, he would need the lights. She didn't like leaving him alone, but he was deeply asleep. He had always been a champion sleeper.

She decided she would risk stepping out of the room for just a moment. She wanted to see the city as they pulled out. She wished she had her cameras.

All three of the others were in the wheelhouse when she came up, their faces lit by a panel of illuminated dials and screens. Damo was at the wheel, Karl and Ellie on either side of him. He spoke in a low voice as they motored slowly away from the marina.

Damo turned the boat around, affording her a sweeping view of the northern headlands, Sausalito, Alcatraz and Oakland.

She knew then that Ellie had been right to make her leave.

She had seen the city from the water many times before.

But she had never seen it like this.

Burning.

30

A LEGION APPROACHES

J onas woke early and alone. Tomi Yates, the local hottie who'd cock teased him so hard in the bar last night, hadn't circled back around for another stroke. But one of her friends had, and she was almost as hot. He'd been tempted. Jonas had been spanking it out for weeks. Figured until yesterday he was for sure gonna get some from one of those sweet-ass Dutch girls who just started at work. Maybe even both.

Because they fucking rocked out to Xurious, man!

But that wasn't gonna happen now. And he had reason to keep everything tidy here in Silverton. Twenty-five thousand reasons. So, he'd been courteous and sociable, and he'd even stood Tomi and her girlfriends a round of shots later in the evening, which he insisted on paying for with his own money. Or Mikey's money, if you wanted to be an asshole about it. But he'd kept a sober head and laid no more traps for himself. A long time before the last customer filed out of Big Al's, Jonas Murdoch had already retired to his free room and masturbated vigorously in the shower before crashing out to sleep the sleep of the just and perhaps the newly wealthy. He still couldn't get online. Cell reception up here in the mountains was shit, but he knew he had to make some money out of the Pendleton traffic. Even if it was just tee shirt sales at the website. Twenty-five large, though. That was a minor fortune, certainly enough for a new start, and he could use one at this point in his life.

Waking sober and hassle-free, he thought, was fucking amazing. Seriously, the trouble you could avoid if you took five minutes to jack off instead. As he dressed in shorts and a tee shirt, pulling on his runners, he resolved to jack off every day he was in this podunk town until he got his reward money. Or it became obvious he couldn't get it without running too great a chance of arrest.

He did resolve to push as hard and as fast as he could to lay hands on it, though. He didn't want to be here too long. That shit in Seattle yesterday and all the madness in the news, that couldn't last. Eventually, things would settle down, and the cops would be looking for him again.

Because he wouldn't be riding today, and there was no gym in town as far as he knew, Jonas wanted to take a light run back down the route he'd climbed on the bike yesterday. A couple of miles would do it. His legs were stiff and sore, in dire need of a stretch, and he'd have to keep his cardio up for when he rode out again. After the run, he planned on taking his breakfast at Big Al's. No sense in turning down hospitality. Then he'd find him some free, anonymised internet somewhere and check in on the pod and the site. And his PayPal account. There had to be some extra in there. He was also gonna polish up his legal research skills. Not to go after Disney and Pendleton this time. He wanted to learn as much as he could about claiming federal reward money. And whether any outstanding warrants for assault and petty theft might interfere with that.

As he dressed, Jonas cursed his stupidity in not giving the sheriff a false name yesterday, but not for long. That was crazy thinking. Despite having meant to do it for years, he'd never set up a false identity, apart from The Centurion, of course, and he was confident the feds would want ID and legitimate bank deets before they'd pay out any reward on Morena.

He took a piss, made sure he had the room key with him and left the cabin in the pre-dawn cool. It was deeply, almost eerily quiet up here in the national forest. No traffic yet on the one road through town. Assholes down in the city were probably still sitting in that monster fucking pile up. He snorted at that. Even if the cops were chasing him right now, they'd have to do it on foot, huffing and puffing the whole way. Probably stopping for a revitalising donut at every 7-Eleven and gas station they passed, too.

Feeling as though his luck had finally broken good, Jonas eased himself into a gentle, almost shuffling run out onto the town's main street. He groaned at the sweet pain of working muscles he'd pushed to near exhaustion yesterday and allowed himself some quiet pride in the strength and fitness he'd worked so hard to build over the last few years. It had saved him yesterday, escaping Seattle. Repaid the investment of hard training when he'd tackled the beaner. And it was a plain and genuine pleasure to be out in the clean air, feeling his potency.

He picked up the pace after a minute, the soles of his Nikes— stolen from the warehouse, natch—slapping on the pavement as he jogged past the site of his heroics. The crowds were gone, and the cash machine had shut down. Move along, citizen. Nothing to see here. He was the only person up at such an hour, and he was able to run out in the middle of the road, rather than dodging around street furniture and other obstacles on the sidewalk, which was littered with paper rubbish and food refuse, the residue of the previous day's mild anarchy. Jonas didn't imagine a tourist trap like Silverton would let its public areas run to seed, but he conceded that the day had got out of hand. Preoccupied with his headlong flight, he hadn't really thought about what any of it meant. If he was still at home, still hauling boxes for Amazon, he would've recorded a piece for The Centurion, riffing on the imminent and inevitable triumph of a genuine American uprising.

Today, he was more worried about opening a new account for his reward money. Be just his fucking luck to score twenty-five grand from Uncle Sugar, only to lose the lot in a fucking stock market crash or banking collapse or something.

As he settled into an easy, loping run at the edge of town, passing the spot where he'd nearly come off his bike, he made a mental note to himself to add another task to his online research later. He needed to know whether people were just being pussies about this run on the banks or whether it was a real thing. If it was going to complicate getting his money, he might be better off just leaving.

Fucking hard to do, though. Turning your back on money like that.

And he'd spent forty bucks on those drinks last night, too.

Man, he really needed to check his PayPal.

Feeling his temper rising with his frustrations, Jonas poured on the speed. He needed a clear head to think this shit through. He passed only a single car, travelling fast, as he accelerated to a sprint through the long curve of the downslope leading back to Seattle. The sun wasn't high enough to have warmed the air at this altitude, and the cool mountain breeze he ran into felt good on his skin. Five minutes of hard running, and he'd started to calm down again. The fucking globalist cucks in Washington weren't gonna let their Jewish banker friends go bust. They hadn't in 2008. They wouldn't now. Jonas would need to make sure that anywhere he stashed his money was federally guaranteed. He was probably at greater risk of an ass fucking by hanging out here too long – up in the woods, waiting on a payday – than he was from a market meltdown.

Even the Chinese thing was bullshit. Way Jonas saw it, those vicious old slants in Beijing had done the American people a fucking solid yesterday. That bitchslap with the drones and shit? That was gonna prevent a war, not start one. He almost fucking laughed at the brilliant, audacious fucking gall of it. Because again, there was no way that Wall Street was gonna let Washington fuck up their balance sheets by going to war with China. All the slants had to do was get their shit locked down. Make their boss level move a *fait a-fucking-ccompli*.

He ran and focussed on his breathing. He tried to let his mind fly out, into the dark green and brown vastness of the forests, and he felt through his soles the hard, fundamental reality of the mountain beneath his tread. It took a while, but in the end, he chilled himself out and was about to turn back when something... *something wrong...* in the corner of his eye pulled him up so abruptly that he almost stumbled over his feet. Jonas stood, breathing heavily, a couple of hundred yards before the road down to the coast turned abruptly into a series of switchbacks to negotiate a steep drop from the high plateau on which lay Silverton and thousands of acres of national forest. He'd cursed those switchbacks when he'd ridden up here yesterday. Felt like they'd added a couple of miles to his trip. He'd have preferred to go straight at the mountain.

Jonas wondered whether the thousands of people dragging themselves up on foot through that zig-zag sequence of hairpin bends felt as he had. They were legion. Because of the switchbacks, the main body of walkers was probably an hour's hike from where he stood. Maybe two from Silverton itself. But there were a few dozen outliers, or forerunners, or whatever, who ranged ahead of the pack. They'd definitely beat the main cohort into town.

"What... the fuck?" he breathed.

But he knew.

Part of him had known last night and refused to believe.

This was it.

He was never getting that money from the government because the government was done. They were done. The social contract was broken.

He turned and ran back for town as fast as he could.

And Jonas moved fast.

HE DIDN'T MAKE the mistake of sprinting the whole way. Matter of fact, he eased up a couple of minutes before the final turn into Main Street. When Jonas entered Silverton, he did so at a relaxed pace that he could have kept up for another hour.

He was very pleased with his fitness, and here it was, paying off again.

The town was not yet fully awake, but there were a few more people about now. Early risers, business owners, and even a gardener in the little public park that divided Main and hosted a statue of... what? The town's founder?

Jonas had no idea, but he jogged past the strangely elongated town square, Big Al's bar and diner, and the Farmer's Mutual. Sheriff Dave's domain was a small modern annexe attached to a much older, grander-looking stone building identified by its signage as the town and county administrative centre. It was still quiet there, but the lights were on next door in the annexe. A patrol car was parked out front, and Jonas could see someone moving around inside.

Given the enormous pear-shaped silhouette, he was willing to bet Sheriff Dave Muller himself was on the job. Probably fixing or delivering breakfast for his prisoner. Jonas took the stairs in three strides and knocked before trying the glass door, which was slightly ajar. It opened freely, and he pushed through.

"Hello," he called out. "You in, Sheriff?"

It had been three years since he'd had reason to cross the threshold of any law enforcement facility. Still, with time served as a bottom feeder in Florida's criminal justice system, he felt like a prodigal son finally returned. Thousands of miles distant, on the wrong coast, and seeming like some malign wizardry had completely inverted the weather, he still recognised the familiar sour stink of body odour, stale pee, lousy coffee and cop cologne. He knew that once upon a time, the carcinogenic reek of cigarettes would have masked some of the stench, but Silverton PD was like all public buildings now in being smoke-free. Fluorescent tubes cast an unflattering white light over everything, draining the scenery of depth and colour. Not that there was much colour to begin with, and most of that was provided by a couple of struggling ferns at a desk Jonas would bet was occupied by the station's administrative assistant. She would be three hundred years old and as mean as a cut snake, or two years out of high school and engaged to one of the deputies. Pregnant, too, probably.

"Jonas," Sheriff Muller said, looking both surprised and pleased to see him. "You taking off on your ride again?"

Jonas smiled ruefully.

"Not just yet, Sheriff. I'm a little sore from yesterday, and to be honest with you, I want to cross all the I's and dot all the T's on that reward you put me in for."

Holding a plate covered in silver foil, Muller seemed satisfied with that response.

"If you're free to wait a few minutes, I gotta deliver up Morena's breakfast. Ham and eggs from Al's, in fact. He got the contract for our catering. Hell of a turn, isn't it?" He rolled his eyes to convey his opinion of that unfortunate irony. "I can be with you in two..."

"That's fine, Sheriff," Jonas said. "But there's something else you need to know."

Muller frowned.

"Yup?"

"You got some trouble headed your way up the mountain. Looks like about a thousand people on foot. Some of them armed. I'm pretty sure they're... well, they're fleeing, I guess."

"Goddamn. What now?" Muller griped. "Just... gimme one minute."

The sheriff disappeared with the hot breakfast for his prisoner and came back before Jonas had much of a chance to check out the office. On first impressions, it was a small operation. Muller reappeared, balling up the aluminium foil from the breakfast plate. He tossed the silver ball into a bin. Wiped his hands on a wad of tissues he took from a desk and indicated with a wave that Jonas should join him.

"Better come along. You can tell me all about it on the way."

They left the office, climbed into the police cruiser parked out front, and Muller keyed the ignition.

"Down the hill, you say? Back towards the city?"

"Yes sir," said Jonas, a little surprised to be riding up front in a squad car. "Where it gets real steep, and the road starts zig-zagging, you know? I went out for a jog this morning. Took me about twenty minutes to run the distance."

Muller nodded as they pulled out onto Main Street.

"I'm guessing you don't work a desk job then?"

"Personal trainer," Jonas ad-libbed. He'd done that once, yet another side hustle for about five minutes after his divorce. Thought it might be a way to grab up some fresh pussy. And it was. But he needed a license and didn't have the money for accreditation. Then he got fucked by Alvarez, and... long story short, he moved to LA for a disastrous three months before fetching up even further away from Miami, in the rainy northwest. Most of the PTs he met were fucking flakes anyway. It would explain his patchy work history the last few years. And he couldn't tell this walking tub of donut lard that he worked for Amazon. Nothing good would come of that.

Muller didn't turn on the siren or even his flashers, but he did put on a good turn of speed as they headed for the edge of town.

"What makes you think they're fleeing?" the sheriff asked. He had to lean back in his seat because of all the extra belly hanging over his utility belt.

"They're dressed for it. Most of them anyway," Jonas said. "Like they're going camping. Some of them are carrying rifles."

"Hunting rifles?"

"Long arms like that, yeah. But AR-15s and stuff, too."

Muller sighed heavily.

"Damn. You really think people are heading for the hills? It seems, I dunno, a bit dramatic."

Jonas shrugged. They quickly ate up the road he'd ridden and run so hard to cover.

"Seattle was a mess when I left," he said. "Like, insanely gridlocked. But all that stuff on the news. And the banks and China. It's gonna freak some people out for sure. You're gonna have some nervous types headed your way. You know. Sort of people would jump at their own shadow..."

"But?" Muller asked, knowing there was more because Jonas had freighted his delivery with that implication.

"But," he said as they sped downhill, the dark green and brown blur of the forest flashing by on both sides, "you're probably gonna have some crazy survivalist types too, and wackadoodle militia and you know, the whole fruit and nut bar."

He was enjoying himself more than he would admit, watching poor Sheriff Dave try to digest all this. But he had his reasons, too. A long game he could see coming into focus.

"Goddamn it," Muller muttered as he wiped some speed off the clock as they closed on the switchback section. "Survivalists I can handle. They just buy up supplies and move on. Leastways, that's what happened last time."

"Last time?" Jonas asked, curious.

"That week in 08. Looked like the banks were going under."

"Ah," he nodded. "Right."

"But some of those militia assholes caused all manner of problems down Oregon way and across in Idaho. I know we had our share, too, but I wouldn't have thought there was too many in Seattle. It's all computer nerds and fancy coffee down there."

Jonas snorted. He couldn't help it.

"It's not a big city, but it is right out on the edge of the wilderness, and you got open carry. A lot of guys in those militia outfits they're not real woodsmen or anything. They're suburban fantasists. And this week is like all of their fantasies coming true."

Muller slowed down even more as they swept around a final curve in the road, and the view opened up over a steep descent through two or three miles of zig-zag blacktop.

"Damn," the sheriff muttered again.

Even Jonas was moved to grunt in surprise. There were many more people in the crowd than he had estimated. Maybe four or five thousand that he could see, and the first of the front runners were most of the way through the traverse. Muller reached across Jonas, excusing himself as he popped the latch on the glove compartment. It dropped open, and he took some binoculars from inside.

He put them to his eyes and frowned at the host, slowly making its way towards his town.

"You seem kinda knowledgeable on this topic, Mister Murdoch. Militias and such like."

Jonas noted the return to a more formal tone of address. He needed to play this just right.

"I used to be a lawyer," he said. "In Florida. Property management mostly. Condos and such. Retirement homes."

That was usually enough to kill anyone's interest in his former occupation. Usually.

"You swapped a salary in real estate law for personal training?"

Good pick-up, Jonas thought.

"It's honest work," he said. "Unlike lawyering."

Dave bobbled his head. He bought that.

"But," Jonas continued, wanting to move the conversation along. "I did have one client in dispute with a militia group who kept using his land without permission for their so-called training weekends."

He put deliberate air quotes around the word 'training'.

"I got to know the type well enough," he said. "These guys won't be any different. Look, see."

Jonas pointed to a small group of similarly dressed men—they were all men—striding ahead of the main cohort. They wore battle dress uniforms, but it was all desert pattern, not forest, and one ruined the already questionable camouflage with a bright orange scarf. Even without the binoculars, Jonas could tell that the uniforms weren't uniform at all. They would all be personal expressions of the owner's particular issues. Over the last few years, Jonas really had "got to know the type well enough", but not because of any property dispute.

Dave Muller was chewing loudly. A tell, Jonas thought, for his growing concern or even anxiety. He had no gum or chaw to work. He was gnawing away at his worries.

"Okay then, just excuse me," he said, mostly to himself, as he performed a quick, three-point turn and accelerated away from the oncoming horde, speeding back towards Silverton. He made a call while driving, undoubtedly breaking a bunch of his own local ordinances and state law. Muller held the phone to his ear while he steered with his free hand. Somebody answered on the other end.

"Hey, Mac. Yeah, it's me. Sorry to call so early, but I'm gonna need you, Dan and Laura Marie on shift early today. We got some trouble coming upslope. Looks like some damn refugee march out of the city. Helluva thing. You can probably see it from your top deck if you still got the telescope up there. Oh, and we better tell Doc Cornwell, too. Figure she's gonna get some work outta this. Blisters and heat stroke an' such like."

Jonas couldn't hear whatever this Mac said in reply. Muller was travelling fast now, but he knew these forest roads well and kept talking while driving. Given their discussion of the crowd's composition, the deputy appeared to have taken up the suggestion of scoping out the mob from his upper deck. The other man confirmed the presence of armed men in at least three separate cadres. A few singletons and families were also coming heavy, but they were more conventionally dressed and armed with hunting rifles.

Jonas wondered where this guy lived that would afford him a line of sight. Somewhere even more elevated, and possibly outside of town. He imagined some dude in his robe, drinking his morning joe and putting one eye to his kid's telescope while he chatted with Muller on his cell. The two men discussed the logistics of a huge crowd suddenly dropping on them from the morning sky and how they might handle the armed elements. Delicately, they agreed.

Jonas kept his own counsel while they talked. The corner where he'd nearly crashed his bike came up on them quickly, but Muller took it at speed with no apparent regard for the laws of physics or the likely consequences of testing those laws. Jonas felt his foot pressing hard on a phantom brake pedal, but the cruiser negotiated the sharp bend with ease, and as they roared into Main Street the sheriff gave his sirens a quick burst to warn a street sweeper out of his way.

He sped on, still talking to Deputy Mac, until they pulled up at the Sheriff's office again.

"Anyway, I'm back now," Muller said. "Get Dan and Laura Marie and meet me here."

He signed off and let go of a long breath.

"Your first ride along?" the cop asked.

"First and last time in a squad car," Jonas lied before adding, "I hope."

"And it appears I owe another favour, son. You know when you're heading out yet?"

Jonas took his time answering. He had to get this right. His lack of any absolute certainty helped with the act.

"Given this, I dunno, Sheriff. If you don't mind, I might let this circus pass through town before I hit the road again."

"Nothing for me to mind, son. We're glad to have you here. Albert most of all. I'm sure you're welcome at his place as long as it's convenient for you to stay. And... er, yeah, probably the right call not to get yourself tangled in with this mess coming up the hill. Whatever it is."

"Yes," Jonas said as they climbed out of the cruiser. Muller had been running the AC, for which he was grateful after his exercise, but now he felt the heat and climbing humidity as he left the chilled interior of the car. "About this mess," he said, jerking his thumb back in the direction they'd just come. "I won't tell you your job, Sheriff, but if this was my town, I wouldn't encourage anyone to linger." He smiled, slightly abased. "I know how that sounds coming from an outsider."

Muller nodded cagily.

"What's your thinking, son?"

Jonas made a show of blowing out his cheeks and staring back down the mountain.

"My thinking is that this bunch you got coming on you now is the first of a lot more."

He looked Muller square in the eye.

"I think the situation's going to get... tough. I haven't read the news this morning. And I've been out of contact, as you know. But you should probably be ready for things to get out of hand down in the city. Feels like they're getting out of hand everywhere. Unravelling. I wonder if you could feed everyone in that mob coming up the mountain and still have enough left over for your own people. City was jammed up bad when I left. I don't think Big Al's gonna be getting a food delivery any time today or maybe even this week. Hate to be the messenger with all the bad news, but..." he shrugged. "You gotta look after your own. Right?"

Muller said nothing.

Not straight away.

He took a good long time thinking it over.

Finally, he nodded as if conceding something he didn't care for.

"Yep," he said.

31

AMERICAN SIEGE

J onas left Muller with those uneasy thoughts. He returned to his cabin, showered and changed into jeans and a black tee-shirt, and went through to breakfast at the diner. The bar, which had hosted seemingly half the town last night, was busy again this morning, but the vibe was different. It didn't feel hungover to him. More like subdued and anxious. He ordered scrambled eggs with Canadian bacon, biscuits, chicken gravy, and all the coffee they could pour. No charge, of course.

He took a booth by the window, looking out over the street, and searched for a newspaper to read. He knew they were full of globalist lies and special pleading for elitist parasites, but he also knew how to filter that shit out. He wasn't a moron. This morning, however, there was nothing to filter.

"No delivery today," the barmaid informed him. "Usually get The Post and The Times from Seattle, but they didn't turn up. Nothing's getting through."

She apologised again with a lift of her shoulders.

"WiFi's free. You want the password?"

That was good to know, but he didn't dare turn on the phone even though he had a rock-solid VPN on his cell. They could track you through those things, and although Jonas doubted he was a priority for the Seattle PD, it was good op-sec to leave no trail. He would still need to find another anonymous way of getting online to check his accounts. He settled down to his breakfast and *Today* on the TV over the bar. Craig Melvin was interviewing some admiral when Jonas speared a fork into his eggs, but the newsfeed switched over to Kristen Welker in Washington before he even had time to start carving up the bacon.

The fork stopped halfway to his mouth.

A banner beneath Welker screamed AMERICAN SIEGE?

And beneath that...

STARVATION!

The muted buzz in the diner dampened to a tense, almost febrile hush as Welker's voice filled the room.

"Congress is meeting in emergency session," she said, in a piece to camera from the steps of the Capitol Building, "but not behind me. All four hundred and thirty members and one hundred Senators are meeting in an unprecedented online session, logging in from dozens of secure and secret locations scattered around the nation."

The buzz came back as Big Al's customers began speculating where their representatives might be hiding and why.

"It's China. China's gonna go nuclear," somebody said a few tables over.

"No, Rosie," another diner at a different table called out. "It's Iran. I read on my Facebook this morning that they're all saying it's Iran."

"Who's saying?"

"My David's in the Air Force, and he..."

Jonas tuned out the idiot chatter and tried focusing on the official fake news on screen. The government would be lying for sure. That's what governments did. But the shape of the lie they threw over the truth could sometimes tell you what lay beneath. Kristen Welker had a full slate of lies and evasions to report on. China's denial of involvement in the previous day's attacks on US military bases. Homeland Security's assurance that all critical domestic infrastructure remained functional and that the President's Executive Order imposing food rationing was merely a precaution against panic buying and hysteria, which "would do far more damage than any limited and largely unsuccessful cyber-attack on a small number of grocery chains." And, most notably of all, at least to Jonas, was something Welker mentioned almost as an aside about the Attorney General 'going missing' for three hours during the chaos and haste of evacuating the executive from DC.

Jonas chewed his bacon thoughtfully.

Three hours.

That was a hell of an extended bathroom break. Especially for the guy running the Justice Department, a rival power centre to the Oval Office on an average day, but possibly the most important challenger to supreme executive fiat in any national emergency. He felt his heart quickening and his thoughts beginning to race.

This was it.

This had to be it; the coup anybody could have seen coming if they'd just opened their eyes and looked.

Jonas hurried to finish his breakfast, ensuring he ate everything on the plate. Nutrition was going to get scarce, that was for damn sure. One of the first things you do in a siege? Cut off the food supply. Starve out the enemy. He observed the other customers, who were mostly still arguing about the meaning of it all. One table of young women he thought he recognised as Tomi's friends had moved on to celebrity gossip. He was almost tempted to ask them if they'd heard about the actresses Pendleton had raped. But he denied his understandable curiosity. If those girls had any sense, they'd be loading up on calories and weapons. But they weren't, of course. They were all sheep. Content to graze.

He left the diner and felt himself passing among them as a wolf.

He had no idea what Muller and the other cops would do about the thousands of people heading for Silverton, but he did know that whatever they tried would not work and was irrelevant anyway. The situation had moved beyond the prosaic measures of a small-town sheriff. As Jonas stood on the sidewalk in front of Al's, taking in the clean air and the warm morning light, a police cruiser sped past, headed downslope for the refugee caravan.

That's how he imagined them. A caravan. For that was the truth of it. They were refugees, the first of millions that he was sure would soon be on the move. Most of them into military camps. Or prison camps. These chumps had no idea. Since 1903, every male in America between the ages of seventeen and forty-five had been legally defined as being part of the nation's Unorganised Militia. They were subject in times of national emergency to military discipline. Not civilian law. Jonas was sure that these days, federal anti-discrimination statutes gathered up every woman in the US between those ages, too. Hundreds of millions of idiots, stuffing their faces with breakfast, none realising they'd just been drafted.

Jonas had to get moving. He had people to find. He didn't know where to look for Dale Juntii, the jarhead he'd met last night at Al's, and he didn't want to draw attention to himself by asking around. But he knew Brad Rausch—*"Damn, but you fucking showed that wetback"* —would be at his auto shop or would be turning up soon enough. And the nice thing about a fuckmaggot, one-street burg like Silverton? All you had to do to find the diner, or the town hall, or the auto shop was take a stroll up and down that street.

Jonas didn't recall seeing Rausch's business back the way he'd come into town, so he headed west on Main, tracking alongside the leafy stretch of lawn that served as the town's centrepiece and gathering place. He didn't imagine Rausch would have his shop in the middle of town. The only businesses that could afford the rent would be living directly off outsiders, and sure enough, he passed one tourist trap after another. Two cafes were open and serving breakfast, but both warned diners that they couldn't process electronic payments. The three cash machines he passed were out of service, and the sidewalk in front of them was littered with discarded transaction slips. A woman sweeping the path in front of her trinket shop smiled at Jonas as he walked past but quickly returned to her chore when it was apparent he wasn't a paying tourist.

Main Street wasn't long. He quickly reached the western end of town and frowned when the streetscape gave way to thick forest not far beyond a small, white clapperboard home with a hand-carved wooden shingle that declared this to be the surgery of Doctor Andrea Cornwell. Jonas stood half-in, half-out of the gutter in front of Cornwell's surgery, wondering whether to go back and check the street on the other side of the town's dividing park when the door to the doctor's rooms opened, and she hastened down the steps.

"Oh," she said, surprised to find a stranger lurking at the end of her garden path. "I'm afraid I can't see patients right now. I have to go help the sheriff with something."

Jonas was just as surprised but put the whole thing together quicker than Cornwell. He had more information.

"That's cool, doc," he said. "I'm not sick. I'm looking for Brad Rausch."

Her face, previously arranged in a pleasant, neutral expression, turned almost vinegary at the mention of the auto mechanic's name. However, she made a visible effort to hide her distaste when Jonas explained that he was looking for a car.

"Thought he might have one to sell me, is all. Just an old beater, you know?"

She had paused on the other side of her gate, keeping it closed between them.

"I'm sure he could help you with that, Mister Murdoch."

She recalled his name.

That was rarely a good thing, but Jonas put it down to her looking after Al Barrett. Of course, she'd remember the guy who saved her patient. A town this small, they were probably good friends. Cornwell appeared to reach a decision. She opened the gate, came through, closed it behind her and pointed to the road out of town.

"If you keep walking, you'll find him about ten minutes down the road. Be careful. There's no path to walk on, and once cars get out of the town limits, they speed up. A lot. They won't have time to see you and slow down on some of those bends."

"Thanks, Doc," Jonas said, keeping it light and breezy. "How's Mister Barrett doing?"

She wasn't expecting the question, and he saw the shadow flit across her face.

"He's doing as well as can be expected. But I'd prefer to have him in hospital, not sitting in bed watching ESPN."

She considered Jonas anew.

"He speaks highly of you, Mister Murdoch. If you should see him, please encourage him to be sensible and get to a proper hospital."

"Sure," Jonas said, the very picture of compassion. "I owe him, after all. Dinner and breakfast so far."

Cornwell excused herself and started walking towards the other end of town. Jonas watched her go before plunging into the forest.

He reached Rausch's place ten minutes later. No vehicles passed him on the forest road, which was good luck. Cornwell was right. There wasn't much of a walking path by the edge of the blacktop. Rausch's auto shop also doubled as a gas station. A 1950s or 60s vintage pick-up was parked on the apron, gleaming in the shafts of the morning sun that pierced the forest canopy. It was a striking contrast to the business premises, which were of an even earlier vintage but not as well maintained. Two later model sedans were inside the garage under repair, and Jonas was pretty sure Rausch had a few more refurbs and rebuilds out the back, but a tall, corrugated iron fence blocked his view.

"Yo! Brad Rausch," he called out, standing beside the pump.

The door to the little shopfront stood open, and Jonas could hear talk radio inside, but there was no sign of the proprietor.

"Hello," he called out again.

Rausch appeared from around the side of the building, wiping his hands on an old rag. His expression was dour until he recognised Jonas. He was a solid fireplug of a man. Somewhere in his fifties but still packing more muscle than flab thanks to a life of hard physical toil. His sullen, slightly florid features lightened some when he saw who'd come calling.

"Hey, champ. What can I do for you?"

The mechanic approached with his hand out, and Jonas shook it heedless of any grime he might pick up.

"Jonas Murdoch," he said, guessing Rausch had forgotten his name. "Might be interested in some wheels if you got 'em to sell."

Rausch's mood, which Jonas assumed was permanently stormy, lifted even further.

"Could be I can help," he said. "What you got in mind?"

"Depends," Jonas said. "Guessing that pick-up out front isn't for sale?"

Rausch smiled. "Nope. My pride and joy."

"Sweet ride. Anyway, seems like I'm up for some reward money for tackling that wetback yesterday. If it pays off, like Sheriff Dave says, I'd like to get me something that can handle cross-country terrain. You got anything like that? For a good price?"

"I do, and the price is great," Rausch said. "For you, a patriot's discount. But it's cheap anyway. Got a Jeep went off the road two years back. Insurance company called it a write-off. But it wasn't. I been putting it back together with spares and stuff. Thought I might drive it down south sometime. Take a swim where the water won't freeze off your balls."

"But?" Jonas said.

Rausch threw his hands up.

"Who's got time? Or the money?"

"Ha, testify, brother," Jonas laughed. "You mind if I take a look?"

"For sure. Come on back," Rausch said.

The mechanic led him through the shopfront, past a rack of tired, faded pornography and stale-looking road food. Twinkies. Corn chips and such like. The radio was loud and crackling with reports of supermarkets nationwide defying government orders to restrict customers to purchases totalling one hundred dollars each. There'd been a riot in Texas when a Piggly Wiggly tried that communist shit on for size. Rausch didn't appear to be listening. He led Jonas through his 'back office', a small utility room piled high with spare parts, stacks of paper, and the second dirtiest toilet Jonas had ever seen. (Numero Uno was the shitter in Mikey's place when he moved in. Jonas had demanded and got a permanent twenty-dollar discount on the rent for cleaning it out and keeping it clean. A bargain. He could never live with a poop throne like that).

The lot out the back of Rausch's shop held three vehicles in various states of repair. The Jeep was the best of them. He let the mechanic talk him through the manifest benefits of owning a pre-loved Jeep and the potentially niggling but barely fucking noticeable issues of buying this particular Jeep which Rausch had hauled off the side of the mountain, where it had ended up on its roof after rolling on a tight bend.

"I won't shit you, Jonas. It had some serious fucking deceleration trauma, worst of which was probably the door panel I had to rip off and the busted ass top cover, but you can see that while it ain't like new, it will surely do."

Jonas had to stop the snort of laughter that tried to escape from the back of his throat and out through his nose.

This was a fucking Frankenstein ride. Mismatched panels. One missing headlamp ("Yeah, I'm planning to fix that.") A badly crumpled fender. ("Still beating that one out.") And a weird, hand-fashioned side mirror on the driver's side.

"Well," Jonas said, "it ain't pretty, but I'm not interested in paying for pretty. Does it go? Is it roadworthy?"

"Hell yeah!" Rausch laughed. "You want we should take a run back into town, maybe down the hill a ways. I know! I can show you where I pulled it out of the ravine. Weren't nothing to it. Insurance weenies didn't want the trouble, is all. Didn't want to pay me for the work, truth be told."

"Amen to that," Jonas said. "Those fucking crooks. They never pay nothing."

He had a natural facility for adjusting his conversation to the level of those around him. It had helped with the hoodlums he repped back in Florida. He knew he was doing it and knew not to overdo it.

"No point driving back into Silverton, " he continued. "Or at least not much beyond town. You hear about the refugees?"

Rausch's face betrayed confusion before turning dark.

"The what? Fucking Mexicans, you say?"

Jonas smiled winningly, he thought, as if at his own stupidity.

"Nah, not that sort of refugee, no. My bad. I was out this morning and saw a couple of thousand people dragging themselves up the mountain from down Seattle way, I guess."

Rausch looked confused again.

"The fuck you say? What's that about?"

Jonas took his time.

This was like fishing. You didn't want to pull too hard on the rod.

Not that he'd ever done much fishing.

He arranged his face into the expression of a man with some hard news he'd rather not deliver.

"You been watching the news?" he said at last, as though finding a way through a difficult patch of trail and emerging onto a clear path.

"I try not to," Rausch admitted. "It pisses me off."

"Yeah. I know," Jonas agreed. "Fucking fake news, right?"

"Fuckin' right," said Rausch.

"Yeah, well, they're still lying and shit," Jonas went on, leaning forward as if to conspire darkly. "But they can't hide what's happening now, not when it's this big."

Brad Rausch furrowed his brow. He was leaning up against the dented driver-side panel of the Jeep. It was quiet out in the forest. The tinny sound of the radio drifted back to them, but Jonas couldn't make out what the voices were saying. Just the quickened sense of threat and danger in their tone.

"China, you mean?" Rausch frowned.

"Yeah, that," Jonas agreed. "But the rest of it, too. The banks collapsing. That's a hell of a coincidence, don't you think? And the internet, too. Another coincidence."

"Not if the chinks did it."

"No, that's right," Jonas said. "But it's happening in Europe too. In Asia. It's everywhere. Why would they do that?"

"What?" Rausch said, looked unsure of his meaning.

"You got any deliveries scheduled this week?" Jonas asked, playing a hunch.

"Supposed to be gas on Thursday."

"Is it coming?"

"Don't see why not."

"You should check."

"Why do that? What do you know, Murdoch?"

"I know the National Guard's been called out and federalised. Saw that on the news back at Big Al's. I know that even though they're blaming China for this attack, China's denying it, and our military is being pulled back *into* the country. Not sent out to give the slants the ass-kicking they got coming."

Rausch's expression was changing from confused to concerned.

"I don't... why would they do that?"

Jonas made like he didn't want to say it, but he had to.

"To defend themselves against an uprising. China ain't the threat. One sub full of nukes can deal with them. But three hundred million pissed-off citizens with the right to bear arms? That's a threat you can't nuke. That's fucking medieval, man. That's a real fucking peasant uprising. And you deal with that shit like a fucking medieval overlord. You send in your army and starve out the peasants. That's what I think this shit is, Brad. And that's why I want that Jeep. I'm out of here. Those refugees coming up the hill? They're the first of a million or so just from the city. A week from now, they're gonna be killing each other for dog food. And I don't think your Sheriff Dave has one fucking clue what's coming."

Rausch glowered at him.

"He ain't my sheriff. I voted O'Shannassy."

Jonas smiled sardonically, "Shoulda voted harder."

The mechanic barked a short, hard laugh in reply.

"Yeah. Too late for that. How many of them are coming, you say?"

"A couple of thousand right now," Jonas said. "First of them will be in town soon. Like, next half hour, if Muller lets them in."

"He will."

"He shouldn't. Food's gonna run out. Food, stores, fuel. Everything."

Rausch's frown grew cavernous.

"Gimme a second," he said before disappearing back inside. The radio cut out. Jonas inspected the Jeep again without having a salesman hovering over him. It was a woeful piece of shit as a repair job, but he didn't doubt it would run. God himself guaranteed redneck repairs. It was good to know he could get to some wheels if he had to. Rausch returned after a minute, looking even darker of mood than before.

"No delivery this week. Some shit about a computer glitch. Messed up the ordering."

Inside his head, a miniature cartoon version of Jonas jumped up and punched the air.

"Figures," he said. "They're cutting us off. They're cutting everyone off."

"Let's get into town," Rausch said. "I wanna talk to Darren O'Shannassy."

"Can we take the jeep?" Jonas asked. "Call it a test drive."

Rausch brightened at the suggestion.

"Sure. You can admire my handiwork. Come on, I'll get the key and shut up my shop."

Jonas followed him back into the shop and noted the location of the keys, hanging from a hook with half a dozen others on a corkboard behind the counter.

Good to know.

32

RALLY IN SILVERTON

R ausch's phone kept buzzing at him on the short drive back into Silverton. It was some ancient piece of Samsung crap with a broken screen, and the third time it buzzed he plucked it out of the cup holder in the Jeep's centre console and tossed it to Jonas.

"If that's my ex-wife, delete the bitch," he said. "She just wants money I don't have for fucking kids that ain't mine."

"You cool with me reading your message?" Jonas asked before taking the phone.

"Hell, yes. Phones in the car are fucking dangerous, man. I get more work off of assholes texting other assholes behind the wheel than I do from drunks. It'll be Sheila, for sure. Or fucking spam. That's all I got coming these days," Rausch grumbled as he rounded the last curve before Doctor Cornwell's cottage on the edge of town.

Jonas read the text.

"Spam," he confirmed. "But not like you're thinking."

"What then?" Rausch asked.

"Fucking Homeland Security, man. Telling you that you're on a budget now. Hundred bucks of consumables until, and I quote, 'the current crisis is over'."

"The fuck is this?" Rausch said.

"Gimme a second," Jonas said. It was difficult to read the text under the cracked screen with the Jeep in motion, but after a moment, he returned the phone to the cup holder.

"Yeah, it's like I heard on the TV this morning. Federal government's imposed food rationing. If you can fucking believe it."

Brad Rausch could not. He pulled over to the curb and took up the phone again. While he was reading and cursing, Jonas scoped out Main Street. A crowd, maybe a few hundred strong, had gathered in the park while he was at the auto shop. He thought most of them were townspeople. They weren't hauling backpacks or tents or any camping gear, not like the small, scattered groups coming into Silverton from the other end of town.

"Goddamnit, how'd these clowns get my number?" Rausch asked, and Jonas almost smiled at his naivety.

"They got everyone's number," he said. He thought he could see the first of those militia yahoos marching in from the climb. "You still want to find this O'Shannassy or get to the store before it's cleaned out?"

Rausch checked his mirrors, flicked the indicator to signal he was pulling back onto the road, and leaned gently onto the gas. Jonas had never seen a more cautious redneck behind the wheel, but he had to allow that this guy's line of work would make anyone a careful driver. Probably hosed a slaughterhouse worth of bad drivers out of their wrecks over the years.

"I'll lay money on the barrel that Mister O'Shannassy's already here," Rausch said, pulling over and parking half a block down from the main body of the crowd. They had gathered around the statue in the town common, which stood directly between Silverton's two grocers. A family-run general store and a much larger Red Apple on the other side of the park. The little store, more of a deli and bakery now that he looked, was occupied. He could see people inside, but the doors were closed, and a couple of dudes stood out front with their arms folded as if to bar the way in.

"Come on," Rausch said, climbing out and slamming the door. "I know where he'll be."

Jonas followed.

He was unsure where this was headed or how he should play it. It was not yet late in the morning, but the sun hammered down from clear blue skies, and the mercury was already climbing toward the hundred mark. He followed Rausch into the gathering, which was growing larger by the minute. A town as small as Silverton, that made sense. Everybody could look out of their windows and see what was happening.

And what was happening?

Jonas thought it felt like the ground was moving under all of their feet. But miles down below. Like some profound tectonic shift had already shunted everything sideways, but the first tremors were only arriving now. He vaguely recognised a few faces, possibly from the bar and diner or maybe from the street yesterday afternoon. He did remember the two YouTube kids, who'd now climbed on the statue and were filming the crowd from above. One of them waved at him, and he waved back, smiling. The townsfolk were abuzz with the news of the rationing. Half of them appeared to be reading the same text Rausch had just received. Some argued in favour of the order. Most did not. Moving through the crowd, keeping close to Rausch, following his thick neck and massive shoulders, he heard snatches of conversation, but it was obvious the message from Homeland Security had cranked up everyone's stress levels. Nobody was talking about collapsing banks or drone attacks now. They just wanted their damn Pop-Tarts and pizza pockets, and they didn't want some bureaucrat in Washington telling them otherwise.

He saw no sign of Sheriff Dave or his troops. The lawman was probably downslope, trying to get a grip on the horde marching on his town. Jonas knew he'd be back soon enough, though. He could see the first of the organised arrivals heading up Main Street. They were an obvious militia crew, tricked out in desert tan choc-chip cammo and tactical rigs fresh from a cardboard box he'd probably humped around Amazon's warehouse before Travis shit-canned him.

Jesus. Was that only yesterday?

It felt like a thousand years ago.

The crowd was packed a little denser on the far side of the town common, out in front of the Red Apple. It seemed hotter here, and people's patience was already frayed to the point of rupture. Jonas could see why.

There were at least six men toting weapons—four axe handles and two shotguns—barring entry to the small supermarket. Dale Juntii held one of the pump-action shotties. He was scowling at the crowd, but when he saw Jonas approaching with Rausch, Juntii grinned and winked at them. As if he was secretly letting them know about a great deal on cheap beer they could get over this way. Even if Rausch hadn't made a beeline for the stocky, square-jawed all-American psycho standing next to Juntii, Jonas would have happily doubled down on any size bet that this enormous asshole was the failed candidate for Sheriff of Silverton, Darren O'Shannassy.

His silvery hair was buzzcut down to the skull, and unlike the cosplay pocket Nazis marching into town at that very moment, his freshly pressed battle dress jacket was appropriately camouflaged for local operations. He had the other Remington shotgun.

"Mister O'Shannassy," Brad Rausch said, raising his voice to be heard over the crowd noise but stopping short of joining the cadre of local heavies on the steps.

"Good to see you, Brad," the man said, "You come to lend a hand?"

Rausch seemed to falter. He was confused.

"You heard about this rationing thing, sir? Is this for real? The government can't do this, can it? Not to us?"

O'Shannassy glowered at him.

"Government can't, but we can. And we will, son. Has to be done if this town is gonna get through the next few days."

"Oh," Rausch said so quietly only Jonas might have heard. "Okay then."

Jonas hung back, not wanting to draw attention to himself, but there was no escaping the radar sweep of Darren O'Shannassy's hard, calculating eyes.

"You're that fella who stepped in and saved Albert yesterday, are you?" he said.

"Yeah," Jonas said. "I was just out at Brad's place. Seeing about buying some wheels."

O'Shannassy's stare was cold but not hostile. Jonas sensed himself being measured and judged.

"Fair enough then. You did some good yesterday, son. Better than that useless sack of shit Muller."

Rausch, Jonas noted, had quietly joined the end of the guard line securing the entrance to the supermarket. It had taken him only a few moments to go from outraged protester to compliant enforcer. The mechanic leaned forward and raised his voice to be heard.

"Murdoch's a good guy, Mister O'Shannassy."

"Didn't say otherwise, Brad," O'Shannassy growled.

He didn't invite Jonas to join the palace guard either.

Not that he was fussed about that. Shit was getting real in Silverton. There had to be twice the town's population of four hundred and some crammed into the common now, with more trailing in from the eastern end of town every minute and locals pouring out of the side streets. The tenor of the crowd was changing, too. The milder, congenial buzz of a neighbourly forum, even one called to deal with a pressing difficulty, was giving way to something heavier.

Jonas had done his share of street-level activism. He'd marched by torchlight in Charlottesville. Run with the Proud Boys in the rolling brawls at UCLA, where they'd finally given those Antifa fags the asskicking they'd been begging for.

But this was different.

This was like the normies had all swallowed the red pill at once. He wasn't an outlier here. The anger he'd carried around for years had suddenly boiled up everywhere.

It was a fucking rush, is what it was. But he'd seen how explosive this shit could be too. And he could see the fuse burning quickly towards the exact place where he stood, with the approach of half a dozen out-of-town militia, all of them carrying heavier weapons than anything O'Shannassy's crew could bring to bear.

And still, there was no sign of Sheriff Muller and his deputies.

The militia types appeared to come on, surfing a wave of crowd noise. He knew these guys, even if he didn't know these exact assholes. The fact they made it into town ahead of the main group, the fact they weren't wheezing and gassing out and sweating like human wheels of cheese, meant they weren't the sort of fat, beta fantasists he'd spoken to Muller about. No doubt there'd be plenty of them on the way up – if they didn't all keel over from heart attacks and heat stroke in the foothills.

But not these assholes.

They looked lean, mean and hungry as fucking weasels. Jonas faded back into the front ranks of the crowd around the Red Apple. He watched O'Shannassy set himself to receive whatever challenge was coming and shuffled back along with everyone around him as the militia strode up and arrayed themselves behind a wiry, middle-aged man carrying an AR-15. He was clean-shaven, save for a neatly trimmed salt and pepper moustache, and his face was flushed with the exertion of the march.

He and his men had definitely marched up here. Not strolled.

They were all red-faced and sweating – but a respectable level of sweat – and Jonas fancied he could smell the stink of their hard trek over the rank stench of the crowd.

"You Darren O'Shannassy?" the man said.

There were no name tags on his uniform.

"Yep. I own this store," O'Shannassy said, surprising Jonas. He hadn't thought of that angle. Figured O'Shannassy was trying out his amateur warlord mojo, not barring the door to his pantry.

"Name's Wolfenden," the man said. "Joe Wolfenden. Your Sheriff Muller said you'd be here. Said to tell you we're just re-supping and rolling through."

"Well, you'll be rolling through. He got that right."

Wolfenden said nothing.

His men shifted slightly in their parade ground rest posture. Nobody raised any weapons or made any challenges, but Jonas felt his balls trying to crawl up inside his body.

Wolfenden spoke again.

"Sheriff Muller said..."

Darren O'Shannassy cut him off.

"Sheriff Muller says a lot of stupid things. And this ain't his store. It's mine."

A few people in the crowd oohed and aahed at that, but the militiaman just laughed softly.

"Uhuh. You plan on opening today? Looks like you got plenty of custom."

O'Shannassy nodded. He held the long-barrelled Remington across his chest. Relaxed but ready to turn on anybody who crossed him.

"I will open in my own time," he said. "And there will be no disorder or anarchy or panic of any sort."

"Sounds like a plan," Wolfenden said, shrugging.

"But you ain't part of it," O'Shannassy said, raising his voice. "Local customers only today."

Wolfenden's men did react to that. Nothing dramatic. Nobody started throwing down fire. But they all turned together, placing O'Shannassy within their firing arcs should they snap up those AR-15s and get to work. The machined harmony of their movement was impressive, Jonas thought. But the people of Silverton weren't as appreciative. Another 'ooh' ran through the crowd, and he was carried back a few more steps as the crush of people around him began to back out of the contested space.

Darren O'Shannassy's shoulders twitched, but he kept the shotgun held low and pointed harmlessly away from any warm-blooded target. He smiled. A cold smile.

"You boys ain't done no real service, have you?" he said. His voice had a natural growl, but he seemed to have lowered it a little, too. Jonas also doubted whether he talked like such a shitkicker in polite conversation. He was acting out his role just as much as Wolfenden. Who said nothing.

"You come in here, tooled up, but you didn't do your recon," O'Shannassy said. "You don't have the high ground."

He grinned. A wolfish expression.

Wolfenden didn't flinch, but a couple of his guys did, their eyes flitting nervously over the crowd, up and down Main Street.

"Captain," one of them said. "DMR high, times two. Roofline, two and four o'clock. Zeroed on you, sir."

Wolfenden grinned now. Not quite as carnivorously, but he made a solid effort to look like he didn't give a shit.

"Just came into town to buy some camping supplies and refill our canteens," he said softly. His trigger finger was still outside the guard of the rifle. "Sheriff Muller said there wouldn't be a problem if we moved on."

"For once, he was right, then. There won't be. You can fill your canteens in the Common. And then you can move on."

Jonas realised the low but strident clamour of the crowd had died away altogether. He thought he could hear the breathing of a thousand people around him. As fascinating as it was watching these two bull goose loonies dance with each other, he was starting to think it might be an idea to get the hell out of the free fire zone.

"I think you should open the store," Wolfenden said. "Now."

"And I think you should get the hell gone."

"That's not gonna happen. You will open up, and we will pay you a fair price for our needs."

O'Shannassy slowly, very slowly, turned the muzzle of the shotgun on Wolfenden.

"No," he said.

The militiaman smiled again.

"That's two guns you have trained on me, shopkeeper. But I can put three times that number on you."

The gasp when his men raised their weapons to point them at O'Shannassy was loud. So loud that nobody heard the two police cars pull up a hundred yards down the road.

But Jonas saw them. He'd been looking for a way out.

"Sheriff's here," he said, and his voice, pitched into the pool of quiet after that collective inhalation of breath, carried over the park. A thousand heads turned, all the gunmen included, and you could feel the tension suddenly come off a peak.

Jonas saw his chance.

He saw two roads leading away from this point in time, heading in two very different directions. He stepped into his future.

"I can help here," he said, pushing his way out of the crowd and placing himself between the two men.

They both looked at him as if he was nuts. And there was a fair chance they judged him right.

But Jonas saw his chance.

"THE HELL IS GOING ON HERE?" Sheriff Muller scowled as he marched into the confrontation between the militia captain and his old sparring partner. He sounded tired and angry, but mostly tired, and the day hadn't even begun. The crowd moved almost gently, like the lapping waves of a low tide. Wolfenden and O'Shannassy tried to speak at once, along with a dozen onlookers, including Dale Juntii and a couple of the militiamen.

"Whoa there, everyone just climb down off of the ramparts," Muller cautioned. His eyes caught Jonas, who smiled helpfully as though he couldn't wait to let ol' Sherriff Dave in on some fantastic joke.

"Mr Murdoch. You want to tell me what's going on here? As an impartial observer. Although honestly, I'm pretty sure I can already guess."

Neither Wolfenden nor O'Shannassy were pleased to cede the making of their case to a third party, but with two more deputies arriving and tenuous control of the situation seeming to pass into the steady hands of Sheriff Dave Muller, each man kept his own counsel. The crowd had started to murmur again, the buzz building quickly, and Jonas stepped forward, turning to Muller and shielding his eyes against the morning sun.

"Sheriff," he said in his most soothing courtroom voice. "I promise you there is less to this than meets the eye." Muller snorted quietly at the attempted humour. He would appreciate the need of it in a tense situation. Jonas inclined his head towards Wolfenden and his men.

"These men," he said, "have had a long hot walk to get up here. I understand you assured them they'd be welcome in town and that nobody would interfere with their freedom of movement, including the freedom to move on."

Muller nodded cautiously. Wolfenden seemed to be chewing over an objection but decided against it. Jonas had pulled on his old court-room persona like a favourite tee-shirt, long lost, now rediscovered. He'd forgotten how much he enjoyed being on his feet in front of an audience and just rolling with the bullshit. He had loved this part of being an attorney. The high-wire act. The rapt attention. Podcasting from his lounge room wasn't the same, although it had kept him in the habit of talking without stopping for hours on end.

"Mr O'Shannassy here," he went on, "has quite reasonably had to secure his business against panic and disorder and not just because of our current difficult circumstances. He, like the rest of us, is now under instruction from the government, from Homeland Security, about the need for temporary rationing of our resources, again because of a short-term crisis which is the fault of nobody here. Not Mr O'Shannassy. Not Mr Wolfenden. And certainly, nobody resident in Silverton. A fair summation?" Jonas asked, drawing both men into his performance.

Neither of the principals had been insulted, nor had Jonas spoken to confer any advantage over one or the other. Both could reluctantly agree that he had just given a fair summary. Nearly a hundred people who had crowded in close to the exchange murmured, nodded, and generally shared their assent.

It had been a long time since Jonas Murdoch had stood before the bench and addressed a judge or a jury. And if hard truth be known, he hadn't been particularly good at it. Probably because he had such shitty fucking clients. And he worked for a third-rate firm. But damn if he wasn't nailing this submission. Projecting his voice across the open-air forum, he had everyone waiting on him to continue.

"Now I'm sure Mr Wolfenden and his men would like nothing more than to conclude their business as quickly as possible," he said, raising his voice like a trained stump speaker and turning to address the crowd, not just Sheriff Muller and the two blockheads. "They look well prepared to handle whatever is going on," Jonas continued, "and all they would require from Mr O'Shannassy, or any retailer who might supply them, are a few basic consumables. Correct me if I'm wrong, Mr Wolfenden. But I don't imagine you will get anywhere near spending the hundred-dollar limit imposed this morning."

Jonas held up his cell phone to remind everybody of the text message they had all received. Everybody but him, of course. Because his phone was powered down so that it couldn't be tracked. The small theatrical gesture, the deployment of a carefully chosen prop, worked well here, as it so often did in court. He saw plenty of people nodding and quietly muttering to each other in agreement. He moved on while he had their indulgence. Muller stared at him as though wondering what he'd set loose on his town. This was not the taciturn outsider who'd ridden into town and let his fists do the talking just yesterday. Nor was he the crude, sly bigot who'd so quickly got Brad Rausch on his side.

Muller didn't know it, but he'd invited the Centurion into his town.

"Mr O'Shannassy, on the other hand, is simply concerned to do the best thing by his hometown," Jonas continued. "Perhaps this rationing order might be lifted by tomorrow. Perhaps it could be more severe by this time next week..."

A murmur ran through the audience at that. Good, he wanted them a little off balance, a little nervous. That way, they were more likely to take direction from someone who sounded like he knew what he was doing.

"With this in mind, Mr O'Shannassy was simply establishing the legal and practical effect of his control over a vital resource. It's a hot morning. We're all a bit freaked out. But I think if everybody can take a breather and agree that we are all in this together, because we are, the rest of this day can run a heck of a lot smoother than the start of it has."

Jonas looked to each antagonist, inviting them to agree with his oh-so-reasonable characterisation of their position. Wolfenden conceded first, gently patting the air with one hand to tell his men to put their weapons away. O'Shannassy nodded and growled, "Fair enough then, I suppose. But he's right about the rationing. Could be this goes on longer than anyone in the government has planned for or is letting on."

"Could be," Jonas agreed. "But sufficient unto the day are the hassles thereof. Let's deal with them first."

"Yeah, let's do that," said Sherriff Dave, stepping into the breach between Wolfenden and O'Shannassy, asserting his ownership of the situation again. "It looks like we got about three or four thousand people humping it up the mountain. We can't have them camping here. That'll be a public health issue within a couple of hours. Be best for everyone if they just picked up whatever supplies they needed, *within reason*," he added quickly when he saw O'Shannassy about to flare up, "and carried on to the camping grounds at Ross Lake. Plenty of space for everyone out there and all the amenities for even more if needed. Toilets, hot showers, camping sites."

"Agreed," O'Shannassy said loudly. "But we need to settle on what constitutes reasonable, Sherriff. Four thousand people spending a ration allotment of $100 each will clean us out. It'll leave nothing for those who actually live here."

Jonas almost smirked at how O'Shannassy quickly settled on the sheriff's higher estimate of the number of refugees. He wondered how many votes this guy had lost in their election showdown. However, Jonas had no intention of losing his leading role in this drama, so he spoke up again.

"Sheriff," he said, "I don't know what information you're getting from the state capital or DC. But it strikes me that, at the very least, you need to know what's happening down the hill, and you have a pretty good resource right here in Mr Wolfenden."

The militia captain looked surprised at that, if not entirely unhappy. O'Shannassy's face darkened. Before he could speak up, however, Jonas was already pushing more of his pieces out across the board.

"Mr Wolfenden," he said, "if I'm right to assume you have pretty basic needs for resupply, can I suggest that Sheriff Muller escorts you into and through Mr O'Shannassy's store while Darren..." He nodded at O'Shannassy to acknowledge the liberty he took using his first name, "... Liaises with the other deputies and town leadership to work out how to handle the surge coming through in the next couple of hours. Because it will need to be handled. Meanwhile, you can brief the sheriff on what's been happening in Seattle and elsewhere. Your information is more current than mine. I left before you did and without due preparations... I was hoping to take my vacation," he smiled innocently and even a little gormlessly. He knew a guy like Wolfenden would enjoy any comparison with his apocalyptic ineptitude.

Nobody could think of any objections. Wolfenden got to play out his doomsday prepper fantasy. O'Shannassy got to revel in his role as a chieftain of the town. And Muller got a debriefing and a de-escalation of a potentially violent confrontation. Everyone was a winner.

Especially Jonas.

THE FIRST PULSE of the main body of walkers had entered the eastern end of Silverton while Jonas was speaking. The town common was now severely overcrowded. People spilled onto the roadway on both sides of the park, and the crowd noise was building up again. Muller detailed two of his deputies to begin organising the crowd. He suggested moving anybody who needed to rest to the shaded fields behind the town hall where the county fair was held each year. Dr Cornwell already had half a dozen cases of heat stress to attend, and she lobbied the town selectmen who were now milling around to open up the administrative building as a triage and treatment point. It was comparatively large, and more importantly, it was air-conditioned. Muller also volunteered to open up one of his two jail cells. Unfortunately, Morena, Al Barrett's attacker, still occupied the other.

Jonas tagged everybody Sherriff Muller and Darren O'Shannassy consulted in the next few minutes. They would all be members of the town's official and unofficial power structure. He noted the due deference Muller paid to Howard Wetsman, the county comptroller and the distance he maintained from Selectwoman Natalie Bochenski, who was obviously allied with the O'Shannassy faction. Doc Cornwell appeared to be held in good opinion by all and acted as a messenger between the rival groups. It wasn't a million miles removed from the shifting protean hierarchies of the Florida Bar. Or the jailhouse gangs he'd repped as a shitbird lawyer for Hondo Alvarez. It was a delicate balancing act, not losing contact with the action at the centre of things but not asserting himself so aggressively that Muller told him to fuck off.

It paid a generous dividend when the lawman asked Wolfenden to speak with him privately inside the Red Apple, and O'Shannassy insisted on being there while they talked, causing the militia captain to demand, in turn, that Jonas act as a mediator again.

"No offence, shopkeeper," Wolfenden deadpanned.

"None taken, but I'm gonna watch you every second you're in my place of business."

Muller rolled his eyes but agreed, just to keep the peace.

"Let's make it quick, gentlemen," the sheriff said. "I want to start moving these people through to Ross Lake as soon as possible."

O'Shannassy unlocked the bolt securing the sliding doors at the front of his market and led the other three inside. Getting out of the sun and into the chilled air was a relief. They walked through the fresh produce stands, laden with summer fruits and green vegetables, past the deli and butcher's counters and through a narrow gap between the frozen goods and liquor cabinets to an ample storage and cold room. O'Shannassy had an office back there and gestured for the others to precede him into the room.

"Nice shop," Wolfenden said in a calm, level tone as they took up whatever perch they could find around the office. O'Shannassy laid his shotgun on the desk on top of a blizzard of paper and in front of an open HP laptop. Wolfenden put his AR-15 down alongside it in something akin to a peace-making gesture. He rolled his shoulders as if glad to be free of the burden.

"Right, Mister Wolfenden," Muller said. "Be quick. What the hell is happening down the mountain? Why'd you decide to hike up here? And how'd those other folks all get the same idea?"

The militiaman shrugged.

"They're smart, I guess. Although not smart enough to have done their prep. I was listening to them all the way up. They each got their own reasons, but bottom line is they know a city is a hellish place to be in a war, so they got out. That's why my team left."

Muller frowned. O'Shannassy scoffed openly.

"Your team? You think the Chinese are gonna invade? That's the dumbest fucking thing I heard of since Medicare for all."

Jonas flicked his eyes from one man to the other. If O'Shannassy meant to upset Wolfenden, he failed. The man just smiled.

"The Chinese are busy with their conquests," he said. "They're not gonna waste blood and treasure coming here. But they could toss off a few nukes to keep us from getting up in their grill."

"Bullshit," O'Shannassy shot back. "If they did that, we got thousands more to send right back."

"That's my thinking, too," Wolfenden said, surprising everyone. "They can't win that exchange. They're making sure they *don't* have to fight a war with us. That's why Seattle is so fucked up. Not just the roads. Nothing is working. You don't believe me, check your stock control systems. Try ordering from your suppliers. It's all over the news. There are no food suppliers any more."

Muller looked at O'Shannassy, who frowned.

"Gimme a second," he said, opening the laptop. He worked the keyboard in silence, save for the clicking of the keys. A minute later, his face looking increasingly dark, he said, "I can't bring up the inventory pages. It should be a live link, but it's like they're not even there."

"And this was enough for you to walk out of the city?" Muller asked Wolfenden.

"Enough for me and plenty of others, Sheriff. A big city can't feed itself for much more than a week. You remember New Orleans, right? That hurricane? That's gonna be happening everywhere in a couple of days. Government's pulling back ground forces from all over and I guarantee you martial law is next. Me and my guys? We are ready for this. We are good to fucking go. So, we're gone."

Because none of you have girlfriends, Jonas thought. But he said nothing.

O'Shannassy was looking at his recent antagonist with a new respect.

"What do you need?" he asked, unbidden.

"Some freeze-dried coffee, long-life milk if you got it. And chocolate," he said almost apologetically. "Daryl, one of our guys, had all that and got caught out of town. We couldn't wait for him. Shit had already gone sideways. We didn't plan to walk out of the city. We had off-road capability, but it was impossible to get out of our goddamn neighbourhoods in any vehicle."

"Except a bike," Jonas put in.

"Not with the loads we're hauling, son," Wolfenden retorted. "Traffic management didn't just collapse. It was weaponised."

"I can confirm that, Dave," Jonas said. "Saw some big pile-ups. Like the lights had been hacked to send the traffic streams crashing into each other. Thought the cops might have cleared it by now."

"Nope," Wolfenden said, almost cheerily. "It's worse."

"Goddamn," Dave Muller said quietly. "This is gonna be an epic fustercluck before it gets sorted."

"If it gets sorted," Wolfenden said.

"What do you mean?" Muller asked.

O'Shannassy was hanging on the reply, too.

Jonas leaned quietly against the wall, taking it all in.

"An attack like this will not go unanswered," Wolfenden said. "Not even by the useless bastards in this Administration. They'll hit back. It'll escalate. And other actors will get pulled in, too. Russia's already moving on Europe, cos she's such an easy bitch. When the rag heads see things falling apart, they'll put the dagger in, too. Syrians have got some good hackers, and they're not as constrained as, say, Moscow. Cos who you gonna bomb if some rando Arab decides to turn off all the safeties in a nuclear power plant? Like the one near Richland?"

Like O'Shannassy, Jonas was starting to warm to this guy, too.

Only Sheriff Dave looked like he wanted to be sick.

"I'll take what you'll sell me," Wolfenden said to Darren O'Shannassy. "And we'll move on. This little town is way too close to the city for my liking. A word of advice for you, Sheriff. You should either evacuate your people to a stronghold, or you should prepare to be overrun by maybe half a million starving scavengers in a week or so."

Nobody spoke for a moment. Jonas broke the silence deliberately.

"There's way more than half a million people in Seattle," he said.

"Yeah," Wolfenden smiled. "But by the time they break out and fall on this place, they'll already be killing each other. They get hungry enough, they'll start eating each other too."

Muller looked horrified.

O'Shannassy wasn't far behind him.

Jonas kept his expression neutral.

This was going so much better than he expected.

33

COWBOY THE FUCK UP

They reached Germantown within fifteen minutes of the time James had predicted. But that was the last of his predictions, which played out. He had two clients here. A retired director of the Atomic Energy Commission. And the CEO of a small technology company, an engineer who had arrived in Maryland from the former East Germany less than a week after the Wall came down. Neither of them were home.

"So much for a hot shower," he said as they stood on the sidewalk in front of the engineer's home. James had no idea whether his guys had fled in panic, if they were travelling, or perhaps just down the road trying to find bread and milk.

"We can stop at a roadhouse and get some moist towelettes," Michelle deadpanned. He felt bad about dragging her across the countryside and through the night. She hadn't complained, not once, but if she was even half as tired and pissed off as he felt, she must have the patience of a saint. James was footsore, and his back was hurting. The laptop in his pack smacked into the base of his spine with every step he took. It was only a light tap, annoying at first, but over a twelve-hour hike, it had become excruciating. He had to take the pack off and carry it in one hand, frequently switching it to the other to balance the load. The switches became more frequent as they trudged through the night.

Dawn broke over Maryland, hot and close. The storms that had swept through the region the previous night had done nothing to break the humidity or wind back the heat. He had no wallet, no access to funds, no way of proving his identity. He'd banked on meeting up with those clients here in Germantown, and now that he could see that wouldn't happen, he was at a loss.

"We should push on," Michelle Nguyen said. "Find a diner or a cafe, maybe a truck stop somewhere back on the main route, get some breakfast."

"You're forgetting what happened yesterday," he said. "There's a fair chance any place we go, they'll have run out of food already. Like the Marriot last night."

Michelle leaned against the rock wall enclosing the engineer's front yard. She stretched her neck and legs and twisted her torso to work the kinks out of her back. James lowered his backpack to the ground. He was thinking of leaving the laptop here, somewhere secure, and getting in contact with the engineer if and when things blew over.

"And you're forgetting where we are, James," Michelle said. "About thirty miles from the national capital. When things unravel, they come apart at the edges. I'll bet that Homeland's rationing system is being enforced in DC. Probably not in the Ozarks, I'll grant you that. But I think we're good for a can of beans and a packet of Twinkies yet."

"But I don't have any money on me. I left my wallet at the White House."

She smiled. He wondered where she found the chill to do that.

"Well, I'm not an idiot," Michelle said. "So I didn't leave my wallet behind, and I've got all my cards and about a hundred bucks in cash. I can pay for your breakfast. But we need to eat and rest, and you need to get your shit together and start thinking this through. Your plan to get home to your parents? That's a good plan. They have access to nutrients, and they are a long way from any kind of population centre. We just have to figure out how to get there. Let's get fed.

Let's find your bank. Get some funds, some credit, some negotiable fucking bearer bonds or whatever it is you guys play with. But let's not sit here by the side of the road whining like little bitches because your plan didn't run exactly the way that you thought it would. I got some sour news for you, Jimbo. This won't be our last setback on the way to Montana. So cowboy the fuck up, and let's get moving."

He blinked.

It was hard to believe he was getting reamed out by a little Vietnamese woman with science-fiction hair, fantasy pirate tattoos and a Hello Kitty backpack. But he was, and it was humiliating, and he wanted it to stop.

James O'Donnell hauled his ass out of the one-man pity party where it'd been sitting in the corner nursing a flat beer, and he set his mind to grinding on how the hell they were going to deal with this.

"You're right," he said. "We just need to find a bank branch open. I've got PIN codes, passwords, even old signature files stored somewhere in their system. We can do this. It's going to take a couple more hours, that's all."

He picked up his backpack again, resolving to hold onto the laptop, as heavy as it was. "Let's find somewhere to eat."

"I feel like waffles," Michelle said.

WAFFLES WEREN'T A PROBLEM. There was an IHOP about two miles further on, strategically positioned across the road from a 24-hour gym. It was crazy busy, and they had to wait half an hour for a table, but the kitchen had no trouble meeting their order for an omelette and waffle combo. An inexplicably bubbly waitress told James they'd been lucky. They got their main weekly delivery just before 'all the trouble'.

"My roommate works the Taco Bell over the other side of town, and they're closed today because they can't re-stock. Bummer, hey?"

"Bummer," Michelle echoed in a mock Valley girl accent as the waitress left to place their order. "I'll bet that's what they say in Seoul as the artillery starts raining down. 'Whoa. Bummer, dude.'"

Sitting in the booth across from her, feeling 100% better simply for taking the weight off his feet, James snorted. "Your mood turned dark. What happened to cowboy the fuck up?"

"Nothing, I'm good. But I couldn't tell whether you were drooling over that waitress or the smell of so much waffly goodness in here."

He blushed. He had secretly been checking out the waitress. She reminded him of a girl he'd dated back in Montana. She'd broken his heart. Michelle laughed at him when she saw the red flush creep up his cheeks.

"Check your privilege, Romeo," she smirked. "And try to remember, I'm paying for you."

Abashed, James returned to his breakfast. The restaurant was as crowded as any he'd ever seen. Staff asked customers to share booths and tables, and those who weren't in a generous frame of mind simply had to wait their turn.

"Wait could be more than a half hour now," their bubbly waitress informed one angry man in a bright yellow shirt. Seemed James and Michelle had got in before the worst of it. Yellow Shirt guy stormed out. Most didn't.

Everybody was talking about the cyberattacks, the banking collapse, and China. But the signal-to-noise ratio was very low, and all that James could discern from the background chatter was that people were freaked out. Chaos seemed to be the organising principle of the day. Some schools had cancelled classes. Some hadn't. Two women at the small table next to James and Michelle worked for the same health insurance company. One of them had received two text messages that morning saying that because of IT problems, the office was closed until further notice. Her friend showed off a message on her phone demanding that staff attend work as usual.

"I just don't know what to do, Jeanie," the woman closest to James said.

"Finish your breakfast," her friend advised.

It was sound advice, James thought as he tuned them out.

"Do you have to check in with work?" he asked Michelle.

She shook her head, spearing a piece of bacon.

"I've been reclassified as a remote asset, remember? I messaged

Panozzo that I was going with you. I emailed Holloway but haven't heard back yet. He's probably a mile underground in the Rockies or something. Panozzo told me to keep my phone charged and turned on and check in once a day by landline or email if I'm out of cell range. But I don't think I'll be missed. What about you? You going to send out your newsletter this week?"

James stopped eating.

"You know," he said, "I'd forgotten about that. Jesus. That's my business. I don't..."

He trailed off. He didn't know what he was going to say.

I don't know that I'll ever send another newsletter.

I don't know if anybody will be around to read them soon.

I don't know what the hell I'm doing anymore.

Michelle picked up the conversation for him as she pushed a wedge of waffle through a puddle of maple syrup. For a small woman, she had a great appetite. Although hiking through the night helped too.

"Let's see if we can get your money sorted out," she said. "We need funds to get across to Montana. That's your job, James." She pointed her fork at him. Maple syrup dripped from a piece of bacon. "That's your responsibility today," she said. "Get it done. We'll get a vehicle of some sort, fill it with supplies, and I will drive. If you want to write something for your clients, tell them to put their heads between their knees and kiss their wealthy asses goodbye, we can do that. Assuming you can get online. But let's deal with our problems first."

Again, he was surprised to be lectured by somebody who looked like an extra from a 1980s music video. But that was exhaustion. That was dumbass male arrogance. He'd spent enough time with this woman to know how smart she was. He was beginning to understand how tough she was, too. Maybe all of this would blow over in the next couple of days, and if they did, James vowed that he would ask Michelle Nguyen out on a date. An actual dinner date, mostly to apologise for dragging her out into the boonies.

"Okay," he said. "Let's finish up and get moving. I need to see if anybody here knows if Bank of America has a branch locally. And if nobody knows, we'll have to find an old-fashioned phone book. My phone is out of battery."

"Mine's not," Michelle said. "But the network is still down."

They both finished every morsel of food on the plates. They'd been starving, and letting food go to waste was no longer an option. James paused as he stood, taking a moment to scan the crowded dining room. He scoped out a large number of working parents with school-age kids. The children mostly looked excited and happy; the parents appeared uniformly worried. One mother was begging her daughter to finish her breakfast. ("Morticia, *please!*") The teen, who was working a whole Goth revival thing, folded her arms, stared implacably at her mom, and shook her head. James resisted the urge to intervene.

Michelle saw him checking out the scene.

She shook her head, a grim expression on her face, and she did not resist the urge to intervene, stalking over to the table and taking out her security pass, all but jamming it into the girl's face.

"Hey! Morticia, my name is Agent Nguyen," she said, disappearing the laminate before the shocked mother and daughter could get a good look at it. "Eat your pancakes like your mom says. It's the law now. National emergency protocols. Wasting food is a federal crime as of today. You *will* eat your fucking breakfast, or I will arrest your sorry fucking Vampirella ass and drag you out of here and into the nearest federal prison with a tanning bed... and sweetheart," she leaned in close, "They all have tanning beds. Now eat!"

The girl was shaking so hard she nearly dropped her fork when she tried to pick it up, but she did eat with her head bowed low. Michelle winked at the mother, who smiled nervously, uncertainly in thanks.

"Holy shit," James muttered as they made their way to the counter, weaving and pushing through the crowd. Its hubbub was gradually building into a roar. "I felt like I was gonna get sent to tanning prison."

"She was a spoiled little biatch," Michelle said under the cover of the background noise. "And it will be a crime to waste a pancake like that soon enough. She needs to harden up. Everyone does."

Michelle paid cash for the meal. A hand-lettered sign by the register informed customers that all sales today were cash-only. James asked the manager, a middle-aged white guy with a little pot belly and curly hair receding fast, whether he knew of a local Bank of America. He did not. He was a Wells Fargo customer. But he did point them towards a man dining by himself at the end of the bar.

"That's Mr Campbell," he said. "I'm not sure which bank he works for, but I'm pretty sure he's with one of them. You can ask him."

They did.

Turned out Roy Campbell was an analyst with HSBC. He lived in Germantown and commuted every day to the capital.

"Not today, though," he informed them. "No point."

"IT down?" James asked.

The banker shook his head. "Not that I know of, no. But my office is in a part of town that's been locked down. Can't get to it, so I'll have to work offsite. Thought I might spend my commuting time having a treat breakfast. I normally get toast at home and eat in the car."

"I hear ya," Michelle sympathised.

Roy Campbell knew where James' local branch was but warned them there would likely be no money in the cash machines and severe restrictions on over-the-counter withdrawals.

"This madness," Campbell said, waving his hand around to take in the crush of extra diners. "Don't normally believe in the government messing with market forces, but sometimes you have to save people from themselves. You know about the withdrawal limit that Homeland and the Fed imposed, right?"

"It's okay," James said. "I'm looking to buy a car. I can use a cashier's check for that."

He thanked Campbell for his time and was about to leave when he paused, turning back.

"Mr Campbell, excuse me, I'm sorry," James said. "We've been on the road. Like literally, we walked here from Washington overnight."

Roy Campbell's eyes went wide.

"My word," he said. "That's impressive. Crazy, but impressive."

"That's what it says on his business card," Michelle teased.

"I'm in the business, too," James said. "I write a newsletter. For investors. Can you give me the short version of what's happening with the banks? I know they had no liquidity problem, not a real one. But do you know how the market stands this morning?"

Campbell leaned back and folded his arms, staring over the sea of diners and out of a large window into the morning sun. He closed his eyes and sighed.

"I wish I knew, son," he said, returning to them. "This was nothing like 2008. It was different. Psychological warfare, if you ask me. Economic sabotage."

"And it worked?" Michelle asked.

"You paid cash this morning, Miss," Campbell said. "You wouldn't have done that two days ago. And like I said, you'll have a helluva time getting more than a couple of hundred dollars in cash from any bank. People have been lining up, demanding to withdraw their savings, all of them. The Dow has been suspended. Most of the foreign exchanges, too. It's a rout, a panic."

Campbell sighed again, longer this time, as if they had tired him out.

"I've seen nothing like it," he continued. "And I started my career in Asia, smack bang in the middle of the meltdown in the 1990s. If I were you, son," he looked at James, "I'd be telling your subscribers to get into bullion."

James said nothing. He just looked at the man.

"Gold is up eight hundred per cent," Campbell said. "That's where the market is."

He smiled almost apologetically.

"But my breakfast is going cold. And it was supposed to be a treat."

They thanked him for his time and left.

The bank was a twenty-minute walk away. There was no rioting in the streets, no looting, no apparent signs of breakdown or chaos, but when they arrived, a crowd was already waiting out front. A much bigger crowd than the International House of Pancakes had attracted. Similar clusters of people had closed in on JP Morgan Chase across the road and a local S&L up the street. James checked his watch.

"It should be open by now," he said.

"No fucking shit, Einstein?" said the man in front of them, turning around to glare at James. Then he saw Michelle and sneered.

He was an intense, barrel-shaped man wearing bright red Bermuda shorts and a loud yellow, short-sleeved shirt. James recognised him. It was the angry guy who hadn't wanted to share a table at IHOP. He must have found a solitary breakfast elsewhere and joined the back of the queue just before they arrived. He was unshaven, and his skin colour was florid. From the dark bags under his eyes, he looked like he'd been up all night searching for lonesome pancakes and a functioning cash machine. James did not engage. He and Michelle moved a few feet away but not so far as to lose their place in the line.

"It'd be good to get a stash of green, you know," she said quietly. "I know that MasterCard and Visa's payment systems got fucking smashed yesterday. I don't know how useful plastic is going to be. Or cashier's checks."

The man in the yellow shirt glared at them, looking like he wanted to get into an argument. James moved further away, taking Michelle with him. He decided he didn't care if they lost their place in the line. Somebody else could bear the brunt of this guy's manifest disappointments with life.

"Me neither," he said. "That HSBC guy Campbell might be right. Maybe not about the gold. People are gonna work out pretty quickly that you can't eat it. But fungible goods, tradable commodities. Food, tobacco, and medicine. They might be as good as currency within a couple of weeks if the situation gets any worse. We need to see how much of that stuff we can get our hands on."

He could see Michelle turning it over in her head. Doing the analysis.

"Agreed," she said at last.

The angry man in Bermuda shorts had moved closer to them again, obviously eavesdropping. They stopped talking, and five minutes later, the bank branch opened. Two security guards, both carrying shotguns, stood on either side of the manager as she announced they would only be allowing six people inside at any one time. The crowd groaned and protested, but the guys with the shotguns looked like they'd been carved out of granite. They weren't going anywhere, and they weren't letting anybody through unless the boss said so. Having arrived late, James and Michelle had to wait another hour and a half before getting in. And by then, another three hundred people had joined the crowd.

"I NEED to see the manager or an assistant manager," James said when he reached the teller at the window. She was deeply unimpressed.

"I'm sorry, sir," the young woman said, "but the Department of Homeland Security has ordered the withdrawal restrictions. We cannot allow anybody to take out more than two hundred dollars in cash during any 24-hour period."

Her voice was so empty of emotion, the words spooling out of her like tape from an old cassette player, that James knew she was repeating a line from a script. Probably a line she'd repeated hundreds of times in the previous twenty-four hours.

"I'm not after cash," he said. "I lost my wallet. I need to establish my ID to access my funds."

She blinked at him.

He started to repeat himself.

"I'm not after cash," he said, but she held up both hands, shaking her head as though a talking horse had wandered up to her window to discuss the futures market for sugar cubes.

"I'll just get Ms Vandenberg," the woman said quickly. "You're going to be her new favourite."

She spoke the truth. Alison Vandenberg was delighted to be able to deal with a customer who wasn't jamming a shopping bag into her face and telling her to fill it up with Benjamins. She did not care that they were unwashed and dishevelled. Nor did she care that it was no simple matter to establish James O'Donnell's bona fides, not with the Internet being so flaky and everything. But Vandenberg threw herself into the challenge with a will. Possibly because it meant she didn't have to deal with the increasingly ill-tempered mob outside.

She had Michelle make a legal declaration that James was a

contractor for the National Security Council and that she, as an officer of the federal government, would vouch for his identity. She took copies of Michelle's ID cards and fixed them to the declaration.

"Can I get a copy of your signature, please?" she asked.

James carefully wrote out his name on a blank piece of paper.

"Excellent," Vandenberg said. "Just give me a minute."

She left them in her office, returning five minutes later, beaming.

"You would never imagine it, but we still have a fax machine here. I faxed your signature to your home branch in Baltimore, and they have confirmed that it matches the one they have on file. We are almost there, Mr O'Donnell; we are almost there."

She pulled over the telephone on her desk, picked up the receiver and punched in a seven-digit number. James thought he recognised it. He hadn't used the number for Bank of America's phone banking service in years.

Vandenberg handed the receiver across the desk, pushing the rest of the phone after it. She seemed to be enjoying herself and gestured for James to put the receiver to his ear and follow the instructions.

He did, and the computerised voice asked him to enter his online pin code.

James punched in the eight-digit number, the same one he used for Internet banking, and handed the phone back to Alison Vandenberg. The banker listened to the automated systems and smiled.

"That's probably the only time in human history anybody has ever smiled at a recorded voice in a phone menu," Michelle said.

Vandenberg's smile grew even wider.

"Indeed," she said. "Now, Mr O'Donnell, is there anything else I can help you with? We have established your identity, and I can provide access to your savings and investments although..." she held up one finger, "not for cash amounts of greater than two hundred dollars."

"I will take my two hundred," James confirmed. "But I need help with finance for a new car. If there's a dealer in town who banks with this branch, I'd be more than happy to do business with them."

Vandenberg nodded enthusiastically.

"Off the top of my head, I can think of two dealerships with accounts here," she said. "What sort of vehicle are you after?"

"A pickup," James said. "Four-seater cab. High wheelbase, extra fuel capacity, a working vehicle."

Vandenberg knew exactly where to send him.

"You need to go talk to Dave Sag over on North Frederick. Would you like me to call and tell him you're coming?"

"Yes, if you wouldn't mind," James said. "And tell him we'll make a direct deposit from my account to his business via you. I need this transaction to go through today. I don't want it held up by any difficulties with electronic funds transfer, payment processing or whatever fresh hell is happening in your world. You can see I have the money. We'll go talk to Mr Sag. He will call you and tell you how much money he wants. I'll sign whatever papers are necessary, and we will drive away before lunchtime."

Vandenberg leaned back in her chair. Satisfied.

"This is the highlight of my day," she sighed. "I'll call you a taxi, Mr O'Donnell. It's on the house. The Bank of America thanks you for your business."

DAVE SAG WAS one of those men who filled a room with his presence. All the way into the corners, up to the ceiling and out through the windows. He could have been a movie star, thought James. But only in Mob movies. He was a happy gangster and never happier than when James explained what he wanted.

"That black GM Sierra AT4 over in the corner, out on the lot," James said. "You tell me your list price. I'm gonna give you an extra ten thousand dollars for it because, Mister Sag, we both know that you are a ten-foot-tall grizzly ass bad motherfucker when you get into it with a soft-headed idiot like me."

Sag grinned, uncertain where this was going but pretty sure he would like it or could at least learn to live with it. All three of them sat in his office at Sag Premium Motors on North Frederick Avenue. The showroom was empty of customers, but all of Dave Sag's staff had turned up because you'd have to be all the way around the S-bend of the world going down the toilet before cutting and running on a guy like this.

"Gotta admit, the ten-foot-tall grizzly ass motherfucker does sound like me," he said. "So, like, you pay me ten grand more than I would screw out of you for the Sierra? Even with all the options?"

"Even with all the options," James confirmed. "Which we won't be taking because I'm driving that bad boy off the lot today."

"I believe it," Sag nodded. "Go on, son."

James said, "You send whatever paper has to go to the lovely Alison Vandenberg at my bank and yours, and you give me five thousand dollars cash back on the deal. And I'll take a spare fuel canister, too. One of the twenty-gallon units."

Sag sucked air in through his teeth.

"Whoa, whoa, whoa! I'll give you the gas, Jimmy Cricket. But you know how hard it is to magic up the green stuff at the moment? Look out the window, son. Go on. I have them cleaned every day. It's a magnificent view out there... of complete fucking idiots losing their nuts over this China thing. People should just calm the fuck down and keep on truckin', you ask me, but nobody does. It's a fucking tragedy, is what it is, son. A Shakespearean fucking tragedy... Until you walked in with this crazy ass scheme of yours, which, to be honest, doesn't sound exactly fucking legit to me, buuuuut..."

Dave Sag spread his hands.

"But," James filled in for him, "what are you gonna do when some guy walks in and says he wants to give you five thousand dollars for free."

"Exactly!" Sag gestured, waving his arms like a cartoon symphony conductor. "Except..." he suddenly cautioned, pinching the air between his fingertips, "I don't know that I can do even two grand on short notice. Let alone five. That's a coupla weeks' worth of this bull-shit withdrawal limit they got going on, you know."

"Yeah. It is," James said, smiling at the game. "If we were talking about you walking to the nearest ATM. But we're not. You got a safe somewhere on the premises, and it'll have way more than five grand in it. You do cash back all the time. It's a great sales funnel to suck in the rubes. And having all that solid puddin' hidden away means you get to take a little bite now and then without Uncle Sam sticking his spoon in. So, I know you got five large, Dave. We both know it. You got it, and I'll bet your competition does, too. I want the cash. You're making a hundred per cent clear on the deal. You want me to sign for a bunch of optional extras you don't actually provide? Keep it legit with the IRS? That's cool, but you give me the green. The only one who loses out is me, paying a two-to-one premium for a wedge of that walking-around money."

Sag's face was a study. James didn't dare look across at Michelle, but he wondered if she could see herself in the man's expression. Like her, he was doing his threat assessments.

"Maybe," he said quietly, "Maybe I could use my own walking around money. Maybe it's not such a good idea to dissipate my liquid funds when we have all this trouble. Like people say."

"Like complete fucking idiots say, you mean," James pushed back at him. He matched the natural rhythms of the man's delivery, a trick he had learned when selling magazine subscriptions in college. "I'll be honest with you, Dave. You really should take a small pile of that cash out of your safe and do it soon. If I was you, I'd turn that folding stuff into things you can eat, drink or shoot out of an AR-15. That's what I'll do with my cash, whether I get it from you or someone else. But if I get it from you, you're making a rolled gold hundred per cent profit. And none of it is going to Uncle Sugar."

Sag narrowed his eyes, turning them like gun turrets on Michelle.

"Didn't you say you work for the feds?"

She replied with a crooked smile.

"Not for the IRS. Nobody likes those motherfuckers."

After a few seconds, the corners of his mouth lifted, and his eyes twinkled darkly.

"Okay. I'll get Sammy to cut you some cheddar. Five grand, but you're gonna pay fifteen over the ask, not ten."

James made a pretence of being wounded by the countermove. He argued, he pleaded, and he played to character. But in the end, he settled, authorising a direct transfer of funds from his working account to Sag's company checking account for forty-seven thousand dollars. Fifteen more than the book price of the base model Sierra he bought. He was happy with that. He'd have paid twenty over and taken quarters on the dollar for the cash back. Cash was king now. People wanted it, and they couldn't get it. The purchasing power of a dollar would spike in the next couple of days. Before everyone realised that, like gold, you couldn't eat money.

Sag presented them with two sets of keys, two Dave Sag Premium Brand Thermos flasks, and a Dave Sag autographed sports bag. His grinning face was stencilled all over the merch.

"Outstanding," said James.

One of Sag's guys had already moved the Sierra to the edge of the lot. James and Dave shook on the deal. You could see the wheels turning inside the salesman's head, trying to figure out the angles on the game he'd just played. Wondering if somehow he'd been played by this chump who'd paid fifteen thousand dollars for a spare can of gasoline. Wondering if he should maybe cash out himself after all. Fill the best off-roader he had with hookers and blow, and get his ass outta town.

They left Dave looking preoccupied and frowning at the long line of customers outside the Safeway across the street.

The Sierra smelled better than James and Michelle when they climbed in. James said he would drive the first leg, a short trip to a Harris Teeter over in Darnestown.

"Good," Michelle said. "I shouldn't be driving right now anyway."

"Why?" he asked. Suddenly worried. "Are you okay?"

She shook her head as if in disbelief at what she had just witnessed.

"I'm fine," she said. "But I can't concentrate. Because I have never been more turned on by a spreadsheet nerd than I am right now."

34

BLOODBATH

I t was late morning, nudging right up on lunchtime when Rick and Mel finally drove away from his cabin by the river. She was right. He'd needed the sleep-in. He was another hour and a half cleaning up storm damage around the resort. Clearing fallen branches from the golf links, mostly. Bretton Woods remained closed, but the responsibility still fell to him. Mel threw a ball for Nomi to chase while Rick tended to the grounds as quickly as possible.

They drove her pickup. His car had taken some hail damage the previous day, and he was worried about a small crack in the windshield. He might otherwise ignore it, but he didn't want the weekend ruined by the screen exploding on them a hundred miles from home. Mel's truck was only a two-seater, but there was plenty of room for Nomi to sit up front on Rick's lap as they drove over to Darnestown to pick up a few supplies for the trip.

They had no reason to turn on the TV at his place, and they listened to music on the short drive, alternating song choices from Mel's phone. She downloaded more music than Rick, and they couldn't stream anything from Spotify.

"You have a lot of songs I don't know," Rick said, scrolling through her playlists as they approached the Harris Teeter at the junction of Seneca and Darnestown roads.

"That's because you don't know much about good music," she teased. "Yet."

"I know there isn't much to be had on your phone," he lobbed back.

His mood was light. He kept glancing at Mel, wondering how he'd ended up with someone like her. Someone way the hell out of his league. Nomi's head lay against his stomach, and her tail thumped as he scratched under her chin. Rick Boreham, who normally moved through the world mindful of all the carefully hidden pitfalls and boobytraps laid for him by fate, was enjoying the doped, almost drifting sensation of being happy.

He'd decided to take Doctor Cairns' advice.

He wasn't going to pay a single damn bit of attention to the news. He was going to spend time with his woman, and he was going to be happy.

"What the hell is this?" Mel said, breaking through his mellow.

The car lot of the 6 Twelve Convenience store was bedlam, with a line of vehicles stretching out onto the road. It was even worse on the other side of the intersection at Harris Teeter. It was like all of Maryland had swarmed the two grocery markets.

"Maybe we should just drive on," Melissa suggested.

Rick frowned.

"Fraid not," he said. "This is the only place I know I can get Nomi's kibble. It's a pain, I know. But we gotta go here. It's part of the program, her diet. They ask me about it every month. Make sure I'm not feeding her burritos or anything. Not that you'd object to that, would you girl?" He said, rubbing her head.

Nomi panted in agreement. No, she would not object to a burrito.

"Babe, I don't know if I can even get in there. Look at the cars."

Rick didn't have to. He could already see what a shambles they were heading into.

"Just pull over here," he said. "We can walk up, get the dog food for Nomi and try somewhere else for our stuff. Might not be as crowded once we get further upstate, away from the capital."

Mel pulled over by the side of the road, cut the engine and engaged the handbrake. They climbed out of the cab, and the morning heat fell on them.

"Man, it's gonna be so good swimming in that lake," Rick said. "Come on, let's get it done."

Traffic was jammed up on both roads, and they could pick their way through the slow-moving vehicles. Rick was amazed at the stuff people were buying. Not just fresh fruit and vegetables. They were cleaning the place out, taking everything. And many customers, she could see, were shuttling back and forth between their cars and the market. Like they had all forgotten something on their first run.

He usually avoided shopping if there were going to be crowds. They set his teeth on edge. He could never quite shake himself of the irrational fear that a car bomb was going to go off. Crazy, because the most likely threat here was an irate shopper getting loud and punchy because they couldn't source their preferred brand of breakfast cereal. But there it was.

Nomi sensed his anxiety as they threaded their way through the crowded lot. She butted her head into his thigh, demanding a pat. He paused, bent down, gave her a rub on her flanks and told her what a good girl she was. It helped.

"Babe, do you want me to do this?" Mel asked. She could see he was doing it hard. That helped, too.

"I might be better inside than out here," Rick said. "It will be cooler, at least."

"True that," Mel agreed, and they pushed on.

If anything, it was even more crowded inside the store. There was no way Rick was leaving Nomi unattended outside, and he led her through the sliding doors into the heaving mass of people inside Harris Teeter.

"Bloody hell," Mel said. "This is a bit of a bloody teddy bear's picnic."

"If the teddy bears were all assholes," Rick muttered. This was like one of the worst souks in Baghdad, with people yelling at each other, gesticulating wildly, even wrestling over items pulled from the almost-bare shelves. It did not help his state of mind.

"Maybe I should go outside," he conceded.

But the shooting started outside at that very moment, and Rick Boreham dropped to the floor, dragging his girlfriend and his dog down with him.

\#\#\#

JAMES AND MICHELLE parked the Sierra nearly half a mile away. It had been a hot, unpleasant walk getting to the market, and he was not looking forward to hauling groceries all the way back. Not that they'd been able to buy much. Most of the long-life produce was already gone from the shelves. No beans. No rice. No tinned foods. The fruit and vegetable displays were half empty, and the butchery was selling offcuts.

Very expensive offcuts.

"This is another one of those setbacks I was telling you about," Michelle said. She was carrying two bottles of olive oil and three boxes of All Bran. James had scooped up six packets of some weird pasta and a bag of potatoes. They'd paid over a hundred dollars for the order.

"Let's blow this popsicle stand," he said. "I want to get further out and see whether we can pick up supplies from the farm gate."

"What, like buy a cow or something?" Michelle said.

"No," James grinned, amused by the idea. "But root vegetables will keep. And summer fruits. Once we get out of the traffic crush, most of our travel will be through open country. We can make pretty good time. We won't need a month's worth of food."

"That's good," said Michelle. "Because I don't think we could buy a month's worth of food here."

They were heading for the front door when James saw the dog. A black Labrador. And he couldn't help himself; he was a dog guy. He was bending over to say hello to this good boy or girl when the glass windows looking out over Harris Teeter's parking lot exploded.

It was Michelle who saved him. Michelle and that dog, he

thought later. If he hadn't bent down to say hello to the lab, the burst of fire might have cut him down. Michelle tackled him and kept pressing him down until they were both on the floor.

Most people did not drop. Most people screamed and ran and fell over each other. One guy tripped over James's leg. A shrink-wrapped palette of bottled water crashed down next to his head. He rolled towards Michelle and tried to cover her with his body. She was going to get trampled. The screaming and chaos grew louder.

He heard more shots. And then shouting. Not screaming and shrieking and the animal sounds of panic, but shouted orders.

"GET THE FUCK DOWN. STAY THE FUCK DOWN. YOU PUT YOUR HEAD UP WE GONNA BLOW IT OFF."

A single booming shot underlined the threat.

"SHUT THE FUCK UP. JUST SHUT UP AND GET DOWN, ALL OF YOU."

James glanced up, still covering Michelle, who was swearing loudly beneath him. His heart lurched. A man was crawling towards him with a knife in his hand. Not a kitchen knife. A killing knife. But nothing as mundane as a bayonet. It was a curved fighting blade, exotic and rare like a special forces soldier might carry. The man's eyes had a faraway look. They were an ocean at night. Dark and cold. Utterly fathomless. James tightened his grip on Michelle. And then he realised the dog was coming too. The Labrador. And a woman. She had coffee-coloured skin and brown ringlets with blonde high-lights. She was advancing across the floor towards him in a fashion similar to the man with the knife. They looked like they knew what they were doing. Even the dog.

James rolled out of the way, and they passed him by. The strange little band snaked around a wooden stand displaying a few sad brown onions. He heard the voice again. A man's voice. It was closer now, inside the store.

"Everybody stay down and stay calm, and nobody else gets hurt."

Nobody else?

Fuck, what was happening? He felt Michelle pushing against him, and he adjusted a little to let her escape from beneath his bulk.

"Sorry," he whispered into her ear. The chaos and panic covered his words.

Somebody yelled, "SHUT THE FUCK UP!"

"It's okay," she said very quietly. "Come on, we have to get out of here now."

She started to back away from the front of the store, staying down on her belly, moving like the man and the woman had, but in reverse.

"You! BITCH! Stay the fuck where you are."

James looked up again. The man was pointing a shotgun at Michelle.

"Stop," James urged.

She did.

It seemed to satisfy the man with the gun. Apart from the weapon and the fact that he was standing when everybody else was on the ground cowering, he seemed unremarkable. He wasn't a Viking berserker, a brigand, an outlaw motorcycle rider, or a gangster. He was just a guy with a gun. He was dressed in jeans and a T-shirt. The T-shirt looked old and dirty, one knee of the Levi's had worn through, and he wore heavy Carhart work boots. More men came in behind him. Four of them.

They looked like guys who might clean out gutters or install drywalling badly for cash. Some were tattooed, but not as extravagantly as Michelle. One wore a beard, but it wasn't sculpted. A couple of baseball caps. Sunglasses. But no masks. They didn't seem to think they had to bother disguising themselves.

"We'll just collect our groceries, folks, and take your money, and then we'll be on our way," said the first man through the door. The one who'd pointed the big-ass Remington at Michelle. The others appeared to defer to him.

James felt a desperate need to take a piss. He was carrying all of their cash with him. He hadn't wanted to leave it back in the truck where it might not be safe. The men fanned out through the shop. They nudged people with the muzzles of their rifles, demanding cash and occasionally a piece of jewellery. One man had to give up his watch. A woman cried as she removed a necklace.

And they took food. The largest of the group, the balding bearded one in a pair of bib overalls and a sweat-stained blue T-shirt, gathered up people's shopping bags, eventually collecting so many that he started dropping stuff on the floor.

"Take it out to the truck, Darrell," said the guy in charge.

Darrell. They were using names and not bothering to hide their faces. James did not have a good feeling about this.

"Hey you, college boy, what's in the bag?"

James didn't realise they were talking to him until a Carhart boot kicked him in the ribs. Not hard; it didn't break anything. But it hurt like hell. He nearly lost control of his bladder.

"All Bran and olive oil," he grunted. "And potatoes."

"Holy shit," the man chuckled. "We got us a real Iron Chef over here. Gimme the potatoes, Wolfgang Puck."

James pushed the bag across the floor towards the boss, who James instinctively thought of as 'Carhart'. He had never felt so powerless in his entire life.

"And your wallet."

"I lost my wallet."

That earned him another hard-booted kick from 'Carhart'.

"Bullshit. Your wallet, loser. "

James had been lying face down, trying to shield Michelle. She grabbed at him as he slowly rolled over, showing his open palms and his face to the man with the gun. When he spoke, his voice shook.

"Seriously, dude. I lost my wallet. My cash is in my front pocket. I can reach in and get it. But I don't have a wallet."

The man levelled the shotgun at his face. James felt as though frozen eels were slithering through his guts.

He reached into his front pocket with a shaking hand, the fingers too numb for fine motor control. He had trouble getting the money. A couple of hundred dollars and a handful of coins eventually spilled out, and he gathered them up and passed them up to the gunman.

A dog started barking somewhere in the store.

It distracted the man. He looked annoyed.

"Leroy, go shut that mutt up. You know I hate that fucking sound."

One of the other men picked his way through the people lying on the floor, moving towards the back of the market. James suddenly felt terrified for the dog. It had to be the Labrador he had seen before. The man called Leroy was carrying some sort of assault rifle. It looked like the type of weapon that could kill everybody in this store as quickly as he could pull the trigger.

Michelle squirmed closer to him, and he fitted his body around her, knowing that it would not protect her from a gun like that. He might shield her from a shotgun blast, however. He could feel her body trembling in terror, like a small animal.

Having taken his food and what he thought was all of James's money, Carhart lost interest in him, moving on to pick over the other hostages, or captives, or whatever the hell they were.

The dog barked again.

"Leroy, I told you," the man shouted.

James felt all of the muscles in his body clenching, waiting for the shot. It didn't come. Not right away. The bandits continued to gather supplies and loot the money and possessions of everybody on the floor. James was starting to shake from the tension when he finally heard the rifle crack. But something inexplicable happened. One of the gunmen cried out and fell to the ground. James jumped at the shot, and his bladder let loose. Michelle screamed. Everyone screamed. And the firing continued.

Three shots. *Crack! Crack! Crack!*

The screaming only grew worse.

Carhart dropped to the floor next to him, but not wounded. He was hiding. Taking cover. His face wore a twisting, shape-shifting rictus of rage and horror. It was a mask slipping from a man who had thought himself in control and suddenly discovered he was not. Suddenly, he was no longer the hunter.

He was the prey.

James saw Carhart's hands gripping and kneading at the stock and slide of his shotgun. A pump action model similar to the Remington James's old man had at home. Carhart was searching inside himself, finding the courage to move, to return fire.

James didn't know what the hell was happening. Just that this guy who'd stood over hundreds of people less than a minute ago had been forced to cower. And his partners, his henchmen, weren't standing up anymore. They were down. They'd been shot.

The front doors of the market rumbled open, and the big guy, the bearded giant in the overalls, came running through.

Two shots stopped him, so closely grouped that they almost sounded like one.

The ballistic crack was loud, but the sickening wet thud and pop of supersonic ammunition striking a human body was also loud and close and terrible to hear. The big man running in with his gun raised continued moving forward, but his momentum was arcing down now. His strings had been cut. His body going loose. His mass collapsed towards the floor, where he fell into a shopping trolley, knocking it over with a bright metallic crash.

Carhart roared and started to climb to his feet. He lifted the shotgun, pumping the slide, ready to spray his shot deep into the crowd.

James didn't realise that he was moving until he moved, launching himself at the man, his arms wide to gather him up in a tackle. He slammed into Carhart. The gun roared, and searing white heat burned the inside of one arm. They went down, slamming to the ground, and James tried to land on him with as much force as possible, to drive out his air, to wind him. But he was not a heavy man nor a trained fighter, and he knew in less than a second that he was in trouble. Deadly trouble.

The gunman wrestled and squirmed and even sank his teeth into James's bicep, biting down hard. He screamed in pain, in violation, but he couldn't let go. He couldn't escape. He couldn't let the man get free access to the weapon. They rolled and struggled, and James found himself caught underneath the other man. An elbow to James's temple stunned him, nearly blacking him out and filling the world with a bright, sparkling meteor shower. A knee or maybe another elbow slammed into his ribs. He started to gas out, to lose breath.

CRACK!

This shot was the loudest of all. And the effect was the most dramatic.

Half of Carhart's skull disintegrated and blew away on an evil wind that carried blood and bone and all manner of dark corruption with it.

James didn't so much shudder as he spasmed with a deep-body convulsion of horror.

The corpse of the Carhart boot-wearing gunman was toppling toward him, threatening to spill its freshly liberated contents all over James's face. Into his eyes and mouth.

A boot shot past him, thudding into the dead man's chest, and the body fell away from James O'Donnell.

He felt that he had gone insane.

He was unmoored from reality.

He could understand nothing.

But he could see Michelle staring wide-eyed at him. And he could see the man who had just saved his life. It was the guy with the Labrador. Holding an assault rifle.

A STRANGE THING happened when the shooting started.

Rick Boreham relaxed.

It was as though he'd been holding himself so tight for so long, waiting for the bad thing to happen, that he had wrenched himself and his soul into a grotesque homunculus trying to fit back into the world. But all of a sudden, the world shaped itself around this dark inner deformity, and he could... relax.

Thinking about it later, Rick was sure he remembered starting to drop and take cover before the big plate glass windows exploded into the store.

Perhaps he'd picked something up in his peripheral vision. Maybe one of the thugs popped a shot off half a second before they hosed the front of the store with semi-automatic fire.

It didn't matter.

He was suddenly back in that place he'd spent so long trying to escape. And it felt like going home.

He would have pulled Mel into cover, but she was already dropping and rolling. Nomi, trained to comfort him when thunder broke, or cars backfired, followed closely, nuzzling him with her snout. Letting him know everything would be okay.

And it would. As soon as he exfiltrated.

He was no longer a soldier, and Mel was no longer a cop. Heavily armed attackers were assaulting the building. The only thing for it was to escape under the cover of the panic and madness. They crawled quickly away from the front of the store. Stayed on their bellies as they crept towards the aisles at the rear. A few other customers followed their example or knew what to do. But most did not. Most people cried out in terror and went to pieces. Rick kept going. At some point, without even thinking about it, he'd drawn the fighting knife he always carried. It wasn't much good for anything beyond quickly slashing open the major bleeders, and he was never going to get close enough to anybody with a shotgun or an AR-15 to do that. But getting it out was more important. He kept crawling forward with the sharpened steel talon gripped in his right hand.

They almost made it out, too. Got all the way to the rear of the store, where they should have been able to exit, except that somebody had blocked off that route. Closed the exit. He cursed. Nomi barked. And they heard the leader of the gunmen order one of his soldiers, Leroy, to "go shut that mutt up".

Rick stopped. There was no way he was letting anybody hurt his dog. They had reached the end of the aisle where he first met Melissa. The pet food section in front of the frozen goods cabinets. He hand-signed to her to get out of the aisle and take cover at the end of the shelving unit. He could see Mel was frightened but functional. She moved as directed. Nomi came to heel next to him on the other side of the aisle.

He heard somebody coming, the one called Leroy. He could see the man's reflection in the glass doors of the freezer unit. He advanced cautiously but steadily, but he stopped about halfway down, leaning forward, peering intently to make out what might be waiting for him.

Rick did not want him reversing and flanking them.

He held up one finger to Nomi. An old game.

How many?

She barked once.

"Leroy, I told you," a male voice shouted. He sounded pissed off.

Leroy resumed his careful advance down the aisle.

Nomi remained perfectly still and silent.

Rick held up his knife so that Mel could see it. He pointed at her and then at his ear. Miming a clapping gesture. She nodded, looking sick.

Leroy moved very carefully, the last few feet of the aisle. Rick nodded to Mel, and she deliberately knocked a bottle of dishwashing liquid to the ground before stepping back and going to the floor in the next aisle over. Leroy hurried forward, his gun pointed at where she had been standing. When he cleared the end of the aisle, Rick stepped up behind him, grabbed a handful of thick, greasy hair and yanked his head back with swift and sudden force, exposing the carotid and the windpipe. He cut both as he kicked out the back of Leroy's knee. The man went down, pawing frantically at the gouts of blood gushing from his wounds. Rick snapped his neck, stripped his weapon from him, inspected it quickly, and moved back down the aisle. Murder in his eyes.

He emerged into the main body of the market and made three targets. He dropped two of them with headshots but missed the third, who was moving, dropping into cover.

The renewed gunfire set off panic among the captives, and his third target disappeared as people screamed and some tried again to flee.

Another armed man, a giant dressed like a cartoon farmer, charged in through the shattered doors. Rick killed him with a double tap to the centre mass.

He moved quickly.

The man appeared a few feet to the right of where he expected him to emerge from cover. Rick adjusted his aim, realising he might not make the shot before the guy got one off. He was caught at the neurological crossroads of fight and flight. Take the shot or take cover?

He never got to make the choice.

Before the shooter could pull the trigger, a civilian tackled him.

They both dropped out of sight as mayhem swept over the store again. Rick ran forward, his muzzle down but ready.

He found the men wrestling behind an empty vegetable stand. The shooter had fought his way into a mount and was about to start clubbing the other man.

Rick Boreham shot him in the face.

35

STAGE FOUR COLLAPSE

An hour later and no cops had turned up. James wasn't surprised. One ambulance had come and gone, taking away four people with serious injuries. The dead, they left behind. Rick Boreham—the guy James had possibly saved by tackling the last gunman—helped triage and treat the wounded. His girlfriend Mel helped too. An army veteran and a former London policewoman, they knew what to do, including for James. Mel cleaned and bound the wounds on his arm, a burn mark from the barrel of the shotgun, and a bite wound from the man he had tackled. James had no first-aid skills and felt utterly useless. He was also dreadfully aware of having wet his pants. Nobody mentioned it. Somebody gave him a Coke. It was cold, and they said it would help with the shock. He didn't know whether that was true or not. But it tasted fantastic. He shared it with Michelle, who sat with him on the floor of the ruined market while other people tried to bring order to the chaos.

After an hour, when it became apparent there might not be any more first responders on the way, Boreham and his partner joined James and Michelle in the manager's office out the back of Harris Teeter. Phil, the manager, looked like he was five minutes away from a heart attack. He had pleaded with them to stay until the police arrived, but when Boreham returned to the office, he said it looked like Phil had gone too.

"Most people have left. There's nobody out there, man."

James and Michelle followed them back out to the main part of the store. His pants were sticky and chafing, and they smelled bad. All of the produce was gone. Most of the shelves were empty. A dozen or so people still drifted around as though in shock. It was a bizarre, otherworldly scene. Like something out of a movie.

"I don't know whether we're supposed to stay here or not," James said. "We're witnesses."

"You're more than a witness," Melissa Baker said. Her English accent sounded like a stage actor's.

"Fuck this," Michelle said. "Give me a minute. I'm gonna make a few calls."

She disappeared back inside the manager's office.

"Dude, you wanna change?" Boreham asked him quietly. "I found these out the back in the staff room.

He offered James a pair of grey drill pants. They looked like they'd fit. He blushed, but the other man waved off his embarrassment. He leaned over and said in a quiet voice, "I shat myself so often in combat I stopped counting."

James thanked him and shuffled away to change in an aisle, where he had at least some privacy, what little the empty shelving could offer. He would have given up all his cash right then and there for a hot shower – and fresh underwear. Instead, when he was done, he returned and stood with the other two survivors. Or were they something else? What did the legal system call people like them?

"I don't know whether you remember or not, in all of the excitement and stuff," James said. "But my name is James O'Donnell."

He held out his hand. Rick Boreham took it with a firm grip. He introduced himself again and his girlfriend, Mel Baker.

"Pleased to meet you, James," she said, as though they had just encountered each other at a tea party.

"And thanks, seriously, man," Boreham said. "If you hadn't tackled that guy, I don't know I'd have gotten the first shot off. He kinda surprised me coming up where he did."

"I don't know why I did that," James confessed. "Honestly, it was a stupid thing to do."

Rick – he had asked James to call him Rick – grinned.

"Nah, you totally had him, bro."

James laughed nervously.

"Yeah," he said. "He was gonna hurt his hand so bad pounding me to a pulp there was no way he could've pulled a trigger on you."

Rick laughed, too. His sense of humour seemed fiercer and more resilient than James's.

"I like your dog," James said. "I probably owe her a cookie or something. I was leaning over to pat her when they started shooting. I'm pretty sure that's why I'm out here talking to you, not in there on the floor. Do you think they'll ever get the rest of those bodies?" He couldn't bring himself to look at them. "You were a cop, weren't you?" James asked Mel. He seemed to recall something about her being a police officer, but the day felt like a jigsaw puzzle he had dropped at his feet.

"There should be law enforcement and paramedics everywhere," she said. She seemed unimpressed with the official response, and James was irrationally embarrassed by that. She'd come all the way to his country, which had no excuse for poorly managing a mass shooting like this after all the practice they'd had, and...

"The old Bill should be here doing the witnesses," she said, abruptly cutting off his meandering line of thought.

And who was this Bill?

"There should be witnesses," she said. "They've all gone. I don't know what's happening, but this is a bloody dog's breakfast. No offence, Nomi."

Nomi, the dog, did not seem to take offence.

Michelle had returned from the manager's office by then.

"What's going on is a stage four collapse," she said. "The police aren't coming. No more paramedics. If Phil, the fruit shop manager, wants those bodies moved, he's going to have to do it himself. We should get going, come on."

Mel, the London police lady, frowned at her.

"We can't just leave the scene of a crime like this. Jesus, it's not even a crime. It's a massacre." She touched Rick on the arm. "Not judging, darlin'. Just saying."

Rick placed his hand over hers and smiled.

James thought they must have been together a very long time.

"Yeah, well, it's not the only massacre today," Michelle said. "It's not even a very big one. Look, you guys don't know me because I didn't introduce myself properly before. My name is Michelle Nguyen. I work for the National Security Council."

She pulled out her ID card and showed them. Melissa Baker read it very closely before giving it back.

"James here was also doing some work for us," Michelle explained. "I've just spoken with Admiral David Holloway, my boss at NSC. He's... not in DC right now. But I briefed him on what happened here. He's going to get a message through to local law enforcement. Not that he thinks it'll be necessary. He advised us to clear the area as soon as possible."

Rick and Mel looked confused.

"We were going to get a cabin for the weekend. On a lake," Rick said. "Can we just do that now?"

"You got food?" James asked.

Rick laughed, but not so happily this time.

"Ha. That's why we came here," he said. "We were gonna pick up a couple of days' worth of groceries. And some dog food for Nomi."

"I got some cheap cuts from the butcher," James said. "If that helps."

"She's supposed to be on this diet," Rick said, but Mel put one hand gently on his forearm again.

"I think she can probably skip the diet today," she said.

"Yeah," he admitted. "Probably.'

"What are you guys going to do?" Mel asked. "Do you live around here? Things are a bit out of hand, eh?"

Michelle gave her a quizzical look. They were standing in the middle of a fucking slaughterhouse. Things were more than a bit out of hand.

"You guys haven't been paying attention, haven't you?" Michelle said. "You can see what's going on here, right? What's been going on the last couple of days?"

Rick and Mel exchanged a furtive smile.

"We've been sort of busy," he said. "Kind of wrapped up in each other."

She giggled.

Jesus Christ, James thought, they've only just hooked up.

"Look," he said. "I feel like we should bring you up to speed. You know, after you saved our lives and everything. I've got a couple of bags of mystery pasta. I think we still have the olive oil if it didn't get smashed?"

Michelle held up a shopping bag. "We're good," she said.

James went on, "We're happy to share our food. We've got a long drive ahead of us, and to tell you the truth, I don't think either of us should be driving long distances today or tonight. We walked here from DC this morning."

"What? The capital?" Mel said. "That's crazy."

"The traffic was crazy," Michelle said.

Rick Boreham looked around the ruined market. Crazy was relative.

"I have some basil and some tomatoes growing in my yard," he said. "I'd be happy to pick them to make up a sauce for your pasta if you like. And if you're serious about sharing that meat with my dog, she'll be getting pretty hungry, and she is a good dog."

"She is a very good dog indeed," James said.

MICHELLE DROVE the short hop to Rick Boreham's place, where James had a long, hot shower. He couldn't believe the luck of this guy. Rick Boreham lived in a charming little cabin in the woods by a river at the edge of a country club. Some people just fell assbackwards into the good life, didn't they?

There were plenty of days when the market made James wish he could run away to a cabin in the woods.

On the other hand, there was that look in Rick's eyes, or rather that complete absence of anything in his eyes, when he was crawling across the market floor towards James with a knife in his hand…

So maybe not such a good life.

Rick kept a small herb garden and a vegetable patch from which he pulled a couple of bunches of fresh basil and five or six plump, impossibly red tomatoes. He took a smaller one and tossed it to Nomi, who wolfed it down in two bites, wagging her tail in Labrador ecstasy. Rick apologised for having only a jar of minced garlic in his little bar fridge, but as somebody who lived on take-out and Uber-EATS, James wasn't judging. Michelle did something to the tomatoes and garlic, which reduced them to a thick, fragrant sauce in a pot on the stovetop, and Mel asked if anybody wanted a drink.

"I got me a thirst that could cast a shadow," Rick said.

"I could straight up murder a glass of wine," Michelle sighed before the light faded from her eyes, and she mumbled, "Oh, sorry."

Rick Boreham tilted his head a little like James examining a really interesting spreadsheet. He found the answer he wanted, walked across the small living room of his cabin and folded Michelle Nguyen into his arms.

"We're good," he said. "You're alive. That's what matters."

James chanced a look at Mel Baker, but she was smiling as if she'd been hugged too.

When Michelle emerged from Rick's embrace, she was crying, but she thanked him and wiped the tears from her eyes.

"I could use that wine," she said quietly.

He made a face.

"I'm not much of a wine guy, but I can get some."

"Oh please, no," Michelle said quickly, "Don't bother." But Rick had a mission now.

"James, you want to come see my club?" he asked.

It was a second before James understood he wasn't joking.

"The country club?" he asked.

"Yeah. I got keys. They got wine. I can leave my boss a note. He's cool."

James asked Michelle if she was cool with that, and she nodded.

"To be honest," she said, "for wine, I'd be cool with you sandbagging another motherfucker with a shotgun. Go."

"She'll be with me, James," said Mel. "I'm even tougher than him." She pointed at Rick, who nodded.

"She is," he said. "Come on. I want to drive your truck. It looks awesome."

James gave him the keys. He did not feel like getting behind the wheel.

They discussed the Sierra on the two-minute drive to the Bretton Woods clubhouse. Like they were just a couple of buds out for some brews. The conversation down-shifted when James told the whole story of how he'd come to buy it.

Rick pulled on the handbrake and cut the engine. The clubhouse was quiet. Deserted. It would typically be jumping with hundreds of guests at this time. It had power. Lights were burning inside. But James and Rick were the only souls about.

"You really think it's that serious?" Rick asked. "You're breaking camp and pulling back to your family's farm?"

They sat in the darkened cabin of the big SUV.

"I thought it was pretty serious when we left Washington," James said. "Michelle, too. That's her job. Threat assessment. But after that... that business at the market today."

He petered out.

Rick said nothing, waiting.

"Man," James went on. "I think you and Melissa should get the hell out while you can. There's a couple of million people in the DC-Baltimore area. They're going to be hungry for real in two or three days. Starving in a week. Maybe the army keeps a lid on it here, but the military's got bigger problems."

"You mean China?"

"No. I mean New York. LA. Chicago. I mean hundreds of millions of people who can't feed themselves. Can't buy food. Can't even get in a car and drive away because the major urban road nets have been sabotaged. Nobody was keeping order at that market today. That's what I think it's going to be like everywhere in a week or so."

Rick stared out into the night. He said nothing.

"We should get that wine," James said after a while.

THEY ATE on the front porch. A simple but beautiful meal, with two bottles of very expensive wine and a six-pack of beer. James threw down a couple of painkillers with his food. He insisted on leaving cash in the resort manager's office to cover the price of the wine. Rick confessed that one of the bottles alone was worth more than his pension for a week.

The day's heat eased into a mild, balmy evening, and Rick burned some incense to keep the mosquitos away.

Violent flashbacks tormented James, but he said nothing of it. Once, he caught Rick looking at him as though reading him like an open book. The veteran nodded at him, and James felt gooseflesh crawl up his arms. But he felt a little better, too, knowing that some-body knew.

Nomi ate all the cheap off-cuts for which James and Michelle had paid so much.

"She's gonna have quite the tummy ache in the morning," Rick said.

"And she's going to fart like a camel tonight," Mel warned.

They drank all the wine, and Rick finished most of the beer. They did not talk about what had happened in the afternoon. Each of them told stories about their families and friends, their lives, and their adventures.

They had all had much more exciting adventures than James.

It was late when Rick and Mel went to bed.

Rick made up a bed roll for James on the floor. A camping mat, a pillow, a blanket and a sheet. It was surprisingly comfortable. Michelle took the couch, and they turned out the light.

James could not sleep. His mind kept replaying the terrible things he had seen that afternoon. He did not imagine he would ever be able to sleep through the night again, but after ten or fifteen minutes, Michelle Nguyen quietly climbed off the couch and came and lay with him under the sheet on the makeshift bed on the floor. She wrapped her arms around him and held him tight, and he soon forgot about things best forgotten.

IN THE MORNING, with Rick supervising, they packed the Sierra for a long trip and all four of them, and Nomi, drove away from the cabin by the river.

EPILOGUE

The desert darkness was hot, even in the deep of night, but not four hundred feet below ground. Down there, in the bio-hazard vaults of Project Blue, the air was held to a constant chill, just above freezing. General Panozzo wore his fur-lined parka. The two Green Beret soldiers with him wore summer-weight BDUs but did not complain. They would not be here that long.

Only Professor Bruce waited for them. The other technicians and scientists had clocked off at the end of their shifts. They had told Panozzo back in Washington that Bruce rarely left the facility. He looked it. His skin was sallow, almost jaundiced under the fluorescent lights, and his eyes had sunken back into his skull. He looked... wrong.

Just being in the same room as the man made the skin crawl behind Panozzo's testicles. He ignored the sensation.

"Gentlemen," Bruce said. He grinned. Or at least he skinned thin, grey lips back from the yellowed teeth hiding behind them. "A great day. A great and terrible day."

"If you don't mind, Professor, we're on a schedule."

"Of course, of course," Bruce said. "Things fall apart. The centre cannot hold. I do understand, General. I understand only too well. Come, come along. I have your package ready."

He led them from the outer lab through a series of clean chambers and scrubber locks into the vault.

A medical suitcase, heavy and grey, waited on a stainless-steel table for them. It was already sealed. Biohazard warning stickers stood out in bright red and yellow on the slate grey casing.

"As promised," Bruce said. "More than enough. More than enough."

Panozzo felt weak and a little dizzy. As though just being in proximity to the contents of the case was enough to kill him. It wasn't. He knew what was in there. They were all safe. But his voice, when he spoke, still sounded watery and thin to him.

"I confirm, Professor, that we are taking receipt of three hundred doses of the HPAI B1 subtype coded 848-AB. Please sign."

He handed the virologist an iPad and a stylus.

Bruce signed with a flourish.

"Thank you," Panozzo said. "Sergeant?"

The Third Special Forces Group sergeant stepped forward, took the iPad from Professor Bruce and handed it back to his colleague. He turned back to the Nobel Prize-winning scientist and killed him with a spear hand strike to the throat. It took Bruce a little while to die, and Panozzo was pursued from the vault by the desperate choking and scrabbling sounds of a man gasping out his last breath through a shattered windpipe. The soldier who had killed Professor Bruce carried the body out of the lab over his shoulder. He would dump it in the desert an hour later. The other non-com carried the heavy medical transport case.

It was very late.

The only Project personnel on base were guards who had been rostered off for the night, replaced with more of Panozzo's men. Nobody looked twice as the General and his escorts carried a dead man and a heavy biohazard containment case out of the facility. The Project sat within an army transport depot deep within California's High Desert region. Panozzo and the soldier with the case drove five minutes west to the airfield that serviced the base.

Three aircraft waited for them there.

Army Medical Corps technicians separated the contents of the case into three smaller carriers, after which agents from the CIA's Special Activities Division took responsibility for the packages. Two agents escorted each case onto a plane and flew west to catch connecting flights from Edwards AFB.

Within twenty-four hours, dozens of unwitting contractors hired by Special Activities would deliver the tailored variant of the Avian flu virus to more than a hundred locations throughout China. But by then, General Panozzo had returned home, written a letter of resignation that he left on the desk in his study, and retired to his garden, where he put a pistol into his mouth and pulled the trigger.

Zero Day Code is concluded. The story will continue in *Fail State*.

John Birmingham

PO Box 437

Bulimba, Queensland 4171

Australia

 Created with Vellum

ALSO BY JOHN BIRMINGHAM

The *End of Days* series.
Zero Day Code.
Fail State.
American Kill Switch.

The Axis of Time.
Weapons of Choice
Designated Targets
Final Impact
Stalin's Hammer
World War 3.1
(World War 3.2 & 3.3 coming in 2024)

A Girl Time in Time.
A Girl in Time.
The Golden Minute.
The Clockwork Heart (coming in 2024)

The Cruel Stars series.
The Cruel Stars

The Shattered Skies
The Forever Dead (2024)

Dave vs the Monsters series
Emergence.
Resistance.
Ascendance.
A Soul Full of Guns.
A Protocol for Monsters.

CHEESEBURGERGOTHIC

Hi. It's me, JB. If you liked this book and you'd like more of the same, sometimes for free, please join me over at my blog/book club/dive bar on the internet.

At the moment, it's hosted on Substack, but it kind of moves around, and wherever it ends up, it's *always* called CheeseburgerGothic.

Just throw that into el Goog or whatever AI chatbot runs the world now, and I'm sure they'll hook you up. I give away free stories there at least once a month. And my faves—everyone who signs up at the Burger is my favourite—get steep discounts on new releases.

Everyone else? Well, my friends, don't be like them.

I look forward to seeing you there.

www.ingramcontent.com/pod-product-compliance
Lightning Source LLC
Chambersburg PA
CBHW021952050726
47495CB00022B/489